D1553487

AMERICA AND THE BRITISH IMAGINARY IN TURN-OF-THE-TWENTIETH-CENTURY LITERATURE

AMERICA AND THE BRITISH IMAGINARY IN TURN-OF-THE-TWENTIETH-CENTURY LITERATURE

Brook Miller

AMERICA AND THE BRITISH IMAGINARY IN TURN-OF-THE-TWENTIETH-
CENTURY LITERATURE
Copyright © Brook Miller, 2010.

First published in 2010 by PALGRAVE MACMILLAN® in the
United States—a division of St. Martin's Press LLC, 175 Fifth
Avenue, New York, NY 10010.

Where this book is distributed in the UK, Europe, and the rest of
the world, this is by Palgrave Macmillan, a division of Macmillan
Publishers Limited, registered in England, company number 785998,
of Houndmills, Basingstoke, Hampshire RG21 6XS.

Palgrave Macmillan is the global academic imprint of the above
companies and has companies and representatives throughout the
world.

Palgrave® and Macmillan® are registered trademarks in the United
States, the United Kingdom, Europe and other countries.

ISBN: 978-0-230-10376-4

Library of Congress Cataloging-in-Publication Data

Miller, Brook.
    America and the British imaginary in turn-of-the-twentieth-
century literature / Brook Miller.
        p. cm.
    Includes bibliographical references and index.
    ISBN 978-0-230-10376-4 (hardback)
    1. English literature--American influences. 2. National
characteristics, British, in literature. 3. National characteristics,
American, in literature. 4. United States--Relations--Great Britain.
5. Great Britain--Relations--United States. 6. United States--
Civilization--British influences. 7. America--In literature. I. Title.

    PR129.A4M55 2010
    820.9'35873--dc22   2010012672

A catalogue record of the book is available from the British Library.

Design by Scribe Inc.

First edition: November 2010

10 9 8 7 6 5 4 3 2 1

For Chrissy

Contents

ACKNOWLEDGMENTS

This book began as a dissertation project chaired by Pat Brantlinger, whose participation was a stroke of good fortune. Our conversations and Pat's generous comments transformed what was a niggling idea into an adventure of reading and discussion, transformative for project and author alike. At Indiana University, Steve Watt was tireless even when I was tiresome, and I continue to lean upon his counsel in academic and scholarly matters. The advice and models provided by Joanne Wood, James Eli Adams, Eva Cherniavsky, Susan Gubar, and Andrew Miller helped in countless ways as well.

Material and intellectual support from the wonderful people of the University of Montevallo and the University of Minnesota, Morris, were crucial. I am grateful for funding from the University of Minnesota's Office of the Vice President for Research, which provides an exemplary model for supporting young faculty. The warmth and collegiality at the University of Minnesota, Morris have made this the work of many. Special thanks to Brad Deane, Janet Schrunk-Ericksen, Michael Lackey, Tammy Berberi, Roger Wareham, Tom Mahoney, Leann Deane, Jayne Blodgett, Eva Wood, and Peter Bremer for their many forms of assistance and encouragement. Thanks to Dominic Scheck for outstanding work during the production stages of the project. Most of all, thanks to Sandy Kill and her staff for heroic work in obtaining the books, articles, and other texts needed to complete this work at a remove from a research library. Without your help, the work of composition would have been infinitely more difficult. Thanks to Brigitte Shull and Lee Norton of Palgrave Macmillan for their outstanding guidance.

Parts of this manuscript have been published previously. Parts of the introduction and Chapter 1 first appeared as "The Thousand Glassy Eyes: Britishness and American Culture in Travel Narratives and Cultural Criticism" in *America in the British Imagination*, Cambridge Scholars Press 2007, and is published with the permission of Cambridge Scholars Publishing. A version of Chapter 5 first appeared as "Holroyd's Man: Imperialism, Fetishism, and America in *Nostromo*" in Nostromo: *Centennial Essays* (*The Conradian* 29.2) published by Rodopi Press in 2004. A version of Chapter 6 first appeared as "Maggie's *Morceau*: America and Human Commodities" in *Symbiosis: A Journal of Anglo-American Literary Relations* 7.2 (October 2003). Exchanges with the editors of *The Conradian*, *Symbiosis*, *Modern Fiction Studies*, and *America in the British Imagination* improved my work immeasurably. Mistakes and misjudgments in this text are my own; the success of the book is partly theirs. Special thanks to Allan Simmons, a model of the talented and generous editor.

Thanks to the Modernist Journals Project for permission to reprint the illustration that follows the conclusion.

Deepest gratitude to Bob Bergman, Jack Kolaya, Linda Kolaya, and my siblings and many friends for their help and patience. Thanks to Andrew Carroll for being a model of productivity and still making time for an old friend. Thanks to my father, Craig Miller, for his encouragement.

Thanks to my mother, Helen Bergman, for her engaged interest and for being both parent and friend. Something beyond thanks to Parks, Eek, and most, Cools, who made this possible and provided the reasons to do it. You are my life.

INTRODUCTION

Books on America are as the sands of the sea for multitude.

—*Times of London,* April 19, 1900

For many generations the person who rejoices in the name of "Britisher" has comfortably divided the known Universe into Himself and Foreigners, with a further confidence . . . too deep to need expression, that these two classes are respectively placed by Providence in a sphere that may roughly be described as "All Right," and in various zones of outer darkness . . . but a suspicion has become . . . planted in his breast that the American is not as other foreigners are.

—Theodore Cook

Americans are often unaware of the accommodations forced upon people the world over by their nation's emergence as an economic, military, and cultural "superpower" in the twentieth century. For the superpower of the nineteenth century, Great Britain, America's rapid rise engendered a wide range of responses, from anxious to humorous, that sought to make sense of the United States in terms of its relation to Britain. This book argues that related changes occur in British self-representation during this period and that texts featuring Anglo-American[1] relationships provide fertile material for documenting the rise of contemporary British attitudes toward nationality and culture. In writing about America, British writers intervened in the discourse of what their nation was and might be.

This introduction will briefly examine the pressures that altered Anglo-American relations and how the conversations that arose from these pressures recast what British authors valued in their nation. Then I'll introduce the central theme circulated within these discussions—the elevation of culture and self-cultivation via contact with culture over the national character—in British literary discourse with particular reference to Matthew Arnold's commentary about America. Finally, this section will consider the theoretical underpinnings of a question that connects the readings in the chapters that follow: how do narrative representations of America participate in a wider shift from national character to culture in British self-representation?

The answers to this last question are, unsurprisingly, many and contingent. In Anglo-American discourse we discover the republic in many costumes: as a "daughter" or "cousin" of Britain; as a "tabula rasa"; as a breakaway colony; as an "English-speaking people"; as a beacon in the pursuit of liberty; as a crucial trading partner; as an imperial threat, partner, and competitor; as a mutual member of the Anglo-Saxon race; as a mutual inheritor of the legacies of "Teutonic origins"; as a source and embodiment of "modernities" both cultural and economic; as a vacation spot; as a worshipper of British culture; as a critic of British culture; and as the site of a virtual infinity of personal relations for British citizens, the overwhelming majority of which remain lost to us.

In examining key political and social events and ideas that had a shaping, and thus uniting, effect upon the realm of the personal, and in examining a variety of key literary texts that express and query the shifting British views of America circulating with these ideas, this book participates in the development of the emergent field of transatlantic studies, or Atlantic studies. Literary scholarship increasingly resists the paradigm of national literatures that has been dominant since the introduction of modern literary studies into university curricula. A recent turn toward circum-Atlantic histories enhances our grasp of the complexities of literary production and other published writing within the Americas, Europe, and Africa. The work of Paul Giles, Paul Gilroy, Amy Kaplan, Joseph Roach, and many others provides a foundation for teaching and scholarship in what Susan Manning and Andrew Taylor describe as "reading transatlantically" (11).

This book, in focusing on British perspectives regarding the United States, may seem to resist this trajectory, and thereby to be aligned with traditions of cultural studies that this new movement opposes, reifying national character and culture as categories of highest value. The relative lack of material from writers marginalized from the national narrative—including women—may seem to affirm a focus upon traditional, hegemonic voices.[2]

This is largely the result of the prolific, interrelated writings that registered shifts in Anglo-American relations during this period. I argue that British cultural criticism at the turn of the twentieth century operates within what Ann Ardis and Patrick Collier have described as a "transatlantic print culture" and promotes an evolving British ideal of cultivated citizenship; that is, it uneasily and differentially circulates between the national and the cosmopolitan, promoting the salutary effects of contact with British culture. The voices that echo throughout this book demonstrate ambivalent allegiances to, on the one hand, the enduring value of their national affiliations and, on the other, the rhetorical modes that unite both national and transnational political and cultural communities as loci of the values necessary to preserve or restore the health of the national community. Rather than reifying the national, this book seeks to illuminate the cultural stakes of transnational contacts from the perspectives of cultural critics deeply impacted by political and social context and deeply affiliated with intellectual communities to and for whom their insights are directed. Anglo-American relations become a key staging ground for the importance of cultivation, while the emergence of a transatlantic readership complicates an older rhetoric of national differences.

The educational component of this cultivated ideal—what Leslie Butler calls "educative citizenship"—reflects the dual scholarly conversations in which this book participates (14).[3] While the movement toward transatlantic literary studies is energized by pressure exerted upon international borders by recent scholarship in American Studies, many scholars focused upon late nineteenth- and early twentieth-century British culture are revising models of domestic hierarchies, especially between "mass" and "high" culture.

My approach blends these perspectives, drawing upon the transnational and the national as malleable, performative forums in which power is both affirmed and resisted and in which multiple, popular, and relatively neglected discursive contexts are illumined as sources for narrative. Indebted to Armitage and Braddick's notion of "*Cis*-Atlantic" history (national or regional history within an Atlantic frame), this book examines how a variety of international pressures, emanating from or attributed to America, impacted British discourse about national character and culture. Additionally, the maturation of transatlantic print culture meant that domestic discourse often was consumed by, and indeed written for, a complex transatlantic readership. At the same time, the materials I consider reflect a belief that in order to fill in gaps between Victorian and modernist literary history, we should heed Duncan Bell's call to delve into the "murky shallows" of popular, influential discourse and connect it to literary production (22). Throughout this book, but particularly in Chapters 2 and 3, Anglo-American discourse is drawn from sources not heretofore considered in scholarly discussions of the period: commentary from Anglo-American newspapers as well as mainstream papers, speeches and notices from cultural commentators and about public events like the King Alfred Millenary, and material from popular fictions offer a sense of the rich, broad discursive context in which cultural texts appeared. Doing so illumines the "profound overlap" between high and mass culture in Britain, explored by Aaron Jaffe and a host of recent modernist critics (Jaffe 88). It also provides a means of disentangling the nationalist and literary programs of turn-of-the-century writing from the *grand recits* propounded by older scholarly approaches by making the production and simulation of a transatlantic public sphere visible. That is, where transatlanticism opened up scholarly conversations to hitherto neglected, marginalized voices, it also functioned as a forum in which competing, often hegemonic forces engaged in discourses about identity and cultural value.

Grappling with this overlap involves disentangling strategic assertions of a "great divide" from our older conceptions of its actuality. My method is to read assertions of this divide transatlantically by tracking how stagings of Anglo-American encounters and relations reflect a variety of arguments about schisms affecting modern British life—schisms that certainly involved realms of cultural production but that also, and often in combination, involved claims about temporal, national, racial, imperial, and gender divides that separate a cultivated citizenry from its antagonists, or even from self-realization.

Here texts about and that include references to the United States perform acts of cultural criticism that simulate the function of "national narratives" for British readers. In an influential essay, Donald Pease describes national narratives as "having constituted literary forms wherein official national fantasies were transmitted to a 'national people' that they aspired simultaneously to consolidate and represent" (40). The articulation and dissemination of

British national narratives is a plural historical phenomenon, deeply intertwined with the domestic and international discourses of the day and both rhetorically strategic and reflective of the perspectives associated with particular audiences. In the texts considered in this book, they are sometimes evoked through fictional British characters encountering fictional American characters and sometimes indirectly, through tonal cues meant to create a shared sense of values between narrator and reader.

By grounding commonality in models of outward-looking acts of criticism calibrated to train a reader's analytic refinement, these texts complicate the work of the "national narrative" considerably. These texts reveal twinned themes—the celebration of Britain as a repository of culture, rather than as a contemporary power fueled by the might of the character of its subjects, and the celebration of subjectivities for culture; that is, subject positions derived from exposure to, and bent upon the preservation of, cultural legacies, artifacts, and ideals. In this manner educative citizenship is trained in a new relation to the national narrative, one in which, paradoxically, the essence of nationality involved a sense of temporal displacement in which the self guards, seeks, preserves, or laments the passing of an imaginary time in which the *natio* and the national culture were coextensive.

In addition, the programs promoted through "national narratives" evolve during the time period in question. By the end of the modernist period, according to Jed Esty, modernist writing "promoted . . . the redemptive agency of *culture*, which is restricted by national or ethnolinguistic borders" (3). This thematic involved a new emphasis upon national culture as an object of study separated from the *natio* (used in this book as a term for the populace as a national community). The period examined here represents a transitional moment in the turn toward culture, in which a complex patchwork of theories of "immanent" cultural superiority, coming from racialist, religious, and other discourses, continued to play an important role in defining the terms of national identity. I offer this perspective while conscious that, in claiming that the turn of the century represented shifts toward the "culturalism" Esty explores, I am offering a "prehistory" of what is already a "prehistory" for Esty, who argues that late modernist writing anticipates a transition other critics have assigned to post-World War II English culture. The story of the emergence of culture as an autonomous entity is, as any reader of Raymond Williams knows, a virtual epic, but the turn of the century, perhaps partly because of the cosmopolitan character of many of its leading cultural figures, plays an underappreciated role in these transitions.

Cultural discourse about America helped renegotiate the terms of the national narrative from an emphasis upon character to culture. This involved the emergence of critical perspectives that questioned the viability of mid-Victorian concepts of identification. As Patrick Brantlinger puts it, "Some modernist writers . . . already approximate the critical recognition of what is fetishistic about the very construction of national identity" (*The Reading Lesson* 7). The intensive transatlantic intercourse with America and Americans, whose national narratives overlapped, usurped, and competed with their British counterparts, provided an important stimulus for thinking outside of older categories. The American story was widely and loudly broadcast within the discursive fields the writers in this study traversed. Above all, this critical consciousness emerges not in radical opposition to British ideologies, but with and through them. It is part of a cultural turn that sought to preserve rather than destroy.

British Analyses of America and British Society at the Turn of the Century

Analyses of America are not, of course, unique to British authors. From Hegel to Baudrillard, the roster of European intellectuals who trained their attention upon America is impressive by any accounting: Talleyrand, Fichte, de Tocqueville, Stendhal, Beauvoir, Baudelaire, Buffon, Crèvecoeur, Heine, Nietzsche, Heidegger, Burckhardt, Schopenhauer, Goethe, Gramsci, Kafka, Freud, Lacan, and Derrida represent just a few of the figures who engaged the subject of America, often describing "Americanization" as a force threatening European culture beginning as early as 1800, "during the first period of modern globalism" (van Elteren 7).

Yet British writings around the turn of the twentieth century compose the subject of this study. Why this narrow window? Stephen Spender, in *Love-Hate Relations*, mused that the figure of the American has played a key role in British evaluations of their own status: "The relationship was a kind of measuring instrument on which the English and Americans read off national

strengths and weaknesses . . . The American is at first a 'colonial';
then, after independence, free but still culturally dependent; then
self-sufficing, but in need of European crutches; then decidedly
adolescent, brash and self-assertive . . . then rising high above the
worn-out shell of Europe" (4).

The time frame examined here, focusing upon the mid-1890s
through the first years of the twentieth century, corresponds to
the penultimate stage of Spender's chronology. How did British
authors reconceive the status of the national culture in this transition from mastery to exhaustion, and what role was America
imagined to play?

While the character of the United States has been a subject of
intense scrutiny in British writing literally since the day the American Revolutionary War ended, at the end of the nineteenth century
two notable phenomena occurred: first, the number of published
travel narratives about the United States more than doubled; second, America and Americans became staples of British fiction.
Whether writing about the realities of domestic social life or fanta-
sizing about the far reaches of the empire, British writers brought
America and Americans into the fabric of their fictions even when
their subject had little to do with the United States.

To account for these phenomena, I will briefly mention changes
within British society and in Anglo-American relations (the first
chapter explores this history in more detail). The period between
1870 and 1914 witnessed the abundant growth of new traditions
in British and, more widely, European society.[4] These new rituals, emblems, and institutions promoted a national cultural ideal
accessible to legions of newly literate citizens and helped reconcile
antagonistic social groups by offering images of aristocratic privilege as the shared weal of the public.

Meanwhile, Anglo-American relations shifted dramatically as
well. Residual tensions over the Civil War, Britain's increased diplomatic isolation with the international politics of imperialism, a
border dispute in South America, debates about the gold standard, Irish politics, America's growing debt to Britain, American
publishers' ongoing resistance to international copyright standards, and Britain's relative decline as a sea power and industrial producer all impacted exchanges between the two nations.
Indeed, several British politicians and commentators suggested a

formalized political bond between the nations, partly as a way of sustaining British influence.

These proposals failed, but what would become, in Winston Churchill's idiom, "the Special Relationship" was realized in intensified Anglo-American interactions, facilitated by increased tourism and travel; a spike in Anglo-American marriages;[5] scholarly exchanges; growth in the availability of literary, scientific, and cultural texts on both sides of the Atlantic; and a proliferation of race discourse about Anglo-Saxon superiority and the role common "Teutonic origins" played in making the two nations beacons of liberty and progress. This mutual affirmation led to rather surprising results: at the close of the nineteenth century, for example, municipal governments held American Independence Day celebrations in London and many of Britain's smaller cities.

Among these interactions, disputes over international copyrights dominated transatlantic discussions of literary issues. Many of the British texts about America—from the travel narratives explored in Chapter 1, to the newspapers and periodicals of Chapter 2, to the novels, short stories, and essays considered in the remainder of the book—contain direct references to the problems of Anglo-American copyright.

The issue both divided and united Anglo-American cultural commentators, and disputes grew steadily through the nineteenth century. The passage of the Chace Act in 1891, which secured international copyright after decades of antagonism between British and American writers, publishers, and others, stands as a signal achievement, promoting closer Anglo-American literary relations and contributing to a richer sense of a shared cultural conversation between intellectual elites from both nations. According to Robert Colby, the Chace Act stimulated "Anglo-American literary symbiosis," evidenced by increasing numbers of British texts on American publishers' catalogs and vice versa, increasing transatlantic ties between authors' societies, increased notices of books from across the pond in periodicals, and the weekly journal *Literature*, produced by the *London Times* and promoting "a cosmopolitan outlook" that included William Dean Howells and Henry James as contributors to an "American Letters Department" (130).

While a success achieved by coordinated efforts by authors and publishers primarily from London and New York, the Chace Act did not remove tensions entirely. The limitations of the legislation, from the perspective of British publishers and authors, included rules that forced publishers to have American editions typeset at considerable expense or risk having their books printed by American firms.[6] The effect of this was, according to James West, that "the American printing industry was protected from British competition, and the American book market remained relatively inaccessible to British publishers" (305). The circulation of texts in transatlantic print culture was markedly asymmetrical, with periodicals subject to different lengths of delay across the Atlantic, but generally flowing more freely than books; nonfiction British books made even more limited appearances.

These commercial and literary frustrations were writ large in the metaphors through which British commentators described America and Anglo-American relations. During this dynamic period, British narratives about America and Americans shifted from comparativist analysis to what Daniel Rodgers calls an "aesthetic framing whose keys . . . were culture, custom, and time" (39). As Catherine Armstrong, Roger Fagge, and Tim Lockley describe it, British cultural critics depicted America as "on the one hand . . . a land of personal freedom and individualism, of boundless economic opportunity and broad social equality. On the other hand America has been perceived as having a self-confidence bordering on arrogance where higher culture is usually subsumed by materialism, where the poor can be easily left to fend for themselves, and where foreign policy can be dogmatic and aggressive" (2). These characterizations were resonantly antithetical to cherished and threatened qualities associated with British national identity. James Epstein, surveying the role America played in the Victorian imagination, emphasizes that in British texts "America was . . . imagined, debated and theorized" as "the site of 'the modern,' . . . entail[ing] a desacralization of tradition, an assertion of openness and freedom unbounded by the past or history, a restless desire to move within the horizon of an always imminent present . . . [and] a national and individual doctrine of self-referentiality" (107–8).

On the whole, analyses of America and Americans entailed a paradox—on the one hand, the authors relate the self-conscious anxieties of Americans to the textual, tautological nature of American national legitimacy;[7] on the other hand, the economic nature of some American aspirational narratives leads to a sense of (often monstrous) homogeneity. That is, these critiques simultaneously invoke a materialist view of U.S. culture and a critique of its ideal-ist ideology. A central assumption of these critiques is that Amer-ica's flaws stem from the void of an absent, or erased, cultural tradition. In asserting a materialist perspective upon American culture, these authors implicitly invoke the redemptive authority of English culture. Their cultural analysis is framed by a cultural-nationalist view of their own identity, a perspective in sync with the "invented traditions" of the end of the nineteenth century and with the analytic bent of the model of educative citizenship promoted in transatlantic discourse.

In the texts considered in this book, thematic unities in the rep-resentation of Americans reflect a common fund of assumptions shared between narrators and implicitly attributed to British read-ers. British writers used critiques of the United States to legitimate what Krishnan Kumar, following Stefan Collini, has declared the "Whig interpretation of literature," which "proclaimed a distinc-tive tradition of English literature that could also be said to consti-tute the cultural soul or essence of the English nation" (219).[8] This facilitated one of the central dynamics of the texts we'll be examin-ing: their subtle evocation of a sense of British cultural superior-ity even while criticizing the British or English public. As literary culture filled in the void left by a waning sense of national spiritual life, proponents like Matthew Arnold promoted the "study and dissemination of culture . . . in missionary terms" (Kumar 220).

ARNOLD'S AMERICA AS OBJECT LESSON

Kumar's comments about Arnold are a reminder that the cultural turn so capably analyzed in modernist criticism has its own longer history. For Raymond Williams and a host of critics writing in his wake, Arnold played a crucial role in articulating culture as a central locus of British value and in pointing to criticism as a means of pre-serving culture.[9] Despite his prominence, Arnold should be under-stood as a participant in a busy transatlantic conversation about the state of Anglo-American society and the value of culture.[10]

Even while prescribing a renewed engagement with "the best that has been thought or spoken," or "culture," Arnold was con-cerned about the perception that this pedagogical advocacy was in fact a replacement for religion: "Both here and on the other side of the Atlantic, all sorts of objections are raised against the

'religion of culture,' as the objectors mockingly call it, which I am
supposed to be promulgating. It is said to be a religion proposing
parmaceti, or some scented salve or other, as a cure for human mis-
eries; a religion breathing a spirit of cultivated inaction" (*Culture
and Anarchy* 48). Arnold's reference to criticism on both sides
of the Atlantic reflects, as we'll explore in the second chapter of
this book, the significance of transatlantic publishing flows, particularly in mass-circulation newspapers. British cultural elites were
increasingly conscious of American readers in the late Victorian
period. Against accusations of the passivity of the project he's out-
lining, Arnold describes men of culture as "firmly bent on trying
to find . . . a firmer and sounder basis for future practice . . . and
believing this search . . . to be . . . of yet more vital and pressing
importance than practice itself . . . we may . . . do more . . . we poor
disparaged followers of culture, to make . . . the frame of society in
which we live, solid and seaworthy" (*Culture and Anarchy* 134).
This pedagogical function for culture, and for the practice of cultural criticism especially, makes Arnold a proponent of literature,
art, and other elements of "civilization" as essential to reshaping
the nation and avoiding political catastrophe. For Arnold, culture
was attractive because it offered "disinterestedness" (rather than
class interest) as a basis for nonpolitical writing.

In *Culture and Anarchy*, Arnold repeatedly wields the threat of
becoming like the United States as the tip of his pedagogical gibes,
describing Americans as provincial and warning English readers that
such a fate may await them as well. His vision of culture is grounded
in literacy and social criticism informed by the traditions of English
literature. A healthy critical apparatus would provide an ameliorative
force in an era in which mass politics degrades British idealism.

More than a decade after the publication of *Culture and Anarchy*, Arnold clarified his views of American culture in "A Word
about America," "A Word More about America," and finally "Civilization in the United States." In these texts, he moves from criticism that Americans are provincial to an emphasis, finally, upon the
want of "beauty" and "distinction" in American culture. Arnold
continues to insist that England needs reform and that his examination of America fulfills the purpose of helping him shape his
reform program.

In some respects, Arnold's new essays represent a retreat from
the strong positions regarding American provincialism he offered

in *Culture and Anarchy*. In "A Word about America" (1882), Arnold insists upon Anglo-American identity, asserting that he regards Americans as "simply 'the English on the other side of the Atlantic'" ("A Word" 2). America is different only in terms of its class composition—while England has an aristocracy and working classes, America seems to consist entirely of a vast middle class: the Philistines. American Philistines are "the great bulk of the nation, a livelier sort of Philistines than ours, and with the pressure and the false ideal of the Barbarians taken away, but left all the more to himself, and to have his full swing" (7). Here aristocratic "false ideals" do not hold sway, but Philistine hegemony results in an excessive valuation of the "powers of industry and conduct" (10). For Arnold, "the building up of human life, as men are now beginning to see, there are needed . . . the power . . . of intellect and knowledge, the power of beauty, the power of social life and manners. And that type of life which our middle class in England are in possession is one by which neither the claims of intellect and knowledge are satisfied, nor the claim of beauty, nor the claims of social life and manners" (10). This negative assessment of American and English Philistinism comes in the larger context of a critique of class divisions; on this subject Arnold makes a key distinction between the two countries. In "A Word More about America" (1885), Arnold argues that a rigid class structure "hampers and falsens" individual thinking, and he recommends establishing social institutions on the basis of ideals rather than "by what one can oneself gain from it" (41). American institutions are strong because they reflect the homogeneity of the American people.

While homogeneity is conducive to good institutions, it is also a key target in his final writing on Americans, "Civilization in the United States" (1888). Arnold's ambivalence toward homogeneity reflects a moderation of his position in *Culture and Anarchy*. Indeed, it reveals that as Arnold became clearer about the role of culture, he began to view it in aesthetic rather than sociopolitical terms. Insofar as this shift mirrors a generally growing unease about American power on the global stage, it reflects a movement toward the representation of America and England in symbiotic relations, not for *realpolitik* purposes, but because each nation's character could fill the lack of its opposite in a mutually useful relation. Simply put, this model imagined the merger of American energy with British refinement.

In this final essay, Arnold isolates the keynotes of civilization, locating "the great sources of the *interesting* [in] distinction and beauty: that which is elevated, and that which is beautiful" ("Civilization" 54). To Arnold, America has "little to nourish or delight the sense of beauty" (55), particularly urban areas. Conversely, Arnold believes Americans are "restless, eager to better themselves and to make fortunes" and thus "the inhabitant does not strike his roots lovingly down into the soil, as in England" (55). English difference thus stems partly from an identification with place, while American rootlessness and materialism are mutually reinforcing. Moreover, Arnold returns to the claim that America is pervaded by Philistinism because Americans "came originally, for the most part, from that great class in English society amongst whom the sense for conduct and business is much more strongly developed than the sense for beauty" (55).

Arnold points to Abraham Lincoln as an illustrative example. Lincoln embodies the "serious Philistine" as a "typical American . . . shrewd, sagacious, humorous, honest, courageous, [and] firm . . . but he has not distinction" (56). This lack is not Lincoln's fault, but reflects, rather, an impoverished culture. Distinction is characteristically ambiguous, though it is in part the "discipline of awe and respect" developed through contact with elevated cultural objects. As Epstein puts it, to Arnold "America lacked, and would continue to lack Culture because of its failure to establish the crucial hierarchies separating high from low, polite from vulgar, art from mere entertainment, hierarchies on which cultural taste and judgement [*sic*] depend" (Epstein 117). Such a calculation no longer necessitates a center-periphery model of culture in which England represents the vanguard, trailed by its "provincial" allies. Instead, the temporal markers of culture shift to emphasize modernity, and the forms it brings, as the chief threats to culture.

Arnold lambastes the American press as a prime cause of this want of distinction. In particular, America lacked the strong literary culture and critical tradition he promoted in *Culture and Anarchy* largely because of the dominance of newspapers (Epstein 118). Arnold's essay attempts to stage this difference by responding coolly and incisively to inflated and defensive claims in the American press. He emphasizes his and his cultivated readers' superiority by performing the results of contact with the national culture he has described.

We thus encounter a return, with a key difference, of Arnold's critique of England in *Culture and Anarchy* in the concluding remarks of "Civilization in the United States": "I once said that in England the born lover of ideas and of light could not but feel that the sky over his head is of brass and iron. And so I say that, in America, he who craves for the *interesting* in civilization, he who requires from what surrounds him satisfaction for his sense of beauty, his sense for elevation, will feel the sky over his head to be of brass and iron" ("Civilization" 58). How are we to take the distinction Arnold makes here between the diagnosis of England in *Culture and Anarchy* and the diagnosis of the United States? The difference resides in subtleties of phrasing: when he considers the English, he is describing alienation from a cultural inheritance. When he describes Americans, however, as "craving" and "requiring," Arnold offers a rhetoric of failed growth. Whereas England is distracted from an interest in culture, America has never possessed any culture of which to speak. English culture requires a *return*, while American culture remains an oxymoron.

Arnold's rhetoric of homogeneity and provincialism was widely influential in literary and political circles. The shifts in his logic reflect a more general, evolving, tension around how to make sense of the United States in temporal terms. Was America lagging behind Britain in the march of cultural progress? Or did America embody modern forces threatening to pollute British culture?[11]

In the period when American industrial and military growth began to impact British dominance, descriptions of the United States can be viewed as strategic communications, both exhorting and reassuring a readership particularly conscious of "the condition of England" and interested in distancing themselves from the agencies causing a relative, or at least perceived, decline. For example, British readers may have taken comfort in the assessment of historian and diplomat James Bryce that American life was homogenous and monotonous and therefore lacked the rich differences in speech, culture, and politics discoverable in the English countryside. Such discourse ran counter to the tide of changes impacting the British domestic scene. Rodgers notes that "by the last quarter of the nineteenth century there were . . . uprooted peasants" in massive numbers in both the United States and Europe: "In England by the century's end, scarcely more than a quarter of the people lived in the county in which they had been born" (49). The critique of

American homogeneity provided a flexible position from which to articulate British superiority; on the one hand, it could be used to describe America as "laggard" in the march of nations along an axis of civilization; on the other, it could be used to identify America with a modernity that threatened to flatten out cultural distinctions. In either event, the critique of homogeneity was bound up with liberal discourse about the way homogeneity, along with egalitarianism, produced the institutions leading to America's rise.

Between Arnold's heyday and the turn of the twentieth century, the sense of cultural crisis infected rhetoric about the relations between the implied readership and the *natio*, shifting from declarations of the superiority of the British character and culture toward exhortations to restore and cultivate British culture. For example, the critic Edmund Gosse worried, in 1883, about "American materialism and democratic sentiment invading culture itself, degrading literary taste and dismantling the canon" (van Elteren 12). At the turn of the century, Gosse reframed his position to account for Britain's imminent decline. In 1901, Gosse published "Culture and the Small Nations" lamenting the impact of the Boer War upon the prestige of Britain. Pointing to the nation's loss of international influence resulting from this declining prestige, Gosse considers the opportunities availed a less powerful nation: "Deprived by its position of . . . material advantages and mental disturbances, the small nation has time to devote itself to culture . . . The advantage to a small nation is seen to lie in cultivating quality instead of quantity" (97).

These speculations are particularly remarkable in light of the historical reality of the moment when, in 1901, the British Empire seemed to be at the height of its powers. Yet as a number of historians and literary critics have argued, prominent British writers expressed uncertainty about the tenure, purposes, and ethics of their power, worried about changes on the domestic front, and longed for a steadier, more confident era. Debates about empire, jingoism, "little England," and the like took on a variety of forms, and at this moment, in particular, each side in these debates had a stake in claiming to represent the nation's interest. The divide Gosse posits—between material advantages and culture, between quantity and quality—reflects a line of tension that spread through these debates and effects a remarkable linkage between economics and identity. Moreover, these tensions reflect debates over international posture and prestige as much as over economic policy or the canonization of particular cultural works.

Arnold's program met with resistance of various forms, of course. The historian Edward Freeman, for example, resisted the institutionalization of literary study on the grounds that its claims to cultivate the individual subject were nonempirical. Mark Hampton, in *Visions of the Press in Britain, 1850–1950*, suggests that changes in journalism around 1880 also worked against the cultivating idealism that Arnold promoted. With the emergence of the New Journalism, the educational purposes promoted through the papers, particularly in opinion pieces, are replaced by a new ideal of the press as a "representative agency" (Hampton 75). While this analysis seems valid, the articulation of this representativeness within the increasingly fragmented reading public manifests in an emphasis upon identity claims. These claims themselves had educational subtexts, revealed through the performance of identities in narrative features and the editorial rhetoric of the papers. The "representative" nature of the New Journalism, as I hope to show in Chapter 2, simulates what it proposes to represent.

These journalistic exercises in "representative" identity performance paralleled a tonal shift in advocacy for high culture from a pedantic mode to the performative. Indeed, literary performance increasingly sublimates its advocacy of a cultivated ideal in response to the cacophony of voices and fabricated controversies embodied in popular journalism. These pressures, then, did not negate the Arnoldian project so much as they sublimated and refigured it, fusing it with disparate political interests and manifesting it indirectly, through performative rather than pedantic means. This strategy manifests widely in both middlebrow and self-consciously literary texts, dispersed along the wide range of the late nineteenth-century political spectrum.

PERFORMANCE, PEDAGOGY, AND THE AMERICAN OTHER

The role of the other in self-definition is the subject of extensive theorization and historicization, particularly with regards to Great Britain. Linda Colley, for example, makes the influential claim that "after 1707 . . . [the British] came to define themselves as a single people not because of any political or cultural consensus at home, but rather in reaction to the Other beyond their shores" (Colley 6).[12]

In the cultural conversations considered here, the stakes and narrative strategies employed in analyses of the United States reflect a nuanced history in these self-defining reactions to the other. Fredric Jameson suggests this much by arguing that in the late Victorian and modernist periods, "'imperialism' designates, not the relationship of metropolis to colony, but rather the rivalry of the various imperial and metropolitan nation-states among themselves . . . The proto-typical paradigm of the Other in the late nineteenth century . . . is the imperial nation-state" ("Modernism and Imperialism" 48–49). One could certainly make arguments similar to this book's based on the German other, the Russian other, or the French other, but the American case was central to the economic and social flows of the British public sphere.

Indeed, the sense of critical consciousness—that is, conscious-ness of the ideological operations of national narratives—implicit in the texts considered here point to the subtle operations of ideol-ogy exposed by the cultural turn. Typically, analyses of ideologi-cal processes focus upon the subject coming to identify with the characteristics promoted and disseminated through the symbolic order. This is described as "imaginary identification" because it involves self-fashioning in response to given models of subjectivity, and it reflects how identification might appear to work in a soci-ety deeply invested in notions of the national character. However, what Jacques Lacan calls "symbolic identification" also operates within the ideological process. J. A. Miller formulates the distinc-tion between imaginary and symbolic identification as the dif-ference between "'constituted' and 'constitutive' identification:" "imaginary identification is identification with the image in which we appear likeable to ourselves, with the image representing 'what we would like to be', and symbolic identification, identification with the very place *from where* we are being observed, *from where* we look at ourselves so that we appear to ourselves likeable, worthy of love" (Žižek, *The Sublime Object of Ideology*, paraphrasing Miller 105). What is the nature and character of identifying with the sym-bolic order? Slavoj Žižek argues that this occurs not through "posi-tive content . . . but only by its positional-relational identity . . . *pure difference is perceived as Identity*" (Žižek, *The Sublime Object of Ideology* 98–99). In the cultivated national narratives considered here, this "positionality" observes the living nation in fragments, while locating the "substance" of the nation in metaphors for the shared perspective from which the fragmented nation is observed: faith, tradition, and discourses inflected with ideological content such as the gender dynamics of chivalric conventions. These metaphors are accompanied by a range of metaphors for America. Rob Kroes has identified "spatial metaphors, where America, in contrast to Europe, is seen as flat and flattening . . . [and] temporal metaphors, where America is portrayed as lacking a sense of history . . . [and] the underlying metaphor of America as lacking the European sense of organic cohesion and integrity" (xiii). The chapters that follow explore the many permutations and combinations in which these metaphors appear, while trying to identify dominant formations with particular social, political, and literary interests.

Underlying these textual convergences is an essential dynamic linking the textual readings in this book: the articulation of the purposes and ideals of educative citizenship via a positionality identified with the national culture rather than the national character. This positionality is articulated through the observation of alterity. Specifically, the observation of the American other provides a means of performing a cultivated persona developed through contact with British culture while using American examples as object lessons for pedagogical messages delivered to a British audience. This duality of performance and pedagogy itself serves an important ideological function along the lines suggested by Donald Pease and Homi Bhabha. By promoting identification with the "warner" rather than the "warned," the narrative deepens the reader's connection to the message itself; nothing indoctrinates so much as being (mis)recognized as one of the indoctrinators.

To explain the wide variety of narrative and characterological forms that promote these forms of identification, I follow Edward Said's proposition that the superiority of colonizer to colonized does not entail a rigid form, but is instead a flexible positionality. In contrast to Said's colonial model, however, this positionality manifests a performance not only for the "other," but also for conationals who fail to live up to the "best which has been thought and said" (Arnold, *Culture and Anarchy* 5).

Homi Bhabha notes the temporal dimension of these issues, seeing the nation divided by "the tension signifying the people as an *a priori* historical presence, a pedagogical object; and the

people constructed in the performance of narrative, its enuncia-
tory 'present'" (*The Location of Culture* 211). This tension is managed through the temporality shared by the narrator and reader;
both in and out of the "present" performed in fictional texts, the
narrator and reader may mutually embody the ideal values of the
national culture by witnessing the characters learning through time
and moving toward a community that simulates its values. Observing the other enfolds Bhabha's pedagogical discourse within the
performative voice of the national subject. The representation of
an other, and particularly of the crises of identity endemic to that
particular other, provides an instance for merging the positional
voice with its lost, venerated object while proclaiming the modern
crisis that makes this merger impossible.

If the performative reflects temporal presence by being enun-
ciative, the pedagogical compares the present to another moment
by being exhortatory. In recent work on the construction of Englishness, Ian Baucom holds that (following Benedict Anderson)
national discourse exhibits a "will to homogenize the present by
submitting it to the sovereignty of the past" (4). To Anthony Easthope, "as the particular mode of collective identity made available
by modernity, national identity is caught up in the new forms of
subjectivity: it is desired with special intensity . . . and that desire
overlooks the fact it is *more* manifestly an effect of construction"
(55). In fiction and in a variety of political and cultural texts, this
"overlooking" of the construction of one's own nation is facilitated by embodying modernity in a force or figure opposed to the
unified nation. The temporal present involves the disunified nation
under the continual pressure of the agents of modernity. Modernity itself takes the form of an antagonistic state or other presence,
rather than a process. The values of the "lost" nation manifest in
figures under erasure—both in cultivated figures who bear witness
to, or seek, the ameliorative properties of immersion in culture:
coherence, unity, and refinement.

How does "positionality" fit into the intertwining of history
and ideology? As I am using the term, positionality designates
an *effect du text* rather than a presupposition. What do we take
away from literature? I am reminded of the famous remark that
understanding is what remains once we've forgotten what we've
learned. Our understanding of a text—or more broadly, of a subject or even a culture—is not manifest in memorized content but

in the remainder of an affective relation the learning subject has imagined he feels with the material. The contents that remain are organized in terms of their status as legitimating supports for this affective relation.

WILDE'S AMERICAN PERFORMANCE

Oscar Wilde provides a strong example of how the positionality associated with the cultural turn enfolds pedagogical messages in performativity and confrontation of the American other. Wilde's 1882 tour of America and his subsequent writings illustrate the performative opportunities available through Anglo-American dynamics. Booked in conjunction with the run of Gilbert and Sullivan's send-up of British aestheticism, *Patience*, in the United States, Wilde's function was to provide a living exemplar of the dandy. Wilde cannily used this awkward position as a platform for promoting a vision of cultural renaissance largely drawn from Walter Pater's writings, professing a desire to "bring beauty" to the United States. Yet where Arnold relied upon reason and persuasion, Wilde capitalized upon his ironic position by staging himself as an embodiment of this culture.

His lectures were spectacles, but they were also serious, "dealing largely with large matters . . . at moments [Wilde] implied . . . that his renaissance was a recurrent phenomenon in history, [but] at moments he insisted that the present awakening of the spirit was more thoroughgoing than its predecessors" (Ellmann 165). Wilde's renaissance manifested a cultural spirit quite at odds with the bourgeois pleasures of Gilbert and Sullivan. For Wilde, "To disagree with three fourths of the British public on all points is one of the first elements of sanity" (Ellmann 165).

Wilde's tour was reported and speculated about feverishly in the newspapers on both sides of the Atlantic, and ultimately brought him some money and enormous international fame. Wilde's passage into celebrity reflects the power of what, in the second chapter, is described as the "Anglo-American public sphere:" a system of discursive flows that promoted, pursuant of self-interest, a sense of a shared culture between Britain and America. The cultural symptom of *Patience* becomes, through this performativity, legitimated as an arbiter of British culture.

Wilde's tour was successful in this regard because his quotable wit enabled a maturing transatlantic print culture to turn the visit into a media event. Moreover, the qualities Wilde embodied as a British aesthete resonated with differences in aestheticism across the Atlantic and with the stereotypes and self-fictions held by each nation's commentators. As Michele Mendelssohn argues, "Often disdainful of materialism and commercialism, British Aestheticism was largely the story of aspirational culture among the middle and upper classes. By contrast, American Aestheticism . . . was proposed in a more popular, smilingly consumerist form" (Mendelssohn 13). Wilde's trip rendered him emblematic, but elusive; his cultural criticism, by contrast, emblematized his subject while performing an elusive authority.

Wilde would refer to America repeatedly in his aphorisms and other works. In "The Decay of Lying," Wilde contrasts English empiricism with American materialism and fabulation. The English are "a degraded race, and have sold our birthright for a mess of facts" (Wilde, *Portable* 977). America, by contrast, is "vulgarizing mankind . . . [with] crude commercialism . . . [a] materializing spirit . . . indifference to the poetical side of things, and . . . lack of imagination" (980). Yet these characteristics, paradoxically, are the result of the fiction of their own earnestness. In adopting George Washington as a national hero because he is "incapable of telling a lie," Americans have done great harm to culture and beauty. The irony is that the story of the cherry tree is "an absolute myth" (*Complete Works of Oscar Wilde* 980). Wilde's turnabout here wonderfully captures many of the themes of the travel narratives we'll explore in the next chapter—America's callow pretensions are the result not only of inexperience but also of ideological zealotry.

In offering this critique, Wilde does not want the reader to be "too despondent about the artistic future either of America or of our own country" because "society sooner or later must return to its lost leader, the cultured and fascinating liar" (*Complete Works of Oscar Wilde* 980, 981). As a performance of a cultivated sensibility, Wilde substitutes wit for sober pedagogical lessons, but pursues a similar purpose; cultivation entails a return that legitimates British culture.

This book presents a variety of images of Americans and the Anglo-American relationship at the turn of the twentieth century. By moving from texts featuring Anglo-American bonding to others focused upon Anglo-American antagonisms, I hope to suggest the outlines of how notions of Britishness still familiar today were forged partly through transatlantic discourse. The complexity comes from at least two sources:

1. Discourse around this topic was overtly political, so modulations and emphases upon forward-looking or nostalgic images of the Anglo-American relation persist in what Raymond Williams has called "residual" and "dominant" discursive patterns.
2. As the objects of both historical accident and cultural fantasy, representations of the Anglo-American relation are activated rather than spontaneous, strategic and reactive instead of fundamental and natural (Williams 124).

The chapters that follow examine the specific iterations in which the positionality outlined in this introduction manifests. The first chapter traces the dominant chords in the culturalist turn initiated by Arnold in select British travel writings about the United States. The second chapter tracks the rise of an Anglo-American public sphere that reached its height in debates about the possibility of Anglo-American reunification in the late 1890s. The third chapter probes the high-water mark of Anglo-Saxon racialism, which witnessed the emergence of British pedagogical discourses aimed simultaneously at America and the British bourgeois to honor and defend British culture and tradition. Chapter 4 examines how a popular text, *Dracula*, reimagines the Anglo-American relation to invigorate an enervated British society. Chapters 5 and 6 examine literary transpositions of America's emergence as a threat to British hegemony, first in terms of empire and subsequently as the vanguard of capitalism. Taken together, the book points to this apotheosis as an important terrain for the recalibration of British identity.

While our narrators thus probe Americans and American culture and perform "symptomatic critique" of how culture reflects material and historical conditions, this book attempts to perform the kinds of readings Žižek describes as "extracting the kernel of enjoyment . . . articulating the way in which—beyond the field of meaning but at the same time internal to it—an ideology implies, manipulates, produces a pre-ideological enjoyment structured in fantasy" (*The Sublime Object of Ideology* 125). For many writers, the "enjoyment" of their writing involves the instruction of and identification with an implied middle-class British reader. In doing so, these writers articulated early critiques of mass culture that share remarkable similarities with contemporary cultural criticism.

CHAPTER 1

THE TRAVEL BOOK

PERFORMING BRITISH CULTURE IN AMERICA AND ON THE PAGE

O my America! my new found land,
My kingdom, safeliest when with one man manned.

—John Donne, "Elegy XIX: To His Mistress Going to Bed"

It is a vulgar error to suppose that America was ever discovered. It was merely detected.

—Oscar Wilde, *The Complete Works of Oscar Wilde*

There is no easy starting place for surveying British writing about America. Long before the founding of the republic, writers like John Donne used the associations of America with wilderness as a trope in their work. From almost the first day of the foundation of the American Republic, British writers were busy sending back to London their reflections upon American geography, government, manners, culture, and commercial progress. Along with other forms of writing engaged in the process of describing, analyzing, and evaluating America, including journalism, fiction, poetry, drama, business reports, and the endless stream of unpublished correspondence, travelogues record the psychosocial transition that accompanied America's emergence as a world power and the uneasy position of Britain at the turn of the twentieth century.

This transition is inchoate in the contrast between Donne's and Wilde's pronouncements on America. For Donne, America is a relatively stable vehicle for characterizing his lover in mock-imperial terms. The romantic language of discovery and conquest is a rhetoric of assertion, the uncertainty of which is signaled by the doubled use of "man" at the end of the lines. That is, the possibility of other men points to the insecurity not only of possession but of discovery itself. The speaker's own projected desire becomes the stuff of what makes America America.[1]

Wilde, too, records suspicion of the rhetoric of discovery. Where Donne's lines engage a drama of the individual subject, Wilde's assume a social perspective—how one views America marks one's own sophistication. In so doing, Wilde references the plenitude of discourse about the subject. By replacing discovery with detection, Wilde coyly points to America as both unromantic—a pest or a threat—and symptomatic of cancers within the home culture. Where Donne's America is a projection screen, Wilde's is a palimpsest.

This chapter examines a variety of travel narratives to give a sense of the changing rhetoric of authorship in British texts about America through the nineteenth century. In particular, the texts provide evidence of the emergence of several tropes—intertextual reference to other travel narratives and discourse about the United States, ideological analysis of American nationalism, and coordinated critiques of Americans and ordinary British subjects. These tropes contribute to the complexities of narrative voice in each text—in a positionality combining pedagogical messages offered via the American example with British performances of culture. This positionality permits the travel narrator to critique, à la Arnold, America and British Philistinism while performing a cultivated British persona.

In his 1948 anthology *America through British Eyes*, Allan Nevins offers an annotated bibliography that reveals the extensive range of British travel writings about America, listing over 350 authors and claiming "this bibliography does not pretend to be exhaustive—for a complete list would require too much space" (Nevins 503). The titles he does include range from the informative, as in Thomas Cooper's *Some Information Respecting America* (1794), to the descriptive, as in William Woodley's *The Impressions of an Englishman in America* (1910), to the contrarian, as in Thomas Brothers's *The United States of North America as They Are; Not as They Are Generally Described: Being a Cure for Radicalism* (1840), and finally to the analytical, as in William T. Stead's

The Americanization of the World (1902) and Philip Burne-Jones's
Dollars and Democracy (1904).

PERFORMING CULTURE
IN THE TRAVEL NARRATIVE

The generic conventions of the travel narrative are suited for articulating positionality through a rhetoric of self and other. According
to Mary Louise Pratt, as sentimental travel narratives replace "survival mode" literatures as bourgeois literary entertainments, they
imaginatively invoke the "domestic subject" of Euroimperialism
by producing the "rest of the world" for European readers (Pratt
4–5). Additionally, in its focus upon the reflections of the author-
narrator, the travel narrative is particularly reliant upon fostering
social and class identification with the audience. As the century
progressed, writers became increasingly attentive to the history of
literature about the United States. The narrative personae of later
travelogues tend to be well read in the literature of travel about the
United States and interested in identifying their culture as what
distinguishes them from Americans.

There has been some debate over the status of knowledge in the
travel narrative. Richard Rapson, writing in 1971, viewed British
travelers in America as "amateur anthropologist[s] perceiving the
fundamental ways of behavior and thought of a culture" (211)
who "furnish the historian with a positive way of talking about the
contrast between the nineteenth-century New World and twentieth-century United States" (190). Yet more recent critics have
avoided debating whether America really was as the British observer
claimed. The resulting analysis is therefore rather solipsistic—with
Wilde, what the British text reveals is Britain itself. A variety of critics have expressed this in similar terms. William Sharpe describes
Charles Dickens's *American Notes* thus: "America . . . becomes
important not so much as a literal place but as a moral foil to
Europe, a kind of ethical scheme that suggests the best and worst
of what civilized society has been and might become" (Sharpe 48).
And Peter Conrad, in a book-length study of British travel fiction about America, argues that "because America offers . . . an
incarnation of your most recondite and specialized fantasies, in
discovering America you are discovering yourself. Europe equips
you with a hereditary, natal self. America equips you to invent a

self better adjusted to the individual you have become since out-growing the impositions of birth. The Victorians felt threatened by America for this very reason: it was a society in which people conferred values on themselves, not the kind of society represented by Victorian novels, in which the attribution of character is soci-ety's enfranchisement of creatures who have no reality outside it" (5). Both Sharpe's and Conrad's statements reflect valid insights into travel discourse, even if they are based on a rather problematic typing of the Victorians. The paradoxical truth of these statements is probably the result of an elision of the operation of stereotypes within British cultural discourse—Conrad's claim wrongly assumes the truth value of stereotypes that portrayed Victorians as staid, yet it correctly posits the existence of a British discourse of threat surrounding the United States. What Conrad may ignore, then, is the function America played in consolidating a sense of identifica-tion between writers and readers who identified with nationality, European cosmopolitan identity, or both. That is, Conrad glosses the imaginary processes at stake in representations of America and Americans: he ignores the ways in which Anglo-American dis-course served an ideological purpose for defining the parameters of contemporary Britishness.

Christopher Mulvey considers this problem in travel writing by both American and British authors about their nations' respec-tive transatlantic counterparts. Mulvey notes a temporal trope that describes Britain in terms of actuality and America in terms of potential. In British texts, Mulvey finds "a pervasive fiction . . . of the gentility of the writer and reader" (7). This positionality includes an embrace of the John Bull stereotype, and according to Mulvey, "the Englishman travelling abroad was likely to turn himself for the duration of his travels into a caricature self" (15).

Mulvey's assertion of the importance of this positionality is born out in this chapter and elsewhere in this study. Yet his claims about gentility and embracing John Bullishness overlook the influ-ence of visions of cultural reform; key changes in the image of John Bull and the other dominant national icon, Britannia; and broader changes in British society and the nation's international position.

In Matthew Arnold's critiques and cultural program (see the Introduction), and the texts examined in this chapter, analysis of America is framed by a comparative dimension—how Americans differ from the British—and a temporal dimension—what forces are presently pressuring Britain, or civilization, toward cultural anarchy. Through the rhetoric associated with these elements, the narrative voice performs characteristics associated with British difference and with cultural sophistication. In style, tone, and manners, we discover the stuff of an idea national self in place of a nonexistent society animated by Arnoldian cultural values. This positioning functions as a supplement in something like the Derridean sense: it stands in for culture by advocating for it. The temporal dimensions of this role lead to an emphasis upon temporal differences between the United States and Britain as well as reflections upon modernity itself. The supplementary nature of the role, in which the self performs culture (in the face of a society that has failed to embrace it), manifests in an urbanity that inflects cosmopolitan values into an otherwise nationalist project. This urbanity manifests primarily in three ways supplementary to the comparativist analysis of America and Americans:

1. Performance of intertextual mastery, in which the narrator's perspective reflects awareness of other opinions about America and Americans
2. A focus upon the limitations of the American and British publics
3. Emphasis upon privacy in contrast to the homogenizing and stultifying effects of public discourse, often manifested in personal anecdotes

These themes develop through the travel narrative of the nineteenth century. In performing culture in these ways, travel narrators establish the terms of an ideal British subjectivity and articulate the failures of both British and American subjects to rise to them.

The rhetoric offers a distinction that reflects a pedagogical purport, however: while the critique of John Bull types takes issue with the Philistinism of their character, critiques of Americans emphasize ideological indoctrination, often enabled by the national embrace of capitalism, republican institutions, and egalitarian ideals. This difference permits a multiplicity of British subjects along an axis of varied levels of cultural achievement, one constant of which is a common grounding in national tradition. This commonality with the narrator (and implied reader), and the contrast with the inexperience and ideological blinders revealed in Americans, make the travel narrative an effective stage for an indirect pedagogical discourse for modeling a reformed national self.

SHIFTING ICONOGRAPHIES

The twin icons of nationality, John Bull and Britannia, themselves illustrate changes in British self-representation at the close of the Victorian period. Britannia, a Roman-inspired figure who had been appropriated by Queen Elizabeth, generally embodied national ideals. At the end of the nineteenth century, she appears with greater frequency as a "semidivine" figure who embodied the nation itself, rather than its people. John Bull, by contrast, was from the beginning an attempt to articulate the national character. He appears first in John Arbuthnot's *The History of John Bull* (1713), contrasted with the Dutch figure "Nic Frog" and the Duke of Marlborough. Bull was "an honest, plain-dealing fellow, choleric, bold, and of a very unconstant temper; he . . . was very apt to quarrel with his best friends, especially if they pretended to govern him" (Arbuthnot 9). Despite this curmudgeonliness, Bull was also generous to a fault.

This character has survived into the present, still celebrated in contemporary advertising, such as the following web copy for "John Bull Ales": John Bull was "hard-headed, down-to-earth, averse to intellectualism . . . the embodiment of honesty, generosity, and zest for life which the common people had." Presumably, the consumption of John Bull Ales puts one in touch with this "personification of the spirit of the British nation."

Yet Bull's appearance as an advertising icon rests on a crucial difference: where Arbuthnot's figure operates via an energetic presence, confronting allegorical crisis, the modern advertisement offers John Bull in a "history" page, described in the past tense as a nostalgic icon, literally laid out in amber hues.

The difference is an ephemeral manifestation of the temporal dynamic at the heart of the evolving discourse of Britishness. Through the nineteenth century, Britannia was "elevated to higher moral planes, echoing her Roman origins, shown as semi-divine and often clad in Greek robes," a development closely tied to Britain's increasingly spiritual adornment of its imperial interests (Matthews 817). Bull's evolution in the nineteenth century was facilitated by the emergence of middle-market papers like *Punch*.

In particular, in the 1840s, cartoonist John Leech refined the character of Bull into a "more cultivated and restrained [version] . . . for increasingly reverential Victorian audiences" (Matthews 819). John Tenniel, also a cartoonist for *Punch*, continued this trend, making "John Bull . . . continue to look like a member of the gentry"—specifically, "from a simpleminded rustic into an English country squire"—and this image would extend into the early twentieth century (Matthews 819, 817). Yet as the Victorian period progressed, "critics observed that farmer John Bull was an anachronism, out of touch with the realities of an industrialized and urbanized nineteenth-century Britain" (Matthews 819). Such criticisms allude not only to material realities but also to the doctrines of (often pedantic) duty and service to the poor characteristic of the mid-Victorian period.[2]

The turn of the century witnessed a widened split between evocations of an ideal self cultivated through contact with culture, and the traditional, unrefined figure of John Bull. Indeed, as we will see, in this period, Bull returns in the character he possessed before the intervention of Leech, Tenniel, and others. After examining two texts that keyed the turn toward an Arnoldian vision of culture, we will consider the social changes that led to the sublimation of Mulvey's gentility and the emergence of a split between pedagogical and performative images of the British within individual texts.

COMPARATIVISM AND GENTILITY IN PRE-ARNOLDIAN TRAVEL NARRATIVES

Alexis de Tocqueville's 1835 *Democracy in America* provides a useful starting point because it predates the British writing focused on in this chapter and because many of the analyses of America and Americans are offered via comparisons to England and Englishmen.

The book was enormously influential, especially in Great Britain (Rapson 6). While not himself British, de Tocqueville was conscious of the volume of English discourse about the United States: "The English make game of the manners of the Americans, but it is singular that most of the writers who have drawn these ludicrous delineations belonged themselves to the middle classes in England, to whom the same delineations are exceedingly applicable; so that these pitiless censors furnish, for the most part, an example of

the very thing they blame in the United States; they do not perceive that they are deriding themselves, to the great amusement of
the aristocracy of their own country" (251). While the ironies of
English middle-class deprecations of Americans provoke laughter
among the aristocracy, de Tocqueville has a last, if muted, laugh.
His intertextual mastery locates English opinion about the United
States within the confines of self-interest, and his own positionality is cosmopolitan—he performs a detachment from class and
national prejudices in favor of taste, as revealed in diction like "ludicrous" and "pitiless," both of which point to unrefined, prejudicial
sensibilities. De Tocqueville's comparison of the United States and
England culminates in a brief chapter titled "Why the National
Vanity of the Americans Is More Restless and Captious than That
of the English" (631). De Tocqueville argues that while every free
nation exhibits "vainglorious" patriotism, Americans are especially
grasping, eager, and jealous to exact praise for their nation. By
contrast, the English, exhibiting their characteristic reserve, "stand
unmoved in their solitary greatness, well assured that they are seen
of all the world without any effort to show themselves off, and
that no one will attempt to drive them from that position" (de
Tocqueville 253). This difference in national vanity is a reflection
of England's aristocracy and American democracy as well as of
the difference in relative international prestige and power. For de
Tocqueville, the stability of English taste comes from the imitative
tendencies of the lower classes. Stable social classes lead to stable
regimes of taste that throw "a pleasing illusory charm over human
nature," which, though misleading, nevertheless provides "a noble
satisfaction" (de Tocqueville 252).

By contrast, American homogeneity results from taking "not any
particular man, but Man himself as the object of their researches
and imitations" (de Tocqueville 255). De Tocqueville's criticism
of Enlightenment humanism, and by consequence liberal individualism, provides a problem for British travel writers repeatedly
through the nineteenth century. British travel writers, themselves
the representatives of middle class interests, were forced to elide
or explain away the contradictions inherent in adopting a position
similar to de Tocqueville's. Their own dependence upon individualist social and economic developments (or, to put it better, upon
the leveling effects of nineteenth century capitalism) gave the lie
to accusations that America suffered from excessive individualism.

In the years of greatest British prosperity and before the franchise had been extended by the 1867 Reform Bill, this contradiction could be glossed over rather easily. Americans' bad manners and primitive social conditions served as mutually explanatory for one another. As American industrial dominance, or even its eventuality, became apparent, and Britain's class structure lost much of the rigidity de Tocqueville celebrated, British travel writing began to evince a multitude of anxieties about America. The example America represented in some cases became ominously incorporative—social homogeneity, even modernity, in Britain does not merely repeat developments in America but issues from it.

In the middle of the nineteenth century, travel writers glossed the contradictions involved in adopting a position like de Tocqueville's by elaborating the temporal and subjective processes required for taste, refined judgment, and courtesy to develop. Charles Dickens's travelogue of 1842, *American Notes for General Circulation*, emphasizes privacy, property, and private education as the keys to culture. The public is for Dickens antithetical to culture, and his criticisms of America hinge upon his association of the young country with materialism and the stupefaction of independent reason by America's suffusion of public ideologies.

American Notes is the record of a six-month journey to the United States that was part pleasure trip, part note-gathering journey for his novel *Martin Chuzzlewit*, and part contentious lecture tour in which Dickens spoke rather unpopularly about the need for an international copyright law.

Dickens begins with an apology for the opinions to follow because his task has been to "resist the temptation of troubling my readers with my own deductions and conclusions" (266). He proceeds to declare Americans "by nature brave, cordial, hospitable, and affectionate," and praises the combination of this predisposition with "cultivation and refinement in educated Americans" (266). Dickens adds that these supplementary characteristics are "natural . . . to the whole people" but are deficient among the masses as a result of several "blemish[es] in the popular mind," including "Universal Distrust" and the love of "smart dealing" (266, 267).

Dickens frames this complaint in terms that anticipate Matthew Arnold's analysis and reference one of the central value hierarchies linking a diverse array of Victorian texts: the tension between the

Real and Ideal, or Material and Spiritual. As Dickens puts it, "It would be well . . . for the American People as a whole, if they loved the Real less, and the Ideal somewhat more" (270).

Dickens dramatizes this fault in the conclusion. In need of new traveling boots, he asks a bootmaker in a small town to call upon him. Dickens receives the bootmaker "lying on the sofa, with a book and a wine glass" (272). The author's contrast with his subject appears in the bootmaker's neglecting to remove his hat upon entering this scene. His rudeness is compounded as he launches into the business transaction: "[He] inquired if I wished him to fix me a boot like *that*? I courteously replied, that provided the boots were large enough, I would leave the boots to him . . . that I would be entirely guided by, and would beg to leave the whole subject to, his judgment and discretion. 'You ain't partickle, about this scoop in the heel I suppose then?' Says he: 'We don't follow that, here.' I repeated my last observation" (Dickens 272). Dickens's courtesy, judgment, and discretion are translated as being, or not being, "partickle" about one's demands as a consumer. The contrast between Dickens's "courtesy" and the bootmaker's combination of stupidity and poor manners becomes comical as the bootmaker bumbles through the transaction, oblivious to the social graces Dickens is modeling for him. Heightening the effect, the bootmaker is intensely concerned about appearances, rushing to the mirror to scrutinize himself midtransaction.

Dickens then gives ideological context for the attitude that prevents Americans from developing taste and manners. The bootmaker muses over the boot again, "after the manner of Hamlet with Yorick's skull; nodded his head, as who should say 'I pity the Institutions that led to the production of this boot!'" (Dickens 273). He then leaves rather brusquely, only to reappear a moment later to wish Dickens a "good afternoon" (though it is evening, in fact). The effect of this "amusing incident"—though Dickens does say it is "not the rule or near it"—is to illuminate the absurdly intense republicanism of Americans (273). The bootmaker is indoctrinated in, not guided by, American values.

The pedagogical aspects of the travelogue expanded in the multiple introductions written for various editions, repeatedly reemphasizing the proper standards for passing judgment. The unpublished introduction of 1842, titled "Introductory, and Necessary to be Read," insists that the reader refrain from judging the book on standards other than those established by its own "design and purpose" (Dickens 275). Proper criticism and reading, Dickens implies, issue from observation, reflection upon the Ideal to which a real object, person, or event owes its form, and careful, limited judgment levied only after a sufficient amount of experience has been processed. In this aesthetic theory, we see Dickens's rather tenuous linkage between intellectual property, taste, and good judgment. His descriptions here of the Press take on a note of irony—they are "veracious and gentlemanly . . . high authorities" with whom Dickens must dissent on the grounds that "in asserting my liberty and freedom of speech while I was among the Americans, and in maintaining it at home, I believe that I best show the high worth of [my] welcome [in America]" (276). Unlike the conclusion to *American Notes*, here Dickens presents his reception in America in a positive light, crowded with "old readers" who welcomed him warmly, rather than surrounded by a "vulgar herd who would flatter and cajole a stranger into turning with closed eyes from all the blemishes of the nation, [offering] . . . an iron muzzle disguised beneath a flower or two" (277). Dickens presents American readers with a choice between the "vulgar herd" led along by the press and more distinguished private readers whose intercourse through literature involves a sense of chivalry, ceremony, and honor. Dickens in effect seeks to instruct as much as to tell.

Dickens's 1842 Introduction may reflect the way the text was embroiled in Anglo-American political and cultural politics. In an insightful chapter on the book history of *American Notes*, Jessica DeSpain argues that newspaper responses to the travel narrative, and its American reprintings, reposition Dickens from a "great British champion of democracy" to "in essence . . . an enemy of the American state" (28).[3]

Perhaps as a result of the way the book became "a contact point for discussions of American national identity," Dickens continued to make additions to the text, including an 1850 "Preface to the Cheap Edition" and an 1868 postscript (DeSpain 68). In the former, Dickens takes his most combative stance, ending the brief piece defiantly declaring that to interpret him "as viewing [America] with ill-nature, animosity, or partisanship, is merely to do a very foolish thing, which is always a very easy one; and which I have disregarded for eight years, and could disregard for eighty more" (279). Dickens here treats his readers as "childish" and "unscrupulous"; it is no accident that this readership is the one he associates with the "vulgar herd" in the 1842 introduction. Yet in his final word upon the subject, Dickens makes a rather dramatic about face, particularly with regards to the Press, by declaring, "How astounded I have been by the amazing changes I have seen around me on every side . . . [including] changes in the Press, without whose advancement no advancement can take place anywhere" (280). The postscript reprints a speech Dickens delivered at a public dinner given by the *New York Press* in 1868. While he begins, then, with praise, he humorously chides the Press for an ongoing lack of veracity: "I rather think that I have in one or two instances observed its information to be not strictly accurate with reference to myself" (Dickens 281).

In these late editions, Dickens not only tailors his message to particular audiences but also extends the dialogism within *American Notes* outward into the discursive context of its reception. This performative move toward intertextuality positions the text itself as a vessel of culture. It anticipates the dynamics described in the next chapter, in which the simulation of an Anglo-American public sphere makes performativity and the commodification of British culture key processes in negotiating revised images of Britishness.

While engaging in a similar examination of the failure of American institutions to foster taste and culture, Robert Louis Stevenson offers a more gloomy perspective. Stevenson's "Across the Plains" was written during a trip across the United States in 1879. Aboard a transcontinental train, Stevenson encounters a great deal of unkindness toward European emigrants by conductors who seem bent upon making the journey unpleasant. For example, the train pauses every so often so the passengers can de-train and have a meal, but the conductors refuse to give them any warning. Yet after receiving unexpected attention and sympathy from a newsboy who had consistently kicked him as he passed through the aisles, Stevenson reflects that the boy is emblematic of "that uncivil kindness of the American, which is perhaps their most bewildering character [*sic*] to one newly landed" (38). Behind the rudeness of American life, Stevenson consistently sees a generous impulse.

Stevenson's essay suggests that egalitarian ideals de-individuate by legitimating the treatment of individuals as mere parts of a crowd to be disciplined and controlled by those given authority over it. While this homogenized public may appear antithetical to the perspectives of some critics, in fact they are of a piece—democratic ideals merely divide people, destroying civility, regimes of taste, and the personal relations necessary to foster them. The ascendancy of these ideals, and their effects upon privacy and culture, paradoxically result in inegalitarian forms. As Stevenson notes, America's devotion to equality "does not extend so low down as to an emigrant" (35).

The lack of manners and underlying kindness of Americans that Stevenson notes links his perspective to early to mid-nineteenth-century writers such as Dickens and Frances Trollope, who note Americans' lack of polish as a sign of their relatively primitive state of civilization and (in Dickens's case) of a desire for validation in their commerce with British travelers. While Stevenson concurs in his assessment of American manners, he attributes them to a different style of governance and a different ideology. For Stevenson, America's rudeness simply differs from European snobbery:

> The American way of conducting matters of business is, at first, highly unpalatable to the European. When we approach a man in the way of his calling, and for those services by which he earns his bread, we consider him for the time being our hired servant. But in the American opinion, two gentlemen meet and have a friendly talk with a view to exchanging favours if they shall agree to please. I know not which is the more convenient, nor even which is the more truly courteous. The English stiffness unfortunately tends to be continued after the particular transaction is at an end, and thus favours class separations. But on the other hand, these equalitarian plainnesses [*sic*] leave an open field for the insolence of Jack-in-office. (Stevenson 24)

Stevenson's analysis of the origins of class prejudice in England illustrate the way a sense of shared gentility between reader and writer was discarded, or sublimated, during the Victorian period. Transatlantic analysis becomes increasingly attuned to faults within British society and derives a sense of positional superiority from textual mastery and cultural refinement. Finally, Stevenson's focus upon business practices, and their relation to culture and national character, becomes a keynote of the travel writings of British authors around the turn of the century.

LATE VICTORIAN AND EDWARDIAN
TRAVEL WRITING ABOUT AMERICA

The intervening years between Dickens's and Stevenson's commentaries and the turn of the century brought rapid changes to British society, heightening anxieties about culture. The 1873–1896 "Great Depression" was stimulated in part by European imperial competition, and the Edwardian period witnessed an extension and institutionalization of a changed national economic focus. Not strictly a depression, this period of slowed growth was experienced as a downturn in the wake of Britain's heyday as an economic world power: "a period when the terms of trade had moved against Britain was succeeded, after 1860, by one in which they rapidly and then slowly moved in her favour till 1896–1914" (Hobsbawm, *Industry and Empire* 119). Also, it was a period in which domestic industrial production occupied a less significant role in providing economic health than at the height of growth in the mid-nineteenth century. As Hobsbawm notes, "the international position of the British economy . . . became increasingly dependent on the British inclination to invest or lend their accumulated surpluses abroad" (*Industry and Empire* 120). Britain lost the competitive advantage that made it "the workshop of the world" (a title with which Hobsbawm takes considerable issue) because it had invested heavily in durable industrial equipment and was reluctant to modernize. Its competitors succeeded by imitating and improving upon British processes, creating advanced infrastructures and machinery that challenged, and in some instances, surpassed Britain's. Britain was forced to turn increasingly to finance and formal imperialism as a means of maintaining economic strength as its dominance as a manufacturer of textiles and machinery waned.

At the same time, Britain maintained its prominence in finance. Enormous flows of capital circulated through London in the form of the British pound, which became the currency of international trade. While new tariff barriers created by imperial competitors to protect fledgling industries limited Britain's expansion of its domestic industry, British finance flourished. A notable exception was the United States, which resisted the adoption of a gold standard. Nevertheless, British finance provided an arena for international trade well into the twentieth century. Thus, through formal imperialism and through taking advantage of the legacy of its dominance in world trade, Britain retained its place among the great powers. According to Hobsbawm, "Britain . . . escaped from the Great Depression (1873–96)—the first international challenge—not by modernizing her economy, but by exploiting the remaining possibilities of her traditional situation" (*Industry and Empire* 125).

These economic changes prompted the emergence of new figures within Britain who posed an implicit challenge to the traditional stoic, liberal figure of John Bull. Foreign elements, particularly from Britain's imperial friends and competitors, appeared upon the London scene. Hobsbawm appraises the situation: "The somnolence of the economy was already obvious in British society in the last decades before 1914. Already the rare dynamic entrepreneurs of Edwardian Britain were, more often than not, foreigners or minority groups . . . The 'guinea-pig' director, an aristocrat put on the board of an often louche company for the publicity value of his name, became common. His obverse was the genuine bourgeois who, unlike his predecessors in the Anti-Corn Law days, imagined himself, and indeed became, the 'gentleman' of the Forsyte saga type" (*Industry and Empire* 142). These developments were coupled with an increasing prominence of royal ceremony in British national life. The British monarchy had been private and insular in the first half of Victoria's reign (up to about 1870), but increasingly made its presence felt in the late Victorian and Edwardian periods. After 1870, the monarch came to represent not only the head of the social order but also the head of the nation as well. This increased attention to ritual was in part a response to international pressures—the economic competition between Britain and Germany, Russia, the United States, and others was projected upon the screen of state pomp and circumstance. For Cannadine, "the enhanced and ritualized public face of the British monarchy was but one example of a more general proliferation of new or revived ceremonial . . . not only at the level of the head of state, but in a more widespread manner as well" ("The Context, Performance and Meaning of Ritual" 138). While competition with other imperial states provides one explanation for this phenomenon, the growth of mass literacy, new national newspapers, faster transportation times, and other aspects of modern society fostered an increased national attention to ritual and ceremony with which not only the aristocracy but the members of the "nouveau riche" and even the newly literate could identify. Further, attention to national iconography became more important in a period of strong social divisions and the growth of anarchist, feminist, labor, and socialist movements.

These pressures provoked a divide in which "the ceremonial shadow of power was cast over the monarch, [but] the substance increasingly lay elsewhere" (Cannadine, "The Context, Performance and Meaning of Ritual" 133). The ceremonies and rituals of British civilization memorialized the nation's history as an imperial power while providing a source of imaginary stability in a fragmenting, modern world. National symbols, which offered the citizen a nostalgic vision of past glory, provided a defense against the effects of modernity.

Royal ceremony was only one element in an array of cultural inventions that helped consolidate a new sense of Britishness in this manner. Hobsbawm notes that during this period "the characteristic mythical Britain of travel posters and *Times* calendars emerged . . . The heavy encrustation of British public life with pseudo-medieval and other ritual, like the cult of royalty, dates back to the late Victorian period, as does the pretence that the Englishman is a thatched-cottager or country squire at heart. But . . . at the other end of the social scale, the same period saw the emergence of a very different social phenomenon, the characteristic 'traditional' way of life of the British urban working class" (*Industry and Empire* 142). A number of critics have analyzed the crystallization of value dichotomies in British culture during this period. We are particularly concerned with how middle-class aspirations are reflected in the increased attention to pseudoaristocratic tradition and how the discourse of taste operates to unite diverse socioeconomic interests in the imagined field of "high" culture by articulating a national cultural mission.

While Britain experienced "encrustation," as Hobsbawm describes it, America also followed a campaign of legitimation and aggrandizement between the 1880s and World War I, redesigning the capital, adding new rituals to the calendar of the president, and constructing national monuments. For British commentators, the juxtaposition between the two nations provided a way to designate British ritual "traditional" whereas American rituals were self-serving inventions for the mollification of a consumption-driven public. This new sensibility about history inflects the temporal themes of late nineteenth-century British commentary about the United States.

Further, these cross-cultural comparisons assuaged growing anxieties about the displacement of the British economy from global ascendancy. Daniel Rodgers notes that the emergence, in response to this phenomenon, of new transatlantic stereotypes that contrasted America and Europe in terms of economic growth: "By the last decades of the nineteenth century . . . reassuring republican contrasts had begun to jostle more and more frequently in American minds with a rival, aesthetic framing of the Old World-New World relationship, whose keys were no longer oppression and liberty but culture, custom, and time. Against the slow, organic forces of Old World growth, they set the New World's raw, competitive unfinishedness" (39). Moreover, Rodgers notes several British social reformers promoting these themes: "Samuel Barnett thought America's people had 'no conception of the state as an entity, no idea of America as a whole, no national consciousness' . . . Ramsay MacDonald concluded that 'no one can conscientiously set the country down as much more than a money making and imitative nation, vitiated by an atomic conception of democratic liberty and equality.' John Burns reiterated the theme: the promise of America was 'circumscribed and impeded by the undue exaltation of the Unit over the Aggregate, of the Individual as against the Community, of the Monopoly as against the State'" (43). The contrast between these perspectives and the emphasis upon America's republican institutions, noted in Dickens's *American Notes*, partly reflects the conceptualizing of the state in Arnoldian terms at the end of the nineteenth century. As we will see, later British writers did examine Americans' pride in their republican institutions as well as its values.

James Bryce was a statesman, historian, and became, in 1907, ambassador to the United States (in fact, a bust of Bryce sits in the U.S. Congress to this day). Bryce explicitly investigates the relationship between republican institutions and the development of culture in *The American Commonwealth* (1888). In this oft-cited work, he focuses primarily upon the homogeneity associated with American life. America lacked local variety in its architecture, landscape, and people. As a consequence, American tastes tended toward a lack of refinement and distinction. Without great variations to discern between, the national character became merely gray manifestations of the nation's egalitarian ideals. This theme shaped the writing of a large number of travel writers in the late Victorian and Edwardian period who focused upon this homogeneity despite taking a diverse array of positions regarding the United States. Such a response to homogeneity may, in fact, explain similarities between the positionalities of these writers even while they differed.

Bryce also provides a key example of the changes in British political beliefs and the national self-image at the turn of the century. In delivering a speech at a girls school in North London in 1897, Bryce claims that it was upon women that "the maintenance of the high standard of literature and culture mainly depended, because it was every year becoming more and more apparent that Englishmen were wholly occupied either in business or in sports." In a speech on changes in national ideals at the Economic Students' Union in December 1900, Bryce compared the national character to its state "40 or 50 years ago," finding that (according to the summary reported in the *Times*—note: all quotes here are from the article summarizing Bryce, not Bryce's own words) "there was rather more in the old ideals of the moral element and less of the material element than there was to-day; there was, too, rather more of a sanguine spirit, and the golden age seemed nearer then than it seemed now" ("Mr. Bryce on Changes in National Ideals" 13). Bryce's lament encompasses the passing of national idealization of liberty, noninterference and republicanism, nationality, and cosmopolitanism. He notes that "freedom of opinion . . . and freedom of action . . . was rather more in men's minds in the fifties . . . than in the present day" and that at the time of his speech "the true enemy of liberty and democracy was not [perceived to be] monarchy, but money, and the power that money exerted" ("Mr. Bryce on Changes in National Ideals" 13). As a result, the emphasis upon republican decentralization had fallen away in favor of concern with the corruption of politics by commerce and the appearance of new forms of capital (see Chapters 5 and 6 in particular for my analysis of this). Bryce notes, with some trepidation, that the doctrines of laissez-faire and noninterference have largely been abandoned, and with these doctrines, the British belief in national sovereignty as a fundamental aspect of a productive, happy international world order also disappeared. This "cosmopolitan" view of nations and a world order composed an enlightened liberalism closely aligned with the liberal individualism found in the national character at home. The nation and the British subject operated in parallel.

Bryce's analysis is useful because it names the terms for British analyses of the United States, but in reference only to British history and identity. Americans' emphasis upon liberty and republicanism would seem, to the eyes of many British observers, a mere blindness to the corrupting influence of money on the political stage. Coupled with the satirical aspects of the old stereotype of John Bull—a preening desire for flattery, a quick temper, and a single-minded pursuit of business—the late Victorian imagination populated its descriptions of Americans with the ghosts of its own discarded national images. Americans' insistence upon the exceptional nature of its institutions and identity, coupled with America's extension of sovereignty over its hemispheric neighbors would seem a travesty of the mid-Victorian consensus. The "cosmopolitan" perspective upon a world commercial and political order would be replaced by a cosmopolitanism that lamented the decay of "character" in Britain while assuming a posture of experience that embodied the experience and cosmopolitan facility of British observation while scrutinizing the intemperate nationalism of Americans.

The pace of British writing about the United States accelerated in this period. Whether from the pressures of competition, a literary consensus created by the imitative dimensions of the genre, some felt reality explainable only through history, or a more generalizable cultural consensus, these turn-of-the-century works focus upon explaining the psychology of a national character formed by the negative forces the United States was perceived to embody.

Moreover, these authors tend to valorize British culture and society by disparaging Americans, and they tend to traffic in negative stereotyping. Moreover, these stereotypes are remarkably similar despite great differences in the authors' aesthetic interests and political commitments. I have selected travel narratives from this period with the intention of representing a range of commitments, from the middle-market newspapers through the Fabian social project, from a nostalgic conservatism to a futurist sensibility, and from a materialist, quasi-sociological analysis to an impressionist aesthetic posture. In each case, however, the analysis of the new

American type provides a foil for articulating British refinement, even while offering criticisms of Britain's national type.

G. W. Steevens's 1897 *The Land of the Dollar* was published by William Blackwood and Sons and went through four editions, suggesting that it enjoyed a substantial readership. Steevens, who worked successively for the *Pall Mall Gazette* and the surging *Daily Mail* at the end of the 1890s, was a prolific journalist and travel writer.

In the text, the critique of American dollar worship implied by the title blends with a conservative anxiety about the effects liberalizing currency would have upon wealth retention. Steevens ridicules American proponents of abandoning the gold standard, an issue that played an important role in the presidential election of 1896. Steevens complains that "nobody in this country [the United States] seems to be quite sure just now what the value of a dollar is, still less what it ought to be" (30). The arbitrariness and mutability of American currency is, for Steevens, a reflection of the American character: "The American is a highly electric Anglo-Saxon. His temperament is of quicksilver. There is as much difference in vivacity and emotion between him and an Englishman as . . . between an Englishman and an Italian. Yet curiously there is just as much difference between him and the Italian . . . behind the flash of his passion there shines always the steady light of dry, hard, practical reason. Shrewd yet excitable, hot-hearted and cool-headed, he combines the northern and the southern temperaments, and yet is utterly distinct from either. He has developed into a new sort of Anglo-Saxon, a new national character, a new race" (Steevens 309). Steevens conflates Anglo-Saxon, national character, and race rhetorics, reflecting the ambiguities that attended these concepts in the minds of many Victorian writers. Steevens differs from British writers who associated hybridity and contact with the other with degeneration. The American is "electric," full of regenerative energy, which makes him both temperamental and extremely focused upon accomplishing the practical goals he sets out for himself. In Steevens's typically vague formulation, "character" and "race" are not only equivalents, but the American version has "developed" recently, in contrast to English and Italians. That is, while Americans' character is presented in comparison to British character, it also holds a different—and mutable—temporal status. In America, the racial alchemy of national character is disturbingly fluid: "From whatever cause, the old element, the English element, the natural leaders of the country, are dying out, and the vacancies are fill[ed] by contributions from every nation of the earth. Will they blend? Will these tributaries of new blood turn the stream of national character into another channel? It is too early to say. It is entirely to be hoped not, for the character of the present American is not one to be lightly lost from the world" (Steevens 315).

For Steevens, American duality reflects a want of culture and imagination as much as it reveals energetic avarice: "The keynote of this character is its irresistible impulse to impress all its sentiments externally by the crudest and most obvious medium. The Americans are the most demonstrative of all the peoples of the earth. Everything must be brought to the surface, embodied in a visible, palpable form . . . If you want to impress your fellows you must do it not through their reasoning powers, but through the five senses of their bodies" (Steevens 309–10). Steevens's description of the hybrid, yet still distinctly Anglo-Saxon, character of Americans emphasizes a lack of subtlety associated with visibility and palpability. For Steevens, American vulgarity is entrenched in what Dickens terms the Material (as opposed to the Ideal). America's emphasis upon the senses leads to a lack of refinement, even a lack of thoroughness: "everything is left, to the English mind, half-finished" (Steevens 312). While historians like Hobsbawm and commentators at the time (such as W. T. Stead—see the end of this chapter) note that America's manufacture of machines that would fail once they had become obsolescent put Britain at a competitive disadvantage, here Steevens is focused upon Americans' lack of deep spiritual reflection.

The pragmatism Steevens associates with American productivity reflects the reversal of English stereotypes emphasized elsewhere in this chapter, but the focus on a lack of thoroughness recalls John Ruskin's critique of the English character in "The Nature of Gothic": "Many a time you [the English reader] have . . . thought how great England was, because her slightest work was done so thoroughly. Alas if read rightly, these perfectnesses [sic] are signs of a slavery in our England a thousand times more bitter and degrading than that of the scourged African, or helot Greek" (Ruskin 85). For Steevens, America's lack of thoroughness represents both pragmatism and a love of display—American work reflects both the spectacular aspects of modernity and modern production strategies (such as planned obsolescence).

Steevens presents America as paradoxical—where he finds pugnacity, institutionalized hatred of Britain, foolish indulgence to children, and cruelty to the elderly, he also finds an exemplary chivalry toward women and a society "magnificently free of intolerance" (313).

Temporally, these paradoxes reflect America's lack of national maturity. With its ongoing celebrations of the Revolutionary War, its "superficial" educational system bent upon continually ginning up anti-British feeling, and its fanatical attachment to its history, Steevens's America is a modern man-child among the nations. Its emphatic public pride signals a lack of privacy, taste, and international perspective. Yet Steevens's American is also the man of the moment: "You may differ from him, you may laugh at him . . . [but] he is essentially the man with whom you are always wanting to shake hands" (316).

Describing Anglo-American relations, Steevens invokes the conversations about formal and informal union addressed in Chapters 2 and 3: "We talk of this country as our daughter, and of war with it as unnatural, unheard of, impossible" (136). The tenor of the British discourse Steevens reports reflects the different maturities of the two nations: "It may not mean much, but the sentiment, if Platonic, is absolutely sincere. But to the American, the champion of arbitration, war is always a present possibility—with anybody at any moment" (Steevens 136). Thus, Steevens associates American reluctance to make firm diplomatic commitments with a belligerent callowness. This character extends to America's behavior on the world stage: American presidents "approach foreign problems without knowledge of the usages of international good breeding, and with one eye steadily fixed on public feeling among the electors at home" (Steevens 140). The implication, here and throughout the text, is that this rude democracy requires British guidance, even if it is reluctant to accept it. Steevens thus reads the pressures driving Britain toward closer ties with the United States in terms that make the latter the true, if unappreciative, beneficiary of these attentions. Such a posture would cumulate in the racialist sentiments trumpeted in Britain in support of America's entry into an imperial war in 1898, discussed in Chapter 3.

Fabian writer and activist Beatrice Webb came to America with a different immediate audience and a different set of political commitments, composing the 1898 *American Diary* while on a visit to study the workings of American local government. Yet she too focuses upon a stable, and culturally deficient, American character, noting "the absence of distinguished talent and of variety of type of the American race" (Webb 148). However, Webb attributes this homogeneity to ideological causes; she offers "the hypothesis that there is something in the way of life and the mental environment of the U.S.A. that hinders or damps down the emergence of intellectual or artistic distinction" (Webb 148). Unlike critics who view American ideals as pervaded by bad faith in their application (and as a result, often, of their hybrid racial nature), for Webb the fault lies within the ideals themselves. She attributes this to two fallacies within American ideology:

> That "all men are born free and equal"; with its derivative that one man is as good as another and equally fitted to deliver judgment on every conceivable question . . . It is . . . Protestantism, [the] assumption that there is no such thing as the expert, and that all men are equally good judges in all questions, that is one of the fallacies that eats away the roots of any American genius by blinding his fellow citizens to his peculiar talent or attainments . . . The Englishman . . . has inherited sufficient experience of affairs to reject the rotten metaphysicals of Protestantism and to perceive that the whole modern theory of division of labour leads straight to increased specialization of particular faculties in particular people, and to the careful selection of experts for the finer work of a complicated civilization. (Webb 149)

In her comparison of the Englishman and the American Webb valorizes specialization as a marker of an advanced culture. Webb's Arnoldian reference to the "finer work of a complicated civilization" reprises the temporal and public-versus-private coordinates of analyses by Steevens and other critics of this period. Unlike these contemporaries, Webb insinuates that intellectual and artistic distinction is fostered by a society with an advanced division of labor, an argument that reflects her Fabian commitments. An advanced division of labor contributes to a strong sense of the state. The second fallacy she discovers in American ideology reflects this position: "The second assumption is perhaps less consciously held, but is more universally acted upon. It is the old fallacy of the classic economists that each man will best serve the interests of the whole community by pursuing his own gain. It is interesting to note that this axiom was invented by English thinkers; but it has never been fully accepted by the English people" (Webb 149). Webb associates American ideals with a naïve individualism and promotes an Arnoldian vision of a culture of experts. She depicts America as a society in which the anarchy of a lack of proper social distinctions and a lack of specialization defeat any promise of cultural development. America is disturbingly homogenous: "All professions, all occupations, resolve themselves into a race for money. However diverse may be the origin and physical environment of a people, if they have but one motive there can be but one faculty. Hence the all-pervading and all-devouring 'executive' capacity of the American people" (Webb 150). The editor of Webb's diary, David Shannon, points out that her strongest conclusions, such as these, stem from a cultural myopia: "So British was she that she was quite incapable of understanding non-Britons. Thus, although she tended to judge American politicians by their intellectual powers or lack of them, she quite consistently judged American intellectuals by non-intellectual standards, primarily by their appearance and manners as compared to their British counterparts" (Webb xii).

Webb focuses, like so many of her counterparts, upon American businessmen as representative figures of the American type. Unlike Dickens with his bootmaker or Stevenson with his paperboy, Webb does not engage in personal anecdote but treats businessmen as an analytical category. Businessmen lack standards of excellence because they lack culture. She notes the "extreme conventionality" of their ideas and asserts that although the prevailing ideology is individualistic, there is in practice great "contempt for the vested interests . . . of the individual citizen. Private enterprise is permitted to trample on the individual" (Webb 13). Webb alludes to a common complaint within American society in the wake of the struggles against monopoly capital in the 1890s: corporations are vested with the rights of individual citizens, and thus the citizen finds her or his own rights circumscribed within contractual relations with an unimpeachable, unassailable corporate might. While such an observation reflects her socialist leanings, Webb's Arnoldian affinities are apparent in her consistent assignations of character to an emergent social type: the "intellectual traditions of the ordinary American business man are a naïve individualism tempered by an opportunist consideration for any new forces that may appear . . . He is . . . an ideal philistine" (Webb 23). As a prototype for this ideal Philistine, the businessman is a "rule of thumb man, destitute of all culture" (Webb 23). Webb's Arnoldian language draws directly from early descriptions of John Bull, associating British culture with the creation of sophisticated, refined subjects.

Philip Burne-Jones's travelogue, *Dollars and Democracy* (1904), focuses upon comment rather than discovery. The author, illustrator, and son of Edward Burne-Jones is conscious throughout that he is recording his opinion of people, places, and structures of which his readership is already well aware. In this intertextual context, in which the subject cannot offer new subjects, the personal impression is dominant. Indeed, Burne-Jones's text contains some of the formal characteristics that distinguished the modernist artistic project from its literary predecessors: a focus upon individual subjectivity, fleeting sensory impressions, an instability of experience, and a conscious reformulation of older artistic conceits.

In his introduction, Burne-Jones stages an impulse to explore America in terms of an exhaustion of the impressions available in Europe. The narrative proper begins with an account of the ennui that drove him from England and the search for experience. This characteristically Romantic trope is supplemented by his appeal to common experience: "Their whole being, physical and intellectual, seems to demand an absolute change of surrounding—to crave fresh opportunities. This, I imagine, is at one time or another an experience common to most of us" (Burne-Jones 4).

This interpellative move is accompanied by an appeal to the values that distinguish the British from Americans. In the preface, Burne-Jones announces a dichotomy between democracy and taste: spending a full year in the United States "has given me opportunities for observing some of the national virtues and shortcomings, from the highest to the lowest (if the Spirit of Democracy will permit such invidious distinctions), such as are not always available to the traveler whose time is more limited" (v). The irony of Burne-Jones's language, describing distinctions as "invidious," serves to position the narrative voice: unserious, dandyish, and focused upon aesthetic pleasures rather than sober analysis. The pose stands in stark contrast to his portrait of Americans, whose seriousness, rudeness of manner, materialism, and myopia go hand in hand.

Burne-Jones is rather unique in focusing upon America's egalitarian ideals without disparaging them or holding them responsible for the condition of American culture: "This doctrine of equality, though of course it lends itself, as the best things often do, to ridicule or ludicrous satire, is in reality a fine idea, and it lies at the root of all that America once held most sacred when she began the new life a hundred years ago—the theory that every man born in the country should have a fair and equal chance—a better chance than he would have had in the Old World; and it is this spirit that has inspired the whole people since it has existed as a separate nation" (Burne-Jones 71). Nevertheless, according to Burne-Jones American idealism fails in its application, particularly among the people who have succeeded financially within the American system. Americans are rather unfortunately prone to fantasy and self-puffery.

The "impressionism" and professed unseriousness of the narrator, however, perform a cosmopolitan cultivation ultimately associated with British culture. Burne-Jones reprises the linkage between American materialism and nationalist fervor to offer a contrasting model of British power and reserve. He describes the boasting of Americans rather ironically: "[In America] manifold excellences can never be outshone, even among kinsmen upon whose dominions the sun never sets" (Burne-Jones vi). By contrast to American self-flattery, Burne-Jones's reference to the British Empire indicates a confidence in British power that many of his contemporaries did not possess. The text thus contains both dandyism and confidence in the stability of a British perspective— indeed, the "dandyish" perspective is not countercultural, but in fact buttresses British cultural claims.

Burne-Jones's staging of his own identity reflects this combination. He identifies himself as characteristically English: "In describing people and things, I have approached them entirely from the point of view of an Englishman, noting especially those details of custom and manner, however trivial, wherein they differ from ourselves" (Burne-Jones vi). On the surface, this passage seems merely to acknowledge that Burne-Jones comes from an English background and that his descriptions depend on his assumptions about the norms of taste learned through his background. On second glance, however, he is implying something more. Namely, he associates the English point of view with an attention to details of custom and manner, with a highly developed ability to collect and order sensory impressions. Nevertheless, he also associates the English character with insularity: "I wonder why it is that an Englishman, starting for a foreign country, so often thinks it necessary to load himself up with articles from home which he could buy just as well or better in the cities he visits abroad. I suppose it is something instinctive in our insular nature" (Burne-Jones 6). Thus while Burne-Jones makes repeated gestures to the common reader and to a sense of shared English characteristics, he is also subtly criticizing the implied reader and using his visit to offer a model for an English aesthetic perspective.

In *Dollars and Democracy*, Philistinism is a threat to civilization, representing a fetishization of pursuits antithetical to culture. He distinguishes between the two nations by noting that while Americans are materialistic, the British are obsessed with politics: "How they talk of money! In snatches of conversation caught in the streets, the restaurants, and the cars, the continual cry is always 'dollars—dollars—dollars!' You hear it on all sides perpetually, and money does truly here, as politics in England, seem to be an end in itself, instead of a means to an end" (Burne-Jones 74). Both points of critique—identifying American Philistines with mindless materialism and British Philistinism with politics for the sake of politics (i.e., needless debate over domestic and international policy)— serve Burne-Jones's attempt to suture an aestheticist perspective with a nostalgic version of the British cultural mission.

Burne-Jones thus attacks the bourgeoisie on both sides of the Atlantic, even while focusing upon the materialism of Americans. To Burne-Jones, Americans' obsession with wealth has become an end in itself, a kind of dead end that the Englishman must avoid. He asks, "What is there, one wonders, that these people can possibly gain from the acquisition of money in any way proportionate in their minds to the importance of the process of getting it? Indeed, it does seem as if the lives of most men in America had for their sole aim and object the making of money . . . It must be the love of the game that keeps them at it; very often it certainly isn't a necessity. They seem to have no time left; no ability to enjoy this money when it is made" (Burne-Jones 74). Burne-Jones thus offers a surprising turn in the theme of different national temporalities—the fetishization of money reflects an unsophisticated, callow culture, and this condition prevents Americans from having time to develop culture. Moreover, the catch-22 of Americans' money worship deprives them of the time for reflection and leisure that is the basis of Burne-Jones's own narrative position. If *Dollars and Democracy* may be said to have a loose didactic project, it consists of modeling the contrast between a leisured, aesthetically interested perspective and the virtually unconscious drive toward wealth of American life.

These circumstances place America, again, in the position of child in relation to its transatlantic parent. Despite some similarities between the English and Americans, for Burne-Jones, transatlantic anxiety circulates only from West to East. He attributes to Americans a "sometimes slightly anxious desire to know just exactly how this great, new, wonderful country—the growth of little more than a century—strikes the stranger from beyond the seas, with his long legacy of prejudice and tradition; and somewhere behind it, too, there lurks the spirit of the truant child, who, having rid itself of all home ties, looks back somewhat wistfully to the place of its birth, perhaps not yet wholly indifferent to parental approbation" (Burne-Jones 18–19). This reimagining of the familial metaphors that structure Anglo-American relations envisions Americans as completely separate from Britain, but nevertheless anxious to please. In this posture, the British stranger figures in the role of parent, as the messenger of tradition to whom the American man-child appeals. Burne-Jones's combination of irony, play, and detachment with a traditionalist view of England links him to other travel writers not dealt with in this chapter, such as G. K. Chesterton. Such a posture seems emblematic of the contradictions that attended the aesthetic pretensions of the Edwardian gentleman.

BRITISH SELF-CRITICISM IN POSITIVE ANALYSES OF THE UNITED STATES

In contrast to the numerous British critics who associated America with a pervasive materialism, Philistinism, and mass culture, others saw in America a valued friend and a necessary aid to Britain in a period of diminishing global influence. For these critics, the act of criticism is itself enmeshed in history; that is, they recognize that their perspective upon the United States, and that of their more negative peers, is dependent upon specific sociohistorical conditions. When exculpating Americans for their faults, they refer increasingly to faults and flaws within the British character. Nevertheless, for these writers Philistinic British culture differs from their own positionality, and they indeed model themselves as figures of British culture incarnate who can offer a valuable corrective to their less refined American cousins. While their opinions about America differ drastically from their more negative counterparts, the refined positionality they model continues to draw upon intertextual mastery, temporal differences between the two nations, analysis of American ideology, and a critique of the public nature of American life.

In *America the Land of Contrasts* (1898), James Muirhead (also the author of the contemporary Baedeker guide to the United States) positions his perspective about America and Americans directly against the trend of associating the United States with Philistinic homogeneity and misguided individualism. Muirhead's title is itself intertextual, designed to attribute to the United States a complexity not granted in most books about America.

Muirhead's awareness of and resistance to reductive readings of the United States is apparent in his appraisal of the most common accusation levied at Americans, materialism. He argues that Americans are associated with greed because of the nation's tremendous economic growth during this period: "The prevalent belief that America is more sedulous in the worship of the Golden Calf than any other country arises largely, I believe, from the fact that the chances of acquiring wealth are more frequent and easy there than elsewhere. Opportunity makes the thief. Anyhow this reproach comes with a bad grace from the native of a country that has in its annals the outbreak of the South Sea Bubble, the railway mania of the Hudson era, and the revelations of Mr. Hooley" (Muirhead 102–3). References to British financial fraud and disasters here remind the British reader not to forget Britain's own history of excessive materialism. Muirhead simultaneously recognizes the dangers of stereotyping and warns of moments of "bad grace" to encourage British readers to engage in disinterested comparisons of the nations.

Yet Muirhead also confirms a number of the stereotypes about Americans offered by his contemporaries: they are rather excessively enthusiastic, they lack refined manners, and they are rather oblivious of the impression they make. Generally Muirhead notes that American society is homogenous, characterized by broad public sentiments rather than class interest. Unlike his contemporaries, Muirhead takes a positive view of the lack of class distinctions in the United States, a point focused on by several of his predecessors. "In America there is less need and less use of this patronizing kindness; there is less kindness from class to class simply because the conscious realization of 'class' is nonexistent in thousands of cases where it would be to the fore in Europe" (Muirhead 378).

Muirhead views class as an "obsolescent institution" that contributes to an inhuman attitude that "frankly and even brutally asserts the essential inequality of man" (91). Whereas other analyses of America tend to displace unfavorable forces within British society abroad, Muirhead carefully distinguishes between American and British variants of particular phenomena. He notes that many of the stereotypes about American businessmen merit some credulity but argues that Americans are not an enormous population of Arnoldian Philistines: "The American man of business, with his restless discontent and nervous, overstrained pursuit of wealth, may not be a more inspiring object than his British brother, but he has little of the smugness which Mr. Arnold has taught us to associate with Philistinism" (Muirhead 83). Here Muirhead acknowledges the prominence of a particular American type, but is focused upon making careful distinctions between different versions. Again, his position regarding Americans is rather more positive than that of other writers.

Muirhead's comments regarding the British affirm many of the characteristics associated with John Bull—a laconic nature, pragmatism, and indifference to the opinions of others:

> The Briton's indifference to criticism is at once his strength and his weakness. It makes him invincible in a cause that has dominated his conscience; it hinders him in the attainment of a luminous discrimination between cause and cause. His profound self-confidence, his sheer good sense, his dogged persistence, his bulldog courage, his essential honesty of purpose, bring him to the goal in spite of the unnecessary obstacles that have been heaped on his path by his own [hubris] and contempt of others. He chooses what is physically the shortest line in preference to the line of least resistance. (Muirhead 91)

Muirhead supports the John Bull stereotype, including the idea that the British are more conventional than other peoples. The British citizen may appear more refined and cultured while traveling in America because he is less adaptable than Americans: "Out of his own class he may sometimes appear less conventional than the American, simply because the latter is quick to adopt the manners of a new milieu, while John Bull clings doggedly to his old conventions" (Muirhead 91).

Overall, then, while Muirhead levels significant criticisms at the United States, he does not share the position that America represents a modernity threatening British culture. Instead, he modifies the typical temporal dynamic by portraying the British as anachronistic figures in need of contact with more contemporary influences and particularly in need of a modification of class-based attitudes.

In *The Future in America: A Search after Realities* (1906), H. G. Wells trains his socialist and sociological gaze upon America, a subject he had engaged in *Anticipations* (1901). As the title suggests, Wells seeks to correct what he sees as the fantastic nature of many previous analyses of the United States. The text is one of the more self-consciously intertextual travelogues in the group examined in this chapter. Wells notes a wide range of sources, from Dickens's *American Notes* to J. Morgan Richards's memoir *With John Bull and Jonathan*. It is an eclectic book, alternating among speculative analysis, impressionistic reflection, and theories of history. In a loose, chatty style, Wells integrates descriptions of American material realities with a growing theory of the "American problem" and how to solve it. Nevertheless, Wells positions himself as an amateur even while demonstrating his polymathic intelligence. He distinguishes himself from the American mind by viewing his absorption and forgetting of details as superior to the rationalistic, excessively archival treatment of knowledge in the United States. He tells an anecdote about a visit to Wellesley College in which he is asked about Tennyson's "The Princess," a poem that celebrates domestic feminine virtues and condemns feminist education. Whether or not Wells is asserting the irony of Wellesley students embracing an antifeminist text, he certainly valorizes his brand of knowledge over theirs: "I had read it when I was a boy, I was delighted to be able to claim, and had honorably forgotten the incident. But in Boston they treat it as a living classic, and expect you to remember constantly and with appreciation this passage and that. I think that quite typical of the Bostonian weakness. It is the error of the clever high-school girl, it is the mistake of the scholastic mind all the world over, to learn too thoroughly and to carry too much" (*The Future in America* 232). Wells's commentary about the Wellesley students as representatives of all of Boston constitutes a specific geographic analysis, but it also reflects his larger sense of the failure of culture in the United States. He repeats themes displayed in earlier anecdotes—the narrator's own, private judgment and faculties are contrasted with the American tendency to draw its opinions and judgments from a rude public sphere. As with previous travelogues, Americans are associated with material values and with a treatment of culture as a commodity. Wells's assertion of a refined personality links ideology to commodity fetishism: while culture shapes the British self, for the American, culture is treated as a possession and sign of prestige. Yet for Wells, as opposed to his predecessors and contemporaries, judgment must be directed upon the present and the future. That is, while post-Arnoldian proponents of culture tend to celebrate the refinement of a persona whose interests turn it away from the material present, Wells mirrors this persona while reversing its interests. He is a reformer cloaked as an Edwardian gentleman.

The Future in America rejects the aestheticism of critics such as Burne-Jones while reasserting the superiority of British judgment to American materialist knowledge. This tendency is surprising in Wells, whose socialist leanings would seem to favor a materialist approach to knowledge. Wells's response to his predecessors in the American travelogue is to continuously, and rather immodestly, disparage his own capacities in the midst of his analysis of the United States. An aside in the chapter "State-Blindness" may stand in for a book's worth of similar dissimulations: "Remember always that I am an undiplomatic tourist of no special knowledge or authority, who came, moreover, to America with certain prepossessions" (*The Future in America* 153). Wells's denial of personal expertise in matters of culture marks his link to Philip Burne-Jones (and others examined elsewhere in this book, including Oscar Wilde and Charles Whibley) as an amateur and impressionist. He differs, nevertheless, from these critics insofar as he envisions collective programs for the betterment of the United States. In this he is a rather direct descendent of Arnold, though with vastly different sympathies.

Wells's diagnosis of the American problem, as he calls it, involves three factors: first, an economic process leading toward plutocracy;

second, the sustained disorder of local and political administration; and finally, the immigration of alien and unassimilable workers. Though Wells is interested in assessing the potential for a socialist future in America, he does not subscribe to rigidly materialist principles. He believes that a nation's destiny is determined more by will than by its resources and capacity for production: "The material factors in a nation's will are subordinate factors . . . The essential factor in the destiny of a nation, as of a man and mankind, lies in the form of its will and in the quality and quantity of its will" (*The Future in America* 13). Wells's vitalism operates within the temporal context of earlier narratives: where Wells judges national "will" from a position of authority, America's will is nascent, and thus scrutinized.

While questioning the "quality" of American will, Wells invokes the rhetoric of judgment that we have seen in other accounts of the United States: "How subtle, how collected and patient, how far capable of a long plan, is this American nation?" (*The Future in America* 15). The English provide a model for the will required of a great nation: "An Englishman comes to think that most of the permanent and precious things for which a nation's effort goes are . . . ends that are not obvious, that are intricate and complex and not to be won by booms and cataclysms of effort" (*The Future in America* 15–16). Wells questions whether Americans' individual willpowers, all directed toward self-interest, are capable of reaching to such a higher purpose: "When one talks to an American of his national purpose he seems a little at a loss; if one speaks of his national destiny, he responds with alacrity" (*The Future in America* 21). Like Arnold, Wells sees the key to the future in a state that promotes culture and education over materialism. Unlike Arnold, Wells sees the pursuit of scientific knowledge as equally, if not more, important than culture. For Wells, the typical American is possessed by an "optimistic fatalism," imagining that greatness consists more in might than in achievement and lasting contributions to Western civilization: "Most western Europeans have this delusion of automatic progress in things badly enough, but with Americans it seems to be almost fundamental" (*The Future in America* 30).

In the chapter "State-Blindness," Wells attributes this critique to the mentality of the American businessman by examining the memoirs of an American advertising agent in London. In *With*

John Bull and Jonathan, J. Morgan Richards reflects upon a life of commercial successes, which included such triumphs as painting the rocks along the Hudson with advertisements for bitters and overcoming public and legal resistance to the introduction of cigarettes in England. Wells's criticism centers on Richards's lack of a communal perspective, and indeed in the cult of commercial values of which Richards was a member. He cites Richards's worship of the British Dr. Parker, whose pamphlet "Ten General Commandments for Men of Business" includes such pearls as "thou shalt not hobnob with idle persons," which Wells mocks as "so glossing richly the teachings of Him who ate with publicans and sinners" (*The Future in America* 159). Wells does not doubt the sincerity of the memoir, but asserts that it is "a fair sample of the quality and trend of the mind-stuff and the breadth and height of the tradition of a large and I know not how influential mass of prosperous middle-class English, and of a much more prosperous and influential and important section of Americans" (*The Future in America* 160).

Wells views this group, particularly in America, as a powerful opposition to "any decent public purpose": "In the face of the great needs that lie before America their active triviality of soul, their energy and often unscrupulous activity, and their quantitative importance become . . . adverse and threatening, a stumbling block for hope" (*The Future in America* 161).

However, Richards is only a sample of "an older type of American" (*The Future in America* 161). Moreover, commercialism is a threat to America because of the corrupting effect it has on the national will. To Wells, the American "has an ethical system of a highly commercialized type. If he isn't dishonest he's commercialized. He lives to get, to come out of every transaction with more than he gave" (*The Future in America* 122). Further, what characters like Richards demonstrate is the degree to which the romanticization of commerce leads to blindness to corruption. Wells sees liberal society built upon castles of sand: "In the highly imaginative theory that underlies the realities of an individualistic society there is such a thing as honest trading. In practice I don't believe there is" (*The Future in America* 122). Such commentary gives us further insight into this text's blend of socialism and idealism, in which commercialism taints Western civilization:

In all ages, among all races, this taint in trade has been felt. Modern western Europe, led by England, and America have denied it stoutly, have glorified the trader, called him a "merchant prince," wrapped him in the purple of the word "financier," bowed down before him. The trader remains a trader, a hand that clutches, an uncreative brain that lays snares . . . It is not he but the maker who must be the power and ruler of the great and luminous social order that must surely come . . . The American, I feel assured, can be a bold and splendid maker. He is not, like the uncreative Parsee or Jew or Armenian, a trader by blood and nature. (*The Future in America* 125)

Beneath his critique of the ways in which the realities of commerce are glorified in American society, Wells makes an ethnic and racial distinction that suggests that he believes in some form of essential character.

In fact, Wells sees glimmers of this "bold and splendid maker" in "Young America . . . an altogether different type from [those] . . . who were the backbone of the irresponsible commercial American of yesterday" (*The Future in America* 161–62). Wells's identification of a new American type is implicitly an intertextual comment, and key to his association of the United States with future progress. Wells's textual critique reinforces his distinction between progress and commercialism, between will that contributes to the national purpose and mere self-interest. He, like the Englishman he describes, is patient, collected, and interested in advancing a higher purpose. The writing of this text is itself an anticommercial enterprise—it reflects a commitment to service and progress, to the very higher purposes Richards's memoir fails to grasp.

Yet the racial underpinnings of this argument recall the claims of Steevens. If Young America proffers hope, it is also threatened by mass immigration. The enormous influx of new citizens would seem to make Anglo-Saxon New England society increasingly peripheral to majority experience: "I have tried to make the note of immigration grow slowly to a dominating significance in this panorama, and with that, to make more and more evident my sense of the need of a creative assimilation . . . for synthetic effort, lest all this great world . . . should decay into a vast unprogressive stagnation of unhappiness and disorder" (*The Future in America* 203). Wells's man of culture—undoubtedly one with Anglo-Saxon roots—must assimilate America into a single collective body focused upon advancing the ideals of Western civilization. Thus while Wells is much clearer than most critics about the processes of stereotyping and the ideological components of celebrations of nationality and capitalism, he ultimately validates a discourse of national and racial difference. His horizon ends at questions of historical teleology. While he recognizes many of the limitations of middle-class British perspectives upon America, he also sees interdependency: "Our future is extraordinarily bound up in America and in a sense dependent upon it. It is not that we dream very much of political reunions of Anglo Saxondom and the like . . . But our civilization is a different thing from our Empire, a thing that reaches out further into the future, that will be going on changed beyond recognition. Because of our common language, of our common traditions, Americans are a part of our community, are becoming indeed the larger part of our community of thought and feeling and outlook" (*The Future in America* 18).

Even works that take comprehensive stock of the sociohistorical conditions that shaped Anglo-American politics share with their less objective counterparts a repeated inscription of a new model of British subjectivity. The circulation of British stereotypes about America, and by implication the refashioning of Britishness, was a key element in what Raymond Williams calls the "structure of feeling" of this particular historical moment. The suffusion of this new model of Britishness throughout turn-of-the-century public discourse suggests its urgent relation to British anxieties about changes in its domestic society and a recession of its imperial might. The next chapter focuses upon commerce as a facilitator of and trope within this discourse. What, specifically, are the economic interests supporting debates about and analyses of the United States and Britain in terms of culturalism? How, in light of improved communications technologies across the Atlantic, did the essentially comparative tropes of Arnold evolve into a sense of Anglo-American commonality? And how did turn-of-the-century writers deploy these changes to offer pedagogical messages to the British public while insinuating, via their own personae, the superiority of British culture?

CHAPTER 2

COMMERCE, REUNION, AND THE
ANGLO-AMERICAN PUBLIC SPHERE

Imagine, for a moment, the sensation caused by the opening of the first Kinetoscope parlor in London in 1894. As the viewer presses his or her eyes to the viewing pane, a reel of individual frames, frozen spots of time, accelerate into an illusion of the comic motions of Fred Ott's sneeze, serpentine dancers, Sandow the strong man, boxing cats, and other sundry scenes shot in the Edison laboratory in New Jersey, or outdoor clips of spectacles like Buffalo Bill's Wild West Show. Now, imagine the forces that brought the parlors to London—American émigrés, perhaps at that moment sharing the parlor with the London consumer; intensive interest in Edison's inventions in England; Edison's sales agent in London, Col. George Gourard; reports of the Wild West show and memories of its appearances in Britain. Each of these would imply a shared cultural space between Britain and the United States. No longer was transatlantic "communication" framed in terms of cross-cultural ripostes for home consumption. That is, no longer did the "conversation" have the aspect of two distant ships firing salvos across one another's bows for the pleasure of the audience on deck.

H. G. Nicholas has argued that shared language, history, and shared "Anglo-American consciousness" have played a key role in legitimating American and British claims to cultural superiority (Nicholas 3). While suggestive, the claim fails to come to terms with the contemporaneous sources promoting the existence of a shared consciousness. By examining Anglo-American journalism, we will consider the implications of voices that proclaimed and *simulated* an Anglo-American public sphere, especially how this rhetoric disseminated the pedagogical and performative images of nationality outlined in the Introduction.[1] This is not to suggest that Anglo-American readers did not share mutual values or consciousness, but rather to focus upon the underlying interest that lay at the basis of proclaiming these contiguities.[2]

The Anglo-American public sphere was suffused with debates over empire. The lessons of the American Revolution and the prospect of international isolation, particularly after the Berlin conference of 1884, spurred liberal thinkers like Gladstone, Dilke, Bright, and Cobden to consider giving colonies self-government and promoting an imperial federation that might include the United States. The imperial federationist movement, itself characterized by a divide between commercial and cultural priorities, lent momentum to proposals for Anglo-American reunification.

The legitimating rhetoric of a shared Anglo-American public sphere changed through the nineteenth century, increasingly locating shared feeling in relations between American and British public figures. By the turn of the century, writings invoking an Anglo-American public sphere recast commerce in a negative light. At midcentury, commerce figured as a lubricant protecting the persistence and growth of affection and the strength of federation. At the turn of the century, it was recast as a dangerous commercialism. This shift reflects the emergent positionality described in the Introduction and Chapter 1, in which pedagogical messages to the *natio* are mediated through representations of America and Americans in the voice of refined British subjects.

Toward the end of the nineteenth century, the Anglo-American public sphere was tailored around the London émigré community of Americans and the circulation of political and diplomatic figures through this community. Within Britain, threats to bourgeois supremacy—the expansion of literacy and voting rights, crises in domestic Liberalism, international competition for the empire—expanded this audience. Also, this positionality was suited to American audiences, whose cultural capital rested upon legitimating a mugwump culture within an avowedly egalitarian system. Paradoxically, the need to naturalize new wealth created a market for voices, experiences, and things British whose associations conferred a legitimacy detached from the market, even when those values were themselves subject to mockery and scorn.

This sense of a mutual "imagined community," to borrow Benedict Anderson's phrase, was driven by commercial interest rather than location. For example, papers were published and circulated throughout Europe for American and British travelers embarked on the *grand tour*. The front pages of one such paper featured advertisements promoting leisure and health—an American family home in Paris available to rent; an Anglo-American bank; an English and American agency locating apartments; an English pharmacy; artistic hair-dressing; philatelic catalogues; and merchants selling champagne, teas, pianos, sight-restoring ivory eye cups, anticlairous tonic elixirs, competing toothpastes, medicines, gloves, fashions, sewing machines, English and American books, Clarke's world-famed blood mixture, female pills, and treatises on male sexual health.[3] In addition, ads proliferated for spas, hotels, resorts, and rail and steamer services. Correspondingly, the paper, after brief "notes" carrying English, American, and Continental news, included lists of sights in Paris and Geneva, of the traveling movements of important personages, lists of American and English arrivals at hotels, humorous anecdotes, and a heavy dose of "sporting intelligence."

Advertisements like these offered a common fund of products linking readers into a shared commercial community. While I cannot vouch for the efficacy of Clarke's blood mixture or the sight-restoring capacities of ivory eye cups, the cosmopolitan experience of the *tour* was heavily mediated by a sense of common Anglo-American identity. Banks, books, and service-industry businesses catering to the traveler hailed Americans and British citizens through a common voice.

This specialized example from tourism foregrounds a fundamental characteristic of our topic: The Anglo-American relation was, and is, overdetermined by commercial interests. While previous commentary on transatlantic relations in textual studies and the Introduction to this book assert a psychodynamics at the core of cross- and transcultural representation, it is useful to remember that commerce dominated the relationship. The movement from "gentility" to "culture" thus requires a proviso: images of the cultured Anglo-American reader proliferate in commercial contexts, drawing upon culture to validate consumption.

THE COMMERCIAL CONTEXT OF THE
ANGLO-AMERICAN PUBLIC SPHERE

The assertion that the Anglo-American relationship is fundamentally commercial carries two implications: first, the visible transatlantic relationship was suffused with commercial intercourse, and second, representations of the relationship and of the character of the parties to it occurred in a commercial context. The second implication becomes increasingly visible as we approach the turn of the century. While earlier images figure the relationship in terms of a simple exchange—culture for lucre—or a common selection of commodities, by the turn of the century, a heightened sense of interconnectedness emerged between the two economies. Whereas through the nineteenth century American consumer appetites for British "brand" names like Wedgwood and Chippendale grew, at the end of the century the sense of a shared, if heterogeneous, market space led to complex images such as the following advertisement for (American-produced) Remington typewriters: "Remington Typewriter. By Appointment to Her Majesty the Queen. HRH The Prince of Wales. Contractors to Her Majesty's Government. Leadership means Superiority. Continued Leadership implies Progress. Tacitly acknowledged Leadership over many Competitors shows Undeniable Merit" (*The London American* April 3, 1895, 1). Sold, one supposes, to an expatriate American readership, this American product is pitched through the approbation of the British monarchy and its apparatus as arbiters of quality and, more obscurely, "leadership," "progress," and "undeniable merit." This ad exemplifies the complications of heightened transatlantic interconnectedness. In 1902, Goldwin Smith argued that in America "the craving for aristocracy goes so high that the furniture of a house in an American city, because a Duke has sat on it, fetches extraordinary prices" (*Commonwealth or Empire?* 13). Here, product differentiation processes operating within the Anglo-American market draw upon notions of national culture and identity. The advertisement reflects increasing competition and the pressure for "distinction." Moreover, the complex relations represented between Britain and America themselves mark the author's sophistication: that is to say, turn-of-the-century Anglo-American discourse produces a kind of market for positionality, for the authorial perspective presenting distinctive, consumable images of the Anglo-American relationship.

In his effort to fill in a "gap in the intellectual history of empire," Duncan Bell argues that focusing upon canonical figures to write the intellectual history of the nineteenth century is inevitably misleading because "'great' figures are often unrepresentative (or are only partly so) of the intellectual currents of any given historical epoch" (Bell 22). As mentioned in the Introduction, Bell favors exploring the "'murky shallows,' not only of policy debate but also of general political argument . . . in order to enrich understanding of the way in which the empire was imagined, and the multiple and often contradictory roles that it played in Victorian intellectual life" (Bell 22–23). Bell's "murky shallows" include a range of cultural materials whose sheer volume, even when confined to the limited subject treated here, is unassimilable.

Of the ephemera fostering Anglo-American identification through the commodity, Anglo-American newspapers are both ground and figure, themselves the *sine qua non* "commodity" exhibiting this process. While the papers were not ultimately commercially viable, the repeated appearance of new papers for this market, and the alteration of their content and politics over time, illustrates a strong current in the evolution of Anglo-American relations from an emphasis upon the free market toward the more complex commercial interrelations found at the turn of the century. Carriers of images of the commodity, these newspapers are themselves products designed to attract a customer base and advertising based on distinction and relationality.

THE CIVIL IMAGINARY IN ANGLO-AMERICAN NEWSPAPERS

While the Anglo-American relationship has been dominated by commerce, the history of Anglo-American discourse has been overwhelmingly *private*. The cultural atmosphere was pregnant with communication between and interest in the nations by their counterparts. Katie-Louise Thomas has argued that postal networks and the transatlantic telegraph were viewed as facilitators of a deep sense of alliance between America and Great Britain. In the context of this thriving private communications network, published transatlantic discourse and representations of transatlantic discourse implicitly speak in the name of a far greater polity. Public discourses were fashioned as proxy speech acts, reflecting a range of perspectives communicated in "invisible" forms. Yet occurring across the pages of commercial newspapers and journals, rather than in the particular situation of private communications, these speech acts simulated a public forum that did not, in fact, exist off the page.

Simon During uses the term "civil imaginary" to describe the "cultural space [created by] . . . prose writings which provide representations of social existence from the beginning of the eighteenth century through the period of the classic realist novel and beyond . . . The civil Imaginary is an attempt to order what Steele calls 'the uncontrollable jumble of Persons and Things' in that society . . . It produces representations of manners, taste, behaviour, utterances for imitation by individual lives" (During 142). This imaginary "reproduces everyday life in the public domain . . . replacing the old science of casuistry by the modern domination of the life-world by style and civility . . . [through a] narrator [who] is explicitly socially located in the writing" (During 143). For During, the "civil imaginary" locates a disciplinary function in the observation and recording of the everyday performed by a humorous, but "socially located" narrator. That is, the "rambler," or "spectator" conveys the happenings in a bounded London sphere, and in doing so makes his scrutiny of that sphere an essential part of how his readership relates to it. Thus, the reader who puts down his (or her) paper and returns to the coffeehouses of the city returns to a disciplinary space, having (ironically) internalized the values, mores, and attitudes of the "position" of the spectator or rambler as a form of pleasurable consumption.

The end of the nineteenth century, by contrast, did not have the dominant voices of the Augustans. Yet the autodidactic zeal, particularly for cultural literacy, that Mark Hampton, Patrick Collier, and others associate with newspaper readers in this period facilitated the simulation of an Anglo-American public sphere. While Hampton persuasively argues that the "educative ideals" of pre-1880 newspapers subsequently gave way to the "representative" project of New Journalism, this "representativeness" in fact involved an interpellative function. Editorial voices in the Anglo-American papers articulated a sense of positional superiority and gave the readership a sense of transatlantic print culture as a knowable community pursuing vaguely Arnoldian ends.

Of course, newspapers perform a "civil imaginary" function ipso facto, and it is hardly surprising that Benedict Anderson's theory of nationalism focuses upon the sense of imaginary community forged through the papers. The Anglo-American papers, however, differ by seeking to speak for a transnational public sphere. To do so, they often adopted a mediating position, rejecting the disputatious tone of editorial pages of other newspapers, especially east coast American papers. This moderate voice emerged as technologies such as the steamship, the telegraph, and the radio; demographic changes; and the mature tourist industry made competitive and comparative accounts of the two nations seem antiquated and indeed regressive.

The "civil imaginary" that emerges in the Anglo-American newspapers is thus a simulacrum: the papers' legitimacy lies partly in response to other transatlantic and journalistic conversations, rather than an observatory report upon social conditions in a bounded physical space. As is the case with simulacra generally, the power of distortion usually served commercial purposes by appealing to the anxieties and needs of its reading public.

Anglo-American discourse entered the civil imaginary through a variety of forms of writing. However, travel narratives and Anglo-American newspapers were instrumental in positing an Anglo-American public sphere. As John Barrington has argued, newspapers in the mid-eighteenth century "simultaneously voiced the particular viewpoint of a single province and manifested a wider, transatlantic discourse about America's place in the Empire and the world" (66).

Nevertheless, we will begin with a survey of explicitly Anglo-American newspapers published from 1835 to 1895, focusing upon the identity claims they made regarding themselves and their readership. Then, we will explore the Anglo-American journalism of 1895 through 1905, the height of Anglo-American sentiment.

The *British and American Intelligencer* (1835) announced the themes that would dominate attempts to create an Anglo-American public sphere—commerce, liberty, and republican institutions—in its founding issue upon converting from the title *New Weekly Dispatch*: "The political hemisphere as regards our connection with America is now fast approaching that resplendence and glory which ever accompany the efforts of a people to obtain and maintain their liberty!" (January 18, 1835, 1). Absent are the analyses of American vulgarity so popular in this period, replaced instead with the sober perspective that while "England has hitherto been considered the emporium of the world—how long she may continue to maintain that position is a matter of considerable doubt" and that Americans may be "better calculated, by their politics and feelings, to surpass us, both as to time, circumstances, and ultimate grandeur" (January 18, 1835, 1). Anglo-American public discourse is calculated to overcome "occasional bickerings" between the two peoples and to help Britain overcome insular tendencies: "We ought and *must* be upon the alert, ere our Trans-Atlantic friends, for friends we much certainly esteem them, steal a march upon us, and leave us, vainly endeavouring to bring up our arrears, and lamenting at the same time our own want of caution and liberality" (January 18, 1835, 1). Thus, the editors' "intention [is] to open a new and novel source, by which means the foreign and domestic information of England and America will be connected, and promulgated with decided advantage" (January 18, 1835, 1).

The liberal terms of this mission—profit, mutual communication, and friendship—signify the perceived distance between the two publics. The first correspondent's column foresees the paper remedying "the great want of information displayed by European writers, as to the affairs and political events of the United States, [which] is much to be regretted at a time like the present, when Republican institutions occupy a large share of public attention. The experience of the United States in the practical operation of these institutions, and of her peculiar form of government, is entitled to great weight, and is worth the deliberate consideration of statesmen of all countries" (January 18, 1835, 1).

Interest in republican experiment is part of a larger, antiaristocratic liberal agenda. Europe is characterized as "enslaved, degraded, [and] insolvent" (January 18, 1835, 1). An imaginary letter from Andrew Jackson to King William diagnoses England's financial difficulties as the product of the burden of "the useless paraphernalia of a Court, with its innumerable train of tax-eating cormorants; while the State machinery of the [United States], from its extreme simplicity, works infinitely better" (January 18, 1835, 1). The paper engages Anglo-American relations in comparativist terms, though the results of the comparison favor the United States: American successes are a rhetorical lever for advancing a liberal agenda in domestic and foreign policy.

Such comparativism was modified midcentury. The Crystal Palace Exhibition of 1851, and the subsequent New York Crystal Palace Exhibition of 1853, promoted international commerce as the route to "universal peace," expounded by Prince Albert in his speech to the exhibition. As Louise Purbrick has commented, the 1851 Exhibition offered a "projection of the world as a free market and at peace . . . It was a performance of a liberal dream of international politics being based in commercial relationships, in friendly exchanges. Free trade was idealized as a form of international communication" (Purbrick 8). While promoted in these terms, the exhibition foregrounded Great Britain as the center of such an international community. The crystal palace itself was perhaps its greatest exhibit, the organizing and structuring ediface of a liberal international order.

A surge in international business in the 1850s led to the publication of *The English and American Intelligencer*, beginning in 1855, in Paris, which reported weekly news from "France, England, and America concerning the Universal Exhibition, Commerce, Science and Industry" (February 17, 1855, 1). The paper proffered "that kind of information which is generally looked for by men of business and Foreigners in Paris" and promotes efficiency and the "drawing closer together [of] Old and New World commercial law to facilitate international trade" (February 17, 1855, 1).

The *Intelligencer* differed from its predecessor by focusing upon individual taste and circumstances, rather than extolling American democracy through a comparative framework. This corresponds to the beginnings of tourism as an important market force in fostering the notion of an Anglo-American public sphere. In 1855, the paper witnessed an "unprecedented" rush of American travelers to Europe, and anticipated continued growth in transatlantic interaction fostered by the eventual construction of telegraph wires across the ocean. The paper notes that it offers "the Foreigner" in Paris "useful information" such as a stranger's directory to happenings in the city, business news, and even a technological dictionary to introduce new technical terms from French or English into the opposite language (February 17, 1855, 1).

The momentum of free trade foundered upon the reefs of domestic politics in numerous ways, particularly the ambivalent British relationship to the Union and the Confederacy during the American Civil War. The "Alabama claims," particularly the dispute over the sale of a British-built commerce raider, the *CSS Alabama*, to the Confederacy were not resolved until an 1872 Geneva tribunal establishing international arbitration. While the foreign policy establishment and the newspapers focused upon the politics of Anglo-American relations, the Civil War had a significant impact upon British life more generally. As R. J. M. Blackett puts it, "No other international event . . . had such a profound effect on the economic and political life of Britain" (7). He cites cotton shortages and renewed domestic debates over political reform and about the general efficacy of democracy as the chief indicators of this impact.

While Blackett cites a "staggering" variety of British responses to the Civil War, Anglo-American papers responded to these troubles by shifting further from a comparative framework to robust images of Anglo-American unity (35). At the end of the American Civil War, the *Anglo-American Times* appeared in London predicting a new age of Anglo-American commerce and suggesting that "England and America are united not only in their language and their traditions, in their religion and their literature, but in the stronger ties of mutual interest" (October 27, 1865, 1). Not only did the editors suggest that the traditional sources of national identity were secondary, but the paper's emphasis upon the importance of trade to the Anglo-American relationship verged upon emphatic: "Commerce is the ring with which these two foremost nations of the earth are wed" (October 27, 1865, 1). Unlike the two *Intelligencer* papers, here liberal rhetoric attacked both British traditionalism *and* American nationalism: The paper

> does not believe that the "manifest destiny" of the United States is to swallow up the whole world, nor that the American people are the greatest people the sun ever shone upon. But it believes that they are an active, energetic, honest, and highly prosperous people—that they not only deserve but desire the good opinion of Europe—and that, eschewing all ideas of conquest or dominion over any lands not their own, they desire no contest with any European State, except a friendly contest and rivalry in the race of progress, and the promoting of happiness and civilization on the earth. (October 27, 1865, 1)

This statement could have served any of several functions for the editors' intended readership. First, it asserts a common sense perspective that debunks American self-mythologizing while preserving a positive view of Americans. Second, it invokes all of Europe in a friendly "race of progress" that legitimated liberal ends. But finally, the passage offers a major theme of late nineteenth-century journalism about Americans—Americans' desire for recognition from old Europe, specifically from England.

The *Anglo-American Times* ran stories for a London readership that cast America as a place of extraordinary events and quick emotion, such as an article entitled "Brief and Brilliant Career of a Fast Woman in the Hub of the Universe" about an American grifter named "Nellie." (The status of the American woman would be a subject of intensive interest through the Edwardian period, a subject that is treated in more depth in Chapter 6.) On the death of Lord Palmerston, the paper predicted that the news "will doubtless be received in the United States with similar manifestations of sorrow to those already reported throughout Europe" (October 27, 1865, 1). Additionally, the paper noted the development of cheap excursions to America, a "rage among the reading public" for cheap, regionalist American literature, the threat to the Anglo-American relationship provided by Fenianism, and the possibility of conflict between the United States and a European state (November 24, 1865, 2).

A dominant theme of the paper was to report and dismiss bilious anti-British rhetoric, such as an article titled "England Going to the Bad" published in the *New York Herald* that claimed that "England has culminated" (November 2, 1865, 1). The *Anglo-American Times*' editor dismisses such "silly boasting" as potent only to "disgust sensible readers" (November 2, 1865, 1). Such a tendency, which is expanded at the turn of the century in critiques of the American yellow press, provided a means of confronting both predictions and actual harbingers of Britain's relative decline in relation to the United States and Germany. Thus, in the post-Civil War era we see the beginnings of a simulated Anglo-American sphere, in which the sensible reader—of American or British origin—is united in community with other sensible readers by a mutual censure of prejudicial, ideological rhetoric disseminated by the press on either side of the Atlantic (though especially in America).

The paper's transitional rhetoric is especially pronounced in its transcription of this manner of American editorial, insofar as it simultaneously records the naïveté of American bombast and promotes economic liberalism. In December 1865, the *Anglo-American Times* reprinted an article titled "America and England" from *The New York Evening Post*. The article was written in response to the London *Spectator* arguing that Americans were not likely to go to war with England. "We do not want to go to war with England," the editor writes, because "the example of our successful Republican Government will have much greater power in England, and will be of much greater use to the Liberal party there, if the two countries remain at peare [*sic*], than if they fall by the ears together" ("America and England," 2).

The transition from comparativism to an imagined Anglo-American public sphere coalesced around commercial relations was clear by the early 1870s, when prices on the transatlantic telegraph cable decreased and usage exploded. Two papers deserve brief mention during this period: *The British and American Journal of Commerce*, first published in March 1873, and *The Continental Herald and Swiss Times: An Anglo-American Daily Newspaper*, which first appeared in 1875. Where *The British and American Journal of Commerce* recalls the purely commercial ends of the Anglo-American relation, the *Herald* foregrounds movement toward an Anglo-American public sphere. The former was founded in light of "the settlement of the matter of Alabama claims and the San Juan difficulty" and increasing investment of British capital in U.S. railways and other businesses, creating "reason to expect a continual increase in friendly intercourse" between American and British business interests.

The *Herald*, on the other hand, offered a forum for social intercourse between travelers: "The Continental Herald will insert, Free of Charge, on any date requested, the names and hotel addresses of English and American Gentlemen traveling upon the Continent, on being furnished with the necessary information a few days in advance. Travellers will thus have a ready means of informing their friends when and where they may be found during the course of their tour" (July 27, 1875, 1). By supplying this service, the paper could entice advertisers with the prospect of tapping into a community that was geographically dispersed.

By the 1880s, the rush of European emigrants to the United States was, at least in the publishing sphere, countered by consciousness of the large numbers of Americans visiting or residing in England and Europe. The period also witnessed the rise of cosmopolitan figures who not only appealed to readerships in both nations but also in some instances had a distinctive impact upon the Anglo-American publishing world. Among these, Andrew Carnegie was a towering figure, a Scottish-born American philanthropist whose interests increasingly turned to journalistic writing and to financing the transatlantic periodicals that played a key role in mediating political and literary debate. Carnegie was the subject both of Anglo-American pride and of British anxiety; as Francesca Sawaya suggests, he "pursued . . . 'Americanizing' Europe by subsidizing periodicals in England" (4). Ultimately, Carnegie held a controlling stake in numerous periodicals and newspapers published in Britain, and he repeatedly promoted American institutions and homogeneity as a key to his adopted country's success (Sawaya 88).

With the countercurrent of wealthier Americans a felt presence in London, discourse over the quality and character of American culture escalated noticeably. The newspaper *America*, published in London beginning in 1883, recorded this influx, noting that in 1883 "upwards of 80,000 Americans traveled to Europe," including millionaires and fashionable American ladies among this number (July 15, 1883, 8). In the same issue, *America* announced the establishment of McArmor's American News-Reading Rooms next to the Haymarket theatre, where Americans could go to catch up on the papers from home.

America's content and, by inference, its readership shifted in a suggestive manner in the first year of its publication. It began as an "independent Guide for Emigrants" with scenic descriptions of the elevated railroads of New York, the sights of New Orleans, and the landscape and natural resources of California, Manitoba, and Montana. Yet by July of 1883, the masthead read, "For Americans in Europe," and the paper described itself as "A Fortnightly Review of Anglo-American Social and Political News and Continental Guide for American Travellers." The shift evidently reflects an attempt to capitalize upon the lucrative market of American tourists and émigrés.

In celebrating this community, the paper recasts images of British culture in positive terms: "We Americans, who represent a vast percentage of dyspeptic infirmities, we used to have a sort of sneaky 'corpse–reviver' predilection for Paris . . . [Now] we are beginning to get vastly disgusted with . . . Parisian extravagance . . . and we are taking kindly to the substantial and less ostentatious style of living of old England . . . We have even gone so far as to find the wisest amongst us showing a decided preference for fogs, and everlasting chops and steaks" ("Progress of the Season" 8). While such an assertion suggests a provincial, nostalgic view of England, the traveler also finds the vanguard of international style: "Our *elegantes*, women of the most refined taste as the world knows, have taken to extensively patronizing the swell shops and magasins de nouveaute's of Regent-street and Bond-street" ("Progress of the Season" 8). Following this observation, the writer notes cheaper prices at London shops than their Parisian counterparts. The coupling of the cosmopolitan aspects of London with traditional English characteristics is not, at this juncture, seamless; they represent two distinctive tendencies. Yet it does foreshadow the elite and aspirational contexts in which the merger of the cosmopolitan with the national will occur, a topic covered at the end of this survey and in the next chapter.

This sensibility contributes to the pedagogical split in representations of Britishness described in the Introduction and Chapter 1. In the following passage, a John Bull figure embodies provincial and bourgeois subjectivity:

> The good Briton of the church-warden type is disposed to shirk America as uncomfortable every way; yet he is just the type of man who would derive most benefit going there and back. It is unlikely that the Americans would want to detain him.
>
> But after all, the bigotry and general prejudice of the ordinary Englishman are not very deep. He holds on to them more from pride and obstinacy than from conviction . . . If, when no one is looking, he can examine the controverted matter for himself, see it with his own eyes, and walk round it carefully, smoking a cigar the while, the chances are that he will do that for himself which not all the king's men or horses would be permitted to do for him. Precisely in this spirit, as one leads a shying horse up to the thing at which he shies, and makes him look squarely at it and even touch it with his docile, good-natured nose, we would ask those countrymen of ours who can spare the time and money to cross over and take a look, however short, at the young England over the sea. (January 1, 1883, 1)

Anti-Americanism, here, is a product of a fusty, provincial version of Britishness distinctly separate from the subjectivity performed by the writer and implicitly hailed in the reader.

A different version of this positionality treats unrefined American and British types alike. This appears in a humorous article titled "The American Dude," which "reports" that "a celebrated chemist . . . recently caught a Dude and subjected it to analysis" finding over 99 percent "bicarbonate of cheek" with trace amounts of "essence of gall . . . nitrate of stare . . . [and] tincture of conceit." "Cyanide of brain" is listed as "doubtful," measuring 0.001 parts per million ("The American Dude" 4). His counterpart, "*Dudus Britannicus*" has "much in common" with the American: "Both are reserved in conversation, not from choice, malicious people say, but from necessity. Both are rather attenuated in figure" ("The American Dude" 4). This comic rhetoric, focusing upon manners, taste, and self-promotion, is partly interesting because of the positionality embedded in the humor. The phrase "malicious people say" toward the end of the article gestures toward the writer's reserve even when he is skewering uncouth Americans and Britishers. In fact, the humor turns upon this simulated reserve in a manner similar to *The Spectator* of old.

These developments—the move away from strict comparativism toward a complex transatlantic economy, the emergence of meta-analysis of national types, and the refined positionality associated with culture, refinement, and criticism were accompanied by increased discourse about American culture, particularly whether America had produced cultural artifacts of abiding significance. While Matthew Arnold resoundingly argued that it had none, commercial interest in American writing drove promotion of its cultural value. Beginning in 1884, the magazine *Columbia: the American Monthly in Europe* promised the "highest class of American literature, with illustrations by well-known American artists." The magazine legitimated American culture through fiction and articles on art and science. It also testified to a growing establishment of American émigré, as opposed to touristic culture in England during this period.

By 1895, the London émigré community had its own paper, *The London American: A Chronicle of the American Colony in Europe*. Its "raison d'etre" was to serve "the upwards of ten thousand American citizens permanently resident in and about the

British metropolis, and from the considerably more than one hundred thousand Americans who are annually dispersed throughout Europe in pursuit of recreation, education, and matters of a commercial nature." ("Our 'Raison d'Etre'" 9). The development of this community was accompanied by "very different conditions to those which attended the publication of its generic predecessors . . . [including] a much greater and more comprehensive interest in American affairs [among the daily press]" ("Our 'Raison d'Etre'" 9).

The paper's coverage included reports of quasi-political social associations such as The American Society in London, reports on the social activities of wealthy and prominent Americans and Britishers, and it even reported on the doings of the London Base-Ball Association, which featured teams like the "Remington Typewriters," "Thespian," "Electrics," "Farringdons," "Anglo-Americans," and "Fuller" (which boasted, "at least two of its members are fine athletic specimens of American 'color'") (April 3, 1895, 5).

One article reprised the emphasis upon commercial values in terms of national stereotypes. British manufacturers and merchants are usually "plodding old fellow[s], hidebound by British conservatism. In the face of the wonderful energy [they] meet with everywhere in the United States, [they] goes about [their] work with Old-World slowness. Large sums of the money set aside for the purpose in hand are expended in frequent trips across the Atlantic and in cabling over petty details that a live American would never bother his head about" (December 27, 1895, 10). The gospel of efficiency renders the British businessman anachronistic and no match for his American counterpart.

By 1895, then, the key values of the Anglo-American public sphere were liberal commerce tempered by cosmopolitan culture, notions of kinship and mutual affection tempered by ideas about friendly rivalry, and critiques of both British and American vulgar types. Proponents of this perspective viewed it as the vanguard of civilization, even proclaiming the centrality of Anglo-American relations to world peace, as in the journal *Cosmopolis: An International Monthly* in 1896. The connotations of the name were validated by articles from English, American, French, and German writers, some of which celebrated international cooperation, in particular the success of international arbitration. Yet the review, published simultaneously in London and New York, represented arbitration as a historical effect of Anglo-American benevolence; the resolution of the *Alabama* claim in 1871 "redounded to the honour and prestige of the two great countries . . . and mark[ed] a stage in the civilization of the human race" (January 1, 1896, 406). The articles worry about England's present insecurities in relation to the other imperial powers: "England stands practically isolated in Europe, and no great Power now cares to conceal its hostility" (January 1, 1896, 423).

The journal notes the distress with which England responded to President Cleveland's message on the Venezuelan boundary crisis (see Chapter 5 for more on this) and asserts that the relationship with the United States "dwarfs into insignificance all other political problems" (January 1, 1896, 427). This emphasis, while conveying the extent of England's crisis, also dramatizes how avowedly "cosmopolitan" perspectives serve the national interest.

In light of the conflation of Anglo-American and world interest, it is not surprising to discover increased representations of British identity inflected with cosmopolitan superiority. In this regard, *The Anglo-American*, edited by W. Payne from 1898 to 1901, embodied the maturation of the Anglo-American public sphere.

Published in London, the paper's early issues began with a profile of a prominent "Anglo-American." The paper mixed political and society coverage, including an emphasis upon the social doings of politically prominent Anglo-Americans such as Ambassador Joseph Choate and his wife Caroline; the wife of Chamberlain's parliamentary successor, Sir Herbert Naylor-Leyland, Opposition leader Sir William Vernon Harcourt; and many others. Mary Chamberlain, the wife of Joseph Chamberlain, was described as the most powerful American woman in the empire. The paper included an abundance of human interest stories, juxtaposing small news items to anecdotes about famous Britons and Americans. *The Anglo-American*'s columns supported the idea of a pervasive, and basically societal, public sphere by including reports of visits of Americans in London, clippings from American journals and papers, and regular columns named "John and Jonathan," "Anglo-American Society," "Kith and Kin Gossip," and others focusing upon books, theater, and music. In tenor, the stories tend to emphasize American originality but without the sense of the spectacular and outlandish conveyed in previous papers. For example, a story titled "Mixed Drinks" announced that

"Parisians have caught on to the 'cocktail.' In fact, the vogue of the American mixed drink is at its height." Another story reported the affair of "the Hobson kiss," in which a St. Louis lady named "Miss Arnold" impetuously kisses a British Lieutenant Hobson. Transatlantic romance was in fact a common theme in the paper, which included reports of international marriages and the Jamesian "American wife" (October 1, 1898).

One article, titled "The American Girl" and written by "An English Bachelor," expressed the positionality affected through the Anglo-American public sphere quite explicitly. The article begins with a familiar disclaimer about "the average Englishman['s] view of Americans who 'guess and calculate,' think they can 'lick creation,' talk with a diabolical nasal twang, and rush madly about accumulating 'almighty dollars.'" ("The American Girl" 6). This self-described "cultured Englishman" observes that the "dry climate with the air charged with electricity" creates flighty, highly sensitive, and socially ambitious American women. This gentleman, ironically, is a particular attraction because "American men are so intent on the making of dollars" ("The American Girl" 6). The evident contradiction in the bachelor reproducing the perspective he mocked in "the average Englishman" emphasizes the split between pedagogical messages to the *natio* and performance of the ideal qualities produced by national culture through the Anglo-American public sphere. Yet the example, additionally, provides for a distinction between the American and British national characters: where English refinement involves an acknowledgement of the shortcomings of average Englishmen, American character is the result of environmental determinism.

An unimpeachable unity of the Anglo-American audience was expressed broadly, and structurally, in *The Anglo-American*, through regular features like "Kith and Kin," which reported social gossip and became the lead feature in later editions of the paper. The tenor of such "kinship" claims was often racial—the leader, for example, announces that "deep ineradicable instincts of race" bind the nations. Yet by contrast to more conservative racialism (see the Anglo-Saxonist rhetoric examined in the next chapter), here race claims are contextualized within a liberal framework. The subheading of the newspaper was "One Kin-One Tongue-One Purpose," and the paper featured an epigraph from Gladstone: "I have a pleasure in becoming, in however humble a degree, a vehicle of

English thought to the American mind. The union between the countries is close, and is likely to grow closer still. Honour to all those who seek to corroborate the bond" (September 3, 1898, 1). Gladstone, who passed away in 1898, functions as a guiding spirit of the paper's spokesmanship for strong Anglo-American relations. An occasional poem submitted by James Muirhead (considered in more detail in the Chapter 1) begins with the following Gladstone proclamation: "God Almighty made us kinsmen . . . It is quite plain that as England has a wonderful past, and as the founding of the American state has been a part of that, you have a past committed to you" (September 24, 1898, 1). The embrace of Gladstone's casting of the Anglo-American bond in terms of thought, history, and kinship and the celebration of Gladstone himself reflect the cultural priorities of the Anglo-American sphere at the turn of the century.

Gladstone's extension of the mantle of English tradition to the United States, which was originally delivered at the American Exhibition in London in 1887, speaks to a neglected undercurrent of Anglo-American relations from the late 1880s and reaching its height, and crisis, during the period covered by *The Anglo-American*: proposals for an Anglo-American reunion.

Thus *The Anglo-American* described its "raison d'etre" emerging from the Spanish-American War, which in addition to securing liberties to the Spanish colonies also portended "the reunion of a kindred race too long divided" (September 3, 1898, 1). The paper "come[s] to hasten the advent of AN INEVITABLE REUNION" (September 3, 1898, 1). In promoting this merger, the paper envisions race as a structural, but not catalytic, reason; the bond, ultimately, will make "liberty, civilization, and commerce" prevail throughout the world (September 3, 1898, 1). In the discursive context of the moment, this distinction served two purposes: first, these liberal bromides partake in the currency of turn-of-the-century racial discourse, but they are distinctive from the racialism traced in Chapter 3; second, liberal ends persist as the governing ideology of the paper and were central to how the paper changed between 1898 and 1901.

While the Spanish-American War spurred the sentiment that "the old hostility [was] dead," the rush to union faltered around the dubious prospects of the Boer War (September 3, 1898, 1). The Boer War did not evoke universal American disapproval. For example, a group of émigré American women in London funded the "Maine," a hospital ship that served during the war, as an expression of support. Yet these events did alter rhetoric about union, governance, and commercial priorities significantly. Thus, in 1899 *The Anglo-American* issued a more tentative editorial leader: "We believe with a well-known American writer that Great Britain and the U.S. are 'distinct as the billows, but one as the see'" (June 17, 1898, 8). The paper sees a common "'fellow feeling,' which only close ties of blood relationship could foster," toning down the racialist rhetoric of the initial volumes.

This "harmony of feeling" was reflected in changes in emphasis, such as making "Kith and Kin" gossip the leader of issues in 1901, along with signing the section with the Augustan signature "The Rambler." The paper modifies its statements about world leadership, noting that "to those who have taken a reasonable view of the world's progress . . . it has been clear for a long time that the United States must inevitably excel Great Britain in certain phases of industrial productiveness" (December 28, 1901, 4). Such a realization accompanied a more distant bond: "The Anglo-American alliance that can produce the greatest good to the English-speaking races . . . [is of] two kindred nations following the same high purpose, not only for their own advancement and protection, but for the good of the whole world. Let us by all means keep our industrial rivalry [because] . . . one country is an incentive to the other" (December 28, 1901, 4).

The Anglo-American, like many of its predecessors, included numerous excerpts from other papers and magazines from both America and London, including *Harper's*, *North American Review*, and *Pall Mall Gazette*. As noted earlier, the Anglo-American public sphere was partly constructed out of an imagined "sphere" of conversations in print, rather than more directly from "coffeehouse culture" or the like. Critiquing voices that did not neatly conform to the imagined relationship created a convenient rhetorical mapping between the Anglo-American paper's editorial board, the Anglo-American "public," and political and cultural progress.

The story of yellow journalism has been told before, but here I would like to emphasize the role Anglo-American dynamics played in the naming and demonization of the yellow press as a curse upon both nations. *The Anglo-American*, for example, emphasized that the Anglo-American relationship was *not* disturbed by the Boer War, even as they were refashioning their own mission. In an article titled "America's sympathy with England," *The Anglo-American* writes, "The Yellow Press of the United States and the pro-Boer papers of this country are struggling very hard to convince the world that the Americans, as a people, have very little sympathy with England in the present war." ("America's Sympathy with England" 6).

Yellow Journalism and the Anglo-American Public Sphere

Certain elements of the American press were vilified as the yellow press for threatening the Anglo-American relationship. Sidney Kobre has argued that the Spanish-American War represented the height of Gilded Age yellow journalism. If the war-mongering spirit of 1898 led to increased clamor for tight Anglo-American bonds, the pendulum swung sharply the other way in the face of the Boer War. The polemical tone of these papers was a source of great agitation in the establishment British press during this period, which saw them as a genuine threat to Anglo-American relations. The *Times* of London carried stories in this vein, such as a report that William Waldorf Astor's change of citizenship was prompted by revulsion at the American yellow press, and concludes that his decision reflects "the same interest which all of us have in promoting active friendship between the two kindred nations" (12). Such a project continued in the face of the Boer War, according to the *Times*, within "the more responsible section of the American Press" (10).

While the *Times*'s self-avowed promotion of Anglo-American relations reflects different journalistic standards from the present day, it is partly a response to the trend toward partisanship common in the yellow press. There were considerable material factors—advertising revenues more than tripled between 1880 and 1904, and by 1889 advertising exceeded subscription revenues in the industry. This put pressures upon editorial staff to shape the news in ways favorable to commerce (Kobre 313). According to Kobre, this increase in advertising was crucial to vast gains in American sales of manufactured goods during this period.

The *Times*'s rhetoric also reflects the impact of "yellow" rhetoric upon its own journalistic model. As David Spencer argues, the yellow press embraced a "'ritual approach' to journalism, which treated news 'not as pure information but as high drama . . . [consisting of] struggles between opposing forces" (Spencer 9). This effect was amplified by massive increases in production of the daily newspaper fostered by technologies such as the "cylinder press, the web press, the linotype, and the stereotype" (Spencer 9–10). Indeed, the polemical attitude of the establishment papers at this juncture was partly responsible for the rhetoric of a "great divide" in culture in the early twentieth century so ably analyzed by Andreas Huyssen as crucial to the ideologies of modernism.

Further, the big publishing houses were beginning to radically change their acquisition strategies. According to James West, "New publishers themselves became the originators of ideas that they would assign to proven writers. Doubleday, in particular, saw that the creative process in book publishing could be reversed. He believed that the publisher should 'invent books which the public really wants, or thinks it wants' and then engage writers to create those books for public sale. Much of the famous muckraking journalism of the early 1900s was created in just this way" (West 44).

These changes contributed to the sense of a "great divide" in culture. According to Patrick Collier, "the new newspapers seemed to exercise a mysterious, extra-rational, *mass* influence, transforming readers into a dehumanized conglomerate, liable in the direst projections to becoming agents of anarchy or an easily manipulated mob" (*Modernism on Fleet Street* 15). For literary and cultural commentators, this supported a sense of positional superiority in the domestic sphere and in the Anglo-American public sphere. As Jonathan Freedman puts the matter, "Levels of culture that had long been forming in relation to each other crystallized into sharply different levels of experience" (*The Temple of Culture* 9).

W. T. STEAD AND AMERICANIZATION

The case of W. T. Stead exemplifies how, within the Anglo-American public sphere, British figures apparently unempathetic to Arnold's cultural project adopted a positionality deeply indebted to it. Stead had in fact been the object of a direct attack by Arnold in the late 1880s, in which Arnold identified Stead's editorship of the *Pall Mall Gazette* as an emblematic example of the dangers of the "new journalism," offering pabulum to the masses rather than the educative ideal he espoused.[4]

Yet as Laurel Brake notes, in the 1890s Stead's journalism was "directed to the potentially active citizen rather than to the ordinary consumer, [and] may be counted as attempting to create a counter-public sphere" (Brake 155). The transatlantic popularity of his *Review of Reviews*, and Stead's deep sympathy toward the United States, attests to some linkage between the simulated Anglo-American public sphere and this "counter-public," pedagogical vector.

These thematics came together in Stead's treatise *The Americanization of the World: or The Trend of the Twentieth Century* (1902), in which Stead promotes Anglo-American unification as a means of disciplining the worst tendencies of both the British and American public. The title reflects a teleology around which his pedagogical reflections on the two nations gather force.

The Americanization of the World examines the processes by which America asserted itself as a dominant global economic and military force. Stead makes repeated reference to Richard Cobden's 1835 prediction that America would surpass England in terms of production and international influence, insinuating that contemporary conditions were forecast by Cobden. In addition, *The Americanization of the World* marshals an argument for reuniting Great Britain and America. In this renewed alliance, America would hold a dominant role in the partnership. Between them, the reunited nations would possess enough power to assert a world peace to last through the twentieth century.

Stead's treatise is thoroughly intertextual, referring to a wide range of predecessors and contemporaries, from Richard Cobden, Alexis de Tocqueville, and William Gladstone to contemporary businessmen in Philadelphia. Stead summarizes Cobden's 1835 pamphlet "England, Ireland, and America," which argues that America is superior to England in its governmental system, educational system, and pacifism, and that "our only chance of national prosperity lies in the timely remodeling of our system, so as to put it as nearly as possible upon an equality with the improved management of the Americans" (412). The intercession of almost 70 years witnessed England's greatest period of growth followed by its relative decline among the world economies, returning to the circumstances that prompted Cobden. Stead does not address the roots of British power in that intermezzo period, but he consistently promotes the liberal principles that fostered economic growth.

The Americanization of the World catalogues and comments upon a wealth of materials from liberals and businessmen advocating the idea of Anglo-American reunification, including figures such as Cobden, Dale Carnegie, and jurist A. V. Dicey. The thrust of these articles is that union would benefit both nations, but that for Britain it would prevent slippage from primacy among the world powers. Stead quotes Dale Carnegie's article "A Look Ahead" at length, which argues that unless Britain reunites with her "giant child" she is doomed to occupy a secondary place in the world.

Stead's criticisms of England include the proposition that its national energy has dissipated because of its wide variety of interests. America, by contrast, has achieved a great deal of energy because of its Puritan morality. According to Stead, "All power arises from restraint," and the United States has "accumulated energy which it transmitted to its descendants" (Stead 383). American growth is "that tremendous spring uncoiling" (Stead 147). Stead questions how long this will last, but nevertheless sees it as a reason to yoke together the two nations. In articulating his comparison of the two nations, Stead refers to the cosmopolitan wisdom of a nameless "cultivated Jew, who, born in the Old World, had lived for some time in the New" (Stead 382). This conceit gives voice to Stead's vitalist principles. According to this figure, "the success of the Americans . . . may be said to spring from two causes . . . the concentration of the whole genius of the race upon industrial pursuits . . . [and] the stern discipline of Puritan morality, [which] repressed with iron hand the animal instincts which lead to a self-indulgent life" (Stead 383). For Stead, America's repressive, ascetic nature "accumulated energy which it transmitted to its descendents" (Stead 383).

Stead urges Britain to adopt three of the "American secrets" of economic growth that are available for export: universal education, incentives to increased productive power, and universal suffrage. Stead notes the ways in which Britain's resistance to change in a variety of arenas contributes to its relative decline. Stead observes that in Britain "education is not regarded as a good investment" and that this attitude prevents the mass of the citizenry from feeling concern for the nation as a whole (Stead 148). What "differentiates the Briton from the American" is that British men of culture "resent the demand that the children of the agricultural laborer or the costermonger should receive the best education that the State can give them" (Stead 387). Thus Stead shares in the spirit of Arnold's critique of British education and seems to envision access to sweetness and light for all citizens. Yet Stead's vision differs from Arnold's insofar as his central concern is to restore Britain to international power as an economic producer. While Arnold's vision grows out of a confidence in British economic power and a sense that the effects of such a surplus on the social and cultural structure were the greatest threat to Britain, for Stead, Britain has fallen from dominance, and the cause was being outcompeted by societies more suited to rapid transformations of their systems of production.

Thus Stead is also critical of both the resistance to improved technology and the "extreme division of labor" developing in certain industries in Britain, which requires the employment of far more workers than necessary to complete a job on the grounds that each employee perform only a very specific task and remain idle when the performance of that task is not required (Stead 149). He idealizes workers who can perform multiple tasks. Although his analysis is rather prescient elsewhere, Stead does not anticipate the trend toward a much more narrow division of labor in the name of efficiency that arose in early twentieth-century America. Finally, Stead blames the vestiges of Britain's aristocratic system for the apathetic nature of the citizenry. Aristocracies, according to Stead, "do not tend to develop in the mass of the people a keen sense of citizenship . . . [and] effectively paralyze that consciousness of individual power which gives so great and constant a stimulus to the energy and self-respect of the citizens of the Republic" (Stead 395).

Nevertheless, Stead recognizes the intractability of British invented traditions at the turn of the twentieth century. While he is evidently condescending toward British aristocratic pretensions, he nonetheless sees their importance in a period of relative decline: "Any scheme which necessitated the repudiation of aristocratic distinctions or monarchial bric-a-brac would be fatal to the scheme of reunion. John Bull would have to experience a new birth before he could qualify as an entirely regenerated citizen of the American Republic. He must be allowed to retain his plush-breeched and powdered footmen, his Lord Mayor's coach, and all the paraphernalia and trappings of monarchy and peerage, if only to enable him to feel at home in a cold, cold world, and cultivate that spirit of condescension towards Americans which is his sole remaining consolation" (Stead 414). Stead's analysis of the insular nature and bad faith of "John Bull" reflects his association of national identity with tradition and aristocratic pretensions. He recognizes the condescending nature of accounts of the United States both in society and in travel literature, and he explains it in terms of Britain's relative decline in power.

Stead's global vision is underwritten by his belief in the rationality and essential fairness of the Anglo-Saxon race (a topic dealt with in the next chapter). Both Britain and America have degenerated in some manner—the former into snobbish paralysis and the latter into mere materialism—but reunification would have a salutary effect upon the racial stock. Stead surmises that British Anglo-Saxons would be reinvigorated by the energy and enthusiasm of their American counterparts; conversely, American Anglo-Saxons would benefit from the attention paid by Britain to "the cultivation of the higher soul"—that is, to culture (Stead 164). Stead's vision combines social Darwinist and Arnoldian themes that view the struggle for cultural survival and civilization as stages in a people's development akin to the stages in human development. Stead argues that

> the rush and bustle of modern life, the eager whirl of competitive business, the passionate rush to outstrip a neighbor or a rival—all these things have their uses; they tend to eliminate the unfit, and to give the survivor superior efficiency . . . But this struggle for existence may easily be carried to such a point as to make existence itself hardly worth having. The universal experience of the wisest and best of mankind speaks with no uncertain voice in condemnation of a life that has no leisure . . . Possibly, when the country is a little older, this tempestuous eagerness natural to youth may give way to a more sedate and tranquil spirit, but at present there is very little evidence of that in the United States. (Stead 442–43)

Thus, even while he levels significant criticisms at the institutions that resist change in the name of British tradition, Stead nevertheless posits Britain as the locus of culture and an important corrective for the United States.

Stead ends his book suggesting that the Anglo-American alliance will provide a solution to the problem of America's unquenchable desire and will foster the more reflective spirit associated with culture. In elaborating such a vision, Stead pairs British culture with Eastern mysticism. The union with Britain will provide that "more sedate and tranquil spirit" which finds contentment in "a wealth which arises from the fewness of our wants" (Stead 444). Stead attributes such a vision of contentment to the "Eastern Sage" (Stead 444). If Stead's scheme appears self-contradictory, that is because it merges American desire with its satisfaction in a unified world empire. Such a contradiction seems endemic to visionary proposals such as Stead's—in any utopian notion there is an arrest of the motion of growth and expansion that is necessary to overcome scarcity and achieve the state of permanent surplus on which the utopia is based.

In this case, Stead attributes a transhistorical perspective to certain British figures who might act as a corrective upon American desire. That such a position seems to contradict Stead's criticisms of John Bull reflects the same distancing of the man of culture from both aristocratic and bourgeois consciousness that we have seen elsewhere in transatlantic discourse. That Stead is aware of the ways in which national stereotyping is part of a bourgeois structure of aristocratic aspiration does not deter him from articulating the same kind of positionality that characterizes less analytical contemporary writing.

COSMOPOLITAN NATIONALISM
AND ANGLO-AMERICAN REUNION

The positionality offered in *The Americanization of the World*, and emblematic of much liberal discourse of the period, functioned either to create a distinction between average and civilized Englishmen or to modify the unrefined pragmatism of John Bull. In either case, the disciplinary dimension of the model for English identity was mitigated by reference to American difference. The critiques of John Bull offered in this text, and in newspapers like *The Anglo-American*, point to a doubled signification of Britishness played out through the Anglo-American public sphere.

These odd ideological formations, in which nationality is critiqued, yet affirmed through a detached, cosmopolitan perspective, make sense within the context of Victorian liberalism if we understand how cosmopolitan identity and nationality could be interrelated. In describing the ideological position of J. R. Seeley, Duncan Bell points out that "the nation was not an intolerant political order, the antithesis of wide human sympathies, it was instead an essential component of such sympathies" (Bell 163). Liberal internationalism idealized a world of competing, sovereign nations as the vanguard of progress and civilization. Nationality provided "nonexclusive, nonparochial, attachment to national-political communities," which made a universal religious order possible (Bell 161, 162).

Bell terms this position "cosmopolitan nationalism," and sees Seeley as a representative of a particular version of the narrative of European cultural progress (Bell 161). This narrative was complex at the end of the nineteenth century. On the one hand, cosmopolitan nationalists display latent nostalgia for an imagined age in which the pluralist unity of sovereign nations was oriented around England as the center of world civilization, as in the Crystal Palace Exhibition; on the other hand, these figures are savvy about the ideological nature of nationalism. Taken together, these perspectives result in a position that associates a "right" relation (like Arnold's "right" reason) to the national culture with British superiority even while condemning the vainglorious and deluded nature of nationalist feeling. This dynamic played out repeatedly in the Anglo-American public sphere, particularly through careful calibrations of commerce, culture, and affect.

Proposals for political reintegration of Britain and the United States date back at least as far as 1780, when Edmund Burke advocated virtual representation for the United States in British Parliament. Similar proposals had been articulated before the American Revolution, notably by Adam Smith (cited in Bell 68–69). In the late 1890s, however, two prominent British figures, A. V. Dicey and Joseph Chamberlain, pushed for a more formal alliance. Dicey, in 1897, "advocated common citizenship for Americans and Englishmen, his proposal—by his own admission—'fell flat,'" primarily as a result of Anglophobia in the United States (Gossett 223).

Joseph Chamberlain proposed a formal alliance in a May 1898 speech in Birmingham, England. In light of British support for the United States in the Spanish-American War, Chamberlain's proposal was endorsed by nearly all British newspapers and by a large number of American papers as well (Gossett 223). This led, later that year, to the founding of the Anglo-American League "in order to keep alive the cordial relations which had been established . . . the League resolved at its first session . . . 'that every effort should be made in the interests of civilization and of peace to secure the most cordial and constant cooperation on the part of the two nations'" (Gossett 225).

The failures of Chamberlain's proposal for formal Anglo-American unification and Dicey's common citizenship were attended by analysis and compensatory gestures intended to preserve the good feelings accrued between the peoples in the mid- to late 1890s. The internationally famed American admiral and author Alfred Mahan lauded the continuity of a "community of interest, present and future," between the two nations emphasizing "material" before "spiritual" "identit[ies] of interest" (Mahan 123).

Social organizations emerged during this period to promote strong Anglo-American ties, speaking to the currency of the Anglo-American public sphere as a locus for business activity and cultural activity alike. The Anglo-American League, the Anglo-American Alliance Society, and the Atlantic Union all flourished at the turn of the century. As *The Anglo-American* reported, the Atlantic Union was targeted toward the "influential classes" and sought to bring Americans in England into British homes with the hope of providing them with an appreciation of English taste. The Anglo-American public sphere promised a clubby atmosphere in which commerce masqueraded as the natural habitus of the cultivated.

While the majority of these associations appeared in London, Gossett notes that soon after the failure of Chamberlain's proposal, the "Anglo-American League was formed in New York" and that the membership included an impressive list of prominent Americans (Gossett 225). Yet "the American organization soft-pedaled the racial bond between the two countries" (Gossett 225). This de-emphasis reflects the non-Anglo-Saxon identification of prominent Americans, especially Teddy Roosevelt. Yet it also reflects a reluctance by Americans to commit to a formal bond.

The loose bonds of influence manifested in countless other ways—in addition to literature and journalism, sport and education provided key venues for British influence with the United States. In the field of education, for example, "Oxford, Cambridge and the British public schools [profoundly] influenced elite American secondary and higher education . . . culturally, architecturally, organizationally, recreationally, and in terms of curriculum, teaching methods and attitudes to race, class and religion" (Chamberlain 1). The Rhodes scholarships were established in 1902, and other exchanges followed. Taken altogether, "This web of connections was of diplomatic significance because it gave Britain a network of influential friends at the heart of the American establishment" (Chamberlain 1).

GOLDWIN SMITH AND THE
VALUE OF COMMERCE

These attempts to strengthen, and even formalize, the Anglo-American alliance and the continued cultural currency of publications and organizations promoting this bond suggests that the simulated Anglo-American public sphere was a sustaining principle of Anglo-American relations at the turn of the century. Attempts to locate other bases for Anglo-American unity (and, simultaneously, British distinction) will be charted in Chapters 3 and 4. While commercial ties were crucial, at the heart of liberalism there lay insecurities created by the indifference of market forces to the continued importance or power of any particular group. As a result, even liberal thinkers tended to position commerce in a subordinate role, as a crucial lubricant within an affective transnational relationship.

Goldwin Smith's late writings demonstrate the tensions within and among economic liberalism, Anglo-Saxon racialism, and national identity played out in the public sphere. Smith wore many hats—acclaimed historian, prolific journalist, and public activist for a variety of causes while residing in England, the United States, and finally in Canada. His peripatetic career and his reputation as a particularly insightful critic of nationalist biases make him a useful illustration of the interrelations of liberalism and Anglo-American relations and for the cosmopolitan-national positionality made available through the Anglo-American public sphere, through the end of the nineteenth century.

Influenced by John Stuart Mill and an admirer of Richard Cobden and John Bright, Smith was a self-described Manchester school liberal. Throughout his writing life, he also professed faith in the superiority of Anglo-Saxon civilization (*Dictionary of*

Canadian Biography 4). In writing repeatedly about the emergent power of the United States in relation to the British Empire for a transatlantic audience, Smith negotiated and renegotiated the tensions between his primary commitments.

According to Elisabeth Wallace, Smith believed that "Americans and English liberals were united by blood and by a common allegiance to the cause of Freedom, which rendered a 'league of the heart' natural and morally desirable" (Wallace 888). Bell emphasizes Smith's understanding of this race bond "in broadly cultural terms [including] . . . shared language, religion, sensibility, traditions and institutions" (Bell 189). Smith's racial beliefs had a vague, Lamarckian biological basis, in which nationality was grafted upon race to create strong, independent nations linked by race but flourishing in a competitive commercial world order. The relations of commerce to race, and their impacts upon culture and nationality, were not programmatically theorized. Instead, Smith parroted "the influences around him . . . in a pallid, synthetic form" (Bell 191).

This lack of ideological purity makes Smith's writings a helpful gauge of the evolving status of commerce within the emergent sense of an Anglo-American public sphere. I will trace how discourse about commerce, especially in relation to a "league of the heart" evolves through Smith's writings. This motif involves increasing suspicion of commerce as a facilitator of international affections and reflects historical changes that include geopolitics and economics.

Commerce occupied an elevated position in Smith's early writings. In his 1861 *Lectures on Modern History*, Smith argues that "the laws of production and distribution of wealth [were] . . . the most beautiful and wonderful of the natural laws of God . . . To buy in the cheapest and sell in the dearest market . . . is simply to fulfill the commands of the Creator" (*Dictionary of Canadian Biography* 2). The greatness of the English was attributable to its industrious, inventive racial stock and to an insular environment that led to a "flourishing commercial spirit" (Bell 193). The Celts, by contrast, were described as a "weaker race, generally unreliable, prone to superstition, and not fit for self-government" (Bell 192). In the United States, Smith displayed strong distaste for Irish immigrants, whose influence might enervate America's promise.

In the wake of the international uncertainties of the early 1880s and the persistence of Anglo-American antagonisms, Smith became less sanguine about the racial character's power to engender a league of the heart. In an 1888 address to the Canadian Club in New York titled *The Schism in the Anglo-Saxon Race*, Smith opens by celebrating "British institutions, the American Republic, and other accomplishments" of Anglo-Saxons (19). He offers an uneasy image of latent Anglo-American affection, claiming to hear "amidst the cannon of the Fourth of July" a "cheer . . . of mutual affection and Anglo-Saxon patriotism" (23). Smith laments the extremity of Anglo-Saxondom's characteristic independence: "It is the weakness of self-reliance pushed to an extreme, which breeds division and isolation. Races such as the Celtic race, weaker in the individual, are sometimes made by their clannish cohesiveness stronger in the mass" (19). Commerce is neither sacred nor a key to affective bonding; indeed, a published volume of the speech opens with the following lines: "pray God that England no more / stand wroth from her daughter apart, / Pray God one blood and one tongue / Be one in hand and in heart."[5]

Smith's authorial self-presentation through much of the 1880s and the beginning of the 1890s reflects a similar ambivalence. Through the 1880s, Smith single-handedly published *The Bystander* from Toronto. This "monthly review of current events, Canadian and general," gave him a platform for commenting upon politics, religion, the arts, and society. As "the bystander," Smith assumed a character meaningful within, yet detached from, the transatlantic public sphere. When not publishing *The Bystander*, Smith published articles in a variety of periodicals based in London, Boston, and New York.[6]

By the turn of the century, Smith's anodyne vision of a league of the heart seemed impossible. Instead, Americans confronted the stark choice that provides the title for his 1902 book *Commonwealth or Empire? A Bystander's View of the Question*. As the "bystander," Smith counsels Americans to "fulfill the special hopes humanity has" invested in them by avoiding the lure of "European Imperialism" into "a career of conquest and domination over subject races" (Smith 2). Disgusted by the Boer War and the jingoism drummed up in England by its advent, Smith rejects "the dream[s] of Anglo-Israel . . . [and] Anglo-Saxon domination" as equally "fatuous" (Smith 46). This moderated racialism is based on worries that imperialism threatens "the wild stocks of humanity" as well as world literature (Smith 55). Of any formal imperial federation, Smith sees "commercial gain [as] . . . the real object, commercial cupidity . . . the sustaining principle" (Smith 49). Even a vision of the universality of "the language of the Anglo-Saxon race" becomes simply "a trader's dream" (Smith 53). Rejecting visions of the American character as a "mystical gift of blood" from Teutonic and, more immediately, British sources, American energy comes from the "blend[ing]" of "half a dozen races" into a spirit of "restlessness and enterprise" (Smith 46).

Smith's vision of transracial enterprise appears to recast his earlier celebration of commerce as a salve between racially linked nations into an internal vision of national unity. In this, Bell's suggestion that "nationality is grafted onto race" in Smith's writings takes on a changed complexion. Here, nationality is a blend of restless, competitive racial forces.

Domestically, however, commerce has begun to displace the pillars of public morality: "Wealth, with little regard to its issue, is becoming almost an object of our social worship" (Smith 9). Smith sees the rise of plutocracy as especially corrosive, threatening America's republican institutions by fostering a "craving for aristocracy" and promoting a disastrous entanglement in imperialism in the name of kinship with Britain (Smith 13). Smith views discussion of closer Anglo-American ties with cynicism: "The aristocratic and plutocratic party in England is enfolding in a loving embrace the American democracy as a long lost member of the family, whose relationship was unfortunately hidden from view at the crisis of Secession" (Smith 51). While the Civil War reference is a prod at Britain's commercial links with the Confederacy, the similarities between the conservative view and Smith's earlier rhetoric mark the degree to which Smith's position has changed (as well as reflect very different historical circumstances).

As Smith develops his polemic against plutocracy and commercialism, he analyzes how culture has naturalized increasingly venal motives. In Britain, "the outbreak of Jingoism [was accompanied by] . . . an inflation of monarchial sentiment, and a perceptible disposition to revive the personal power of the Crown" (Smith 35). Smith reports that Americans living in Canada for two years become eligible for any number of British "Peerages, Baronetcies, Knighthoods, and minor badges of rank" (Smith 13).

Thus we find Smith at the turn of the century, a voice emblematic of the fluidity permitted by the Anglo-American public sphere analyzing the cupidity of romanticized visions of Anglo-American relations and of the role of commerce itself. Rhetorically, his shift here to a primarily American audience reflects market conditions and validates the power of the Anglo-American public sphere as a commercial instrument. Ideologically, Smith moves away from shared culture, as it merely consolidates the authority of aristocracy, validates the imperialism promoted by conservatives, and provides a flimsy veil over naked commercial interest. Smith's own positionality as the "bystander," then, is maintained through disinterested cultural criticism. Moreover, in doing so he locates the themes that dominated Anglo-American discourse during this period: the substance and role of race, nostalgia for a restored culture based on tradition, fears of the emergence of transnational capital, and anxieties about the domestic commodification of culture. In the subsequent chapters, I trace how each of these themes circulated in the Anglo-American public sphere. In each case, the theme was renegotiated in the Anglo-American context to subtly assert the flexible positional superiority of the British.

CHAPTER 3

THE WHITE ATLANTIC

ANGLO-SAXON RACIALISM AT THE TURN OF THE TWENTIETH CENTURY

Gigantic daughter of the West / We drink to thee across the flood, / We know thee most, we love thee best, / For art thou not of British blood?

—Lord Alfred Tennyson

"What curious attitudes he goes into!"
"Not at all," said the King. "He's an Anglo-Saxon Messenger—and those are Anglo-Saxon attitudes. He only does them when he's happy."

—Lewis Carroll

If this era witnessed increased British scrutiny of the American system, a need to confront an impending crisis in international power, and proposals for reuniting the two nations, what discourses were employed to justify the last of these rather than another approach? Especially in the face of pervasive anti-British rhetoric and the continuing political advantage in America of, as one historian puts it, "twisting the lion's tail,"[1] what convinced British thinkers and the public that a formalized alliance was natural and would triumph over contemporary antagonisms? That is, what convinced readers that brotherhood and commonality, rather than animosity, were the essence of the relation between the two peoples?

The story of British racial ideologies has been described before, but this chapter traces the sublimated forms expressed through

Anglo-American relations. The role of race in Anglo-American discourse varies, but at the turn of the twentieth century, it only infrequently appears as a strict biological designator of inherited characteristics. Part of this sublimation involves viewing race as a psychological phenomenon, in which instinctive antagonisms and empathies ground individual and communal perceptions of the other.[2] While the psychological model of race still natural-izes difference and commonality, Anglo-Saxon racialist discourse increasingly manifests in the associative and classificatory assump-tions of narratives and criticism, providing a forum within which performances of the cultivated ideal described in the Introduc-tion occurred, and sometimes operating as a subtext. These forms straddle the performative and pedagogical, drawing upon a cul-turalist rhetoric to promote British superiority—in empire and in international affairs—while confronting the nation's failure to live up to its legacy. In turn, visions of racial reintegration are offered as a means of guaranteeing national, and world, progress.

THE KING ALFRED MILLENARY

In 1901, the opening of the Edwardian era in Britain was marked by commemorations of three deceased leaders. Queen Victoria's funeral in February and President McKinley's funeral in Septem-ber preceded the millenary celebration of the death of the Anglo-Saxon King Alfred. Each of these commemorations prompted reflection upon the relationship between the two nations.

Historian Frederic Harrison, in proposing the Alfred celebra-tion, says "I trust that, in the first year of the twentieth century, the English-speaking world may unite in its tribute of homage to the hero-saint who was the true father (if any man can be so styled) of our common literature, 'the model Englishman,' . . . the herald of our civic and religious organization" (Bowker 4).[3] The empha-sis upon the international nature of the event, and the sense of Alfred as a "model Englishman," along with the rhetoric of his argument—"I trust that"—indicate his opinion that strengthening Anglo-American relations are inevitable and link the transatlantic bond to a national ideal. Promoting a ritual of joint Anglo-Amer-ican memory, Harrison's paternalism contrasts sharply with the triumphalist rhetoric associated with jingoism, both at home and abroad. He pursues a vision of common tradition that would tamp down renewed Anglophobia kindled by the Boer War.

The proposal frames this vision in cultural terms, emphasizing limitation and refinement as the keys of "true human greatness": "It is true that the field of Alfred's achievements was relatively small, and the whole scale of his career was modest indeed when compared with that of his imperial compeers . . . It is *quality* not *quantity* that weighs in the impartial scales of history . . . That which tells in the end is the living seed of the creative mind, the heroic example, the sovereign gift of leadership, the undying inspiration of genius and faith" (Bowker 5). Recalling Edmund Gosse's commentary on culture and the small nation (referred to in the Introduction to this book), Alfred represents an embodiment of the *personal* contrasted to the expansive and aspirational qualities of "his imperial compeers" (Bowker 43). Harrison envisions a man of action, but as an emblem of cultural continuity and the integration of various forms of social activity: "Alfred represents at once the ancient monarchy, the army, the navy, the law, the literature, the poetry, the art, the enterprise, the industry, the religion of our race" (Bowker 5). During the millenary events of 1901, Harrison elaborates upon this portrait by linking restraint and his personal example, rather than violence, to the forging of the modern nation: "He was the purest, the noblest, and the most venerable hero of whom our race could boast. He made England one, not by conquest, not by fraud, but by wisdom, justice, and moral force" (Harrison 78). That Harrison was the mouthpiece for such a perspective was no small irony—he was specifically and repeatedly targeted as an illustration of the forces ranged against culture by Matthew Arnold in *Culture and Anarchy* some 30 years earlier.

The contemporary significance of this ideal was emphasized by novelist, historian, and critic Sir Walter Besant, who claimed "the tale of Alfred . . . should be always fresh and new, because at every point it conceived every successive generation of English-speaking people" (Besant 7–8). Besant sees an Alfred monument as a corrective to excessive pride in empire, noting "in the minds of many a feeling that we ought to teach the people the . . . meaning of our Empire" (Besant 8–9). This pedagogical function of the memorial underscores how the worship of cultural continuity implicitly naturalizes class interest as national interest. The public resurrection of Alfred symbolism identified nationality with a respect for limits and hierarchies while shoring popular confidence about the implicit value of the British imperial enterprise. Note the Arnoldian language in Besant's description of Alfred's significance: "Great as were the achievements of Alfred . . . Alfred is, and will always remain, the typical man of our race, call him Anglo-Saxon, call him American, Englishman, call him Australian—the typical man of our race at his best and noblest . . . I am quite sure and certain that the mind of the Anglo-Saxon at his best and noblest is the mind of Alfred; that the aspirations, the hopes, the standards of the Anglo-Saxon at his best and noblest are [those] . . . of Alfred" (Besant 9). The terms of such a description—Alfred as "typical" example of the "best"—evokes differentiation within the body politic, suggesting the discourse of cultivation described in the Introduction.

In grouping Americans and Englishmen into a common race, organizers paid close attention to celebrating the American stars in the firmament of the Anglo-American public sphere. Anglo-Saxonism had great traction in elite circles in America, from visions of the Yeoman Republic to Henry Adams's seminar on Anglo-Saxon studies at Harvard, and even to Theodore Roosevelt's convoluted race ideas. Eric Kaufmann's *The Rise and Fall of Anglo-America* (2004) provides an incisive analysis of racialist rhetoric in the United States in this period, and Thomas Dyer's *Theodore Roosevelt and the Idea of Race* (1992) links the president's racial ideas to domestic and foreign priorities. Kaufmann argues for the development of an "American ethnicity," which by the mid-nineteenth century viewed "the era of the Yeoman Republic, described by Jefferson in an allusion to both the Bible and King Alfred's Anglo-Saxons [as] . . . a Golden Age for America, to which it should return" (Kaufmann 24). This ideology coexisted, according to Kaufmann, with liberal cosmopolitanism in a form of "double-consciousness" (Kaufmann 31).

Although American Ambassador Choate was forced to miss the millenary celebration because of the assassination of McKinley, Americans, especially American professors, are heavily represented in the lists of attendees and subscribers. In the fall of 1901, several months after the celebration in England, there was a celebration in New York at St. Paul's chapel. Plans were made for the establishment of a permanent collection of Anglo-Saxon literature at the New York Public Library, for an ongoing transnational lecture series, and for celebrations of Alfred's life throughout the United States.

With the newly crowned King Edward as its chief patron, the events of the millenary celebration included an exhibition at the British Museum, visits by luminaries to key Anglo-Saxon cites, the unveiling of the King Alfred statue in Winchester, with a reading from Lord Rosebery, and a street procession. Later that year a naval cruiser, the *King Alfred*, was launched.

Besant's and others' casual invocations of race testify to the pervasiveness of racialist ideas at this moment. The millenary was a culmination of Anglo-Saxon rhetoric disseminated from elite members of British culture, the volume of which had risen to a height in the late 1890s. While the Rhymers Club was meeting to chart the future course of British poetry, the poet laureate, Alfred Austin, wrote longing poems about King Alfred, including "England's Darling" and "The Spotless King," as well as a biography *Alfred the Great: Containing Chapters on his Life and Times.*

There were cynics about the production of Alfrediana. A *Times* reviewer of Bowker's book *Alfred the Great* complained "there is more than a trace of hyperbole. The butter . . . is spread very thickly upon the thin bread of fact" (August 10, 1899, 18). The review goes on to dispute the millenary's value as anything more than a remembrance: "We cannot agree with the Poet Laureate that through the distance of a thousand years 'Alfred's full radiance shines on us at last'" (August 10, 1899, 18). However, the reviewer does "recognize in Alfred a true hero of our race, and a King more than worthy to be celebrated in an age much addicted to celebrations and anniversaries" (August 10, 1899, 18).

Stuart Anderson contends that "Anglo-Saxonism, as an intellectual construct, provided the primary rationale for the diplomatic rapprochement between the two countries. Anglo-Saxonism linked the British and American peoples, or at least that segment of the population in both countries that had the most direct influence on foreign policy, in a kind of larger patriotism of race" (Anderson 12). The fuzziness of concepts of race at this moment created a flexibility that permitted different ideological perspectives to incorporate racialism into their rhetoric (though racialism generally promoted a Tory politics). It also provided a language of identification within the Anglo-American discursive community that brought legitimacy to calls for deeply integrated bilateral foreign policies. As Anderson puts it, "By the 1890s, nationalism, imperialism, and racism were so intertwined in Western thought that it was difficult to separate the intellectual strands" (Anderson 18). They were also exchangeable—referring to the American race or the British race was not uncommon. These convergences reflect a bastardized popular or diplomatic use of scholarly ideas that, as Hugh MacDougall notes, had largely been abandoned by the academic establishment by this period: "By the end of the century few serious scholars accepted the fallacious identification of race and language" that had been so influential in the mid-nineteenth century (MacDougall 120).

Millenary rhetoric and other Anglo-Saxonist expressions typically articulate pride in the freedoms, cultural and political achievements, and lack of aggression associated with Alfred. Like race itself, these characteristics of the Anglo-Saxon were quite flexible, bending to the circumstances and political interests ascendant in particular moments of articulation. A consistent pattern, however, can be discerned in its nostalgia for a golden age, promoting veneration for culture, tradition, and veneration itself, sometimes even emanating from liberal voices.

Through repeated depictions of the *natio* demonstrating its best self in reverencing, celebrating, and always obeying a naturalized authority, Anglo-Saxonism rhetorically endorses aristocratic hierarchy and refashions the British relationship with America.

With the aim of presenting how these themes are manifested for different audiences, the chapter will examine portraits of Anglo-Saxon racialism in various literary modes at the turn of the twentieth century: from popular "pulp" literature to a celebrated author, and then to an elite journal that trades upon the new traditionalism by inflecting it with sublimated racialist sentiments. The chapter will begin with two late nineteenth-century "future war" novels, Louis Tracy's *The Final War* (1896) and Benjamin Rush Davenport's *Anglo-Saxons, Onward!* (1898). Tracy's novel takes a British perspective, while Davenport's is American, and the contrast illustrates the cultural stakes behind British expressions of Anglo-Saxon racialism.

Subsequently, we will turn our attention to Rudyard Kipling's implicit Anglo-Saxonism in *Captains Courageous*, and relate it to the more overt strategies discoverable in "Recessional" and "The

White Man's Burden." When contrasted with the future war novels, Kipling's work reveals more sophisticated approaches to racialism.

Finally, this chapter will conclude with an aesthetic and content analysis of the literary, cultural, and political publication *The Anglo-Saxon Review*, which further sublimates "race" as a locus of direct identity claims and, in so doing, emphasizes the positional superiority articulated by Kipling, but with a greater emphasis upon cultural refinement. Taken together, the movement from "future war" novel to elite literary review begins to demonstrate the range of manifestations of turn-of-the-century Anglo-Saxonist discourse while suggesting the shifting image of the British national character identified herein. Mapping images of the British self as a product of what Hobsbawm and Ranger have termed "encrustation," with increasingly sophisticated textual strategies, the chapter will consider how a nostalgic, regressive discourse manifested differently in texts targeted at quite different readerships.

A common, even central, theme of literary images of Alfred is manifest in the millenary speeches quoted earlier in the chapter: Alfred's national function as a lawgiver. This identification of Alfred with the law is reconceived in a number of other representations of heroic Anglo-Saxonism and provides a key for the reconciliation of Britain with America and between its own classes. Such a purpose emerges relatively closely antecedent to the material under consideration here. According to Scragg, "It is from the end of the eighteenth century . . . that Alfred—and occasionally the Anglo-Saxons in general—are seen as bringing order and stability to England through the imposition of law" (Scragg 15).

Through this lawgiving function, an emphasis upon the *continuity* represented by Alfred, and the focus upon hero-worship rather than present historical circumstances or, for that matter, Anglo-American relations, the celebration provided an apt symbolic medium for the achievement of the imperatives of recasting Britain's role as a world power: to provide new rituals and heroic examples that emphasized British experience and tradition. In doing so, the event offered a mutually acceptable vision of close Anglo-American relations while providing a pedagogical rhetoric to discipline the emergence of empire-enriched middle classes into public discourse.

Millenary rhetoric thus points to a common dynamic within British Anglo-Saxon racialism, illustrated in this chapter by the millenary, future war novels, Kipling, and the journal *The Anglo-Saxon Review*. Neither simply a group of convenient prejudices nor a fund of self-affirming myths, racialism operates as a disciplinary ideology that naturalizes a conservative worldview through the law-giving function. The narratives of racialism consist in a double movement: first, affirming a shared sense of masculinity that defines and celebrates a certain form of homosocial bonding; second, affirming a posture of reverence and submission to authority that justifies an aggressive national posture in foreign policy in the name of duty. In tandem, these messages imply and legitimate a pedagogical message to the *natio*. These transformations of Alfred's law-giving image, vested in the raiment of Anglo-American relations and world-historical destiny, express a longing for a return to stable domestic hierarchies even as they vaunt Britain's cultural superiority. The law is frequently contrasted with images of mob rule, legitimating the class hierarchies threatened by contemporary economic and political currents. The contrast also supports Britain's imperial identity against liberal internationalist policies that threaten to erode British liberty, sovereignty, and power. This chapter traces different iterations of this dynamic offered to different British readerships.

In "The Anglo-Saxons: fact and fiction," Donald Scragg tracks the treatment of Alfred and other Anglo-Saxons as political and cultural figures in literature through the nineteenth century. The Anglo-Saxons' military successes defined England, and to a degree Great Britain, as a unitary political body, providing a historical context for their importance in national iconography (Scragg 1). Indeed, Alfred's leadership encouraged the development of a conception of Englishness through the production of vernacular translations of Latin works as part of a Christian revival, which in turn made reference to an "English people" (Scragg 4). As Scragg puts it, "The idea of the 'English people' was being promoted amongst the reading public . . . at just the time that 'England' as a political structure was becoming a reality" (4). In addition, conceptions of the "foreignness" of non-Anglo-Saxons are evident in the vernacular literature of this period as well (Scragg 4).

After playing a key role in producing nationalist ideas, Alfred and the Anglo-Saxons subsequently became nationalist icons themselves. Interest in the Anglo-Saxons flourished during the Renaissance and the eighteenth and nineteenth centuries. The stage during this period was particularly receptive to plays about Alfred, which may have appealed to a burgeoning sense of national pride during the growth of the empire. The patriotic song "Rule, Britannia" first appeared as part of a masque titled *Alfred* in 1740, and Alfred is a focus of patriotic discourse in the eighteenth century.

In addition, antiquarian interest in Alfred and the Anglo-Saxons developed as early as the early Modern period (Frantzen and Niles 5). Velma Bourgeois Richmond describes Anglo-Saxon medievalism as "a discourse through which the present, especially its anxieties and discontents, can be articulated through a repository of belief and images [that] . . . served British national interests, and many authors in the years before World War I continued to rely on and exploit the nation's heritage from the age of Alfred" (174). These functions of medievalist iconography— to articulate and assuage cultural anxieties—partly account for the tenor of the cultural analogies linking Anglo-American relations to British domestic anxieties. Richmond notes that Sir Walter Scott's *Ivanhoe* presents a reconciliation of "the virtues of an aristocracy and the strength of the lower classes . . . celebrat[ing] a new 'Englishness'" (174).

Racialism in the Popular Imagination

At the turn of the twentieth century, Scott's model was reframed in the burgeoning field of invasion literature that drew upon an Anglo-Saxon past. Amplifying the Anglo-Saxon inflections of imperial and historical fictions by H. Rider Haggard, Charles Kingsley, Edward Bulwer-Lytton, and G. A. Henty, and attempting to draw upon the sources of Scott's continued popularity, these novels were set in the past, present, or future, and express "Tory sentiments" (Richmond 177–78). Another branch of Anglo-Saxonist popular fiction that will be explored in this chapter, involved future war scenarios that pitted the United States, Britain, and occasionally nations from the Commonwealth against a variety of menaces, ultimately securing world peace.

Richmond describes a steady current of Anglo-Saxon inflected patriotism in juvenile literature through the Edwardian period, including "favorite nursery histories [such as] H. E. Marshall's *Our Island Story* (1905) and *Our Empire Story* (1908)" as well as "enthusiasm for northern stories [such as] . . . M. I. Ebbutt's collection of retellings for children, *Hero Myths and Legends of the British Race* (1910)" (178–79). Richmond identifies Charles W. Whistler as "the most remarkable writer of Anglo-Saxon historical novels for juveniles," notable among numerous others for his prolific output as well as a strong focus upon Anglo-Saxon themes (187). Additionally, the *Boy's Own Paper* and other magazines for Victorian and Edwardian youth were filled with Anglo-Saxon references and sentiments, supplemented by masculinist, imperial movements like Baden-Powell's boy scouts and the cult of sport. Richmond concludes that the vogue for Anglo-Saxonism had a lasting impact, creating the "high sentiments" and feudal language that figure prominently in Paul Fussell's account of the literary catalysts of World War I (192).

There is some terminological disagreement manifest in descriptions of Anglo-Saxonist rhetoric before the nineteenth century. Hugh MacDougall sees this history in terms of two animating racial myths in England: the Celtic, emergent in the twelfth century and associated with Geoffrey of Monmouth, which gave rise to the Arthur legends; and the Teutonic/Anglo-Saxon, which arose in the sixteenth century. According to MacDougall, the Celtic myth stalled after the Glorious Revolution, while the Teutonic/Anglo-Saxon myth reflected "a higher degree of historicity" and "arose in response to complex religious and political needs" and "matured" in step with the rise of England's empire (2).

Yet according to Reginald Horsman, Anglo-American valorization of the Anglo-Saxon period predated a specifically racialist conception of Anglo-Saxonism. Before the American Revolution, writers from both countries celebrated the political and individual freedoms believed to be characteristic of Anglo-Saxon governance (3). In the early nineteenth century, writers began speculating "that blood, not environment or accident, had led to their success. England and America had separated their institutions, but both countries were surging forward to positions of unprecedented power and prosperity" (Horsman 62). At the end of the nineteenth century, Anglo-Saxonism is articulated in conjunction with negative images of Celts or Celtic races. One telling example was the 1896 Olympic success of Boston track star James Connolly, whose Irish roots stirred anxiety about race both in the WASP-y enclaves of mugwump America and in England.

A number of British cultural figures promoted racialist ideas in the early and mid-nineteenth century, including Thomas Carlyle, Thomas Arnold, and Benjamin Disraeli. Nineteenth-century academic disciplines used to define and characterize the Anglo-Saxon race included philology, anatomy, and perhaps most prominently, evolutionary theory. As the knowledge disciplines struggled to create a coherent portrait of the race, interest in an essential connection between the Anglo-Saxons and the characteristics of the contemporary nation grew and spread into diffuse spheres. Charles Kingsley was an important proponent of Anglo-Saxonism in the 1840s, applying the logic of Anglo-Saxon destiny to both foreign and domestic matters (Horsman 76). According to Horsman, Anglo-Saxonist discourse was inflected with the sense of a world-historical status in the mid-nineteenth century: by this time "the simple praise of Anglo-Saxon institutions and freedom, which had assumed such importance in the sixteenth and seventeenth centuries, had undergone a profound change in England. Rather than emphasizing earlier freedom as a basis for internal reform, the new theorists were envisaging a world shaped to the desires of a supposedly innately superior Anglo-Saxon race. There was a firm and increasing belief that what was good for the Anglo-Saxons was good for the world" (77). The arrogance of such claims for the race were tempered and, indeed, sublimated within notions of duty and reverence for culture by the turn of the century.

The development of theories of national character occurred in tandem with evolutionary and race theory, and nationality was inseparable from ideas about race. According to Hobsbawm in *Nations and Nationalism Since 1780*, in the nineteenth century ethnicity becomes "the central, increasingly the decisive or even the only criteria for nationality" (*Nations and Nationalism Since 1780* 102). Clare Simmons sees an infusion of quasi-scientific race ideas into British history throughout the Victorian period. At the beginning of Victoria's reign, Matthew Arnold's father, Thomas, posits a class split between Normans and Saxons. Thomas Arnold was a key disseminator of concepts of national character, and "almost in spite of himself . . . helped create a slightly anti-intellectual environment in which a sense of character, and above all of English character, was seen as the way to social success and also as the standard by which to assess the past" (G. Jones 73). In the 1860s, Walter Bagehot's conceptualization of national character incorporated notions of "use-inheritance"—that is, the idea that the individual's attempts to adapt to his social environment *gradually* created "an hereditary disposition for certain attitudes and behavior" (G. Jones 79). This idea was the centerpiece of Jean-Baptiste Lamarck's evolutionary theory. Bagehot's version emphasized the imitative tendencies of humans. As Greta Jones notes, for Bagehot "the sober appreciation of the process of parliamentary government among English men and the expression of this in policies of certain great statesmen provided an ideal which moulded the character of the English nation" (81). Thus when, as we surveyed in Chapter 1, British critics analyze Americans' ideological credulity as the result of their lack of history and absolute identification with republican institutions, they are transforming a discourse central to mid-Victorian "John Bull"-ish constructions of British identity. Other figures laid the groundwork for conceiving of Anglo-Saxon community, particularly Charles Dilke, whose 1869 *Greater Britain* "gave greater currency to the idea that the English-speaking peoples of the British Isles and the United States belonged to a common, pre-eminent Saxon race," according to Lorimer's "Race, Science and Culture" (16).

These causal theories were often abetted by the scientific community. Herbert Spencer reframed the theory to emphasize the impact of the social environment created by institutions and social circumstances; for Spencer and his followers, the mechanism of change was the environment itself rather than imitation, and the slow process of natural selection was superseded by an evolutionary process caused by the shaping of the members of a society by the aforesaid factors. Spencer and others, operating under the "assumption that the processes of race formation were in large part social . . . provided some rationale for the casual but widespread misapplication of the term 'race' to specific national grouping" (Livingstone 186).

Methodology facilitated applying evolutionary logic to nations and national cultures as well: "With the comparative method as their tool, they bridged the physical and social sciences, maintaining that many indications of parallel cultural development in both living and extinct societies suggested that cultures underwent tensions and struggles similar to those in the biological world" (G. Jones 121). The confused metonymies of such comparativism—is a culture like a species? or an individual member of a species?—lent themselves to the vague operations of stereotype and embodiment endemic to discourses of national character and culture. Specifically, the insinuation of environmental factors into racial heredity offered a structure through which Anglo-American contact could be mutually enriching even as British culture is heralded as the center of world civilization.

The genealogy of Anglo-Saxon racialism is not strictly coupled with the vanguard of science. According to Greta Jones, "By the 1900's Lamarckians were a minority within biology" (84). The scientific community largely abandoned these social models in light of August Weissmann's work in the 1880s. Weissmann's "germ theory" posited that hereditary characteristics were conveyed in a germ plasm that remained unaffected by environment. In addition, the scientific community debated whether all human beings came from a single genetic source. Yet notions of use-inheritance and environmentalism persisted in popular representation.

George Frederickson draws a key distinction in types of racism during this period. On the one hand, "ideological racists" believed in innate, biologically determined differences in competence and capacity; on the other, "missionary" racists operated upon the presumption that the other could be civilized.[4] Representations of Anglo-Saxon unity often lack this clarity, drawing ideas from both camps as convenience suits: that is, no particular set of assumptions can be exclusively credited (or better, blamed) for the racial ideas underlying the turn-of-the-century Anglo-Saxonist vogue. Rather, these theories provided a fund of ideas on which contemporary popular discourse of nation and race was based. The roles of individual and "herd" instinct, the relation of learning and reason to instinct, the relation of evolutionary processes to progress and atavism, the role of emotion, the place of morality, and the basic organizing rubrics of race and nation were cribbed and inferred from scientific texts into theories, treatises, diatribes, and other forms of discourse representing a variety of political and social perspectives, both informing them and being bastardized to conform to the assumptions and ends of those perspectives. According to John Haller, "Obscured by the comparative method of analogy, explanations of biological and social evolution became synonymous in meaning" (98). The period witnessed popularized versions of biological ideas enjoying cultural ascendancy: "The cross-fertilisation of biological and social metaphors was important . . . biology helped . . . create the kind of moral universe in which nature reflected society and vice versa" (Jones 146–47). Stuart Anderson puts the point more emphatically: "So pervasive and influential were [Darwinian notions] . . . by the latter years of the century that any social theory based on Darwinian analogy stood a good chance of winning widespread acceptance. Indeed, for some Britons and Americans, the struggle for existence was a universal formula; they habitually blurred the distinction between the organic development of plants and animals and the social development of human groups" (36).

Other British intellectuals, including Thomas Henry Huxley, Leslie Stephen, and Benjamin Kidd fueled the rise of Anglo-Saxonism by promoting these ideas and applying them to the sphere of international relations. Kidd's 1894 *Social Evolution* was a transatlantic bestseller and emblematic of the Anglo-Saxonist tendency to describe both primitive peoples and the lower classes as children needful of paternal governance (Kohn 6–7). Karl Pearson argued that rival nations, rather than individuals within a nation, were the real players in a Darwinian struggle for existence (Anderson 31). Interestingly, and quite against the Tory tenor of most evocations of Anglo-Saxonism, Pearson's theory was intended to legitimate socialist principles (Anderson 31).

On the Liberal side, James Bryce, whose ideas about Anglo-American relations are touched upon in the Introduction, provided an influential perspective in the Romanes lecture of 1902, *The Relations of the Advanced and the Backward Races of Mankind*. In the lecture, Bryce employs the idea of national character frequently, crossing between nation, race, and region. In "Race, Science and Culture," Douglas Lorimer notes that Bryce "contrasted racial groups by their level of development, but to his mind racial conflict derived less from innate inequality than from the psychology of interracial conflict" (30). Nevertheless, much of Bryce's analysis, and his most striking recommendation, take notions of "blood" quite seriously:

> For the future of mankind nothing is more vital than that some races should be maintained at the highest level of efficiency, because the work they can do for thought and art and letters, for scientific discovery, and for raising the standard of conduct, will determine the general progress of humanity. If therefore we were to suppose the blood of the races which are now most advanced to be diluted, so to speak, by that of those most backward, not only would more be lost to the former than

would be gained to the latter, but there would be a loss, possibly an
irreparable loss, to the world at large . . . It may therefore be doubted
whether any further mixture of Advanced and Backward races is to be
desired. (36)

Bryce's conflation of development with race is perhaps mystified by
his nuanced psychologism, but ultimately it argues *against* racial
mixture and *for* the primacy of peoples descended from northern
Europe, particularly Anglo-Americans, in preserving and improving civilization. The language of "efficiency," additionally, is an
unfortunate precursor of the eugenics movement.

Race was thus a dominant critical category in thinking from
across the political spectrum, but we should be cautious of over-
stating the powers of analogical and biologistic thinking, however,
or of making spurious assumptions about the naïveté of readers in
this period. In 1899, for example, a *Times* reviewer commented
that "There is a good deal of suspicion, which is, we are afraid,
not unfounded, of books which mix up discussions of comparative
anatomy with discussions of social phenomena. The most unwary
tiro is now on his guard against analogies between the organisms,
actual and unmistakable, of the animal world and the so-called
organisms of society . . . Occasionally these analogies are fruitful
in new views; they enlarge the horizon of the inquirer; and they
suggest to him useful lines of inquiry. But forced, persisted in, and
stated without necessary modifications, they are positively misleading" ("Short Notices" 7).

In popular discourse, the celebrated Anglo-Saxon character modified the bluff practicality and energy of John Bull with
"patien[ce] . . . considerat[ion] . . . [high] intelligence . . . [and
impeccable] morals" (Anderson 20). Part of this transformation
can be attributed to the identification of Anglo-Saxonists with the
monarchy. For example, Prince Albert, with his famed refinement,
good manners, and cosmopolitan origins, embodied the Anglo-
Saxon type.

APOCALYPTIC RACIALISM: FUTURE WAR NOVELS

For Anglo-Saxonists, the monarchy evoked reverent feelings that
blurred the lines between the heroic past and an ambiguous present. Victoria's personal lineage and governance symbolized "both

progress and a return to the Golden Age . . . Victoria's very person reinforced the Saxon identity" (Simmons 260). This dual temporality in Victoria worship, and in Anglo-Saxonism more generally, affirmed domestic class hierarchies by manifesting in literature in scenes of reverence and obedience. These qualities were associated with elevated notions of British identity. As Clare Simmons puts it, Anglo-Saxonists viewed "respect for their leaders [and] . . . support for established authority as patriotically English" (261).

This modern transposition of the lawgiving function into muted reverence manifests repeatedly in popular fictions at the turn of the century and, as we will explore in Chapters 5 and 6, manifests in the attitudes of literary writers toward mass culture and modernity itself. The different images of Britishness offered in an American future war novel, Benjamin Rush Davenport's *Anglo-Saxons, Onward!* and a British counterpart, Louis Tracy's *The Final War*, illustrate how this form of Anglo-Saxonism supports British images of its national culture.

These two novels have been selected out of a large number of such "future war" novels—I. F. Clarke counts over seven hundred of them. Tracy's and Davenport's fictions provide representative examples of the genre, and while the former was written by a British author and features textual appeals to a British audience, the latter was penned by an American for an American audience.

The American *Anglo-Saxons, Onward!* repeatedly returns to a core racialism in the phrase "blood is thicker than water." The phrase provides a simple logic for Anglo-American partnership in an international field swarming with intriguing foreigners who use convoluted logic and the lure of self-interest to attempt to sever the partnership. Presented in scare quotations throughout the novel, the phrase functions as a motto of unthinking allegiance, locating Anglo-Saxon kinship in bodily terms. The notion of "blood" manifests in a passionate, even primal desire for serving the nation and race. A number of scenes feature bureaucratic procedures and diplomatic niceties shoved to the side in favor of direct, instantaneous action.

For example, when the commander of a British man-of-war hears of danger to the American president's comely daughter, he bucks a policy that would prevent intervention on the grounds of shared racial heritage. The officer's "bull-dog blood was up in an instant," and he pronounces that he will "be d— if an English

man can stand that. There may be a h— of a row when they hear
of it in England, but here goes, for 'blood is thicker than water'"
(53). This kind of manly feeling is at the heart of Anglo-Saxonist
discourse targeted toward the middle and lower classes, manifesting here and in Tracy's and Kipling's evocations of the Anglo-
Saxon character.

Yet Davenport's portrait of the British recalls old stereotypes.
The familiar image of England as a "bull-dog," accompanied by a
performance of stubborn fierceness, describes a vision of John Bull
associated with pragmatism, vigor, directness, and courage. His
passionate nature, clearly antibureaucratic and anti-intellectual,
verges upon overriding all cerebration. That this character manifests in an officer underscores the subordinate and stereotypical
role accorded the British in this American text.

British author Louis Tracy's *The Final War* also draws upon traditional John Bull imagery. The novel alternates scenes of derring-do,
manly bonding, and moments of class-oriented affect in chronicling
the Anglo-American defense of Britain against a continental plot.
Early in the novel, after Parliament passes a war bill to counter the
incipient threat, the narrator reflects: "The Briton is, perhaps rightly,
accused of being stolid. It is certain that the members of Parliament left Westminster with as much *sang-froid* as if they had just
given their sanction to a new railway bill" (27). The image differs
from Davenport's in emphasizing British impassivity. To foreground
this point, Tracy includes a popular vaudeville air in France, one of
the conspirators against Britain, in a chapter titled "On the boule-
vards": "Ca y est donc, en l'Angleterre, / Fron de boeuf, et plein
d'biere, / Trop de ventre, pour s'enfuir, / V'la un homme, qui
nous fait rire" (So there it is, in England / Forehead [face] of an
ox, and full of beer / Too big a belly, to run away / There's a man,
who makes us laugh) (65). Here the caricature of John Bull as vulgar, bodily, and lacking reason and emotional control appears in its
most hostile iteration. The record of this stereotype provides a false
standard against which to compare actual male British characters,
and it indirectly provides evidence of the bigotry, sneering nature,
and, most important, the mob mentality of the French. Whereas in
Davenport's novel European intrigue is symptomatic of a decadent,
self-serving intellectualism, in Tracy's it reflects the rule of the herd.

By contrast, the novel articulates a vision of ideal Britishness
grounded in some of the qualities traditionally associated with

John Bull, but shaped by reverence for authority, the nation, and moral principles. The energy, pragmatism, and frankness associated with the stereotype manifest as impatience to do one's duty, as in the following prebattle disposition: "Every man in the fleet knew that he was going to practically certain death, but that was of slight import—delay alone was irksome" (Tracy 45). This masculine bravery is not foolhardy; rather, it is part of the call of duty, and personal devotion to its valorous fulfillment. When one commander is assigned a supporting assignment in the initial advance, he "turns scarlet with indignation. 'Do I understand you, sir,' he said passionately, 'that the *Speedy* is to be turned into a post-office'" (Tracy 43).

Scenes like this, which proliferate through the novel, not only create a modified portraiture of John Bull, but they provide opportunities for the articulation of duty within the bounds of the hierarchies of the British state. A letter signed by "Salisbury, Albert Edward, W. E. Gladstone, [and] Wolseley" (figures spanning a range of institutions and holding different ideological positions) urge that "Great Britain is now fighting for her life, and that it is the duty of all her sons, without distinction of class or position, to devote every energy toward bringing the war to an early and successful termination" (Tracy 89). While the rhetoric of the letter suggests a possible leveling of the classes in the service of the nation, the performance of duty in fact reinscribes class hierarchies.

The success of Britain's self-defense is guaranteed by the invention of an electric gun by a common citizen, rather than through the tactical genius of the elite. In applying for an audience with the prince, the inventor, Mr. Thompson, seeks "no reward or self-aggrandisement of any sort. I am above all else an Englishman, and I hope that this fact will be sufficient excuse for my action at this moment" (Tracy 55). Even in the service of saving the nation, the proper Englishman apologizes for intruding upon the attention of someone well above his station.

In counterpoint to displays of proper middle-class modesty, the figures who embody the law-giving functions of Alfred perform attitudes of sophistication and refinement. For example, the text features an illustration of Wolseley with a world-weary, detached expression on his face, with the caption: "I have spent the night in reading, smoking, and thinking—the latter unwillingly" (Tracy 112). Wolseley's reluctance to engage even in ratiocinative work as unbecoming a gentleman represents an attempt to recast the exigency of duty into a cultivated, reluctant mastery. In a particularly affecting speech in *The Final War*, the Prince of Wales lays out the imaginative basis of Anglo-Saxon affiliation: "I depart from established custom in order to utilize this favorable opportunity of conveying to you, and through you to the people of the British Empire all the world over, the sentiments of Her Majesty the Queen at this supremest hour in the history of Britain. Her majesty charges me to say that she recognizes with a delight intensified by life-long conviction, the indomitable faith which characterize the English-speaking people at a moment when such qualities are in the most urgent demand" (Tracy 52). Edward's praise of the characteristic indomitable "faith" of the English-speaking people oddly (but typically) is not given an overt referent. In Chapter 5, we will explore how Conrad employs a similarly fuzzy rhetoric to venerate British culture, and the proper attitude toward culture, even while questioning the behavior of the nation and many of its members.

Here, the prince articulates British secularized faith in the nation as an object of worship. While this reflects a sublimation of the rhetoric of religious destiny, it also points to a complex economy between reader and text. Future war novels, as works imagining the manifestation of a contemporaneously inchoate crisis, and subsequently the overcoming of that crisis as a substitute for a return to a golden age, implicitly have a complex relation to temporality. The narrator guides the reader, even in the most obvious of these future war narratives, into an ambiguous temporal position and an ambiguous sense of mastery over and worship of the heroes. The net result is that this secures a fantasy of transcending the differences between Anglo-Saxon nations and, internally, between leading and working classes.

The end of the future war novel repeats this rhetoric on a grand scale, metonymically hailing the nation's own self-sacrificing submission to its world-historical destiny. At a key moment in *The Final War*, secular nation-worship animates England's call to a world-historical destiny: "Let it be England's glory that she takes up the quarrel on behalf of freedom, honour, and prosperity, and earns anew the gratitude of the world . . . It is a time for cheerful self-denial" (26). The sublimated grandiosity of such visions appears frequently in Anglo-Saxonist discourse. Where *The Final*

War employs religious rhetoric, other texts imagine the nation as a direct instrument of the divine will.

While Anglo-Saxonism drew upon quasi-scientific theories of race, it also found vocal religious proponents, like the bestselling American preacher Josiah Strong, who believed Malthusian population pressures would lead to a competition of races for world supremacy (Anderson 34). Strong associates a "centrifugal" tendency with the race, naturalizing expansion, aggression, and conquest as part of the racial character. Thomas Gossett argues that religious and scientific treatments of race were not incompatible—for Strong, the traditional religious view that God would not create races incapable of self-government was outdated in light of scientific evidence (228). In literary texts, this association of nationhood and divinity promotes attitudes of reverence for authority that naturalize domestic hierarchies and create safe outlets for homosocial bonding. Rudyard Kipling offered the epitome of this attitude.

REVERENCE, MASCULINE AUTHORITY, AND ANGLO-SAXONISM IN KIPLING

Rudyard Kipling achieved more fame that any other British writer for expressing Anglo-Saxonist and generally racialist sentiments at the turn of the century. He had close ties to the United States, marrying an American woman, Carrie, and living in Vermont from soon after their marriage until the height of the Venezuela boundary crisis in 1896. Despite these ties, Kipling experienced America as a place of teeming Anglophobia, even at the height of Anglo-Saxon feeling. He explains it thus: "There is no other country for the American public speaker to trample upon . . . France has Germany; we have Russia; for Italy, Austria is provided . . . Only America stands out of the racket; and therefore, to be in fashion, makes a sand-bag of the mother-country, and bangs her when occasion requires" (Kipling, *American Notes* 58).

Kipling's 1891 *American Notes* reprises some of the themes of the travel literature traced in the first chapter, including American materialism and the linkage between egalitarian institutions and a singular focus upon business. In a passage reminiscent of Robert Louis Stevenson or Charles Dickens, Kipling writes of checking into a hotel: "When the hotel clerk—the man who awards your room to you and is supposed to give you information—when that resplendent individual stoops to attend your wants, he does so whistling or humming, or picking his teeth, or pauses to converse with some one he knows. These performances, I gather, are to impress upon you that he is a free man and your equal" (Kipling, *American Notes* 15). Further, America's egalitarian spirit stunts the development of culture. Encountering a group of well-dressed American women, Kipling expects to hear "the level voice of culture" but finds, instead, "the *staccato* voice of the white servant-girl all the world over" (Kipling, *American Notes* 23). He reflects upon this shock in Arnoldian language: "Revolving in my mind that these folk were barbarians, I was presently enlightened and made aware that they also were the heirs of all the ages, and civilized after all" (Kipling, *American Notes* 24).

More generally, Kipling's disappointment with America rests in its tendency toward mob rule, partly driven by "foreigners" in the country. He fails to find a stable basis for the social contract: "I have striven to find out where the central authority of the land lies . . . It certainly is not in the citizens, because they are governed and coerced by despotic power of public opinion as represented by their papers, preachers, or local society" (Kipling, "From Sea to Sea" 156).

While these disappointments recall the themes of other travel narratives, Kipling tempers his perspective by repeatedly praising the American people for their passion. Aboard a steamer on Victoria's birthday, Kipling witnesses the following scene:

If you ever meet an American, be good to him . . . A small American penned half a dozen English into a corner and lectured them soundly on—their want of patriotism!

"What sort of Queen's Birthday do you call this?" he thundered. "What do you drink the President's health for? What's the President to you on this day of all others? Well, suppose you *are* in the minority, all the more reason for standing by your country. Don't talk to me. You Britishers made a mess of it—a mighty bungle of the whole thing. I'm an American of the Americans; but if no one can propose Her Majesty's health better than by just throwing it at your heads, I'm going to try."

Then and there he delivered a remarkably neat little oration—pat, well put together, and clearly delivered. So it came to pass that the Queen's health was best honored by an American. We English were dazed. (Kipling, "From Sea to Sea" 428–29)

Kipling's juxtaposition of American feeling and English indifference mark his critique of the variety of English refinement manifested in avant-garde literary movements as well as the self-satisfactions of the empire-enriched British public. He turns to America, as he turns to the empire elsewhere, as a source of renewal for national virtues and as a crucible for the forming of British masculinity.[5] He prays for the emergence of a poet to

> compose the greatest song of all—The Saga of the Anglo-Saxon all round the earth—a paean that shall combine the terrible slow swing of the *Battle Hymn of the Republic* (which, if you know not, get chanted to you) with *Britannia needs no Bulwarks*, the skirl of the *British Grenadiers* with that perfect quick-step, *Marching through Georgia*, and at the end the wail of the *Dead March*. For We, even We who share the earth between us as no gods have ever shared it, we also are mortal in the matter of our single selves. Will any one take the contract? (Kipling, "From Sea to Sea" 157–58)

The fullest articulation of the search for masculine renewal comes in his 1897 novel *Captains Courageous*. In this novel, Kipling offers a paean to Americans' unrestrained masculine individualism, but tempers it by locating sources for the central sources of authority of the land in attitudes of Anglo-Saxonist reverence. The narrative celebrates a raw, vigorous masculinity, but places curbs on masculine excess by situating Americans within scenes that invoke natural authority and compel reverence. This oft-violent process parallels portraits of masculine education found in Kipling's other work and depicts a vigorous masculinity that defends social hierarchy as the embodiment of the perfected Anglo-Saxon type.

Kipling's American heroes—a fisherman named Disko Troop and a multimillionaire named Harvey Cheyne—are both masculine in a pragmatic, rational way and possessed of a blunt common sense. Though not social equals, Troop and Cheyne are both forged through work, and their thoughts are dominated by practical business concerns.

The book celebrates the rigorous physical education offered aboard Troop's commercial fishing vessel to Cheyne's son, "a singularly smart boy, the son of a very clever man and a very sensitive woman, with a fine resolute temper that systematic spoiling had nearly turned to mulish obstinacy" (Kipling, *Captains Courageous* 45). Through scenes of corporeal discipline, stoicism, and occasional humor, the boy's natural character emerges into a strong example of American masculinity.

The novel opens with a conversation about Harvey Cheyne Jr. between a German, a New Yorker, and a Philadelphian. While the German sees "Ameriga" replete with insolent, uncultured types, the Americans note a lack of discipline and masculine labor spoiling the child (Kipling, *Captains Courageous* 3). Harvey Jr.'s bluster is prototypically American: "I'm an American—first, last, and all the time. I'll show 'em when I strike Europe" (Kipling, *Captains Courageous* 5). The blame is largely laid upon Cheyne's mother, who has little control over her son. They are headed for a *grand tour* of Europe, which promises to turn young Cheyne into "a holy terror" (Kipling, *Captains Courageous* 3).

A fortunate misfortune—falling off of the steamship taking him to Europe—thrusts Harvey Jr. into the virtuous discipline of life on Troop's boat. After Harvey Jr. complains about being struck in the face by Troop, Troop's son says the injury will "let the shore blood outer you" (Kipling, *Captains Courageous* 17). Suspicion of the comfortable, privileged life is juxtaposed to the world of commercial fishing, with its dangers, masculine challenges, and hard-won pleasures. Through the course of the novel, life at sea molds Harvey Jr. into a masculine subject worthy of the claims he's making, but too reserved to make them. At the end, the meeting of the two figures for masculine authority—Troop and Cheyne Sr.—itself provides a disciplinary lesson, reminding Troop about his natural place in the social order.

Unlike other texts explored in this chapter, *Captains Courageous* does not invoke notions of blood and racial unity. There are occasional gestures, such as the fact that the *We're Here*'s primary fishing rival is the *Parry Norman* (one could certainly read the name *We're Here* in imperial terms). The Cheynes are represented in racial terms: "Father and son were very much alike . . . Harvey had his father's slightly aquiline nose, close-set black eyes, and narrow, high cheek-bones. With a touch of brown paint he would have made up very picturesquely as a Red Indian of the storybooks" (Kipling, *Captains Courageous* 14).

The novel contains its share of anti-British feeling, rooted in the politics of the Civil War: "Old man Hasken he would hev it thet the *East Wind* was a commerce-destroyin' man-o'-war, an' so he declared war on Sable Island because it was Bridish"

(Kipling, *Captains Courageous* 12). Hasken's antagonism is of course irrational, steeped in a history that, if not irrelevant, at least occupies an outsized place in the American imaginary. His language maps this irrationality with the strain of jingoistic stubbornness latent in the lower classes, a strain that pertains to the more heroic Troop as well.

The novel's lack of declarations of racial solidarity speak to the fact that, first, *Captains Courageous* is about America, with Britain figuring primarily as a humorous source of uneducated Americans' outrage and disdain; and second, the American figures operate surrounded by foreign nationals, whose insufficiency naturalizes white American leadership. This condition manifests itself particularly in Troop's attitudes toward other boats. When the *We're Here* encounters a group of boats huddled together in the Grand Bank, he tries to avoid it because of his fierce self-reliance and because "he objected to the mixed gatherings of a fleet of all nations" (Kipling, *Captains Courageous* 76). While most of the boats are from Massachusetts, the "crews drew from goodness knows where" (Kipling, *Captains Courageous* 76). The international crews Troop disdains represent a mere conglomeration for the sake of money: "Risk breeds recklessness, and when greed is added, there are fine chances for every kind of accident in the crowded fleet, which, like a mob of sheep, is huddled around some unrecognised leader" (Kipling, *Captains Courageous* 76). Though muddled, this passage tellingly associates internationalism with a crowd or mob mentality: while Disko Troop is himself a member of the working class, the conflation of nationality and "mob logic" facilitates Kipling's portrayal of the *We're Here* as a salutary environment. Troop's son, Dan, also reports that he "mistrusts furriners," and despite the potential for his vernacular speech to undermine this claim, he has good reason (Kipling, *Captains Courageous* 109). Indeed, the Troops's xenophobia operates in a larger logic of common sense associated with white Americans and is crucial to legitimating the structures of authority that pervade the novel.

The *We're Here* also has an international crew, but each member is so thoroughly acculturated to Troop's values as to resemble a familial group. Troop's hierarchical community, which eschews pure profit in favor of the avocation of fishing, replaces the anxious femininity of Harvey's mother with a masculine substitute for the domestic sphere: "The little rocking *We're Here* looked so deliciously homelike . . . There was a warm glow of light from the cabin and a satisfying smell of food forward, and it was heavenly to hear Disko and the others, all quite alive and solid, leaning over the rail and promising them a first-class pounding" (Kipling, *Captains Courageous* 108). This domesticized masculine community subsequently finds an analogue in Harvey Cheyne Sr.'s railroad empire.

The *We're Here* provides a safely hierarchical space for the interrelation of Anglo-Saxon and other subjects. In addition to a whiny, cunning Portuguese sailor, the cook is a "coal-black Celt with the second sight"—a figure whose mysticism is mitigated by feminine affect and stereotypical confusion (Kipling, *Captains Courageous* 322). Kipling's hybrid figure recapitulates an association between blackness and Irishness in British and American caricature in the nineteenth century. For the purposes of this chapter, however, it underscores the way sublimated Anglo-Saxon ideas underlie the narrative economy of the novel.

By the end of his time on the *We're Here*, Harvey Jr. has become "a recognized part of the scheme of things," learned humility and courage, and developed a strong work ethic (Kipling, *Captains Courageous* 67). His natural capacities emerge in his skill on the boat, leaving only the question of restoring him to his place in the social order. Upon news of his son's rescue, the patriarch returns.

Martial values—honor, service, and loyalty—combined with a sense of the deep imprint of the leader's personality upon his environment shape Cheyne's empire in terms notably similar to Troop's ship. When a telegram from Harvey Jr. arrives in San Francisco announcing that he has been saved and is in Gloucester, Massachusetts, Harvey Sr.'s authority spurs immediate action: "He signed . . . to move to the Morse, as a general brings brigades into action. Then he swept his hand musician-wise through his hair, regarded the ceiling, and set to work, while Miss Kinzey's fingers called up the continent of America" (Kipling, *Captains Courageous* 119). Through the telegraph and the force of Cheyne's name, the secretary facilitates an unprecedented 60-hour passage across the country that unites competing business interests and repairs the relations of Cheyne and his lieutenants with disgruntled workers. In linking two self-made male authority figures from different social classes, Kipling is affirming a central American ideal.

Moreover, the mapping of modernity with masculine action provides a disciplinary function that, like the domestic order located aboard the *We're Here*, rescues self-assertion from venal self-interest. The corporation becomes a unified body, almost a tribe, to facilitate the Cheynes's passage under the sign of Harvey's stern judgment: "He paid his obligations to engineers and firemen as he believed they deserved," dismissing the selfish interests of union-men (Kipling, *Captains Courageous* 124). The remarkable speed achieved is not simply an instance of cowering, selfish union men coming to heel under Cheyne's mastery; rather, Kipling casts the moment in chivalric terms. In a decidedly clumsy plot device, Mrs. Cheyne's poor health moves into a crisis mode when Harvey Jr.'s survival has been discovered. Kipling celebrates the spectacle of modern technological prowess and business might along with a narrative of sentimental feeling grounded in Cheyne Sr.'s reverence for his wife: when Mrs. Cheyne calls, "the master of thirty millions bowed his head meekly and followed [his maid to his wife]" (Kipling, *Captains Courageous* 118).

Cheyne Sr.'s role is not simply to play the neglectful parent, however. He is focused, driven, and represents not only a sterling example of American masculinity but also the opening of the frontier itself: Cheyne's story is "the story of forty years that was at the same time the story of the New West," in which he sought "his own ends, and, so he said, the glory and advancement of his country" (Kipling, *Captains Courageous* 142). Cheyne's liberal idealism is, as with his treatment of the unions, grounded in the notion that market exchange produces maximum fairness and achievement. It is a force for good—thus, Cheyne tells how he had "bested his enemies . . . [forgave] them, exactly as they had bested or forgiven him in [his youth]; how he had entreated, cajoled, and bullied towns, companies, and syndicates, all for their enduring good" (Kipling, *Captains Courageous* 143).

While *Captains Courageous* thus secures a subtle reconciliation of vitalizing action with restraint and reverence, the sources of the latter are ambiguously located. For the narrative serves as a corrective to the older men on two fronts as well—Troop learns to temper his rather obstinate independence, deciding that he will "never stand on my own jedgements again" (Kipling, *Captains Courageous* 134). Troop, that is, learns that his proper duty to his superiors (Cheyne owns a number of cargo freighters) requires that he not think for himself in larger questions, only when it comes to locating cod. On the other hand, Cheyne Sr.'s fierce individualism itself needs tempering. With characteristic foresight, Cheyne insists that his son get a college education, because "sit-down-with-your-chin-on-your-elbows book-learning . . . pays . . . and it's bound to pay more and more each year in our country—in business *and* in politics" (Kipling, *Captains Courageous* 144). Cheyne Sr.'s emphasis upon what "pays" is a problem—while the frontiers of American capitalism have produced a vital American masculinity, its commitment to common sense tends toward the base commercialism Kipling and other British writers associated with the "new imperialists." The solution is not a turn to textual "culture," but rather a scene of communal reconciliation as the location of the faith required to foster more laudable qualities.

At the end of the novel, Kipling returns to the discourse of "civilization" by replacing the restless, emasculating *grand tour* with a ceremony that evokes tradition, heritage, and memorialization as the keynotes of a shared culture. The novel ends, quite gratuitously, with a ceremony on the Massachusetts coast memorializing fishermen lost to the sea. The commemoration helps reconcile the masculine heroes, both deeply suspicious of a mob mentality and of the degenerative effects of civilization and domesticity. After occasional poems stir common feeling, the ceremony culminates with a litany of the dead. In this moment the women weep, the townsfolk squabble, and the three figures of masculine prowess—Disko and the two Cheynes—are deeply, but silently, moved. The display of masculine affect—Cheyne Sr., for example, has a face "all in hard lines, as though it had been cut out of bronze"—exists as a nearly invisible trace upon the masculine subject (Kipling, *Captains Courageous* 155). This scene recapitulates the scenes found in *The Final War*, yet involves a deep integration of the two sides of the disciplinary contract. The keynotes of the American character—vital energy and muted emotion—are here combined with a reverence for tradition.

Captains Courageous thus draws a distinction between venal self-assertion and a situated heroic masculine identity. Masculinity is defined not through feats so much as the provision of order and the authority of the natural leader. While references to the Anglo-Saxon race or to icons like Alfred are absent from its pages, the novel provides an imaginative reconciliation of American individualism and energy with Kipling's notions of imperial virtue in the same key. The giving of the law and the clothing of this scene in rituals of masculine affect and submission link *Captains Courageous* to Kipling's other messages about empire and the United States.

In conceiving a tale of masculine adventure in the United States, Kipling does for America what he had done for India in *Kim*: the tale legitimates America as a crucible of masculine virtue, opposed to the decadence he associates with European cosmopolitanism. Depicting the disciplining of this masculinity within the structures of naturalized hierarchy, Kipling "hails" the United States into the imperial attitudes he asserts more directly in his poetry. Here he does *Kim* one better, however. If the key to the legitimation of the imperial crucible is the way its circumstances summon innate, but suppressed, inactive qualities derived from a heritage located outside the scene of action, in *Captains Courageous* the crucible and the virtues it conjures are identical. The novel narrates the development of American masculinity, characterized by mastery and humility. In doing so, Kipling commutes the aggression of future war novels into a vision of sovereign kinship, a healthy alternative to the twin mob rules of egalitarian democracy and liberal internationalism.

These values, along with the rhetorical act of writing a novel about American masculine development targeted to an Anglo-American audience—make *Captains Courageous* a logical antecedent of the more famous, and more directly "Anglo-Saxonist," poems that were crucial to the scope of Kipling's international fame and the cultural, rather than merely literary, importance attributed to his voice.

"Recessional" and "White Man's Burden," published in 1897 and 1899, respectively, bookended the United States' entry into war with Spain over the Philippines, an event hailed in Britain as Brother Jonathan's acceptance of the imperial "burden." Britain's support of America's entry into the Spanish-American War in 1898 represented the high tide of popular Anglo-Saxonism.

With its refrain "lest we forget," "Recessional" poses a self-involved present against the fidelity to duty characteristic of Kipling's mythic past, suggesting that reverence for this past, and for tradition, will prevent Britain going the way of other empires. The framing of imperialism as duty, and especially as a time-honored duty conducted with God "in Awe" and under the purview of his "Law," facilitates a contrast between British Empire and the self-aggrandizement of Britain's imperial competitors.

"White Man's Burden" frames these notions of duty within a masculine, and overtly racist, context:

> Take up the White Man's burden—
> Have done with childish days—
> The lightly proffered laurel,
> The easy, ungrudged praise.
> Comes now, to search your manhood
> Through all the thankless years
> Cold, edged with dear-bought wisdom,
> The judgment of your peers!

Imperialism is cast as an interaction between well-intentioned, faithful Anglo-Saxons with sullen, ignorant "devil children," as an earlier line suggests. Moreover, this interaction occurs in the context of a rapacious international environment in which other imperialists stand by, ready to profit from the civilization the "white man" brings to the imperial periphery. On a personal level, the burden is a catalyst of experience, creating hardship and humiliation but, ultimately, honor and wisdom.

As a call to a national audience, the poem rings with a combination of the pedagogical and performative. The narrator performs the voice of enduring faith in imperial values at the same moment that he teaches a lesson about what values sustain the nation. That is, the message of the poem teaches a faithfulness exuded by the confident narrative voice.

Originally written as an occasional poem to celebrate the United States' entrance into the business of colonialism, the poem was addressed to the United States. Read in this context, the performative and pedagogical messages appear differently targeted—the British voice embodies the wisdom grown through hard experience, and America is a place of easy success and the copious self-confidence of an inexperienced power.

"White Man's Burden" was a transatlantic sensation. Published in the February 1899 issue of *McClure's Magazine*, it "'circled the earth in a day and by repetition became hackneyed within a week.' American newspapers printed its heavily edifying message on their front pages as an exhortation to the United States to take up its onerous task of looking after the affairs of the dark peoples . . . a task which might well be hopeless, but which their manly athleticism and moral rigor would not allow them to evade" (Gossett 231).[6]

While these poems have achieved lasting fame as expressions of Anglo-Saxon racialism at the turn of the century, Kipling's heightened celebrity made his own person the subject of outpourings of Anglo-American affect as well. In 1899 Kipling made his final, disastrous visit to the United States, during which he and his daughter Josephine both developed severe pneumonia, from which Josephine later died.

The severing of Kipling's ties to the United States has some symbolic import, for it largely heralds the end of hypermasculine visions of Anglo-American friendship in this period. As the sentimental desire for deeper racial attachments that accompanied the beginning of the Spanish-American War began to fade, Anglo-Saxonism itself would modulate into sublimated forms, as we will witness in the next section.

Yet the moment also crystallized the image of Kipling as an icon of Anglo-American friendship. As Ambassador Choate put it, "Somehow or other [Kipling] reached the hearts . . . of more English-speaking men, women and children of the world than any other living writer. He was cherished equally in the palaces of Queens and Emperors and in the cabins of the poor; and when the sorrowful tidings went out . . . of his sad condition, a response came back to him which . . . must have thrilled his heart with gratitude and pride" (March 6, 1899, 16).

CORRECTIVE TEXTS, CULTURE, AND THE ANGLO-SAXON REVIEW

In the "Impressions and Opinions" section of the first issue of the new *Anglo-Saxon Review*, the reviewer links Kipling to Tennyson:

> There is not very much in common between Tennyson and the young Tyrtaeus of Tommy Atkins and Sergeant What's-his-name; but, if we read Mr. Kipling's sermons aright (and he has hardly written a line which is not part of a sermon) he would say with Pallas Athena in "OEnone":
>
> > Self-reverence, self-knowledge, self-control,
> > These three along lead life to sovereign power.

Yet not for power (power of herself
Would come uncalled for), but to live by law,
Acting the law we live by without fear . . .

It was surely in this spirit that Mr. Kipling cooled the hot fever of the
Jubilee summer with his warning 'Recessional.' (1.1: 245)

The commentator attributes Kipling's national significance to his
ability to calm both the jingoistic British masses and the nascent
imperial energies of the United States (via "Recessional"). The
linkage of reverence, self-control, and the law in the achievement
of power echoes the dynamics illustrated in *Captains Courageous*,
and the secular nature of the description of Kipling's sermoniz-
ing indicates the review's shared project with Kipling: to employ
quasi-religious language to highlight the redemptive properties of
reverence for culture and tradition. The reviewer defends Kipling
against "hostile critics [who] choose to represent Mr. Kipling as
the Laureate of Jingoism" (1.1: 244).

Yet where Kipling's sermons come in memorable poems and
exhilarating action tales, the voice of *The Anglo-Saxon Review*
engages in the highbrow register of classical allusion, quotation,
and analysis. The Arnoldian use of Athena (paralleled by other
Arnoldian statements like "there is a certain connection between
Imperialism and Philistinism"), the situation of a perspective
against the competing claims of other critics, and the nuanced
sense of reception suggest a different set of priorities associated
with a different audience (1.1: 243).

The Anglo-Saxon Review, founded by Lady Randolph Churchill
in 1899, lasted only a few years and cannot be said to have been a
dominant voice in the literary or cultural debates of the moment.
The name mirrors a similarly short-lived magazine called *The Anglo-
Saxon*, which ran in 1849 and 1850 and stressed a more overtly
Christian mission for the Anglo-Saxon race (Horsman 74). Lady
Churchill, born Jennie Jerome, one of the most famous of American women to marry into London society in the late nineteenth
century, announced the journal's purpose to create commentary
of enduring cultural value as a bulwark against the temptation,
as "newspapers and periodicals become cheaper and cheaper . . .
to satisfy the loud demand of the enormous and growing reading
public, with the minimum of effort" (1.1: 1–2). Her solution is

ironically commercial: "The book is published at a price which will ensure its respectful treatment at the hands of those who peruse it" (1.1: 2). The rhetorical combination here bears some scrutiny: the review will provide a bulwark against yellow journalism and pulp literature not by making more elegant commentary available to the general public, but by making it less accessible. It is "the book" itself, rather than the reader, that possesses culture along with an anthropomorphic stubbornness: "It will not be lightly cast aside" (1.1: 2). Indeed, each review is ascribed a life-narrative worthy of a chivalric tale. It is sent out as "an adventurous pioneer . . . [and] its intended fate is to occupy "after a brief, though not perchance unhonoured, stay on the writing-table . . . that Valhalla of printed things—the library" (1.1: 2). Moreover, "he [the review] bears a name which may sustain him even in the hardest of struggles, and of which he will at all times endeavor to be worthy—a name under which just laws, high purpose, civilizing influence, and a fine language, have been spread to the remotest regions" (1.1: 2). Dressed for the "battle of life [in a] . . . costly habit," the review sallies forth as a kind of knight errant, bearing cultural value in its papery body (1.1: 2). While hyperbolic, the politics of displacement implicit in the narrative—of removing Anglo-Saxon culture to a textual, rather than masculine, bodily form—is manifest in numerous other instances in the review, and thus serves to locate it on the extremity of the culturalist end of Anglo-Saxonist rhetoric, as opposed to the tenor of the future war novels.

As the bloom came off of the rose of Anglo-Saxon feeling, the value associated with Anglo-Saxonism was shifted from personal characteristics to cultural artifacts and texts. This permitted a sublimation of prejudicial feeling embedded in notions of Anglo-Saxon superiority into a more subtle valuation of cultural heritage. The *Anglo-Saxon Review* provides a striking example of this sublimation because its content—political comment, literary reviews, and cultural essays—is contemporary. Only infrequently do historical articles appear. Yet the product itself, in its "materiality," to use the current parlance, invokes an aura of hoary, tradition-laden value.

By simulating old texts, the review not only critiques mass culture but also relocates Anglo-Saxonist sentiment to the archive, away from the body and mind. One might read this move in at least two ways—first, as a way of sustaining Anglo-Saxonist sentiment even as its political moment passed; second, and perhaps more convincingly, the review demonstrates how cultural change occurs through the reproduction of the familiar in unfamiliar iterations that reflect reaction and response to what preceded it. The review thus implicitly removes Anglo-Saxonism from jingoism and locates racial consciousness in an elite sphere of taste and good judgment. Here, the representation of national character is sublimated, partly in a conservative gesture of preservation, and partly as an Arnoldian distillation of the best of cultural production.

The impact of such a posture is ambivalent, if more subtle than overt racialism. The *Review* describes a common Anglo-Saxon nature as a predictor of common political experiences in Anglo-Saxon countries. The case of a review of a bestselling book on race is instructive in regard to the positionality the journal modeled in relation to other "races." The *Anglo-Saxon Review* devoted sustained critical attention to French writer Edmond Demolins's *Anglo-Saxon Superiority: To What It Is Due* (1899). The provocative title, the appearance of the book in the wake of the Dreyfus affair, and its compatibility with other popular contemporary books about racial degeneration ensured significant sales in England as well as in France. Demolins's argument was, in fact, more a critique of socialism than of racial characteristics. He divides the English people into three "elements": the Celtic, the Norman, and the Saxon. While Celts introduced a communistic orientation that "never attains social superiority, the Normans, largely mixed in with the rest of the population so as to be indistinguishable, contributed the law of primogeniture, the hereditary nobility, and the House of Lords . . . [and] the spirit of snobbery" (Demolins xii). Each group thus had a degenerative impact upon English society: "Whilst the Celtic element weakens especially the lower classes, by dragging them into labouring pauperism, the Norman element weakens especially the upper classes by promoting Lordolatry, Patronage, and Snobbery" (Demolins xiii). For Demolins, "it is precisely among these two elements—Celtic and Norman—that the socialistic doctrines have found any echo in the Anglo-Saxon world" (Demolins xiii).

In contrast, Anglo-Saxon individualism provides the key to the success of the entire society: "Exclusively by individual efforts, and by personal initiative, without any support from private association or from that great public association, the State . . . the Anglo-Saxon manufacturer and merchant took possession of the market of the world; and they did so, thanks to those social conditions which it is the aim of this book to explain. Men who could do by themselves, without any outside help, what others could only do (and this much more imperfectly) by combining, give thus the measure of their undeniable superiority" (Demolins xxxv). Ironically, perhaps, Demolins's description of the Anglo-Saxon shares close similarities to the old caricature of England as a nation of shopkeepers, and thus with some of the negative characteristics lampooned in the figure of John Bull. The tone of Demolins's book does not lend itself to an ironic reading, but this mapping of Anglo-Saxon superiority with business acumen certainly contrasted with some of the more grandiose evocations of English culture as the shibboleth toward which English spirits keened.

In its review of the book, *The Anglo-Saxon Review* opens by noting that the Dreyfus affair provoked interest in the book and wondering "why are the Latin races giving such painful evidence of political and moral decadence?" (2.1: 248). An attitude of coy reluctance becomes particularly visible when the reviewer considers whether such questions are appropriate to *The Anglo-Saxon Review*: "Under other circumstances we might hesitate to ask the questions in the[se] pages . . . since they imply a general superiority on the side of Englishmen and Americans which even to the serene 'Anglo-Saxon' mind, justly conscious of its neighbors' infirmities, is a large assumption. But France . . ." (2.1: 248). In this remarkable passage, the reviewer eschews racism but makes the point that to eschew racism is a mark of racial superiority. Thus he distinguishes "general superiority" from positional supremacy. By describing the Anglo-Saxon mind in scare quotations and as "serene," the reviewer legitimates Anglo-Saxon prejudices indirectly. Moreover, the reluctance to speak functions as a marker of refinement (by contrast, one assumes, to the "blabbering" Latin races); yet the paragraph is itself, indeed, a speech act. Masked as literary and cultural analysis, the reviewer reinforces prejudices he presumes his audience to share, but to be too polite to say. Such a negotiation of silence and speech as the markers of identity reveals, even in an ephemeral text such as this, the way in which notions of cultural refinement and textual mastery sublimated, rather than displaced, nationalist prejudices. This becomes even more clear when the stakes are raised to the French commenting class more generally: "French commentators, in their present mood of self-deprecation, are . . . inclined to lay exaggerated stress upon those individualistic qualities of self-reliance, practical energy, and almost reckless enterprise, which as they believe has led to the conspicuous material successes of their Anglo-Saxon rivals" (2.1: 253).

In appraising the values manifest in *The Anglo-Saxon Review*'s assessment of Demolins's bestseller, it is instructive to consider just how far off the mark the haughty critique actually was. While the reviewer busily reinforces national stereotypes through tone and insinuation, he fails to notice Demolins's rejection of the ideologies of national and racial character. Demolins argues that human behavior is determined by institutional and social conditions, rather than racial or national qualities. He rejects even the soft essentialism of neo-Lamarckianism, making a strong case for the importance of the national education system, among other social conditions, as the key to Anglo-Saxon success.

The overt valences of an Anglo-Saxon identification dwindled rapidly after the turn of the century: "In part because of an anti-imperialist reaction, the twentieth century has less sense of the Anglo-Saxons and their heritage than any other period of [British] history" (Scragg 5–6). Yet the period did stimulate other forms of interest in the Anglo-Saxon period. In December 1899, the *Times* announced the introduction of a new academic field, Anglo-Saxon linguistic studies, at the meeting of the Modern Language Association. More generally, the medieval values associated with Alfred shaped representations of British culture and character, emphasizing chivalric expressions of affect and duty and coloring Anglo-American relations with a sense of a merger between New World energies and the wisdom, judgment, and refinement derived from a venerable cultural heritage.

It was an always tenuous enterprise. As the statue of King Alfred was being erected in Winchester, England, in preparation for unveiling during the millenary celebration, "one of the guy-ropes broke and a moment afterwards one of the shearlegs snapped under the strain thrown under them, and the whole structure came down with a crash" ("The King Alfred Millenary" 5). Like the statue, the moment of Anglo-Saxon racialism tumbled under the weight of its own ungainliness. Unlike the statue, racialism was resurrected in sublimated forms, as culture is increasingly separated from the body, and modernity itself, rather than any specific menace, becomes its chief antagonist.

While the ascendancy of Anglo-Saxonist identification as a keynote in Anglo-American relations was short-lived, other forms of Anglo-Saxon racialism persist. From fringe groups purporting Anglo-Saxon unity via the Internet to historians of the English-speaking peoples who veil beliefs in racial character within an anodyne rhetoric, the essential allure of racialism—trumpeting one's own tradition and virtues, rather than demonizing the other directly—will doubtless continue to find a voice.

CHAPTER 4

MODERNITY, FABULATION, AND AMERICA IN *DRACULA*

The glory of this world passeth . . . I recall a brief dialogue on the Teutonic in 1889 between the Prince of Wales and a distinguished American: "Fine ship, Mr. Depew." "Yes, Sir, Britannia rules the waves to-day."

—*Times* shipping correspondent, 1899

In *Anglo-Saxons, Onwards!* the narrator repeatedly reminds readers that "no foot ever touched this land!" A sense of the inviolability of national space inverts the imperial trajectory of Anglo-Saxonism, recoding imperial adventures in terms of the greed of international competitors for native soil. Such a turnabout did not necessarily entail self-scrutiny: Lady Churchill writes in the opening number of *The Anglo-Saxon Review* that "Anglo-Saxondom is occupied with its relations to the external world. It looks outwards instead of within" (1.1: 1). On the whole, the decline of British life at home was not directly confronted in the Anglo-Saxonist narratives examined in the last chapter. Yet the difficulties of empire inevitably spurred consideration of its attendant costs, most famously, perhaps, in the "little Englander" movement spurred by the Boer War. Whatever one's view of empire, British domestic life was increasingly perceived as vulnerable, and fears of enervation, stagnation, and even degeneration and atavism proliferated. Anglo-American discourse, correspondingly, had a different relation to this anxious terrain than to visions of a shared public sphere or forms of racial unity.

The differences between racialism and racial panic are instructive. In the previous chapter, racialism served as a disciplinary structure using tradition and a sense of world-historical destiny to legitimate domestic hierarchy. In other texts, however, fears of racial tainting and decline are intermixed with anxieties about the effects of modern economic forces upon the national culture. In the latter, America plays an ambivalent role. At once mythically shaped by the rigors of the frontier *and* a source of economic modernity, the prospect of American exceptionalism posed a potential threat to British hegemony. In addition, the sublimation of race as a critical category takes an additional turn: racial difference becomes negatively signified, marked by the other's—including the American's—embodiment of racial instincts and ideologies. The cultivated ideal becomes a source of communal values to "restore" a fabled social order poisoned by the encroachments of economic modernity and a variety of forms of the authority of the other.

While a number of popular fictions bring together the concerns of Chapters 2 and 3 by considering America's economic modernity and racial composition, Bram Stoker's *Dracula* (1897) represents an important turn in the culturalist program this book explores. Earlier narratives locate cultivation in the practice of cultural criticism and the qualities—judgment, refinement—it endows. *Dracula* provides a particularly rich vein for describing a change in this rhetoric: texts begin to explore the *agency* and *identity* available through myths. That is, while early "culturalist" texts perform culture by revealing the indoctrination of American and domestic others, later culturalism invokes the power of mythmaking in creating a sense of mutual community otherwise lacking on the modern scene. In *Dracula*, the longing for a return to premodern social relations is assuaged, if not fulfilled, by the forging of modern narratives based around feudal values.

The novel mirrors its villain insofar as its reflection of contemporary ideology seems to shape-shift. As the hunt for Dracula runs its course, the narrative focuses less upon exposing and explaining the vampire than upon the development of the band's sense of identity, especially the communications and hierarchies that develop within a close-knit community. Yet in the critical hunt signaled by renewed interest in the novel, critics launch bursts of silver shot at the count, each ball inscribed with key words like

"Irishman," "Oriental," and "Jew."[1] This work reflects a broader critical interest in the intersections of race with a variety of social issues, including class, economic transformation, and imperialism. In what Chris Baldick and Robert Mighall describe as the "anxiety school" of criticism, race often serves as the *sine qua non* basis of the cultural fears expressed and worked through in narrative (Baldick and Mighall 225). This chapter adopts a different, though related position by investigating the instabilities of apprehension, in all three senses of the word: how capturing the count, by reflecting social anxiety, foregrounds how the professionalization and fragmentation of knowledge contributes to modern alienation.

In light of Jameson's insight (explored in the Introduction) that in fiction of this period, the primary other is the imperial competitor, the multinational composition of the band of vampire hunters assumes added significance. Yet Matthew Gibson, in a meticulous analysis of Stoker's meditation upon the Eastern Question and the Treaty of Berlin, views readings of the novel as "a repository of anxieties by a colonial elite . . . [as] too imprecise" (Gibson 8). How, then, do the novel's representations of multiple nationalities operate in conjunction with explicit references to contemporary international tensions? What's more, how is an anachronistic chivalric ideal rendered plausible in light of the conditions of late imperialism?

In *Dracula*, a degenerated Britain requires physical and psychic reinvigoration as well as reeducation in forms of knowledge that have been lost to modernity. This is facilitated partly through contact with American masculinity. Homosocial bonding between the British and an American provides an antidote to the alienation fostered by modern liberal individualism; by restoring camaraderie and clear communication, the British are restored to health. This process, as we shall see, involves the death and memorialization of the novel's American, Quincey Morris.

Stoker's attraction to an American ideal of homosocial union began during his student days at Trinity College when he first encountered Walt Whitman's *Leaves of Grass* (Belford, *Bram Stoker* 39–47). While there has been some debate over the nature of his interest in the homoerotic references in Whitman's poetry, it is certain that Stoker was animated by ideas of hero worship and male camaraderie. In an adoring 1872 letter to Whitman, he writes, "You are a true man, and I would like to be one myself, and so I would be towards you as a brother and as a pupil to his master" (Stoker, Letter to Walt Whitman, 18 February, 1872). Later, he claims to be one of Whitman's defenders in Ireland: "You know what horrible criticism your work sometimes evokes here, and I wage a perpetual war on your behalf" (Stoker, Letter to Walt Whitman, 14 February, 1876). Stoker viewed Whitman as a prophet of male intimacies whose views were characteristic of America and, by contrast, unfortunately marginalized in the repressive notions of masculinity prescribed in Ireland and Britain more generally. He comments upon the special nature of American masculinity in an 1885 speech titled "A Glimpse of America" (later published as a pamphlet). In the speech, delivered to the London Institution, Stoker proclaims that "one of the most marked characteristics of American life is the high regard in which woman is held. It seems, now and then, as if a page of an old book of chivalry had been taken as the text of a social law" (23). The emphasis upon chivalry as an attribute of national, masculine character presages its crucial role in *Dracula*, linking nationality, gender, class, and imperial rhetoric. As we will explore, chivalric discourse establishes the terms for a mythic identity for the band of vampire hunters.

William Hughes emphasizes the importance of American chivalry for Stoker: "America—implicitly white, Anglo-Saxon America—is . . . attractive to [Stoker]. Chivalry has overwritten race and, in doing so, has affirmed it" (Hughes 56). Stoker first presents a comparative portrait of American and British masculinity in his tale "The Shoulder of Shasta." In this tale, a British artist, Reginald Hampden, rescues an American woodsman, Grizzly Dick, from embarrassment in proposing marriage at a San Francisco salon party. Dick represents a masculine ideal: laconic, action-oriented and direct, yet unrefined. Hampden combines this masculinity with social refinement. He is a classic gentleman hero, fashioned in the mold of Sherlock Holmes and the Scarlet Pimpernel. His impeccable manners are accompanied by a scornful view of male society types, and his exercise of social literacy validates American manhood while simultaneously asserting British superiority. Here, Stoker conveys no sense that British masculinity must be regenerated.

Quincey Morris shares several attributes with Grizzly Dick. First, he is a man of action and stumbles in tests of manners. Second, he is remarkably innocent—his social *faux pas* indict the society that requires fine manners even as they mark his limitations. Last, he is associated with the frontier, and is thus aligned against the sense that modern urban society is superior to earlier social forms.

Morris is certainly a romantic figure whose self-reported exploits recast imperial exploitation as adventure. However, at the turn of the century, the cowboy figure evoked America as much as it might have called up ideas of racial union. Buffalo Bill's Wild West Show had traveled throughout Europe and even performed at Windsor castle, offering American entertainments that capitalized on fantasies about the American West.[2]

Additionally, the famed "frontier thesis" offered by Frederick Jackson Turner in 1893 challenged the hegemony of a theory that supported a sublimated racialism. Teutonic Origins theory had reigned as a dominant historiographic paradigm in academic circles for several decades at the end of the nineteenth century. The theory held that British and American democratic institutions had sprung from Teutonic tribes, and that the germ of these origins had passed down through history. The frontier thesis foregrounded the role the American West was supposed to have played in shaping a unique national character, which argued that "in the crucible of the frontier . . . immigrants were Americanized, liberated, and fused into a mixed race, English in neither nationality nor characteristics" (23). At the same time, Turner's analysis of race included Germans as part of the Anglo-Saxon "native stock" of the United States (Kaufmann 51–52). While both theories were, like Anglo-Saxonism, vague enough to be appropriated for diverse purposes, the frontier thesis seemed to British observers to provide an example of American self-mythologizing. As an ideology, however, the myth nevertheless generated a sense of national community.

Numerous critics have commented upon the community forged by the male characters, reading it as a synecdoche either for British identity or for the West. Carol Senf writes that the men form "a remarkable union of sentiment . . . lose much of their uniqueness as individuals and become representatives of all England" (Senf 23). Cannon Schmitt argues that Stoker views England as the cultural apex of the Occident: "At the end of the novel England *is* the West" (Schmitt 33). Such a mapping of England with Western culture sublimates tensions and contradictions within contemporary Britain in favor of a fantasy. By making Britain the herald of western civilization, conflicts within the nation are effectively glossed over. The result is a peculiar amalgam of political impulses presented as a unified expression of the national character. Senf sees the novel as a reflection of Stoker's vexed sociopolitical ideas: as "a *fin-de-siècle* writer . . . Stoker often combined extremely conservative views with progressive ideas, a trait that makes him difficult to classify" (Senf 46). Stoker's ambivalence regarding changing gender roles reflects a more general uncertainty about the forces, technologies, and social movements that we might classify under the rubric "modernity." Stoker records this ambivalence in a wide variety of registers, but of particular interest here is the way in which the modern and the traditional are reconciled by suppressing antithetical elements of each through a narrative of masculine regeneration.

MODERN ALIENATION, MODERN PERMEABILITY

Reproducing an idealized version of England involves negotiating both imperial and domestic anxieties simultaneously. As a reverse colonist, Dracula is a figure from turn-of-the-century anti-imperialist rhetoric, threatening to migrate from the East to invade the nation undetected. Indeed, several critics have noted that the count's Romanian origins link him to contemporary imperial debate over the Eastern Question. Yet his presence in England raises anxieties about the depersonalization of its public sphere, particularly its legal institutions; the count learns to speak English and emulate English customs, as well as to use the legal system to his advantage.[3] He threatens to blend into everyday social life.

That is, the threat posed by the count is in several respects an indictment of the skepticism and alienation characteristic of modern consciousness. One of the vampire hunters articulates this critique of modernity: "Our efforts are in secret; for in this enlightened age, when men believe not even what they see, the doubting of wise men would be . . . at once [Dracula's] sheath and his armour, and his weapons to destroy us, his enemies" (Stoker 279). The causes of such skepticism are many, but they include a general sense of the emptiness, and even the falsity, of ritual, tradition, and memorials. For example, Mina Harker encounters a "very skeptical person" named Swales in the seaside graveyard at Whitby (Stoker 86). Swales calls superstition "all wore out," particularly ghost stories, which are "invented by parsons an' ill-some beuk-bodies an' railway touters to skeer an' scunner hafflin's, an' to get folks to do somethin' that they don't other incline to" (Stoker 86, 87). Swales also points out that, because they memorialize deaths at sea, "in nigh half of [the graves] there bean't no bodies at all" (Stoker 88).

Patricia McKee asserts that Swales's assertions reflect his (and Mina's) "estimation [that] . . . the world is always, on the one hand, assimilable to human construction and always, on the other hand, to be therefore doubted, interpreted, and reconstructed" (McKee 47). She links these qualities to the imaginary possibility that the world is "an expansive circulation of culture" and that Mina and Swales "personify the movements and uses of capital as they enter speculatively into representations of different cultures" (McKee 47). While I agree with McKee's assertion that the world is open to doubt and human construction, it is this very fluidity that Stoker has his vampire hunters resist. Read another way, Swales's revelation explains the skepticism Van Helsing associates with modernity. For Swales, memorials reflect a pervasive bad faith—the sign falsely marks the referent—and moreover, empty memorials signify an exhaustion of tradition. As such, the Whitby graveyard anticipates the emptiness of hegemonic ways of knowing exposed elsewhere in the novel: positivism, legal-juridical notions of citizenship, and liberal individualism.

Apprehending Dracula involves restoring continuity with tradition by reconnecting the tools of modern, rational science to the lost arts of the occult. This regeneration of knowledge is complemented by a transformation in the intimacy and character of personal relations, particularly in the honoring of the dead. Whereas the Whitby graveyard is ultimately barren, figuring the failure of signification, memorialization at the end of the work offers hope for a regeneration of tradition. The death and memorialization of Quincey Morris will, for the hunters at least, provide a sense of continuity and enduring bonding that both subordinates American masculinity and incorporates its sociality into at least one member of the next generation.

This reading of Swales and the graveyard troubles McKee's central thesis as well. The vampire hunters are certainly figures for adventure, and numerous critics have shown that adventure fiction is intimately linked to the circulation of British capital abroad. Yet to argue that the adventurer is a figure for capital is,

I think, to ignore the mystification that the adventure narrative performs. Here the adventurers withdraw from "free circulation" and establish very limited relations with the public. Their culture is not "expansive[ly] circulat[ed]"; rather, it is reborn in spite of the inhospitable conditions of the public at large.

Despite pervasive skepticism and the rather good reasons for it among the public, the unmooring of signs from referents is only partial. The chief indication of this is the fact that Dracula's attempts to simulate Britishness repeatedly fall short. His ineffectuality is surprising, yet it reveals that the alienation caused by modern social organization, customs, and technology is incomplete. Dracula may eventually master each of these fields, but somehow they do not add up to being a British subject. While critics have noted that the surplus of Dracula's foreignness is endemic to stereotyping in general, it also underscores the artifice of modern social life. At the same time, the failure of this simulation preserves Britishness as unperformable, as an essence. Dracula's failure supports a *mythic* Englishness by inverting the lived realities of national identity. As Slavoj Žižek describes it, "*nobody* is fully English . . . every empirical Englishman contains something 'non-English'— Englishness thus becomes an 'internal limit', an unattainable point which prevents empirical Englishmen from achieving full identity-with-themselves" (*For They Know Not What They Do* 110).

Such an apparently paradoxical representation of the immemorial and modern, essential and invented aspects of nationality prevails in other turn-of-the-century British invasion narratives. In John Buchan's *The Thirty-Nine Steps* (1912), for example, German invaders manage to simulate members of the British leisure class, only to be given away by an indelible foreignness in the appearance of their eyes. What ultimately distinguishes the heroic subject, in each of these novels, is the ability to recognize the essence beneath the artifice. That is, the hero sees beyond and through a superficial modern skepticism; he is distinguished by a highly developed judgment. Insofar as the hunters become all England, Britain, or the West, they do so as the representatives of the kind of high cultural literacy urged by Matthew Arnold in *Culture and Anarchy*.[4]

Paradoxically, then, *Dracula* promotes the mapping between nationality and cultural development most characteristic of imperial rhetoric while critiquing aspects of British modernity. By contrast to the British imperialist, Count Dracula brings a certain childishness to the pursuit: "With the child brain . . . [Dracula] learn [*sic*] new social life; new environment of old ways, the politic, the law, the finance, the science, the habit of a new land and a new people who have come to be since he was" (Stoker 339). While more ancient than Britain, the count is nevertheless a child; ethnicities and nationalities exist along an invisible continuum of development understood metaphorically in terms of individual maturation. Though comic, this critique, framed in the broken English of a continental European, suggests a critical distance from British ideology: the comments anatomize Great Britain, particularly British social institutions. This historical perspective on Britain comes from Professor Van Helsing, a Belgian who investigates and eventually hunts down the count. By describing law and science as aspects of "new social life," he implicates the temporality of British power within much longer arcs of history.

Despite the quasi-aristocratic bloodlust that motivates him, Dracula benefits greatly from the modernity of England. While the band investigates Dracula's nature in order to locate a means of dispatching him, what they seek is not new knowledge; rather, their quest requires reclaiming knowledges lost to modernity. Indeed, Belford compares it to "the classical gnostic quest" (*Bram Stoker* 214). As a result, the collective that pursues the count derives its coherence by adhering to an antimodern, chivalric code. As Van Helsing puts it, "We go out as the old knights of the Cross to redeem. Like them we shall travel towards the sunrise; and like them, if we fall, we fall in good cause" (Stoker 278). Van Helsing's comparison of the band to legendary Christian knights would seem to gloss over class distinction in favor of a mythic ideal. Yet the apparently nationalistic character of the pledge may reflect Stoker's own social aspirations. Hughes suggests that Harker's band can be identified with "the gentlemanly caste to which Stoker was perceptibly aligned by birth, education, and inclination [which] was . . . supported through images and ethical values drawn from a nineteenth century appropriation of medieval chivalry" (55). But was this appropriation an example of recoding capitalism, cloaking it in notions of duty and fidelity? Or to the contrary, does this feudalism represent a rejection of and withdrawal from contemporary economic ideals (as we shall see, Liberalism)? Such rhetoric was common in fin-de-siècle Britain, specifically with conservative discourse prominent among white-collar readers who aspired to an elevated social status.

Also, the invocation of feudal values within the context of modern capitalism is not unusual in late Victorian romance novels. For example, Jameson sees in Joseph Conrad's *Lord Jim* (1900) "in the midst of capitalism . . . the aesthetic rehearsal of the problematics of . . . the feudal ideology of honor" (Jameson, *The Political Unconscious* 214). Jameson traces the means by which Conrad simultaneously critiques the devaluation of the empire by trade while evoking an ideology that romanticizes the personal codes embraced in the imperial mission. In a similar manner, Stoker's gothic narrative follows the transformation and bonding of a group of knights pledged to defend British virtue. The group, initially separated by different professions and social statures, comes together through the production of a communal text. The process of creating this text is pivotal in the hunt for Dracula, making this collective act the key to overcoming the effects of modernity. Modern alienation is overcome through the mutual sympathy fostered by shared literacy.

In *Dracula*, this community of personal relations synecdochically stands in for an ideal national community that contrasts with the skepticism of the British masses. Such a social formation implies both anxieties about imperialism and a critique of the decay of Britain's imaginary community. That is, it registers generalizable social fears both about the vulnerability of Britain caused by an overextended and weakened empire and about the failure of a political ideology to neutralize the threat of mass enfranchisement. In terms of contemporary history, the novel takes up the discourse of Liberalism and investigates how mass enfranchisement and immigration threaten Liberal ideals.

Liberal Panic

In *Vampires, Mummies, and Liberals*, David Glover argues that *Dracula* reflects Bram Stoker's complex relation to turn-of-the-century Liberal discourse. He notes Stoker's Anglo-Irish upbringing and Home Rule politics, his advisory relation with William Gladstone, and his interest in science and technology. For Glover, "much of the fear that resides in the pages of *Dracula* reflect[s] the underside of the liberalism to which Stoker adhered, a nightmare

vision of unruly subjects who are unamenable to its formal democratic calculus" (41). During this period, economic liberalism was
under attack from intellectuals such as the Fabians, and the Liberal Party was forced by popular sentiment to support increased
governmental intervention in the relations between capital and
labor. Further, Liberalism's crisis involved the conflict between its
domestic ideals and colonial policies. As Glover puts it, "Stoker's
Liberalism was forever haunted by the return of those flesh-and-
blood identities that Liberalism seeks to neutralize or exclude rhetorically" (13). Nowhere was this crisis felt more painfully than
with regard to Ireland, and Glover reads *Dracula* in the context
of English anxieties about the Irish. Stoker's Anglo-Irish background complicates his apparent "othering" of the Irish in *Dracula*. Also, in making sense of Stoker's Liberalism and Anglo-Irish
background, we must also keep in mind his political roots. As he
put it in his letter to Whitman, he was "reared a conservative in a
conservative country" (qtd. in Belford, *Bram Stoker* 42).

Yet Stoker's conservative collectivism can be explained by more
contemporary pressures within the Liberal Party. By the Edwardian period "new collectivist forms of liberal thought were coming
into prominence and these were often aligned with attempts to
investigate and control the private sphere, the realm of sexual relations and private life" (Glover 20). Whether read as an anticipation
of Edwardian interventionist Liberalism or as a sign of Stoker's
distaste for liberal individualism, collectivism in *Dracula* nevertheless fulfills the function of exclusion that classic Liberalism fails
to accomplish. The crisis that attends both the specialization of
knowledge and the skepticism of modernity is relieved by a restoration of organic community.

The neoconservative courage and chivalry of the hunters is juxtaposed to images of British degeneracy throughout the novel.
While these middle-class professionals are complicit in the alienation and skepticism that characterize modern life, their culpability is diminished by their growth in the course of the novel. By
contrast, other figures for degeneration, both from the working
classes and from the aristocracy, prove static and thus irredeem-
able. One explanation for the links between regeneration and chivalry, and thus for the elusive and paradoxical nature of Britishness
in *Dracula*, is that they jointly reflect bourgeois aspirations for
social mobility. Because the group is identified with "all England,"

the healing of the nation implicitly excludes the lower classes and the remnants of the ancien régime.[5] Otherness within the group is embodied by a woman, a Belgian, and an American.

Glover argues that bourgeois fears of degeneration focused upon two social groups—the "traditionally well-to-do" and the "new poor" (69). Fears of the poor involved mass enfranchisement, mass literacy, and the swelling urban ghettos as loci of disease and social privation. When applied to the aristocracy, degeneration involved the effects of excessive leisure, exposure to immoral, particularly lascivious arts, and inbreeding. In addition, representations of aristocratic degeneration figured the aristocracy as social vampires, feeding off of the productivity of the middle classes. Glover sees Dracula as a composite of these two types of degeneration, fused by the "threat they each posed to the security of middle class society" (69).

This identification resonates with the values of the vampire hunters as well. Although the vampire hunters clearly identify with a chivalric code, their application of that code dissociates it from its traditionally aristocratic class valences. Indeed, a figure named Renfield embodies the unraveling of aristocratic ideology into naked bloodlust. He is a patient at Dr. Seward's mental asylum, and his descent into and temporary reemergence from madness under the scrutiny of Seward and the Belgian physician, Van Helsing, provide one of the major subplots of the novel. The causes of Renfield's madness, and the scientists' inability to explain it, represent both a collapse of the Victorian cult of the gentleman and the danger that modern scientific rationality is partly responsible for Britain's attenuated masculinity. When he is introduced in the asylum, Renfield has recently fallen from an aristocratic position: he claims, in fact, to have "seconded" Lord Godalming's father at a gentleman's club. The count appeals to Renfield's nostalgia for an organic model of social organization, for an England ordered by the aristocratic principles of *noblesse oblige* and personal relations.

Anxieties about the loss of class and social distinctions articulated by Renfield are assuaged by the suture of chivalric discourse with an emphasis upon the intimate collective forged by the production of a shared text. Moving toward a quasi-aristocratic emphasis upon sympathy and literacy, the hunters enforce class distinctions by withdrawing from the professions that underwrite class mobility. Whereas the romance novel traditionally plots the ascension of heroes and heroines to naturalized places in society through trials in a realm of action, *Dracula* promotes a cultivated ideal that resists simple political valences through the building of an ideal *communitas*.

The development of this community requires a shift "from blood to blotter"—from a blood logic to a textual logic. When Lucy Westenra falls under Dracula's power, the men each contribute blood to regenerate her to health. While on some level, blood works—Lucy is improved with each transfusion—the process is unsustainable. In Seward's asylum, Renfield attempts to prolong his own existence by imbibing the vital fluids of other creatures. He conducts this as a quasi-scientific study, keeping scrupulous notes as he feeds less developed creatures to more developed creatures in a pattern that resembles the food chain—flies are fed to spiders, spiders to birds, and he plans to feed birds to cats. His experiment meshes a Darwinian model of life cycles with Dracula's aristocratic blood logic. Seward notes that "what he desires is to absorb as many lives as he can," and he uses the journal as a ledger of his consumption (*Dracula* 75). The results, predictably, are as confused as the count's whirlpool of ideas about race.[6]

Renfield's decline is registered by the collapse of his literacy; his writings degenerate, ultimately becoming incoherent, as Dracula approaches Britain. His findings, though recorded in meticulous detail, are incomprehensible. The result is a text that conflates modern and ancient ideas and that stands as a symptom of crises of Victorian confidence. It provides a figure for the degeneration that characterizes modern Britain.

LITERACY, WRITING, REGENERATION

In keeping with the collapse of Renfield's writing into incoherence, writing is crucial to the potential regeneration of Britain. Literacy and textuality underwrite the realm of action by making the pursuit dependent upon the construction of a unified text. As Mina says, "In the struggle which we have before us to rid the earth of this terrible monster we must have all the knowledge and all the help we can get" (*Dracula* 235). Written in an optative mode, the ordered collection of artifacts, including journals, letters, memoranda, and newspaper articles foregrounds the novel's textual construction while displacing the agency of a central narrative presence. Although the proleptic strategy of the journal entries reflects the characters who produced them, plot resolution depends quite literally upon the synthesis and apprehension of the entries, along with other documents, into a coherent text. Indeed, the suture of each character's subjective, fragmentary experience into a unified journal is metonymic for what Benedict Anderson describes as the "rags and fragments" that bind together the nation. Doing and knowing become inseparable as the pursuit progresses. As Van Helsing says, "We shall go to make our search—if I can call it so, for it is not search but knowing" (*Dracula* 273).

Emphasis upon the importance of the shared diary also suggests that the hunt is related to British anxieties about the massification of culture. Fears about cultural degeneration arose not only in response to empire, but also, as Brantlinger demonstrates in *The Reading Lesson*, in response to mass literacy. Or as Arnold puts it in *Culture and Anarchy*, culture fosters the precious social force that newspapers, the constitutional system, and all three social classes diminish: "right reason."

In *Dracula*, the values, codes, and languages of individual professions have replaced the patriarchal rhetoric of the duties of the gentleman. The return to Arnoldian sweetness and light is facilitated by defending British womanhood. On one level, then, the novel links masculine subjects together through a cultish worship of femininity. Idealized English womanhood represents a shared locus of value in stark contrast to the alienation associated with professionalized discourse and the anonymity and decay of culture associated with mass literacy.

In restoring a sense of duty and chivalric mission to each of the vampire hunters, Van Helsing emphasizes collective action, using science as a resource, and the strength of ethically guided commitments: "We have on our side power of combination—a power denied to the vampire kind; we have resources of science . . . we have selfless devotion in a cause, and an end to achieve that is not a selfish one. These things are much . . . All we have to go upon are traditions and superstitions" (*Dracula* 259). Van Helsing's exhortation is paradoxical—on the one hand the hunters have duty, science, and moral urgency to propel them forward; yet on the other, they have only traditions and superstition to guide them. Read in the context of restoring Britain to health, the terms of his speech indicate a faith in a collective, heroic endeavor in the face of modern skepticism.

Since the community of vampire hunters functions not simply to combat but also to relieve fears about modernity, the group's source of identification and bonding itself incorporates aspects of modern life into the chivalric ideal. That is, the group bonds around a masculine ideal that simulates an order of knighthood but is armed with American Winchester rifles; a kukri knife; legal, medical, and scientific expertise; and the ample capital reserves of Lord Godalming. Glover asserts that while "the vicissitudes of the law and its ethnological and criminological supports suggest a flawed modernity," the group nevertheless embodies "liberal bourgeois order[:] . . . Despite the invocation of archaic symbols, the laying of hands on the golden crucifix, the vampire is 'serious work,' to be undertaken 'in as businesslike a way as any other transaction in life,' informed by all the modern freedoms, freedom of association, freedom to 'act and think,' and free access to the 'resources of science'" (44–45).

For Glover, the invocation of medieval icons is superficial, a mere veil for a liberal (albeit, for Stoker, a "modern" liberal) order. While Glover correctly notes the merger of modern and chivalric elements in the band, in my estimate his assessment of the liberality of the group must be qualified by noting the longing for a fantastic, more integrated past. The cult of the feminine, references to chivalry, and disavowals of public consciousness and profit bespeak a nostalgia for a premodern world in which individual freedoms were subordinated to a collective ideal. Stoker's archaic references seem to indicate a wish to transform modernity, and thus his belief in technology and progress shares some impulses with the socialist utopian visions of William Morris and H. G. Wells. At the same time, *Dracula* clearly seeks its reinvention of chivalry in the more conservative elements of turn-of-the-century ideology: nationality and masculinity.

This restored masculinity and the homosocial bond are both forged through the common aim: defending Western womanhood from penetration by the East. Differences among members of the group are insignificant because of their common aim, and their mutual discourse of inclusiveness and friendship stands as a model for restored chivalry. No one member of the group functions as the central hero—each contributes to a whole that none could have created alone.

In much late-nineteenth-century fiction, British masculinity is a signifier without a full-bodied referent. Given the rhetorical exclusions implicit in representing the hunters as "all England" and given the rhetorical leveling of the bourgeois professions into a code of gentlemanliness, an indirect representation of British manhood was probably unavoidable. Such a conundrum does not seem to hold for narratives in which British heroes traverse the imperial periphery—in these it is less problematic for the nation to be signified in a single body. But on the domestic scene, the act of representing British masculinity involved an imaginary suturing of opposed types. As Glover notes, Stoker attempts "to reconcile two ideals of masculinity that had generally become dissociated by the 1890s, creating a bridge between the expressive man of sensibility and the strong, steadfast man of action" (79). William Hughes offers a related appraisal of Dracula's union of a bifurcated masculine ideal: "Acceptable masculinity is . . . in Stoker's fiction constructed in part through a clash of 'drives.' An 'exchange' takes place, as it were, between the conflicting demands of egotism and altruism, and between sheer strength and the controlling qualities of restraint and purposefulness" (80). Hughes's analysis, while related, places the consolidation of masculinity within the realm of the individual ego rather than among different British masculine types. Since the "man of sensibility" and the "man of action" were ideals rather than definable social categories, Glover's point is perhaps not incommensurable with Hughes's.

The pursuit of the vampire plays an important role in reconciling opposed types and revealing the national character in opposition to the forces transforming modern Britain. Perhaps because of these consolidations, masculinity offers only a rather fantastic quality for identification. It is more simply defined through exclusion than by positive identification. The reconciliation of action and sensibility, or egotism and altruism, involves both defense of womanhood and the restoration of ways of knowing lost to modernity. Through the hunters' quest, the nation is defended, if not entirely restored to health. The novel self-reflexively exposes the indirect definition of the vampire hunters through a succession of character-written texts in which they are both actors and narrators. In these documents, the characters are not only the protagonists of these documents but also the authors and, crucially, readers of them. In this identification with literacy, the actual reader of the novel is hailed into the group by the shared act of reading. This interpellation invokes Britishness through association rather than definition and through a conflation of subject and object, or of the knower and the known, into a vague sense of identity. Further, by implicating textual construction in the realm of action, Stoker bonds together characters whose identification with science, aristocratic privilege, or the legal system reflects the fragmentation of British culture into a babel of irreconcilable discourses.

PERFORMING CHARACTER, CRITIQUING SOCIETY VIA THE IMPERIAL OTHER

How, then, does Stoker both valorize the British character and critique British society in the same stroke? In his original plan for *Dracula*, Stoker appears to have wanted to emphasize the contrast between Britain and another imperial power more directly: on his way to Transylvania, solicitor Jonathan Harker was to have visited Munich. Carol Senf asserts that Stoker originally planned to focus on cultural differences directly and that by removing this visit he strengthens the orientalist binary of East and West.

While a more elitist, conservative rhetorical strategy emerges to defend British cultural and geographic boundaries, that strategy is elaborated in a context in which Britain's national claims have been historicized. In *Dracula*, the invented national traditions that characterize late nineteenth-century Britain bear the signature of their own invention. British culture as a whole is excluded from this national claim, yet British modernity provides the context out of which the novel's heroes attempt to construct a national iconography.

The tenuous nature of this paradoxically modern and antimodern version of the nation is reflected, and partly resolved, by the depiction of emergent imperial rivals. The hunters' bond is tempered by the presence of Van Helsing and Morris, who embody characteristics that the British have lost. Van Helsing's presence in the group troubles the notion that the hunt for Dracula is metaphorically also a quest to recover British masculinity. His leadership, along with Morris's heroic martyrdom, suggests that the novel favors an orientalist binary of East and West over valorization of a particular national identity. Yet if we take the priority of narrative to be the fulfillment of a fundamental lack, Britain's centrality is clear. In contrast to the fundamentally static Van Helsing and Morris, British males undergo significant change through the course of the plot. Stephen Arata argues that the narrative dramatizes the threat produced by a degeneration of British masculinity: "Through the vampire myth, Stoker gothicizes the political threats to Britain caused by the enervation of the Anglo-Saxon 'race'" (630). Van Helsing provides qualities of judgment, particularly an archaeological grasp of lost histories and knowledge, which the British characters lack. Through the pursuit of Dracula, the British recover faith and lost faculties of judgment, if not Van Helsing's scholarly range.

The American is particularly important in facilitating homosocial bonding. Whereas Britishness in *Dracula* is indeterminate, defined through negation, Americanness is synthetic: borderless yet inclusive, quintessentially pluralistic. Moreover, America registers a sort of credulity that contrasts with the skepticism embodied in the British masculine characters. If the ideological work of reconciling modernity with an essentialized notion of Britishness involves invoking an indeterminate facility for discernment and self-restraint, Americanness, by contrast, involves a naïve simplicity that seems utopian. Quincey Morris is in many respects Dracula's opposite. Whereas Dracula is ultimately undermined by his dependence upon codified rational discourse, Morris's martyrdom is irrational, stemming from a heroic disregard for his well-being.

Morris's irrationality is linked to his embodiment of the masculine realm of action. Like Mina, he embodies an excess of an otherwise positive quality that British judgment counteracts. If we accept a dichotomization of masculinity into action and sensibility, Morris is pure "action" without the tempering influence of British "sensibility." During one of the group's meetings about how to track Dracula, for example, Morris suddenly leaves the asylum to pursue a bat that had alighted on the windowsill: "As we were talking Mr. Morris was looking steadily at the window, and he now got up quietly, and went out of the room" (*Dracula* 213). Morris rarely speaks but often acts in this instinctive manner. Moreover, the dominant role perception, rather than discourse, has in determining his will distinguishes him from the other men and further aligns him with Mina, who herself eventually becomes a perceptual medium for Dracula. Both characters ultimately are incapable of resolving the crisis on their own—their martyrdom reflects the need for a regenerated British masculinity rather than a replacement of it.

The key to Stoker's evocation of Britishness lies in the dual movement away from skepticism and professional discourses and toward the process of judgment from the careful ordering of perceptions. In terms of the struggle for a new scientific model, empiricism and materialism are replaced by the subjective data of the perceiving subject, collected and ordered by an interested individual with mature faculties of judgment. The mature British subject refines judgment by freeing himself from the prejudices created by a professional discourse.

At the same time, restoring the faculties of judgment involves becoming sensitive to the importance of narrative structures as a mode of inquiry as well as a means of collective identification. As Seward notes while considering the apparently unexplainable details of Renfield's case, a new receptivity to "story" is a crucial investigative mode: "Several points seem to make what the American interviewer calls 'a story,' if one only could get them in the proper order" (*Dracula* 290). That is, the data do not admit rational scientific conclusions, but they permit narrativization. Through "story," knowledge that falls outside of typical knowledge categories (e.g., the existence of the undead) can be ascertained.

Americanness thus consists of both a certain naïveté and, opposite to vampirism, a continuity between action and language. In contrast to the alienating effects of overrationalized discourse, Morris's language is inclusive and conveys genuine sympathy. He entertains the readers and the British characters in *Dracula* by imitating dialects and using slang. Stoker gives us one example of Morris's language when he writes to invite Arthur to dinner with Jack Seward to "mingle our weeps over the wine-cup, and to drink a health with all our hearts to the happiest man in all the wide world" (*Dracula* 62). Morris reminds his friends that "we've told yarns by the camp-fire in the prairies," invoking the spirit of fellowship and sympathy necessary to fend off Dracula, who by contrast represents the extreme example of how modernity enables an individual subject to exist in isolation (*Dracula* 62). At the same time, Morris occupies a secondary position among the vampire hunters—his proposal to Lucy, for instance, is couched in raw dialect and evokes comedy rather than sympathy.

FABULATION AND AMERICAN DIFFERENCE

Morris thereby embodies America as at once a space of universal sympathy and as immature as compared with Britain. Yet it also demonstrates deep ambivalence. Written over the period in which America began reasserting the Monroe Doctrine, the novel anxiously prognosticates about America's imperial future. As Renfield, in a moment of lucidity, asserts, the Monroe Doctrine will cause the "Pole and the Tropics" to "hold alliance to the Stars and Stripes[:] . . . The power of Treaty may yet prove a vast engine of enlargement when the Monroe Doctrine takes its true place as a political fable" (*Dracula* 215). America is aligned with fabulation, and ultimately the novel's movement away from professionalized discourses toward the creation of a collective story inflects the narrative of the hunt: the group's mutual purpose and understanding leads to the apprehension of the count. This image of American empire contributes to the ongoing critique of rational discourses in the novel. When the obfuscatory power of rational discourses like science and the law are stripped away, Britain's empire is similarly fabulous. Arata takes Morris's presence to signify "a second threat to British power hidden behind Dracula's overt antagonism" (641).

While America is certainly referenced as a potential world power, I believe Morris's presence manifests a more complex relation between American nationalism and the British imaginary. Morris performs a nostalgic function in the sense that he signifies a purity of association between the idealized nation and the self that proves impossible in the context of the heterogeneous composition—perhaps the *inorganic* nature, to borrow Edmund Burke's term—of the modern nation. In ideological terms, the reasserted Monroe Doctrine reflected this function powerfully at the end of the nineteenth century. The doctrine was used as a hedge against European efforts (particularly French) to colonize South and Central America. It legitimated America's claims to territory beyond its boundaries, but the status of those claims shifted radically in this period. As Gary Ulmen explains in his essay, "Universalism Contra Pluralism," the doctrine evolved through the course of the nineteenth century, shifting from a pluralistic paradigm to "a pretext for [Roosevelt's] liberal-capitalist 'Dollar Diplomacy'" (Ulmen 34). This transformation involved invoking universal human interests to justify a foreign policy directed toward expanding American markets. Herein lies the "fabulous" nature Renfield identifies. To the European eye, the Monroe Doctrine represented a naïve credulity about the transformative power of texts. As Arnoldian "culture" attempted to stabilize a modern vision of Britishness through canonization of particular cultural texts, textuality itself becomes a potentially threatening force. In constructing Britishness as skill in reading, Stoker's novel poses the American solution to nationalist dilemmas as simultaneously utopian and insufficient. Exceptional literacy distinguishes the British from Americans, but it also exposes the contradictions latent in imperial narratives. British proclamations about America contain traces of the imperial threat. While America's apparently self-generated authority provides a model for British regeneration, in a skeptical modernity, Morris's presence exposes this weakness. The healing narrative becomes a story of reinvented tradition. By martyring and memorializing Morris, the British transform him from threat to fable.

By rendering Morris into a remembered figure and a displaced contributor to new generations, Stoker eliminates the sense of threat associated with America's emergent power. David Glover notes that comments about America's future are "troubling" because of their "implication for Britain's position in the 1890s" (94). Glover argues that, despite this implied anxiety, Morris's death restores traditional images of the Anglo-American relationship: "Transposed onto the plane of social biology . . . the implicit dangers of imperial rivalry are lifted once Quincey is dead, since he leaves no heir . . . The story therefore concludes on a resounding counter-note: not only is the vampire's threat to hereditary purity vanquished, but the Harkers' marriage becomes a form of hierogamy which subordinates American energy to the triumphs of British breeding" (94). Glover's hierogamy depends on the subordination of Morris to British refinement; what he does not note, however, is the crucial role textualization and literacy play in this narrative process, and why America is consistently associated with the link between story making and the health of the nation.

The production of a fable, then, provides a basic structural framework for Stoker's novel. Its value, as the group acknowledges, paradoxically resides in a denial of its historicity. The final, metatextual turn of the novel reveals the authorship of this contemporary fable. Here Jonathan Harker emerges on the final page as the editor who has bound the collection of texts (and by implication the very novel that the reader holds) together. He denies the historicity of the text: "Every trace of all that had been was blotted out" (*Dracula* 342). The "blotting out" reminds the reader of his or her own position in relation to the text; since it is a collection of dead artifacts, the reader is him or herself participating in the production of a privileged yet paradoxically national imaginary. The will to belief, coupled with "right reason," is offered as regenerative. As Jonathan comments in his final "Note" to the novel: "Our boy's birthday is the same day as that on which Quincey Morris died. His mother holds, I know, the secret belief that some of our brave friend's spirit has passed into him. His bundle of names links all our little band of men together; but we call him Quincey" (*Dracula* 332). Jonathan's message, and Mina's hope, is incorporative: the passage of American bravery into the British child will recommission the national narrative, but with a difference.

Clearly the memorialization of Morris is only one of the ideological maneuvers undertaken by the band of vampire hunters. To represent an idealized Britishness in the midst of a degenerate Britain is a complicated and exclusionary task. So while America is both threat and salve, comrade and subordinate in the logic of regenerating the nation, so might the poor, the Irish, the "Oriental," and a variety of others play equally important roles in the matrix of anxieties woven into the narrative. The novel's lasting pull on us, indeed, stems from the inevitability of reading vampirism as an analogue both of our externalizable fears and our inner conflicts, whomever "we" happen to be.

This flexibility is enabled by the key dynamic traced in this chapter: how racialism is supplanted by an image of British culture associated with homosocial bonding and a textualized community. Through a merger of American instinct and sympathy with European tradition, the novel imagines an idealized synecdoche of the national community. The microcommunity, however, is not recognized by the public at large. Britain's best self survives, but tenuously, in the faith and memory of its select subjects. It is the stuff of legend and myth. As such, it is the only possible solution to the *anomie* of modernity—a fable that, through its romance and grandiosity, could ultimately restore the nation itself. Through this self-mythologizing, the novel begins to define British culture as a locus of national value separate from the modern public and accessible only through faith and careful reading. In the next two chapters, this representation of British culture is itself subjected to the forces of modernity, particularly economic transformations, embodied in America.

Figure 1 Fantasies about Anglo-American union, such as that recorded on this promotional poster, emphasized the role of commerce in the progress of civilization.

Chapter 5

Holroyd's Man

Tradition, Fetishization, and the United States in *Nostromo*

Joseph Conrad's fictions have been at the frontlines of debates about the status and role of British stories about empire. Famously, critics have argued about Conrad's sublimation of imperialism into a realm of ideals, especially in *Heart of Darkness*. While this old chestnut usually circulates around questions of Conrad's own beliefs, less attention has been devoted to Conrad's portraiture of how the preservation of cultural value depends on fiction-making, and even upon a willful self-deceit. This project, in step with Stoker's in *Dracula*, reimagines the "educational ideals" of the Arnoldian cultural project into tenuous forms of bad faith. As we'll see, in the novel *Nostromo* it also depends on a troubled view of Anglo-American relations.

In his late essay "Confidence" (1919), Conrad offers a perplexing homage to the profession he pursued before becoming a writer: "The seamen hold up the Edifice. They have been holding it up in the past and they will hold it up in the future, whatever this future may contain of logical development, of unforeseen new shapes, of great promises and of dangers still unknown" (Conrad, *Notes* 159). Conrad celebrates seamen as the keepers of civilization, supporting its institutions, and defending it against an uncertain future. The key terms in this essay, "confidence" and "edifice," imply that British traditions are unsteady, marginally anachronous, and even, perhaps, necessary fictions. The metaphor situates the edifice in an ambivalent temporal and spatial position, opposing a static domestic culture to dangerous territory beyond the home front. Moreover, threats to the edifice exist in a fluid, uncertain future. Unlike his imperial novels in which a protagonist attempts to embody British ideals in his person, by the writing of "Confidence" Conrad valorized collective imperial work in the context of the alienating effects of modernity. That is, his portrait of British imperial traditions validates the work of an entire class of men rather than the actions of a solitary hero.

This chapter argues that *Nostromo* (1904) plays an especially important role in articulating Conrad's notions of tradition and empire and that it does so with a special focus on American capitalism. In particular, the novel reflects a growing understanding of the relationship between individualism and commodity fetishism. While Conrad's protagonist, Charles Gould, embodies the cultivated ideals of British culture, he becomes an emblem for an older version of imperial governance that serves the interests of viciously exploitative imperialists from elsewhere. Unlike Conrad's earlier novels, *Nostromo* manages to validate the British Empire's ideals while coolly examining the relationship between idealism and modern economic processes. Gould's values are anachronous and the pedagogical message offered by the novel is thus paradoxical: keeping faith with outmoded values offers the text's only model for personal integrity and continuity, but it depends on necessary illusions that themselves are appropriated by the forces of late capitalism.

Conrad's previous novel, *Lord Jim* (1899), abounds in images of the protagonist as an embodiment of the European, specifically British, *mission civilisatrice* in Southeast Asia. As Jim leaves the *imperium* for the "undiscovered" island community called Patusan, Marlow imaginatively transfers him from anxious modernity to atemporal traditions: "At the first bend he lost sight of the sea with its labouring waves forever rising, sinking, and vanishing to rise again—the very image of struggling mankind—and faced the immovable forests rooted deep in the soil, soaring towards the sunshine, everlasting in the shadowy might of their tradition, like life itself" (149). The passage centers on a contrast between sea and land—"labouring" waves face "immovable forests." The metaphorical significance of these images is clear: the sea and forests are figures for mankind and for eternal tradition. Jim passes from one to the next. His departure from "struggling mankind" suggests an escape from modernity and temporality as well as a homology between adherence to tradition and individual maturity. Conrad's solution to the degraded conditions of modern empire is to invest his hero with British ideals, valorizing the British "mission" despite an ongoing critique of the workings of modern empire. Marlow's celebration of tradition is couched in highly romantic, Orientalist terms: "His opportunity sat veiled by his side like an Eastern bride waiting to be uncovered by the hand of the master. He . . . was the heir of a shadowy and mighty tradition!" (Conrad, *Lord Jim* 149). Jim's spatial movement eastward carries him into an idealized moment of imperial history. The British "mission" is guided by an invulnerable faith, resistant, as Marlow puts it, to "official morality" (23). Conrad opposes the individual will to officialdom, criticizing Jim's romanticism but ultimately validating his individual desire to break from modern empire's degraded conditions. Through Marlow's constant reiteration, the novel distances imperial ideals from their tainted materialization in a modern economic context.

Analyzing Conrad's writing has long meant coming to terms with this ambivalence toward fin-de-siècle empire. His major fiction is simultaneously nihilistic and nostalgic, exposing the faults of imperialism—British, French, Belgian, Spanish, Dutch, and American—while attributing those faults to imperial competition. For Conrad, the racist and exploitative practices that constitute imperial work are partly redeemed by the ideals behind them, particularly fidelity to tradition. Reflecting this, his work celebrates British imperialism by distinguishing it from Britain's competition. In *Nostromo*, Conrad uses the emergent phenomenon of American imperialism, sanctified by the reinvigorated Monroe Doctrine, as a model for imperial otherness. By associating the United States with insidious new forms of capital development, Conrad indirectly legitimizes Britain's imperial tradition.

AMERICAN IDEOLOGIES AND THE MONROE DOCTRINE

Nostromo was written during a tense period in Anglo-American relations. Images of America's growing power were resonant with British subjects who kept up with the news in the 1890s and early twentieth century. Having recovered from tensions fostered by Britain's ambivalent support of the Union in the Civil War,

Anglo-American relations were stimulated by a dramatic rise in imperial competition and common threats. The two powers provided mutual support in the Spanish-American and Boer Wars. At a moment of British insecurity in its own position within the "concert" of European powers, American foreign policy messages were intensely scrutinized. Thus McKinley's 1900 State of the Union address was analyzed in the following terms in the *Times* of London: "Phrases concerning Germany and France are possibly more cordial than the sentence in which friendly relations with England are asserted and dismissed. He is not less friendly to England, but thinks a guarded expression of friendship most prudent" ("The President's Message" 5). American popular opinion also was subject to British interest: one of the *Times*'s American correspondents reports that "the President's Message is good-humoredly received by the country . . . The Washington dispatches which have flooded the country lately are responsible for the opinion which widely prevails that Europe is following the American lead, following reluctantly, but still following" ("The President's Message" 5).

The power relations behind McKinley's rhetoric and British commentary had been anticipated decades earlier, in J. R. Seeley's 1883 *The Expansion of England*. Seeley then argued that the growth of the United States and Russia threatened to "reduce [England] to the level of a purely European Power looking back, as Spain does now, to the great days when she pretended to be a world-state" (237). At the turn of the century, the appearance of American assertions of its prerogatives and leadership, along with strong support for the Boer cause emanating from within the United States, forced Britain to assess her future prospects in relation to America's. This led to a retailoring of images of the Anglo-American relation. In particular, American foreign policy and military strength played a key role in shaping both diplomatic and imaginary relations between the two powers.

Often America's new international prominence was greeted with rhetoric that recapitulated the paternalism of earlier portraits of the Anglo-American relation examined in this book. Analyzing President McKinley's comments on the Boxer Rebellion of 1900, the *Times* writes that "The Chinese crisis has afforded the United States an opportunity of going through a dress rehearsal of its new part as a member of the concert of the Great Powers . . . There has been unmistakable evidence of inexperience and that lack of self-control which characterizes so many *débuts*" ("President McKinley's Message" 6).

In the late 1890s, assertions of the Monroe Doctrine promoted what Gary Ulmen calls "a policy of global interventionism" involving an "unresolved dichotomy between an imperialist and a universalist impulse" that persists to this day (5). By "universalism" Ulmen means that the United States increasingly justified intervention in foreign disputes by invoking "universal" interests such as stability, economic development, international justice, and human rights. In negotiations over the Hay-Pounceforte Treaty and the assertion of the Drago Doctrine and the Olney and Roosevelt corollaries to the Monroe Doctrine, this universalism was pursued under America's claims for moral sovereignty over the Western hemisphere. Discussions of "pan-Americanism" proliferated in British newspapers and worries about American control over the isthmusian canal negotiated through the Hay-Pounceforte Treaty struck British observers as ominous.

Writers in Britain, including Conrad, identified this universalism as an ideological cloak for the exploitative pursuit of national self-interest. For Conrad, tradition provided a defense against the rapacious tendencies fostered by international imperial rivalries. In "Autocracy and War" (1905), Conrad details the relationship between modern imperial rivalries and the expansionist logic he terms "Prussianism," in which national ideals are made to serve economic motives.

This sentiment is fully developed in *Nostromo*'s critique of American neoimperialism. Like *Lord Jim*, the novel features a charismatic British leader, Charles Gould. The romance of the saving British imperial ideal, however, occurs within the broader context of American capital development, which disrupts the narrative of progress associated with Britain's civilizing mission. By contrast to the tradition of missionary stewardship pursued by British interests, the United States finances political revolution as an expedient to economic exploitation. But by focusing on an American financier, the novel overlooks the British role in financing the new imperialism: London, after all, developed an ascendancy in banking and finance precisely during the period in which her naval and production advantages were disintegrating.

MATERIAL INTERESTS AND HISTORICAL CHANGE

Nostromo interrogates the possibility of integrating an idealized vision of British imperial work into the modern conditions of capitalism and imperialism. A key difference between *Lord Jim* and *Nostromo* is thus that the earlier novel posits a radical division between tradition and modernization, while the latter seeks to locate British ideals operating within a modern imperial context. If *Lord Jim* is partly structured around a nostalgic escape from modern commercialism, *Nostromo* questions whether "material interests" are a source of progress or ultimately create a vicious cycle of oppression and revolution. In fact, *Nostromo* begins with these opposed views of history as a framing device.

The reopening of the San Tomé mine provides the novel's central dramatic action, as well as a primary point of ambivalence in terms of the discourse of imperial work and modernity. Its reopening, along with the building of railroads and telegraph wires, represents the coming of a modern age that supplants the moral authorities of the past, particularly the Catholic Church. A minor figure, the British railway man, explains it thus: "We can't give you your ecclesiastical court back again; but you shall have more steamers, a railway, a telegraph-cable—a future in the great world which is worth infinitely more than any amount of ecclesiastical past" (Conrad, *Nostromo* 63). The valorization of an internationally oriented and economically directed future over the ecclesiastical past suggests a *telos* in history toward a "great world" of international communication and commerce. Conrad both develops and interrogates this vision by juxtaposing it against a pessimistic, circular model in which modernity simply repeats a historical pattern characterized by imperial exploitation.

Critiquing or complementing the railway man's view of modernity, a legend of "two wandering sailors—*Americanos*, perhaps, but *gringos* of some sort for certain" posits an imperial pattern of fetishization and corruption: "Their souls cannot tear themselves away from their bodies mounting guard over the discovered treasure. They are now rich and hungry and thirsty . . . tenacious gringo ghosts suffering in their starved and parched flesh of defiant heretics, where a Christian would have renounced and been released" (Conrad, *Nostromo* 40). In this "strange theory of tenacious gringo ghosts," the relation between capitalism and religion is reversed (Conrad, *Nostromo* 40).

The opposition between ecclesiastic and material values in the two narratives suggests a tension that Conrad develops throughout the novel: Is history circular or linear and progressive?

Thus we are confronted with two possible interpretations of the labors of Charles Gould, a Sulaco-born Englishman whose father, like the gringo ghosts, found himself unable to get away from the San Tomé mine. Gould's father, after attempting to abandon the mine, is granted the Gould Concession in perpetuity, effectively imprisoning him in the country and leading to his early death. The decision to reopen the mine defies the wishes of the father, who had a premonition of a similar fate for his son. By opening the mine, however, the younger Gould affirms a progressive notion of history.

These competing models of historical process are tested through the efficacy of imperial projects in fostering positive social change. In each, imperial work is the engine of history, though in very different ways. Gould embraces the sense of mission associated with a progressive view of history despite the decidedly mixed legacy of European activity in Costaguana. He believes that the mine's reopening represents the beginning of a better future for Sulaco's destitute and oppressed: "What is wanted here is law, good faith, order, security. Anyone can declaim about these things, but I pin my faith to material interests. Only let the material interests once get a firm footing, and they are bound to impose the conditions on which alone they can continue to exist" (Conrad, *Nostromo* 100). For Gould, capitalism is legitimized by its eventual promise of democratic institutions. As he sees it, the pursuit of material interests and the pursuit of justice are inextricable.

Nevertheless, in order for "material interests" to become established, a transitional, less democratic leadership is necessary. In this context, Gould's work is charismatic, for it must bridge the gap between Costaguana's uncivilized present and its future modernity. Gould's devotion to the mine and his self-transformation into a symbol of the importance of "material interests" make him an example of Max Weber's charismatic leader. Unlike Jim, however, whose charismatic *imperium* brings peace, security, and justice to Patusan, Gould's is outwardly directed—to legitimizing the mine and Sulaco, more generally, as good investment opportunities. In fact, his personal leadership comes to stand in for the mine's legitimacy as he represents "the embodied Gould Concession" for foreign investors (Conrad, *Nostromo* 190). As the novel progresses, he becomes obsessed with the mine, thinking it "symbolic of abstract justice" (340). This reflects a key shift in his thought: while at the outset he believes that developing material interests leads to progress, in the latter half of the novel he no longer distinguishes between development and justice.

Emilia Gould painfully witnesses her husband's transformation. At the beginning of *Nostromo*, she distinguishes his commitment to the mine from that of the American capitalist Holroyd, whose objective seems to her the "most awful materialism" (Conrad, *Nostromo* 99). Initially, she sees the silver as a symbol of a greater principle: "By her imaginative estimate of its power she endowed that lump of metal [the reopened mine's first bar of silver] with a justificative conception, as though it were not a mere fact, but something far-reaching and impalpable, like the true expression of an emotion or the emergence of a principle" (Conrad, *Nostromo* 117). As threats to production transform the mine's value from means to end, however, Emilia Gould observes its corrupting effects on her husband.

Gould's transformation, from idealism to fetishism, thus provides an internal textual critique of his "ray of hope": faith in capitalism devolves into a fixation on its means rather than its objectives. Weber links this process to modern economic transformation, particularly the rationalization of labor. In *The Political Unconscious*, Jameson notes that "rationalization involves the transformation of everything into sheer means" (250). Unlike Jim, who breaks from history, Charles Gould is instrumentalized as its agent. His charismatic leadership is part of the process of legitimizing and enfranchising American economic imperialism.

The transformations that take place over the course of the novel are, in fact, revaluations: like the silver, Gould's leadership becomes an instrument rather than an agent. Daniel Bivona, among others, sees a homology between the silver and the pun on gold in Gould's name (1998). This points to a distinct difference between *Nostromo* and *Lord Jim*. If Jim's success and failure constitute a nostalgic moment of imperial work in which charismatic legitimacy is derived from Jim's embodiment of the West's humanist ideals, particularly British ones, Gould's charisma is directly related to the market and the economics of the imperial encounter. His value is a source of speculation for international development capital. For example, the European "representatives of those material interests that had got a footing in Sulaco under the protecting might of the San Tomé mine . . . [felt] deference . . . [to] Charles Gould, to whom they were paying their court, [as] the visible sign of the stability that could be achieved on the shifting ground of revolutions" (Conrad, *Nostromo* 182). The deference for Gould and the silver are virtually identical: they "rallied round Charles Gould, as if the silver of the mine had been the emblem of a common cause, the symbol of the supreme importance of material interests" (230). Both Gould and the silver are appropriated as symbols of a progressive, capitalist vision of history. Their value, determined by their position in a particular system of generating wealth, is conferred from without; yet representations of it depict both Gould and the silver in terms of a valued essence.

Martin Decoud, who many critics have argued functions as a mouthpiece for Conrad, provides a running commentary on Gould's transformation, linking it to his nationality. He describes the English character as both relentlessly practical and narcissistically idealistic. On the one hand, he notes that "It's a part of solid English sense not to think too much; to see only what may be of practical use at the moment" (179). At the same time, this pragmatism is based on misty idealism: an Englishman "cannot act or exist without idealising every simple feeling, desire, or achievement. He could not believe his own motives if he did not make them first a part of some fairy tale" (199). For Decoud, English dullness and idealism are parts of a self-serving delusion: as he puts it, "Those Englishmen live on illusions which somehow or other help them to get a firm hold of the substance" (215). The narrator, who asserts that Gould embodies conflicting forces of pragmatism and sentimental idealism, partly validates his claims about the English character: In Gould "the strictly practical instinct was in profound discord with the almost mystic view he took of his right" (340). Decoud reverses Gould's claim that material interests produce justice as a by-product; for Decoud, English idealism produces material accumulation as its by-product.

THE NATIONAL FETISH

But if Gould fetishizes the silver and is homologous *to* it, does the logic of fetishism apply to him? That is, is he himself a fetish object as well as a fetishizing subject? In a limited sense, yes. The

American financier of the mine, for instance, takes great pleasure in the thought that his Costaguana project is not merely financial: "He was not running a great enterprise there . . . He was running a man!" (98). The economy of the fetish, in which an object is assigned a value far in excess of its usefulness, is much like the logic of market exchange, albeit in exaggerated form. Unlike the process of valuation in capitalist exchange, however, in fetishism the subject overvalues the fetish object even while conscious that the object is being overvalued. Thus a high-heeled shoe may be valued as an erotic object even though the beholder "knows" that it is just a shoe. Indeed, part of fetishization's pleasure stems from the chasm between reason and drive; the pleasure of the fetish originates in sublimated mastery.

Recent criticism has explored the fetishistic aspects of national identity. As Patrick Brantlinger argues, nationality is based on the fetishistic misrecognition: Although the national subject knows that his or her identity is a fiction, he or she embraces it as a "practical solipsist," aware of the bad faith involved but unmoved by this awareness (*Fictions of State* 4). For Conrad, nationality was a kind of fetish *par excellence*, an overvalued fiction of identity that was the locus of international tensions. In fact, nationality is crucial to understanding the process by which Charles Gould is transformed into the "embodied Gould Concession." From the novel's outset, Gould is represented as an ideal English type: Gould "looked more English than the last arrived batch of young railway engineers, than anybody out of the hunting-field pictures in the numbers of *Punch*" (Conrad, *Nostromo* 72). His outward appearance, moreover, matches his character: the head of Gould's Sulacan security staff, Avellanos, declares that "Carlos had all the English qualities of character with a truly patriotic heart" (73). Whether the addition in this passage is explanatory (patriotism is part of the English character) or ironic, it corroborates Gould's identification of English pragmatism as the central tenet of his family's and nation's character: "In Costaguana we Goulds are no adventurers. [Uncle Harry] was of the country, and he loved it, but he remained essentially an Englishman in his ideas" (85). According to Gould, the English character consists of stoicism, pragmatism, and simple idealism. Moreover, Gould's representation as an ideal type is merged with archetypal figures of gentility and national strength. At one point, for example, Gould "suggested an officer of cavalry turned gentleman farmer" (90). According to Avellanos, who affirms that Gould's "English, rocklike quality of character" is "his best safeguard," Gould's representativeness of national virtues provides the basis for his legitimacy (101).

Moreover, this English "bullishness" is distinctly anti-intellectual. In contrast to the cosmopolitan Martin Decoud, Gould rarely speaks, relying on his devotion to the mine to speak for him. Decoud, though, is anything but laconic: his speeches and letters proliferate as his vision of the Occidental Republic comes into being. Decoud and Gould share a belief in progress, but through very different means. Whereas Gould promises a "ray of hope" in economic development, Decoud forecasts an awakening of the Republic of Sulaco into being: "We Occidentals . . . have been always distinct and separated" (175). Decoud's assertion echoes the Romantic nationalism voiced by figures like Johannes Herder, who conceived of the nation as preexisting its historical being and having lain dormant, often as the result of repression. In such a position, self-invention is rhetorically conceived as reawakening or restoration to a natural state. Decoud makes full use of this rhetoric: "Nature itself seems to cry to us 'Separate!'" (176). Yet this brand of nationalism turns out to be a sham; Decoud invents the revolution to secure his obsession with Antonia Avellanos, and the revolution indirectly serves the interests of American and European capitalism. Decoud's twin desires, for Western culture and love, mark him as an agent of the forces of degeneration in Conrad's masculinist logic.

In contrasting Gould and Decoud, Conrad differentiates between contrasting models of historical change. Gould's faith in material interests reflects an antirevolutionary view of history, whereas Decoud's nationalism reflects the bad faith of the modern condition. Unlike *Lord Jim*, in which modernity is embodied in the specter of the native other as a crowd, in *Nostromo* Conrad develops a portrait of the colonial consciousness in which a nationalist revolution paradoxically leads to greater dependency on foreign investment interests. The Sulacan people are left with neither an improved civilization nor the prospect of profiting from their natural resources. It is troubling that the cynical and imitative psyche of a native—not the colonizing—subject bears immediate responsibility for this increased dependency. Conrad is in this sense a debunker of nationalist illusions; he holds tradition, rather than identity politics, as the surest guarantor of progress.

Decoud is a hybrid figure, possessing "a Frenchified—but most un-French—cosmopolitanism, in reality a mere barren indifferentism posing as intellectual superiority" (Conrad, *Nostromo* 152). His intellectual pretensions ally him with the "theme of the alienated intellectual" Jameson identifies with *ressentiment* (*The Political Unconscious* 200). A cosmopolitan *poseur* who reinvents himself as an intellectual leader of the people, "the Journalist of Sulaco," Decoud occupies a liminal position. He foments the birth of a new state, but the revolution ultimately secures the subordination of his people to exploitative development schemes. Decoud's bad faith undermines his critique of British imperialism.

From Conrad's perspective, Decoud is a member of the colonial *élite* whose idealization of European intellectualism is tantamount to a desire for the forms of Western civilization without its substance, its moral work. By making him a hybrid of cosmopolitanism and colonial *anomie*, Conrad effectively uses Decoud to blame modern fragmentation on a spirit of effete dandyism and bad faith. The superstructural symptom of modern economic transformation becomes a primary cause of the deterioration of the imperial mission. While Gould is ultimately wrong about history, for Conrad, colonial desire and Britain's imperial rivals drive imperial history's vicious cycles.

In his critique of Gould, Decoud reveals a nihilistic spirit that is a source of historical contingency, the self-conscious invention of a romantic, national narrative. His "Occidental Republic" is a sham, but one that comes into being anyway. This mapping of the colonial subject with bad faith provides one route for legitimizing the British imperial mission despite its problematic status. In *Nostromo*, Conrad does not turn to a nostalgic imperial fantasy as in *Lord Jim*; instead, imperial ideals become necessary illusions to sustain hope for progress in an era otherwise characterized by nihilism. If *Nostromo* fails to provide a sustainable narrative of progress, it insists that modernity is a threat to British imperial ideals from without rather than from within.

Through Decoud, then, Conrad illustrates the efficacy of a moral system founded on tradition even while exposing the delusions necessary to support such a system. Decoud finally breaks down and commits suicide after being isolated from Costaguana.

He kills himself not because he exists in bad faith but because his position is merely critical, offering no ideals toward which to work and around which to construct meaning. As Conrad puts it, "In our activity alone do we find the sustaining illusion of an independent existence as against the whole scheme of things of which we form a helpless part . . . He beheld the universe as a succession of incomprehensible images" (Conrad, *Nostromo* 413–14). By contrast to Decoud's narcissistic self-reflection, Gould finds his "sustaining illusion" in pursuing the realization of his ideals through the mine.

Conrad's sustaining illusion, I suggest, is a remarkably modern version of the culturalist project. Disappointed with the turn in imperialism, despairing about the nature of domestic society, for Conrad the "cultural turn" involves investing in a value system apparently negated on every side but that, as a form of faith, is the only tenable path for the thinking (read, reading and writing) subject. Nevertheless, the novel registers an evisceration of the individual from history and the replacement of heroism by the rule of economic forces. Gould's imperial work provides a necessary sustaining illusion, but ultimately fails.

MODERNITY AND AMERICAN CAPITAL

While Decoud's *ressentiment* is directed at Gould's belief in the ray of hope available through "material interests," the power of American capital, which has fashioned Gould both as fetish and charismatic leader, presents a far more odious threat. Conrad recognizes the United States as Britain's successor and worries that it threatens the British imperial ideal. In their shared idealism, Gould and his American financier, Holroyd, are parallel figures. They are linked as sentimentalists about their work—"businessmen are frequently as sanguine and imaginative as lovers" (93)—yet their romantic optimism has important differences. Gould is committed to the "ray of hope" in progress, but Holroyd sees the project as part of a modern crusade. The financier is a queer blend of forces, combining the imperialism of Caesar with a hybrid racial composition of a specifically American kind: "His massive profile was the profile of a Caesar's head on an old Roman coin. But his parentage was German and Scotch and English, with remote strains of Danish and French blood, giving him the temperament of a Puritan and an insatiable imagination of conquest" (94). Holroyd's mixed origins reveal tensions between the universalist and imperial impulse and recall Ulmen's diagnosis of turn-of-the-twentieth-century American foreign policy.

In fact, Holroyd's management of Gould provides a metonym for the changed landscape of Anglo-American relations, as evidenced by Britain's boundary dispute with Venezuela in 1895. In this crisis, the United States forced Britain to arbitrate in an American court. Britain responded that the Monroe Doctrine, never recognized in international law, did not apply. President Grover Cleveland addressed both these arguments in a famous speech on December 17, 1895: "While it is a grievous thing to contemplate the two great English-speaking peoples of the world as being otherwise than friendly competitors in the onward march of civilization and strenuous and worthy rivals in all the arts of peace, there is no calamity which a great nation can invite which equals that which follows a supine submission to wrong and injustice and the consequent loss of national self-respect and honor, beneath which are shielded and defended a people's safety and greatness" (Mr. Cleveland A1). Cleveland's notion of a friendly rivalry in pursuit of progress differs drastically from Conrad's. Cleveland positions the United States as the defender of universal values against wrong and injustice. This presumed right to intervene in the name of "justice" finds its fictional reflection in Holroyd's puritanical temperament and imagination for conquest. Like Cleveland's assertion of American prerogatives, Holroyd's capital recognizes no objections.

Gould's agency as an instrument of history is thus circumscribed within a larger interest, represented by Holroyd, who is himself a cluster of corporate forces organized around an ailing body: "Thus spoke the considerable personage, the millionaire endower of churches on a scale befitting the greatness of his native land—the same to whom the doctors used the language of horrid and veiled menaces" (Conrad, *Nostromo* 94). Here Conrad is not presenting American imperialism as naïve, but as an aged body in need of revitalization. Indeed, Holroyd's illness, and its apparent amelioration, becomes a trope for American capital's parasitic nature.

Gould's transformation parallels a more obscure change in Holroyd. While Gould's fetishization of the silver drives him into a kind of insanity, Holroyd's interest in the mine as an investment also deepens as well: "Costaguana had become necessary to his existence; in the San Tomé mine he had found the imaginative satisfaction which other minds would get from drama, from art, or from a risky and fascinating sport . . . Even in this aberration of his genius he served the progress of the world" (322). Holroyd's embodiment of modern capitalist expansion is complete: Even his intellectual shortcomings serve the cause of progress. But Holroyd represents not only the vanguard of capitalism; he also offers himself as a representative of the United States. Indeed, he makes the linkage between modern capitalism and his country explicit, proclaiming not simply that the United States has taken over the mission of progress but that it represents modernity itself: "Time itself has got to wait on the greatest country in the whole of God's Universe. We shall be giving the word for everything: industry, trade, law, journalism, art, politics, and religion, from Cape Horn clear over to Smith's Sound, and beyond, too, if anything worth taking hold of turns up at the North Pole . . . We shall run the world's business whether the world likes it or not. The world can't help it—and neither can we, I guess" (94–95). By exempting the United States from temporality, Holroyd makes a nationalist claim for the country's mission, much like claims to "Manifest Destiny." Unlike nationalist rhetoric locating the nation in an immemorial past, Holroyd, who comes from a country that has no such past, links his country with futurity. Conrad's reading of American imperial pretensions maps those ambitions with the coming of a new age dominated by mass culture, insofar as "everything" will be dictated from the central source of this commercial behemoth.

Holroyd's statement mirrors the reinterpreted Monroe Doctrine by invoking American sovereignty over the Western hemisphere. In particular, he articulates Theodore Roosevelt's position on America's strategic sphere of influence, which guided American policy on Panamanian independence and the construction of the Panama Canal in 1903 and 1904, the years in which *Nostromo* was completed and published. But more than that, the *hubris* of this passage is indirectly a declaration that Americanization means the propagation of a global mass culture. Holroyd's final comment—"and neither can we, I guess"—indicates an unconscious force behind American growth that may represent the greatest threat of all. In contrast to the individualist gospel of fidelity that animates Conrad's view of British values, the United States represents the threat of commercialization and the displacement of historical agency from individual to impersonal forces. Here, America is modernity itself.

Indeed, the novel's end registers a subtle transformation in the new Occidental Republic in its early years of independence. As the narrator puts it, "Material changes swept along in the train of material interests. And other changes more subtle, outwardly unmarked, affected the minds and hearts of the workers" (Conrad, *Nostromo* 417–18). As the republic modernizes, Anglo-American relations begin to reflect American hegemony. In one of the closing scenes, British Captain Mitchell leads a visitor through the Americanizing Sulacan landscape. Mitchell, a kind of touristic historian who validates and justifies the sham revolution and the American presence, notes that "the United States, sir, were the first great power to recognize the Occidental Republic" and recounts a tale of "how the United States cruiser, *Powhattan*, was the first to salute the Occidental flag" (Conrad, *Nostromo* 403, 405). New American businesses accompany these diplomatic landmarks, and Mitchell refers to a growing American community in the republic. Yet his anecdotes do not cover over the grim realities of a country created to support and protect the extraction of silver by outside interests. The juxtaposition of his patriotic narrative and the people's building resentment expose the vacuity of Gould's hope for progress through material interests. Emilia Gould sees the artificiality of progressive narratives most clearly: "There was something inherent in the necessities of successful action which carried with it the moral degradation of the idea. She saw the San Tomé mountain hanging over the Campo, over the whole land, feared, hated, wealthy; more soulless than any tyrant" (Conrad, *Nostromo* 431). Mrs. Gould's vision of the mountain as a tyrant brings the narrative full circle to the question of how developing the mine fits into the region's history. Here, as with the tenacious *gringo* ghosts, modern development merely repeats the exploitation of the native peoples by outsiders.

A secondary character, Dr. Monygham, makes the clearest statement of how modern imperialism repeats the vicious cycles of the past: "There is no peace and no rest in the development of material interests. They have their law, and their justice. But it is founded on expediency, and is inhuman; it is without rectitude, without the continuity and the force that can be found only in a moral principle . . . the time approaches when all that the Gould

Concession stands for shall weigh as heavily upon the people as the barbarism, cruelty, and misrule of a few years back" (Conrad, *Nostromo* 423). Insofar as the concession portends a repetition of barbarism and misgovernance, Monygham affirms the vicious historical cycle forecast in the legend of the *gringo* ghosts. Gould's desire to use material interests as an instrument of democracy has been misguided; democratic revolution makes the hegemony of such interests a *fait accompli*. Dr. Monygham is a mouthpiece for Conrad's analysis of rationalization: in modern life, the economic becomes its own system, detached from "moral principles." The development of material interests is "inhuman"; expedient and amoral, it severs one's sense of historical continuity and fosters *anomie*. Unlike any of the other characters, Monygham recognizes the complicity of material interests in enacting a return to exploitative practices. Yet his comparison is to the "misrule" of a native *élite* before the Sulacan Revolution. He equates Gould's materialism to barbarism, leaving open the possibility of a nostalgic view of British missionary idealism.

That Monygham's vision of the Occidental Republic reflects Conrad's pessimism about new forms of imperial development is evidenced in "Autocracy and War," in which Conrad explores the contemporary conflict between Russia and Japan, the death of Russia's claim to great power status, and the dangers posed by German imperial ambitions. In diagnosing the issues underlying these circumstances, Conrad voices many of the concerns about imperialism manifest in his fiction: "Industrialism and commercialism . . . stand ready, almost eager, to appeal to the sword as soon as the globe of the earth has shrunk beneath our growing numbers by another ell or so. And democracy, which has elected to pin its faith to the supremacy of material interests, will have to fight their battles to the bitter end, on a mere pittance" (Conrad, *Notes on Life and Letters* 107). The repetition here of "pin[ning] faith" on "material interests" suggests the mapping between Gould and misdirected democratic impulses in *Nostromo*. Further, it bolsters the association between Holroyd and "commercialism." Conrad's claim that commercialism will as soon turn to "the sword" as to democracy reveals his deep-seated suspicion of democracy's premises and efficacy. He views the history of capitalist expansion and development pessimistically, and his late attempts to legitimate

British tradition focus on finding ways to disentangle tradition from the imperial present.

The conclusion of this passage suggests that Conrad sees containment of unbridled imperial competition as the only hope for release from rapacious commercialism in the future: he predicts that democracy will fail unless "some statesman . . . succeeds in carrying through an international understanding for the delimitation of spheres of trade all over the earth, on the model of the territorial spheres of influence marked in Africa to keep the competitors for the privilege of improving the nigger (as a buying machine) from flying prematurely at each other's throats" (Conrad, *Notes on Life and Letters* 107). The vision of a world parceled out into spheres of influence confirms Conrad's pessimism about a national democratic future, although it indirectly validates the Monroe Doctrine. Most pointedly, the passage completely deflates the myth of progress that legitimated empire: "improving the nigger," itself a blunt travesty of the civilizing mission, is in fact a matter of cynically and even brutally creating new markets.

Finally, then, the ambivalence manifest in Conrad's representations of imperialism stems from his inability to reconcile the imperial ideal with its actualization. As he puts it in "Autocracy and War," "It is the bitter fate of any idea to lose its royal form and power, to lose its 'virtue' the moment it descends from its solitary throne to work its will among the people" (Conrad, *Notes on Life and Letters* 86). In this reassertion of the divide between ideals and realities, Conrad's use of a monarchical image to describe ideas reflects his distaste for the political culture created by mass enfranchisement and a more literate populace. But if he seems particularly ambivalent about "the empire," and, for that matter, empires, during the period from 1895 to World War I, he shares this sentiment with several European thinkers.

Throughout his career, Conrad searched for ways to reconnect the modernization of British imperial work with tradition. This search resulted in notions like "the Edifice," which reflect an acknowledgement that in a modern context collective ideals are necessary fictions, pragmatic forms of misrecognition. Having critiqued the degenerative forces of modern imperial competition in *Lord Jim*, Conrad repeatedly maps the antiheroic forms of economic imperialism on other imperial powers, particularly the nascent American one. Conrad's apparent complaint against the United States as the source of ominous modern economic processes was a self-interested critique commonplace at the turn of the century.[1]

By associating modern capital with the American character, Conrad displaces anxieties about Britain's emerging market structures. Assertions about the glorious past and future of British seamanship in the wake of the World War I thus reflect an increasingly conservative view of British history.

Figure 2 The American cowboy represented both a source of masculine vitality and a counterpoint to the refinement of the English gentleman.

CHAPTER 6

AMERICANIZATION AND HENRY JAMES

Go where you will in England and you will find the impress of the American mind, the results of American ingenuity.

—Sir Thomas Lipton, 1901

I object but to two things in America; the pie, and the hotel child. Not until that child is made into the pie will I tolerate either.

—George Augustus Sala

They came by rail, they came by foot. Where Dickens, in 1842, had comically contrasted his person with the American commercial energies of a nervous, preening bootmaker, by the turn of the century, the boots themselves were making a pilgrimage to England. According to one report, American boots began appearing *en masse* in London shops in 1892. In 1901, the *Times* reported on "American Competition in the Boot Trade" from the Shoe and Leather Fair in Islington. In addition to the footwear, "the machinery in motion constitutes one of the most important and instructive features of the exhibition . . . it is largely of American origin" (7). American production practices and equipment, as well as American products, were in the early stages of the flood tide that would sweep Britain in the twentieth century. Railway equipment, matches, electrical machinery, and appliances came in, provoking analysis and worries about American commercial energies as well as the values, tastes, and cultural practices that might trail in their wake. "Americanization," as it was frequently called, pitted the "electric" American character against Old World experience, variously figured as refined, durable, corrupted, and antiquated. In confronting Americanization, British observers debated whether they were confronting modernity itself. As one writer put it, "The new era, as represented in the United States, certainly affects me personally with distaste and misgivings" (Watson 789).

Frederic McKenzie's 1901 polemic *The American Invaders* catalogues the various industries in which America had moved from being a customer of Britain to a competitive threat or even a dominant supplier.[1] The invasion proceeded "unceasingly and without noise or show in five hundred industries at once. From shaving soap to electric motors, and from shirt waists to telephones, the American [was] clearing the field" (2).

This rising tide had in fact been gathering momentum since the so-called recession of the 1870s. U.S. investment overseas focused upon new technologies, especially new production technologies. This emphasis stirred anxieties about American trade practices that went beyond pure competition to the challenges of modernity itself.

Sir Thomas Lipton noted that "American money poured into England and American methods [have forced] England to move at a rate of speed that her system will not stand. Confusion follows, and the cry of 'Commercial Invasion' is heard throughout the land" ("The American Invasion: Sir Thomas Lipton's Views" 8). America's advantage, to Lipton, consisted in a "marked capacity . . . to follow the spirit of progress set by the buying public" ("The American Invasion: Sir Thomas Lipton's Views" 8). Lipton, along with many others, mapped the difference in national characters in terms of American understanding of modern commodity capitalism. Specifically, this mapping entailed a projection of the shift from production- to consumption-based economies onto the shadowy terrain of national difference.

Stephen Schwarzkopf points to P. T. Barnum's tours of Britain in the mid-nineteenth century as "a centre-point for all those who saw the core of 'American values' and the 'American character' in commercial advertising and the ideology of consumerist waste of resources" (136). The association of advertising and consumerism with the lack of culture in America gained momentum at the turn of the twentieth century, as American advertisers played a key role in McKenzie's invasion, and British advertisers found themselves struggling to compete with American sloganeering and advertising techniques (Schwarzkopf 140–41). Thus, Americanization seemed visibly ideological as well as material in character.

The meaning of the American invasion was debated in terms that reflected these international and temporal tensions and their impact upon British culture. American Earl Mayo, writing in *Forum*, saw "aggressive Americanism" as a transforming force in London: the observer traveling from

> Bank to Piccadilly Circus through the Strand and Pall Mall atop a London bus . . . will view "American" tailor shops, "American" tobacconists, "American" shoe stores, "American" bars and restaurants by the score, and even "American" patent medicines and soda-fountains. In many places he will find a more specific welcome extended to him in the signs before the shops, such as "Outfitters to American tourists" and "American patronage solicited." If he looks through a newspapers he will not only observe the effect that American typesetting and stereotyping machinery have exerted on its appearance, but he will find also that a great deal of American news . . . is being published. In the restaurants he will find American dishes; on the book-stalls he will see American books; and everywhere he will hear characteristic American expressions. (568)

By contrast, a British respondent in a subsequent issue of *Forum*, journalist H. W. Horwill saw the proliferation of American shops as simply part of England's cosmopolitan adoption of foreign goods. Horwill responded in like terms to a litany of Mayo's claims about "yankomania," in which the British "acquire some of the characteristics of his Yankee cousin": a decline of social customs for chaperoning, increased use of hotels and restaurants for private affairs, interest in technical education, use of American colloquialisms in speech, and American spellings in printed texts (566–67). In arguing that "Mr. Mayo considerably underestimates the receptivity that England habitually shows to ideas coming from outside," Horwill rejects the notion that Americanization has suffused world culture: "The time has not yet come, though many of her sons seem to regard it as already arrived, when Columbia may assume the chair of Professor of Everything" (235, 242).

In Mayo's boasts and Horwill's rebukes we find questions of culture and changing commercial dynamics intertwined. In this, Britain's identification with Arnoldian culture provided a locus of enduring value. Even Mayo admitted that "in the study of the classics and the liberal arts England, of course, has nothing to learn from America" (570). Other critics were less sure, however, about the permanence of this in the face of American social incursions.

THE AMERICAN WOMAN

American women in the British marriage market were viewed, depending on one's perspective, as either a particularly vital- izing or a destructive force. Mayo sees these women possessed of a "grace, brightness, and . . . adaptability" that makes them "immensely popular" (569). Yet they seemed nefarious to one *Times* correspondent who hoped that only British subjects would be allowed at Edward's coronation because American women would use the event "as a means of advertising themselves" (November 22, 1901, 3).

The height of invective against American women was per- haps voiced by the British gothic writer H. B. Marriott Wat- son in a 1903 article in the journal *Nineteenth Century and After, a Monthly Review.* Watson claims the American woman "has undertaken to annex as much of Europe as is practicable" (788).[2] The American woman's imperial tendencies, coupled with the insidious nature of American values, are a threat to culture itself: "She is anarchical. The State has been built upon certain sociological facts as foundation; the American woman is destroying these" (Watson 789). These facts include culture, beauty, art, wisdom, and humanity, none of which "is the final consideration in those eyes which see beyond all such trifles the omnipotent symbol of power evolved by the genius of moder- nity . . . a dollar" (Watson 787).

Lipton's, Watson's, and even Horwill's tone signal a sophisti- cated, rational sensibility threatened, or at least affronted, by the incursion of American forces upon their own sense of identity and culture. The tension between the diluvian tropes of American incursion and the singular, private self point to a growing asso- ciation of America with an unconscious, imperial drive to possess, control, and by these, ultimately destroy British culture. The debat- ers of "Americanization" would map an economic transition with an older discourse of national difference, and in so doing would generate types who managed the trick of this dual embodiment.[3]

Henry James is famously situated at the heart of the "international" theme, and his chronicling of the Anglo-American (or American-European) relation writes, and rewrites the tensions and possibilities inherent in a meeting of old and new world sensibilities. From early novels like *Roderick Hudson* (1875), *The American* (1877), and *The Portrait of a Lady* (1881) through the end of his career, the "international theme" preoccupied James's considerable analytic talents. Additionally, James's cosmopolitan allegiances align him with the positionality described in relation to the British authors traced in earlier chapters.

Here I examine James's difficult masterpiece *The Golden Bowl* (1904), followed by *The American Scene* (1907), which records James's voyage to the United States after a two-decade absence, immediately in the wake of the publication of *The Golden Bowl*. James articulates a critique of the impacts of commodity capitalism upon private human relations in these texts. In so doing, he negotiates a cosmopolitan positionality. James's relentless qualifications and increasingly difficult prose function as aesthetic tools for, as Michael Anesko has put it, "Build[ing] a readership for his writing both in his native land and in his adopted country" (120). James was not purely commercial and clearly struggled with the call from both sides of the hyphen of his Anglo-American identity. Yet, by analyzing English, American, and European societies vigorously, James offers a distillation of culture as a preserve from mass society and the penetration of privacy by economic interest.

CULTURE AND PERFORMANCE IN *THE GOLDEN BOWL*

On the occasion of James's seventieth birthday, friends and admirers presented the author with a Charles II porringer and dish, gilded in silver, along with a commission to John Singer Sargent for a portrait that today hangs in the National Portrait Gallery in London (Edel 5:484–87). We may wonder what James thought of this gift, inspired by his novel *The Golden Bowl* (1904). By contrast to the flawed bowl of the novel, the gift was truly valuable, the "real thing" as one of his characters might have put it. The dish and portrait were part of a series of canonizing gestures made in response to the Nobel committee passing James over, highly public and intended to memorialize his contributions to literature.

James may have viewed them with some irony, for *The Golden Bowl* explores relationships between legitimacy, cultural authority, and the exchange of antiquities. In particular, James focuses upon how the American-European marriage resembles the market dynamics of art collecting. In this novel, the acquisition of important pieces of European art by a self-made American millionaire upsets European mores and effectively makes American money the *sine qua non* of value. Likewise, marriage in the novel involves an asymmetrical exchange of financial security for culture and pedigree. In both cases, stability is restored only when the valued commodity—whether human or material—is removed from the public sphere and secured as a possession. This transformation, which centers on an Italian aristocrat and the daughter of an American millionaire, provides an important counterpoint to critical claims that in *The Golden Bowl* James finally finds a way to make his European-American marriages work. While the marriages succeed, it is at the cost of the reification of European culture in the service of American self-legitimation.

The Golden Bowl deploys several motifs to render an analogy between American-European marriage and the threat posed by American capitalism to European culture. Images of imperial legitimacy; tropes of commodification, public visibility, and representation; and images of authorship relate cultural artifacts to the interpersonal relations that govern two marriages of American wealth to European culture. James situates these motifs among reflections about modern economic values that transform the relationship between subjectivity and commodities in capitalist societies. The dramatic action of the narrative, understood thematically, involves control over the split, commodified subjects who embody European culture. While in the first half of the novel these characters use their duality to secure a limited form of freedom, in the second half American capitalists hamstring their human commodities by forcing them to conform to the representative public functions they had been performing. Thus the first half of the novel offers an exploration of the subversive freedoms available in a market system, and the second half demonstrates that those freedoms are limited compensations for the dehumanizing aspects of social relations driven by the market. Finally, the difficulty of James's writing and aestheticist presentation of the action links these issues to debates about his position as a novelist.

American millionaire Adam Verver's invasion of Europe challenges and appropriates European imperial traditions in the name of modern commodity capitalism. *The Golden Bowl* begins by staging empire as the banal material of a flourishing market economy. In the opening scene, Verver's daughter's fiancé, Prince Amerigo, muses about the relation between London's leisure and commercial areas and "an Imperium" (James, *The Golden Bowl* 43).[4] London's antique shops are stuffed with goods that suggest "the insolence of Empire," which the prince mentally links to the "legend of the City to which the world paid tribute"; Edwardian London succeeds Rome as an imperial center (James, *The Golden Bowl* 43). Similarities between the British and Roman Empires are reinforced by parallels between ancient and modern strategies of legitimation.[5] Shops commemorate present-day empire by collecting and employing the imperial icons of the past: the titular golden bowl is discovered among a wide variety of imperial antiquities, including "a few commemorative medals of neat outline but dull reference; a classic monument or two, things of the first years of the century; things consular, Napoleonic temples, obelisks, arches, tinily re-embodied" (James, *The Golden Bowl* 115). This mixed pile includes both Roman and French imperial artifacts and reflects an appropriation of imperial icons of the past. As Patricia Crick observes, "The First French Empire liked to reproduce the artifacts of ancient Egypt and Rome in order to authenticate its own Imperial image" (584).[6] Indeed, the prince muses upon imperialism as a political and commercial process of self-legitimation. Here we see a repetition of the process of imperial legitimation, yet it occurs in the context of a postimperial, capitalistic world. The artifacts of empire are not locked in the vaults of national treasure houses; rather, they are tourist trinkets, on sale in a Bloomsbury shop.

This commodification of imperial iconography references a contemporary phenomenon that appalled James. James derided the Diamond Jubilee of 1897, which celebrated Victoria's reign and the reach of her imperial dominion, as "a drab commercializing of national sentiment" (Edel 4:178).

Odious as they may be, imperial motifs in *The Golden Bowl* are circumscribed by the threat posed to European culture by American capitalism. America represents the vanguard of homogeneity and massification, the primary threats posed to culture by modern economic realities. Edel traces a gradual shift in James's view of Europe and American-European encounters: in his early work, Europe is both primary and unabashedly corrupt, but by the late 1890s James viewed Europe as "a splendid façade of civilization . . . [which] concealed a life of liberty, and . . . offered a veil of public decency, codes, and standards of judgments, with which to protect 'the private life'" (Edel 3:237). One reason for the shift was James's concern about the increased American tourist traffic he witnessed in London and in parts of Europe. Whereas in his early career, Americans abroad could be found traveling alone or living in small communities, by around 1890 he reported an influx of Americans into Europe *en masse*. James increasingly worried about the impact masses of bourgeois Americans would have upon Europe—the observers of European culture had become a social force in their own right. In a notebook entry that foreshadows the imperial metaphors of *The Golden Bowl*, he compared them to the Barbarians who invaded the Roman Empire: "The deluge of people, the insane movement for movement, the ruin of thought, of life, the negation of work, of literature, the swelling, roaring crowds, the 'where are you going?', the age of Mrs. Jack, the figure of Mrs. Jack, the American, the nightmare . . . The Americans looming up—dim, vast, portentous—in their millions—like gathering waves—the barbarians of the Roman Empire" (Edel 3:379). In this nightmarish montage, James records his anxieties about an American invasion of Europe. By referencing Barbarians, James insinuates that the American presence—or at least the presence of certain kinds of Americans—involves an unsettling of stable imperial forms. Additionally, by employing "the figure of Mrs. Jack," one of James's particularly social American acquaintances, James feminizes these images of cultural invasion and degradation, anticipating the modernist "great divide" chronicled by Andreas Huyssen in *After the Great Divide*.

James was more ambivalent about America's imperial ambitions. In 1895, James lamented that, with regard to the dispute with Britain over Venezuelan borders, President Cleveland made the United States sound "like one of those big European powers, particularly the Germany of Bismarck" (Edel 4:154). Moreover, he called the Spanish-American War a "deep embarrassment of thought" (Edel 4:238). Yet when he considered America's initial forays into imperialism, he could not help but consider affinities with England's imperial policy: "To live in England is, inevitably, to feel the 'Imperial' question, in a different way and take it at a different angle from what one might, with the same mind even, do in America. Expansion has so made the English what they are—for good or for ill, but on the whole for good—that one doesn't quite feel one's way to say for one's country 'No—I'll have *none* of it!' It has educated the English. Will it only demoralize us?" (Edel 4:239). Vindicating the English experience, James leaves open the possibility that imperialism will benefit the American character. The comparative nature of this comment anticipates themes that emerge in *The Golden Bowl*: even while the American invasion is figured in terms of the Barbarians, America's expansive tendencies are considered homologous to Britain's legacy of imperialism. That is, *The Golden Bowl* critiques American cultural imperialism while attributing its lineage to European conquest.

Adam Verver is the source of both the money and values that threaten to unmoor European culture. He is in Europe to purchase art for a new museum in "American City" in an unspecified part of the American Midwest. In the order he creates, both persons and commodities are evaluated not simply for market worth, but also on the basis of whether they can transcend that value. Verver's taste has been formed by his "exposure to the currents of the market" rather than "instruction in culture" (James, *The Golden Bowl* 142, 143). That is, he derives value from the laws of supply and demand, from the possibility of exchange rather than from cultural standards. Verver attempts to purchase and possess what is priceless, looking constantly for "civilization condensed, concrete, consummate" (James, *The Golden Bowl* 142–43). He obsessively pursues authentic, priceless cultural artifacts: "He was, as a taster of life, economically constructed . . . It was all at bottom in him, the aesthetic principle, planted where it could burn with a cold still flame; where it fed almost wholly on the material directly involved, on the idea (followed by appropriation) of plastic beauty, of the thing visibly perfect in its kind" (James, *The Golden Bowl* 179). Verver seeks the "real thing," a category that includes persons as well as art. For example, Amerigo represents the "real thing," the perfection of a type. This logic applies also to his marriage to Charlotte, an American woman who has abandoned the United States for European culture. She is described as "the thing classed and stamped as 'real'" (James, *The Golden Bowl* 178). Verver paradoxically desires to condense and concretize civilization while appropriating its ineffable quality, the very characteristics that elude or are spoiled by commodification.

Thematic references to America as a nascent imperial power are thus complicated by the bourgeois nature of Verver's aesthetics and the homologies between antiquities and cultured individuals. The shaping of imperial images by modern economic processes is particularly pointed when applied to individual subjectivity and interpersonal relations. In particular, commodification in human identity transfigures and represses alienation and relations of domination. James's critique of modernity involves the impact of commodification upon psychological and psychosocial dynamics.

The Golden Bowl turns on a logic of parallel human and material commodities, in which the former seek freedom *within* their status, but in so doing submit themselves to the traceability and strictures under which the latter is placed. The bowl is both symbol and symptom, repressing Charlotte's and Amerigo's dependency while providing evidence of their affair. Unable to support herself and relying upon the kindness of wealthy friends like the Ververs, Charlotte comes to London to buy a wedding present for Maggie (despite the fact that Maggie is marrying Charlotte's once and future lover, Amerigo). The bowl she selects (and that Amerigo attempts to reject) is aesthetically pleasing but contains a structural flaw immediately noticeable to the prince's refined eye. The crack has a variety of potential resonances, but its most immediate context is its reference to Amerigo and Charlotte's affair. Its imperfection, introduced into Maggie and Amerigo's drawing room, is a visible symbol of adultery. It stages a contrast between American and European faculties for valuation. Finally, it stands as a symbol of the Verver's cultural project—their acquisition of culture is tainted by the nature of the acquisition.

Nevertheless, in *The Golden Bowl* the commodities in question bear the traces of precapitalist aristocratic society and are valued because they enhance social prestige. That is, the novel demonstrates the way in which aristocratic lineage could itself become a tradable commodity that differentiated the bourgeois subject from his peers. The two subordinate characters in the narrative—Amerigo and Charlotte—attempt to secure a position as equal subjects by trading their links to culture as commodities. Inevitably, the people who control the money assert their privileges over their human commodities. By the end of the novel Amerigo and Charlotte are described as the kind of "human furniture" necessary to decorate a fashionable salon (James, *The Golden Bowl* 574).

Images of authorship reflect James's consciousness of the coercive power of his art and the relation it had to modern economic forces. In his analysis of James's self-positioning as a novelist in relation to Britain's aesthetic movements, Jonathan Freedman asserts that James contributed to the "full commodification of high art" (*Professions of Taste* xxvi). Moreover, this contribution "negated [aestheticism's] subversive play of irresolute possibilities and helped accomplish the full delineation of a zone of 'high culture'" (Freedman, *Professions of Taste* xxvii). Freedman argues that James's fiction embodies a response to his experience of the mediation of British aestheticism through American commodity culture, particularly advertising. James professionalized novel writing, partly through an increasing focus on formal strategies, and partly through numerous treatises on the craft. According to Freedman, James "remodeled the figure of the aesthete into that of the Jamesian high art novelist—a figure, like the aesthete, of supple and ample consciousness—but one who, unlike the aesthete, is capable of acts of sustained and disciplined creativity and dedicated professionalism" (*Professions of Taste* xxv). Freedman views *The Golden Bowl* as the "apotheosis and collapse" of this process, seeing simultaneously James's fullest exploration of point of view technique and a consequent return to the indeterminacies of the nonprofessionalized aesthetic. Freedman's argument about James and aestheticism relates to Verver's "economically constructed" taste insofar as he participates in America's appropriation of European cultural forms and the subsequent commodification of high art (James, *The Golden Bowl* 179). Yet James's novel also emphasizes the parallels between these processes and changes in interpersonal relations. Verver, for instance, sees individuals as a "numerous array"—an image suggesting that a person's value can be quantified as the sum of his or her component parts (James, *The Golden Bowl* 129).

Nevertheless, in the first half of the novel, entitled "The Prince," Amerigo's discretion and refinement allow him to subvert the rationalization of human relationships. James evidently understood the limited freedom associated with commodity fetishism. Prince Amerigo muses constantly upon British and American values, providing a critical perspective upon Anglo-American culture. A descendent of Amerigo Vespucci, the prince attempts to view his marriage as a second stage of his familial conquest of America. At the same time, he recognizes his marriage as an attempt to escape from his "antenatal history['s] . . . ugliness": "What was this so important step he had just taken but the desire for some new history that should . . . contradict, and even if need be flatly dishonour, the old?" (James, *The Golden Bowl* 52). For the prince, marrying into Verver's millions means rejecting a heritage and embracing modernity: "He was allying himself to science, for what was science but the absence of prejudice backed by money? His life would be full of machinery, which was the antidote to superstition . . . [He accepted] the developments of the coming age" (James, *The Golden Bowl* 52). In rejecting superstition the prince is allying himself with the modern; yet at the same time, he recognizes in the Ververs' modernity a "laxity . . . of the romantic spirit" which makes them too accepting and, thus, incapable of appreciating "the real thing" (James, *The Golden Bowl* 52). He finds himself constantly among the rich, separated as by "plate glass" from the rest of the world. His background, while in some ways degenerate and regrettable, nevertheless provides an archive of worldly experience that sharpens his critical faculties and allows him to see through the Ververs' modern romanticism.

At the same time, the prince lacks the clarity possessed by Verver—throughout the novel Amerigo is troubled by his "inability . . . to conclude" (James, *The Golden Bowl* 152). In this deficiency we may see the potentially subversive indeterminacy that Freedman attributes to preprofessionalized aestheticism. In fact, in the prince's absorption of the social logic of the Ververs, James may be identifying the power of the aesthetic to transcend commodification by appropriating and confounding its terms. At the same time, such a process merely inhabits the logic of commodification and fails to hinder its penetration of social values. The prince's conundrum is that he is a commodity as well as a critic, bound by the ideology of market value in his evaluation of the Ververs. As such, the prince embodies many of the difficulties James and his contemporaries explored within the purview of high art (and that literary critics experience in their institutional positions today). Thus while he is a key mouthpiece for James's critique of the leveling of cultural traditions and distinctions by American capitalism, he is also a figure for James's sense of the futility of such a project.

Amerigo's conundrum is that his acquisition of the Ververs is also an acquisition by the Ververs and that the terms of this mutual acquisition are determined by Adam Verver's education in culture through the market. While he secures the independence to rekindle an affair with Charlotte, their freedom is intimately tied to their role as commodities possessed by the Ververs. Adam and Maggie have an extremely intimate and, as some critics have suggested, quasi-incestuous relationship. They prefer each other's company to anything else, and they spend long days together with Maggie and Amerigo's young son, the Principino. When Verver marries Charlotte, both Amerigo and Charlotte see the marriage in contractual terms: "He had seen her . . . dealing always . . . with the duties of a remunerated office" (James, *The Golden Bowl* 263). She performs "the act of representation at large and the daily business of intercourse" for Adam Verver (James, *The Golden Bowl* 262). This business involves doing the "worldly" for the sentimental, sheltered Ververs, who are horrified by "the greater London bousculade" of society, which they view as the "brutality of mere multitude, of curiosity without tenderness" (James, *The Golden Bowl* 264, 265). Charlotte's, and eventually Amerigo's, role is to represent the Ververs socially, which involves securing them a position in society without exposing them to public scrutiny. Charlotte and Amerigo engage in the "act of representation at large and the daily business of intercourse" for the Ververs (James, *The Golden Bowl* 262).

By conceiving this role in business terms, Charlotte and the prince justify their frequent trips into society together. Also, they view their renewed affair as compensation for the function they perform. The power of this conception is partly mitigated by its irony—by constructing their sense of freedom upon exchange and compensation, Charlotte and Amerigo embrace the logic that made their romance impossible. They accept, to a degree, Verver's "economically constructed" values and see their marriages as business arrangements. Yet they fail to perceive that their autonomy depends on maintaining the façade that marriage is a shelter from public economic values.

Paradoxically, then, the prince's justification for the affair depends both upon the logic of market exchange and upon a romantic transcendence of that logic. The prince derives his agency from his commodity status, and the double-consciousness he experiences reflects the fact that his value is not his—that it is conferred rather than innate. While he conducts the affair, and while he and Charlotte represent the Ververs socially, Amerigo experiences a radical sense of alienation. As his body is "engaged at the front" of English society, "something of him . . . was left out; it was much more when he was alone or when he was with his own people—or when he was, say, with Mrs. Verver and nobody else that he moved, that he talked, that he listened, that he felt, as a congruous whole" (James, *The Golden Bowl* 270). The alienation he experiences is more than simple loneliness; he feels that "'English society' . . . cut him in two, and he reminded himself often, in his relations with it, of a man possessed of a shining star . . . something so ornamental as to make his identity not complete, ideally, without it, yet who, finding no other such object generally worn, should be perpetually and the least bit ruefully unpinning it from his breast to transfer it to his pocket" (James, *The Golden Bowl* 270). Amerigo's split self involves unstable dichotomies between lineage and selfhood, exteriority and interiority. His lineage and culture are ornaments that authorize his position in the social economy, yet their display foregrounds his otherness. The assertion of dependency on ornamentation signifies his lack of internal congruency; his need to escape history is juxtaposed against his need to trade upon that history. The metaphor of transfer from visibility to invisibility is in effect a hiding of his place in an older network of social relations for the sake of his agency in modern society. At the end of the novel, the fate of this "shining star" provides one gauge of the status of the prince's revived marriage to Maggie. At the conclusion of the novel Amerigo and Maggie are on the verge of reestablishing sexual intimacy, but whether this renewed relationship promises to restore the prince or complete his fragmentation is rather ambiguous.

Thus, Amerigo's bifurcation is the keynote of his commodification. The language in which James couches the star metaphor suggests an underlying relation between the prince's self-concept and the commodity form. The comment that his star is "something so ornamental as to make his identity not complete . . . without it" provides one of those paradoxical assignations of value that, as much as the obscurity of his plotting, contributes to James's difficulty. That the ornamental is deeply linked to selfhood for the

prince, and perhaps for the narrator, suggests an underlying relation between display or decoration and notions of self-congruity.
The act of self-display not only serves to define one's social place;
it also retroactively confers a sense of identity upon the self.

The complex coordinates of identity that characterize the
prince's conundrum suggest James's dilemmas as an American
high art novelist in Edwardian London. In his exploration of subjectivity in James's novels, David McWhirter suggests that James's
New York Edition "explor[ed] his own cultural, authorial, and
personal identity under the sign of [a] revisionary model of selfhood" (16). Constantly revising his personal identity in search of
an equilibrium between aristocratic manners and the conveniences
found in American values, the prince seems to embody in fiction
the dilemmas James experiences as an artist. Both seek remunera-
tion for their aesthetic judgment and critical perceptions even while
training those faculties upon ideological analysis of the institutions
that make this commodification possible. Amerigo is caught in a
vicious paradox—his notions of self involve an unchanging essence
and continuity with tradition; at the same time, his limited agency
depends on social recognition and the privileges accorded as a
result. Only through social representation can Amerigo be himself,
yet in the London society in which he circulates, his congruous
self is simply not recognized. To achieve limited freedom he must
accept fragmentation.

As Amerigo's meditation upon his congruity suggests, a fully
realized sense of selfhood can only come through private relations,
through interpersonal communication not mediated by public
economic ideology. To paraphrase Leon Edel's comment (quoted
earlier), James increasingly valued the role European culture and
manners played in protecting privacy. Yet as the inevitable exposure of the affair testifies, the private sphere is a construct—a place
removed from commerce only insofar as it subsists upon surplus
value. As the plot unfolds, the private sphere is revealed to be a
component of the public order of exchange and alienation misrec-
ognized as an escape from it. We may consider *The Golden Bowl* a
work of social and ideological criticism insofar as it reveals erasure
of the ways in which the private sphere is dependent upon modern
economic realities.

The major transitions in the novel, between Amerigo's perspective and liberal interpretation of his marriage contract to Maggie's

awakening and exercise of a newfound mastery, also mark a transition in the relations between private and public spaces and the freedoms they allow. Amerigo and Charlotte's relationship reveals the illusory nature of the freedom secured through their public functions. For the privacy they secure by performing the "business of social representation" for their spouses turns out to be an illusion. They conduct their affair in the public sphere, which makes anonymity and secrecy unsustainable. Public spaces document the activities of their inhabitants through physical traces and the memories of others. Thus, documentation links Amerigo's bondage to his past and his attempts to secure personal freedom in the present.

Early in the novel, the public documentation of antiquity and lineage provides a link between competing motifs of value and social position. Fanny Assingham, the matchmaker for Maggie and Amerigo, comments upon the documents that legitimate the Prince in the British Museum: "There's a whole immense room, or recess, or department, or whatever filled with books written about *his* family alone" (James, *The Golden Bowl* 96). The family history "of such people is known, root and branch, at every moment of its course" (James, *The Golden Bowl* 96). Amerigo comments upon how the existence of these histories contributes to his sense of double-consciousness: "There are two parts of me . . . one is made up of the history, the doings, the marriages, the crimes, the follies, the boundless *betises* of other people . . . those things are written— literally in rows of volumes in libraries; are [*sic*] as public as they're abominable. Everybody can get at them . . . But there's another part, very much smaller doubtless, which . . . represents my single self, the unknown, unimportant . . . personal quality" (James, *The Golden Bowl* 47). According to Amerigo, this highly public history has robbed him of a better pecuniary situation. The financial instability wrought by his history is disabling, forcing him to marry into wealth. History itself, according to Amerigo, is imprisoning, even if it constitutes the vast majority of the self. Lineage, however, performs a kind of advertising function for Amerigo, attracting Maggie's attention. Maggie points this out explicitly—"what was it else . . . that made me originally think of you? It wasn't . . . your particular self. It was the generations behind you" (James, *The Golden Bowl* 47). Maggie offers the prince's documents as a source of liberation, though she does not seem cognizant that this liberation involves a base commodification of his family name. Maggie's different evaluation of his family's public history provides a new iteration of a characteristic Jamesian figure—the American who idealizes Europe, particularly European aristocracy. In this case, however, James explores how American economic ascendancy shapes the romanticization of Europe. James represents wealthy Americans in Europe throughout his work, but here Americans dictate the terms and values that mediate Anglo-American relations in an unprecedented manner.

These distinctive views of documentation and lineage are merged in a startling image at the end of the novel: to save their marriage, Maggie decides to

> move indefatigably while he [Amerigo] stood fixed in his place as some statue of one of his forefathers . . . Such a place as Amerigo's was like something made for him beforehand by innumerable facts, facts largely of the sort known as historical, made by ancestors, examples, traditions, habits; while Maggie's own had come to show simply as that improved "post" . . . she was to have found herself connected in the fashion of a settler or a trader in a new country; in the likeness even of some Indian squaw with a papoose on her back and barbarous beadwork . . . [Maggie's territory] would be doubtless that of the fundamental passions. (James, *The Golden Bowl* 549)

Maggie's recognition of "her having had, in respect to him, to 'do all'" while Amerigo remains "still as a statue" places her in a superficially subordinate position to the prince—he holds a revered place while she is likened to "some Indian squaw with . . . barbarous beadwork" to sell (James, *The Golden Bowl* 548). At the same time, Amerigo is effectively converted to a lifeless piece of art while Maggie's activity is commercial, industrious. We might see this image, indeed, as imperial: though a squaw hardly represents a typical imperial figure, the reference to "a settler or a trader in a new country" suggests a colonizing figure (and perhaps a romantic conflation of colonizer and colonized). Like many American frontier romances, Maggie's narrative implies a kind of innocent industry territorializing an undiscovered country. While she romanticizes her incursion into "the fundamental passions," Maggie is nevertheless penetrating new territory—her exploration is metaphorically an imperial act. Indeed, bringing her beadwork to the passions is an image of commerce invading the interior of the self, and of the penetration of the private sphere by the public.

In short, Maggie's metaphor for her marriage both mirrors earlier comments about Amerigo as a "morceau de musée" and significantly alters them. The difference is that, by the end of the novel, Maggie has mastered European social forms. The limited freedom obtained through Amerigo's representational function is foreclosed once Maggie begins to exert control through European social forms. As a result, the prince becomes very much like a statue—immobile, detached from real human relations, revered but deprived of individual agency. Amerigo is rendered a silent symbol, a muted *object d'art*.

This crucial shift in the novel reflects the broader social context created by the modernization of Britain. The imperial theme introduced at the beginning of the novel—that British culture has amassed the booty of older empires as a form of self-legitimation—and a renewed theme of documentation depict Britain as a rationalized society in which public traceability eliminates privacy and personal freedom. The imperial center is monitored by a panoptic disciplinary gaze: as Fanny Assingham puts it, "People are always traceable, in England, when tracings are required . . . Murder will out" (James, *The Golden Bowl* 418). The traces that lead Maggie to the truth seem, on the one hand, incredibly painful—learning of her husband's and mother-in-law's infidelity destroys her innocence. At the same time, Maggie's contact with evil is a source of remarkable empowerment. If the traces of Amerigo and Charlotte's affair persist in a public network of social relations, Maggie's use of these traces places her in a position of considerable disciplinary power. By controlling the knowledge she has gained in public, Maggie obtains control over the private relations between the two couples. Her loss of innocence is simultaneously a gain of social power. Threatening, sadistic aspects of Maggie's empowerment lace the resolution of the novel with ambivalence about both feminine and American power.

The shift between the first section of the novel, "The Prince," and the second, "The Princess," involves the replacement of Amerigo's tropes of imperial legitimation and public representation by Maggie's romantically couched metaphors of authorship and domination. In the second half of the novel, repressed relations of domination are exhumed and exert terrible discipline upon the "human commodities," Charlotte and Amerigo. Whereas "The Prince" stages multilateral exchanges of culture and wealth under the sign of empire, "The Princess" reveals repressed relations of domination through Maggie's awakening to the "sweetness" of her "sense of possession" of Amerigo (James, *The Golden Bowl* 339).

Maggie's fall from innocence is a source of liberation; similarly, her new knowledge of evil, as Fanny Assingham had predicted, is simultaneous with the development of a "more analytic consciousness" (James, *The Golden Bowl* 339). Maggie, that is, develops a kind of double-consciousness herself—she becomes cunning, but that cunning is partly targeted at perpetuating romantic views of what essentially becomes a proprietary relationship. This is a significant difference between Maggie and her father, who embodies a less complicated sense of the relation between wealth and power. Adam Verver's mind has an automatic quality about it: he is described as "the man in the world least equipped with different appearances for different times" and as "the representative of a force—quite as an infant king is the representative of a dynasty" (James, *The Golden Bowl* 267). By contrast, Maggie is conscious of her awakening and engineers the fate of the two couples. Her masterful performance of manners to exert power indicates that she has developed the ability to manipulate the divide between perception and truth that heretofore characterized only figures who embodied European culture.

The result is a peculiar mixture of innocence and manipulation, good intentions and a sadistic desire to hurt Amerigo and Charlotte. Once Maggie discovers the bowl and the affair, she begins to carefully stage encounters with her husband and the rest of the group. Her goal becomes to end the affair and take hold of the situation without compromising her father's innocence—throughout the latter half of the novel she thinks of him as a "child," a "spotless lamb," and the like. After the bowl has been smashed, Maggie reflects upon the bowl's enduring value in her confrontation with Amerigo: "Its having come apart makes an unfortunate difference for its beauty, its artistic value, but none for anything else. Its other value is just the same—I mean that of its having given me so much of the truth about you" (James, *The Golden Bowl* 455). Here aesthetic ruminations about the bowl give way to its status as a document, a public object revealing Amerigo's infidelity.

After confronting Amerigo with the bowl, however, Maggie refuses to fully disclose who does and does not know about the infidelity: as she puts it, "Find out for yourself" (James, *The Golden Bowl* 464). Instead of simply uncovering hidden truths, the document functions here as a source of power. By refusing to make her knowledge fully public, Maggie begins to manipulate the gap between public appearance and reality that heretofore had been Charlotte and Amerigo's source of freedom. Moreover, by doing so she begins to control the behavior of the adulterous couple.

With Amerigo, Maggie finds an almost sadistic pleasure in using what he does and does not know against him: she feels "with her sharpest thrill how he was straitened and tied . . . visibly, palpably, traceably, he stood off from this, moved back from it as from an open chasm now suddenly perceived" (James, *The Golden Bowl* 457). By wielding the possibility of full exposure as a threat, Maggie makes Amerigo's behavior transparent—rather than reflecting a state of double consciousness, Amerigo's responses are palpable, traceable, visible. The disciplinary aspect of Maggie's power play does not involve full exposure, but rather the threat of exposure. Instead of exposing Amerigo to public scorn and, to refer to an earlier metaphor, breaking him into component parts, she "straitens" him by forcing him to conform to the very public image he has created for himself. That is, instead of forcing him to shed his façade, she effectively makes him become the façade itself. His private, "smaller self" is paralyzed. As her section unfolds, Maggie pursues a similar disciplinary strategy for Charlotte and Fanny Assingham, paralyzing their private agency by making them public functionaries.

Fanny Assingham, who facilitated Maggie's marriage and has worried over her culpability for the affair, is disempowered and reduced to a parodic symbol of an artificial peace. In a desperate attempt to suppress the truth about the affair, Fanny smashes the bowl and exhorts Maggie meekly to ignore the truth it reveals. Maggie, however, recognizes that Fanny would simply have her suppress history for the sake of the *status quo*. That is, Maggie sees that her peacemaking would ultimately confine her in a disempowered position. For Fanny, equilibrium, rather than truth, is everything. After the interview, Maggie orchestrates a group visit to Fawns that includes the Assinghams. From Maggie's perspective, Fanny's presence is figured in a rather comical image of power: "She was there inordinately as a value, but as a value only for the clear negation of everything . . . She knew accordingly nothing but harmony, she diffused restlessly nothing but peace—an extravagant expressive aggressive peace, not incongruous after all with the solid calm of the place; a kind of helmeted trident shaking *pax Britannica*" (James, *The Golden Bowl* 470). The irony in this image—Fanny as an armored, weapon-brandishing preserver of a false peace—reflects the bad faith Maggie sees in Fanny as well as signaling Maggie's new control. Like Amerigo, Fanny is reduced to "a value," a person whose identity has been appropriated for its public utility. Worse, that value, like Amerigo's, proves antiquated—it stands only for "the clear negation of everything"—and Fanny has become, like one of the Bloomsbury shop's imperial antiquities, a decorative object valued for its reference to a discarded past.

In addition to recalibrating Fanny's value, the image makes an implicit commentary upon Britain's *pax Britannica*. In this sense, James both ironizes Britain's imperial moralizing and relegates it to the past—Britain's imperial icons are merely antiquities collected by America for its self-legitimation. Maggie's assumption of power thus indirectly reflects American imperial pretensions around the turn of the century refracted into the private sphere. While certainly the assumption of power revises the fates of earlier American heroines, in this case the incursions of a modern business mentality and references to foreign policy reflect James's deepening understanding of how cultural politics are shaped by economic processes.

Maggie's transformation thus indirectly functions as a critique of American culture. As a figure for the romantic idealism associated with American cultural imperialism, Maggie threatens to master European culture in order to further America's own imperial aggrandizement. Indeed, James presents America in a particularly ominous light insofar as her empowerment involves a sadism that the other narratives lack. As Maggie's control over the other characters tightens, her sadistic tendencies increase: the narrator notes her "fascination of [*sic*] the monstrous, that temptation of the horribly possible, which we so often trace by its breaking out suddenly . . . in unexplained retreats and reactions" (James, *The Golden Bowl* 487). Maggie's sadistic temptations involve a desire to expose the relations of power that exist beneath the couples' veneer of equality and equanimity.

The plot culminates in a famous scene at Fawns, the Ververs' English country house. Adam, Maggie, Charlotte, Amerigo, and the Assinghams have a dinner party, and afterward they retire to play bridge. Maggie excuses herself from the game to take some air. Looking in at the players through a window, Maggie reflects that "her companions . . . struck her as almost consciously and gratefully safer . . . they might have been figures rehearsing some play of which she herself was the author" (James, *The Golden Bowl* 488). Maggie's empowerment is figured as authorial discipline, claiming the requirements of integrity and continuity to justify control. Seeing them seated at their leisure, playing cards, "positively brought home to her that to feel about them in any of the immediate, inevitable, assuaging ways . . . would have been to give them up, and that giving them up was, marvelously, not to be thought of" (James, *The Golden Bowl* 489). While Maggie flirts with an attraction to the monstrous possibility of exposure, here she puts herself in the position of a steward. She recognizes that the only way to preserve both marriages is to separate Amerigo and Charlotte from one another. In particular, this means countering the sexual threat Charlotte poses both to Maggie's marriage and to her father. The final scenes of the novel chronicle Maggie's effort to protect Verver and stabilize her marriage by decommissioning the sexual threat represented by Charlotte.

Continuing the inscription of public and national metaphors in the private relations of the Ververs, the disempowerment of Charlotte is depicted through images of state. After excusing herself from the bridge match, Charlotte follows Maggie onto the verandah and into the garden. Maggie views Charlotte as "the creature who had escaped by force from her cage," refiguring Charlotte's earlier freedom as a threat (James, *The Golden Bowl* 492). Charlotte attempts to intimidate Maggie by professing ignorance about what has caused a rift between them, and she moves the conversation to a well-lit drawing room that, as Maggie reflects, appears to be "appointed for some high transaction, some real affair of state" (James, *The Golden Bowl* 495). Knowing that Maggie does not want to create an open rift, Charlotte maneuvers her into a sisterly embrace just as the rest of the party comes looking for them.

The embrace takes on, as the narrator puts it, a "high publicity" (James, *The Golden Bowl* 499).

At this juncture, Charlotte succeeds in manipulating Maggie by giving publicity to their apparent reconciliation. In the final chapters of the novel, however, Maggie exerts mastery over Charlotte through similar means. Charlotte's power, throughout the novel, has stemmed from her proficiency in society—she has secured her marriage by offering the Ververs an opportunity to achieve a social position. Maggie now intercedes in a similar manner. After the bridge scene, Maggie confronts her father with the "fatuous" and "selfish" nature of their social arrangement (James, *The Golden Bowl* 502, 505). She denigrates the personal and private relations she enjoyed with her father by invoking his public mission, proposing that Verver has been her victim. Verver, recognizing her desire, decides to go back to American City. The idea has a "clearness" for Maggie that "almost dazzled her": "She saw Charlotte like some object . . . [wavering] in her field of vision, saw her removed, transported, doomed" (James, *The Golden Bowl* 512).

After Verver puts forward this idea, Maggie's perceptions of him change. Instead of being her affectionate father, she begins to perceive him as a public figure: he becomes "the 'successful' beneficent person, the . . . great citizen, the consummate collector and infallible high authority" (James, *The Golden Bowl* 513). Further, Verver becomes "public [and] . . . inscrutable," his inner thoughts increasingly obscure as the novel concludes. It is testament to the transformation Maggie undergoes that while Amerigo's section contains numerous accounts of Verver's thoughts, by the end of Maggie's section they have become entirely inaccessible. He has, in a sense, become one of Maggie's public functionaries as well.

Verver rededicates himself to his collection for American City and thereby seals Charlotte's fate, leaving her no recourse but to represent European culture in the Midwest. James records this revised relationship, through Maggie's eyes, in terms of imprisonment: "The likeness of their connexion [*sic*] wouldn't have been wrongly figured if [Verver] had been thought of as holding in one of his pocketed hands the end of a long silken halter looped round her beautiful neck" (James, *The Golden Bowl* 523). Here Maggie's fear of Charlotte as an uncaged beast is relieved by her imprisonment. The couple, unable to reach greater physical intimacy (the text suggests, in fact, that Verver may be impotent), learns to "live in the perfunctory" hours of the day, serving the public interest together (James, *The Golden Bowl* 524).

By the end of the novel, Charlotte has fully transformed into a public functionary. Her public utility, in contrast to the first part of the novel, is harnessed in the service of Verver's art collection. She assumes the duties of overseeing the removal of the artworks back to America, making Fawns "peculiarly public" as porters and construction workers descend upon the place. Moreover, this new duty penetrates her sense of selfhood; she acts and feels as a mere reflection of her husband, "having eyes at present but for the clock by which she timed her husband, or for the glass—the image perhaps would be truer—in which he was reflected to her as he timed the pair in the country" (James, *The Golden Bowl* 549). This rather disturbing image of Charlotte is complemented by Maggie viewing her as encased in glass, "frantically tapping from within by way of supreme entreaty" (James, *The Golden Bowl* 552). In addition, the "silken halter" image recurs in several forms at the end of the novel, emphasizing both the sense that she is a defused threat and the way this change marks her, both outwardly and inwardly, as a domesticated beast.

The leave-taking between the couples reinforces the sense that private, interpersonal relations have been abandoned in favor of public functions and social position. After receiving a telegram from Charlotte, Maggie announces that the Ververs will come "in state—to take formal leave. They do everything that's proper" (James, *The Golden Bowl* 560). Maggie supports the impersonal character of the visit. When the prince suggests that he make a personal break with Charlotte, Maggie responds, "'Aren't you rather forgetting who she is?' . . . It was the very first clear majesty he had known her to use" (James, *The Golden Bowl* 571). Maggie's assertion places Charlotte into the public role of her father's wife, and the prince perceives that this reflects Maggie's own development, a mastery of aristocratic manners. The prince and princess receive the Ververs in the front hall among "ranged servants," (James, *The Golden Bowl* 571) and the Ververs themselves appear "conjoined for a present effect as Maggie had absolutely never yet seen them" (James, *The Golden Bowl* 572). In this state, the "amount of correction to which Charlotte had laid herself open" is obscured by "the shade of the official, in her beauty and security": officialdom functions as a "cool high refuge," in which she "refer[s] to her husband and remembers her mission . . . of representing the arts and the graces to a people languishing afar off and in ignorance" (James, *The Golden Bowl* 572). In lieu of maintaining a social position in European society and the opportunities such a position offers, she instead will bring European taste to the masses of American City. Given that, for Charlotte, America is antithetical to good taste, her fate is particularly grim.

This final scene interweaves discourse about the public nature of the couples' final meeting with tropes of ownership. During the visit, Verver takes a last look at a particularly valuable painting he has given to Maggie. It is one of the objects Verver esteems most, and Maggie reflects that "in leaving the thing behind . . . he was doing the most possible toward leaving her a part of his palpable self" (James, *The Golden Bowl* 573). Verver's gift is more than simply a symbol of his love for Maggie; it is also a sacrifice. The painting stands in for Verver's physical presence, underlining both the impossibility of their continued intimacy and the degree to which their emotions are communicated through material objects. Verver has, like Amerigo, given up his "smaller self" to abide by Maggie's new order.

Though Verver is linked to Amerigo in their mutual self-sacrifice to Maggie, the scene makes their difference abundantly clear. While Maggie and Verver share a last moment of "abiding felicity" looking at the sacred painting, Amerigo and Charlotte sit down to tea. By contrast to the father and daughter, whose possessions function as vehicles of sympathy, the latter couple unconsciously adjust themselves to harmonize with the scene around them: "Mrs. Verver and the Prince fairly 'placed' themselves, however unwittingly, as high expressions of the kind of human furniture required aesthetically by such a scene . . . to a lingering view, a view more penetrating than the occasion really demanded, they also might have figured as concrete attestations of a rare power of purchase" (James, *The Golden Bowl* 574). Amerigo and Charlotte are figured as "furniture," functional objects positioned to legitimate, aesthetically, the material high culture in the room. Maggie's (or the narrator's) excessively penetrating perspective makes an important point about both the marriages and culture generally: Amerigo and Charlotte's cultural pedigrees and social facility naturalize the excessive concentration of art objects in the room, yet their own presence, when scrutinized, marks the economic as the horizon of all human activity. Culture is only a particularly rarefied type of economic activity. Moreover, Maggie views them not as culture incarnate but as culture commodified for mass consumption: they sit as though waiting to be "appraised, as a pair of effigies of the contemporary great on one of the platforms of Madame Tussaud" (James, *The Golden Bowl* 574). That they have become living effigies of the greatness and corruption of European culture indicates the degree to which Maggie has succeeded in imprisoning them within the very public selves they had used to mask their infidelity. Instead of unmasking them and sequestering them to the private sphere, Maggie imprisons them within their social personae.

These images of Amerigo and Charlotte's imprisonment, and even paralysis, within their social functions suggest a similarity in their fates. Indeed, Maggie reflects that Amerigo's restlessness reveals the "virtual identity of his condition with Charlotte's situation" (James, *The Golden Bowl* 559). Nevertheless, she sees a difference in his remaining captive "by his own act and his own choice" (James, *The Golden Bowl* 559). For Maggie, it was "as if she was succeeding with him beyond all intention" (James, *The Golden Bowl* 559). The prince's self-imprisonment suggests a kind of penance through which he hopes to restore the sanctity of his marriage and his personal honor.

This project involves alienation from his deepest sense of self, specifically from the value system that shapes and thus distinguishes his aesthetic and social judgment. By the final scene of the novel, the taste that seemed to evolve from his noble ancestry has abandoned him entirely: "Taste in him as a touchstone was now all at sea . . . for who could say but that one of her fifty ideas, or perhaps forty-nine of them wouldn't be exactly that taste by itself, the taste he had always conformed to, had no importance whatever?" (James, *The Golden Bowl* 563). Maggie's "fifty ideas" are not described in detail, only that "she had been going about him these three months . . . with a maintained idea—of which she had never spoken to him . . . but what had at last happened was that [he perceived] the presence not of one idea but of fifty, variously prepared for uses with which he somehow must reckon" (James, *The Golden Bowl* 558). Since Amerigo is in fact imagining a whole range of values where Maggie has only pursued a set idea, his misconception and inconclusiveness become the very bars of his imprisonment, elusive and ultimately illusory values to which he now attempts to conform. By thus being induced to react to the unknown desires and intentions of his wife, the prince loses his personal freedom.

To conclude that Amerigo is entrapped by a need to conform suggests that his young American wife's awakening into an understanding of European double-consciousness is both liberating and threatening. Maggie's new power undermines the refined European taste, flattening the very distinctions she has paid so dearly for by reeducating Amerigo with her 50 ideas. Her narrative is a tale of cultural imperialism displaced into the sphere of private relations.

Finally, the shift from Amerigo's perspective to Maggie's marks not only a historical transition, the change from formal empire to the cultural imperialism enacted by American capitalism. The shift from tropes of imperial self-legitimation to public iconography and from cunning resistance to a panoptic disciplinary regime also parallels the first two phases of imperial occupation: from conquest justified by symbols of imperial legitimacy to the construction of public icons that legitimate an established authority. Thus while James represents the threat America poses to European culture, through the narrative he also traces the initial phases of American occupation, accepting American hegemony as a *fait accompli*.

For James, the paradox represented by Americans' desire to develop their taste was that their forms of self-improvement led to a degradation of the very culture they mimicked. At the same time, though, James clearly notes the parallels between this process and the processes that historically drove European imperialism, particularly the British Empire. His position reflects a final ambivalence about traditions and culture. James's reactionary tendencies are complicated by a recognition that American imperialism is at once new and simultaneously a troubling legacy of the European culture he embraces.

This ambivalence is perhaps most effectively depicted in a figure who appears only briefly in the novel, Mr. Crichton, the curator of the British Museum. To this guardian of the national culture, America's appropriation of European art seems both tragic and an inevitable part of American ascendancy: "He could feel for the sincere private collector and urge him on his way even when condemned to be present at his capture of trophies sacrificed by the country to parliamentary thrift . . . He was almost consoled to see such lost causes invariably wander at least one by one, with the tormenting tinkle of their silver bells, into the wondrous, the already famous fold beyond the Mississippi" (James, *The Golden Bowl* 426). Mr. Crichton's resigned attitude toward American appropriation of Europe's and Britain's art treasures resonates with the novel's commentary about America: at once threateningly accumulative and at the same time deeply romantic, America's ascendancy portended an unhappy fate for James's professional ideals about culture. Like Crichton, James became increasingly resigned to Americanization as the fate of Europe.[7]

JAMES'S OWN "RETURN OF THE NATIVE"

Soon after the publication of *The Golden Bowl* in 1904, James arrived in a transatlantic steamer in Hoboken, New Jersey. From Hoboken, James rode a train into New York City, where he took pleasure in observing its vitality, and indeed saw a superficial harmony between nature and science in "the extent, the ease, the energy, the quantity and number" (James, *The American Scene* 72–73). Once James walked through the city, however, this harmony was badly disfigured by the stark, overwhelming presence of skyscrapers and the pulsing masses along Wall Street. James viewed the skyscrapers as America's repugnant "contribution" to the traditions of European architecture. They become "the most piercing notes in that concert of the expensively provisional into which your supreme sense of New York resolves itself" (James, *The American Scene* 77). This provisionality reflected America's lack of history and, further, the lack of "credible possibility of time for history" caused, in his view, by the predominance of commercialism. He saw a pervasive "ugliness" in both rural and urban landscapes caused by what James called "the complete abolition of forms" (*The American Scene* 25). In this paradox—America is "history-less," but forms have been "abolished" rather than simply absent—we see the Jamesian emphasis upon cultivated tradition as the stimulant of new cultural production and his distaste for revolutionary movements, both political and artistic. Through a drama in which James invoked a Burkean notion of the sublime, James came to see the skyscrapers as a "conspiracy against the very idea of the ancient graces" (*The American Scene* 89). As he stood before the gleaming new buildings, James began to feel overwhelmed.

He saw a linkage between pervasive commercialism and the arti-
fices at the root of America's dramatic expansion: the skyscrapers speak with an architectural "vocabulary of thrift at any price
[which] shows boundless resources, and the consciousness of
that truth . . . of the finite, the menaced, the essentially *invented*
state, twinkled ever, to my perception, in the thousand glassy
eyes of these giants of the mere market" (James, *The American
Scene* 77). The emphasis upon menace, invention, and a pervad-
ing watchfulness sent James into a kind of sensory overload, in
which his sensations "testify to the character of NY" but nevertheless "kept overflowing the possibility of poetic, of dramatic
capture" (James, *The American Scene* 82, 83). James's moment
of capturing the effect did come, however, when he named the
sensation in terms of the discourse of the sublime: "The vast
money-making structure quite horribly, quite romantically justified itself, looming through the weather with an insolent cliff-like
sublimity" (*The American Scene* 83). This sublime effect comes
from the merging of the skyscrapers with the weather, the way
the building towers over a church, and, crucially, the experience
of a pushing male crowd. In its homogeneity and density the
crowd nearly overwhelmed reflection in its "sounds and silences,
grim, pushing, trudging silences, of the universal will to move . . .
an appetite at any price" (James, *The American Scene* 83–84).
James's victory against this crowd is artistic—he survived it and
captured it in *The American Scene*. Nevertheless, the drama of
the sublime foregrounds the artist's difference from Americans
and indeed associates them with a horrific, unthinking appetite
that is the very antithesis of James's refined, restrained ideal.

The effect of the artist's encounter with the sublime generally entails a moment of panic, in which human reason is stunned
by nature's vastness. Here James deploys this logic to insinuate a
sense of menace into the mechanization of life in America. Yet his
sublime involves the horrors of a formless, incessant human aggre-
gation. Immediately after his description of Wall Street's skyscrapers, James reports his horror at the constant flow of immigrants
through New York's Ellis Island—he sees this as an "act of ingur-
gitation on the part of our body politic and social . . . that never,
never, never stops" (*The American Scene* 84–85). The experience
creates a "sense of dispossession" that haunts his sense of national
belonging. The inversion implicit in this idea, that immigration

robs James of his nationality, points to how closely he—along with many of his contemporaries—associated ideas about nationality with race. The result is that "free existence and good manners . . . are too much brought down to a bare rigour of marginal relation to the endless electric coil" (James, *The American Scene* 89). Thus James, like many analysts before him, employs electrical metaphors to convey his sense of America's energy and subordination to commercial interests.

The converse of James's association of Americans with a monstrous body of unceasing appetite is his portrait of the commercial equivalent of the cultural ideal. In contrast to the messy, voracious muddle of the streets of New York, in Florida James finds quiet and a semblance of good manners in the opulence and sense of enclosure of an expensive seaside hotel. At first the Poinciara Hotel strikes James as a "supreme illustration of manners . . . [and] fresh and luminous" (*The American Scene* 438). By contrast to the horrific sublime of New York, "the sublime hotel-spirit . . . operates by an economy so thorough that no element of either party to the arrangement is discoverably sacrificed" (James, *The American Scene* 438). An apparently generous interchange between hotelier and customer becomes emblematic of an exchange between the spirit of commerce—the "hotel-spirit"—and the spirit of national life. In this interchange, "the hotel-spirit is an omniscient genius, while the character of the tributary nation is still by struggling into relatively dim self-knowledge" (James, *The American Scene* 439). Thus James sees the national character as a "tributary" to the spirit of material gain, as only dimly self-aware, and as ultimately adjustable. This mutability reflects, again, the lack of history and culture to give the American a stable sense of self and, importantly, an absence of distinction and "the jealous cultivation of the common mean" (James, *The American Scene* 442). This hotel-spirit creates and shapes national appetites, leading ultimately to an absence of individuality and variety, and dimness of "distinctions" (James, *The American Scene* 442).

James's critiques of the homogeneity and commercialization of American culture are in a sense sociological accounts of the impact of commercial values. However, it is crucial for James that this analysis convey not objective detachment but rather an intensely personal performance. Thus the hotel-spirit and adjustable national life are not simply analyzed but recorded as antithetical to the well-emphasized spirit of his narrative persona, the "restless analyst." The analyst is an "agent of perception" who "would take [his] stand on [his] gathered impressions, since it was all for them . . . that [he] returned" (James, *The American Scene* 4). He returns to the United States not so much for the place itself, but rather for the impressions that his perception shapes and gathers. He is emphatic on this point: "I would in fact go to the stake for them" (James, *The American Scene* xxv). James's valorization of the "cultivated sense" as not merely the key to acute perceptions and good judgment but in fact as an "enrichment" of the subject matter differentiates his persona from the Arnoldian project. James's man of culture, "acute as an initiated native" while ennobled by immersion in English culture, *enriches* reality through his refined sensibility (*The American Scene* xxv).

In *Writing the Self: Henry James and America*, Peter Collister elegantly argues that James "assemble[s] . . . his American self in the text of *The American Scene*" (3). Noting that James's preferred title, had it not been taken, was *The Return of the Native*, and that James here claims that "one's supreme relation . . . was one's relation to one's country," Collister traces how "America has now become what Europe had earlier had been for the 'yearning young' [James]—his indirect way of referring to himself" (6). The dynamic is one of performance, rather than direct identification: "*The American Scene* records the continuing accumulation of material in the configuration of self as the most impressionable and painstaking of observers confronts a continent both known and mysterious. It is a landscape of fearsome incompletion and absence of boundary, which holds incomprehensible messages challenging James, as the text records, to find expedients in writing the self" (Collister 7). This model ingeniously treats the national sphere as a space that facilitates selfhood only through the subject's attempts to come to terms with it through writing. The notion of writing the self asserts a set of positive cultural values while exposing the problem of representation for what it is—always linked to the negotiation of identity.

Such a figure, whose perceptual powers in a sense make the cultural object observed, has aligned himself with a nonnational, acculturated readership. Indeed, he has performed his status as a citizen of culture by articulating one's "supreme relation" in terms of "restless analysis" rather than passive embodiment. *The American*

Scene, finally, transforms the strategy, witnessed throughout this book, of using the rhetoric of narrative address to valorize British culture by making culture itself the domain of the refined self, performed within particular national contexts for the sake of legibility.

An interesting coda to James's cultural performances occurred in the spring of 1914, when American painter John Singer Sargent's portrait of James was slashed by a militant suffragette with a hatchet. According to the *New York Times*'s report of the incident, the portrait "was acknowledged on all hands to be the greatest picture of this year's exhibition of the Royal Academy" ("Militant Ruins a Sargent Picture" May 5, 1914, 6). That James's image, produced by an American inducted into the Royal Academy, could be the object of such a symbolic action speaks to the degree to which he had ascended into the elevated ranks of British culture.

CONCLUSION

The full story of what Paul Giles has termed "transnational fictions and the transatlantic imaginary" stretches far beyond the limits of this study (Giles *Virtual Americas*). In incisive and capacious work, scholars including Giles, Laura Doyle, Susan Manning and Francis Cogliani, Jane Garrity, and many others have begun mapping this paradigm, which promises to have important impacts upon the boundaries of literary studies. A vast range of images of America, especially after the emergence of the notion of a "Special Relationship" in World War II, has been, and continues to be, profoundly interwoven with British conversations about its culture and identity. In concluding this book, I suggest the directions British discourse about the United States pursued after the turn of the twentieth century, focusing in particular upon the treatment of America in the influential London-based journal *The New Age*.

As this book has illustrated, British writers used representations of the United States to offer pedagogic messages to the *natio*. Through these stagings of transatlantic affiliation and difference, aspirational models of British identity were sublimated into critical acts and refined perspectives. As we move into the twentieth century, criticism itself becomes more sophisticated, taking account of both the imaginary nature of the "America" produced as an object of criticism and of the agency of myth in producing a sense of community.

Examining the critical writings in an early modernist review might seem an unlikely coda to a study that began with Matthew Arnold's cultural prescriptions. Yet the writers and editors of *The New Age* practiced forms of cultural criticism that display deep affinities with Arnold and other critics of British modernity and the ascent of American influence.

In the spring of 1907, Holbrook Jackson and A. R. Orage purchased *The New Age* with a five-hundred-pound contribution from George Bernard Shaw and Theosophist banker Lewis Alexander

Wallace. Though initially charged with presenting a Fabian perspective, Orage—who would edit the journal until 1922—sought a wide variety of social, economic, and aesthetic positions, often determinedly rejecting Fabian orthodoxy. As Wallace Martin explains, the list of contributors included in *The New Age* reflects Orage's belief that there were two types of periodicals—representative and presentative. While the successful representative journal acted as a mirror, winning subscriptions by parroting the values, perspectives, and interests of a bourgeois readership, the presentative periodical attempted to offer work that "belong[s] either to oblivion or to the history of culture, depending upon the extent to which [it] anticipate[s] and shape[s] cultural development" (3). According to Martin, Orage "deliberately attempted to make *The New Age* a presentative periodical which would mediate between specialized fields of knowledge and public understanding, and encourage a vital relationship between literary experimentation and the literary tradition" (3).[1] As a result, "*The New Age* provides a comprehensive record of the emergence of modern culture from its Victorian and Edwardian antecedents" (3). Martin's claims are supported by the startling range of authors who contributed to the review, names like Mansfield, Wells, Chesterton, Shaw, Belloc, Marinetti, Pound, Muir, Gorki, and Sinclair.

Although tuned to radical political registers, Orage's notions of the purposes of journals are reminiscent of the ideals of cultivation and educative citizenship outlined in the introduction. But what's really at stake in the "presentative" aspect of the journal for its readership? According to Orage, the readers of *The New Age* were "Matthew Arnold's fourth class, the class, namely, that lies outside the three weltering masses, and is composed of individuals who have overcome their class prejudices" (Orage 280). As Martin comments, *The New Age*'s readership was hailed as an "intelligensia," distinct from both the unlettered masses and the bourgeois intellectuals who wrote for and read "representative" journals (8). Orage's choice of Matthew Arnold's model may seem odd given the socialist program the journal espoused, for between Arnold and Marxist ideas lay deeply opposed visions of the springs and meaning of cultural change. Yet the journal's rhetoric engages the pedagogical and performative dynamics visible throughout this book, accommodating its readership's pride in difference with its national bearings by producing a British ideal paradoxically threatened from within and without and qualitatively superior to its national cohort.

With these ideas in hand, we can turn to the more limited topic of my discussion: how, and why, *The New Age* represented American culture. In writing about the United States, *New Age* writers participated in a long conversation that had been unusually busy since the turn of the century. With uncertainty manifest in Anglo-American relations through most of the publication of the journal, sentimental notions of racial or cultural brotherhood became the target of ridicule. Note, for example, how the phrase found in Anglo-Saxonist texts is mocked in the Max Beerbohm cartoon that follows this conclusion: the image features an aging, beggarly John Bull pleading to an uninterested Brother Jonathan in a mock-Dickensian whine, "O Sir, please Sir. Do let us young Anglo Saxons stand shoulder to shoulder agin the world. Think of that there Mayflower. O Sir, Sir, ain't blood thicker than water?"

Such British commentary upon the Anglo-American relation demonstrates an acute consciousness of the accumulation of preceding commentary and offers metadiscursive evaluations of its own. H. G. Wells comments upon the tenor of Anglo-American discourse in a 1910 article in *The New Age*: "Europe has despised America profoundly for nearly a century because it took its geographical advantage for virtue and valued things by their price in dollars . . . [and] bought beauty instead of making it" ("Roosevelt" 341). Other critics, like Francis Grierson, characterize America as possessed by the most "materialist decadence" of any nation in the modern world (Grierson, "Materialism and Crime" 341). The American public is variously described as possessed by pervasive ennui, a hunger for spectacle, neurasthenia, nihilism, disillusionment, imitativeness of Europeans, provincialism, worship of aristocracy, and—worst of all, perhaps—prejudiced views of the English. Americans are familiarly figured in two basic iterations: first, as the avatars of insidious, irrational modernity characterized by unstinting consumption and aggression; or second, as naïve, backward, and ingratiatingly desirous of English recognition and approval. Interestingly, the first of these descriptive regimes is usually applied when English culture is associated with hallowed tradition, while the second manifests when English culture is associated with vitality, common sense, and national success.

Such contradictions circulate throughout the journal. On the one hand, Orage's addresses to his imaginary "intelligentsia" depended, as we will see, upon identification with a national culture and with the production of Arnoldian notions of cultural amelioration. On the other hand, the journal's socialist politics led to criticism of both cultures, with America representing an extreme version of the ills that afflicted the English nation. In the latter line, the journal is rife with attacks on plutocrats, magnates, and trusts, and the American capitalist is repeatedly singled out as a particularly vile type. The most entertaining portrait of the American fat cat is perhaps Maxime Gorki's satirical account of an interview with an American millionaire.

Avowing a fascination with "the steel King, the Copper King, and all the other kings of the [American] Republic" and a belief that they must "have no resemblance to the rest . . . of our species," Gorki imagines his subject as the very picture of excessive consumption (Gorki 368). Possessed of three stomachs and 150 teeth, they yet must hire a train of servants to premasticate their constant banquets so they might pursue "the mere swallowing process thereof" (Gorki 368). Gorki imagines that, on holiday, millionaires affect to wear at least eight coats and six pairs of trousers, chew "two pound a gulp" tobacco, and snort "a pound a pinch" snuff (Gorki 368). Indeed, his "predominant fancy was of a nondescript being grasping the whole globe in his prehensile clutches, and pressing it towards [a] mysterious mouth [that] sucked, gnawed, and chewed our entire planet, with a greedy saliva exuding from his lips" (Gorki 368). Gorki is disappointed.

Instead, when he goes to meet a real, live millionaire, Gorki finds a "clean-shaven visage . . . with a somewhat greenish hue" breakfasting upon "an egg, a small cup of tea, [and] a fourth of an orange" (Gorki 369). He is astonished, moreover, to discover a man characterized by the "infantile naïveté" that the thousands who worked for him at subsistence wages were "satisfied," even appreciative (Gorki 369). In paternal fashion, he is committed to preaching the gospels to them every Sunday so they are not overcome by sin, especially not unrighteous envy of their employer. The millionaire does express difficulty being "an American and a follower of Christ at the same time" because Christ was "a bastard" and "in America, not only God but even an ordinary Clerk . . . dare not be born out of wedlock" (Gorki 370).

Despite his prudery, the millionaire loves the arts, especially theatre: he says, "I simply love to watch the young women in decolletee [*sic*] dominating the situation! I have a powerful pair of glasses" (Gorki 371). He, in fact, hopes to become something of an art impresario—inspired by his love of cock-fighting, the millionaire would like "to hire a pair of good [European] kings . . . [to] box each other . . . daily." As he reflects, "One can surely devote half an hour to Art after lunch!" (Gorki 372).

Gorki's satire, in addition to being entertaining, is interesting for the kinds of insights it offers. First, by noting the millionaire's subscription to self-serving doctrines about labor, religion, and art, Gorki identifies the ideological functions of Weber's protestant work ethic. Second, however, by beginning the piece with his own misconceptions, Gorki pokes fun at looking at America through the lens of caricature. Like the portrait of Adam Verver in Henry James's *The Golden Bowl*, Gorki's millionaire is a misguided idealist, mastered by a belief system that suits his interests. Yet where James's portrait emphasizes the ultimate inscrutability of a Verver, Gorki's interest is in the way the "revaluation of all values"—seeing everything through the lens of money—makes a mockery of any notion of transcendent, universal values.

It is just such a problem that runs through much of *The New Age*—unlike earlier texts, in which critiques of the United States analyzed American ideology while ignoring the prejudices of British subjects, in this journal, a pervasive critical awareness of the operations of ideology supplements, and sometimes destabilizes, this conventional frame.

This is manifested in intellectual responses to the spectacle of Theodore Roosevelt traveling the United States and the world at the end of the Edwardian period. In a 1910 article, H. G. Wells argues that "the Roosevelt that now engages so much American and European attention is manifestly no finite human being at all, but one of those colossal monsters as artificial as king carnival, which journalism, photography, caricature, and the immense possibilities of reverberation in the modern world create. Roosevelt has ceased for a time to be a man in the European mind, and has become a giant, a chimera'" (Wells, "Roosevelt" 340). If modernity creates a particularly distorting lens, the ensuing perspective can also be regressive. As another writer puts it, Roosevelt is "essentially middle class [and] . . . very faithfully the typical successful American of 50 years ago . . . [with his sense of] his own infallibility, of the monumental superiority of his own country, and contempt of the foe and the foreigner" (Lloyd 243). For this critic, these "old ideals" provide a comforting image for the American middle classes, lending nostalgic value to crass materialism and jingoism.

Critiques such as Gorki's and Wells's (and we can add numerous contributions from Hilaire Belloc, G. K. Chesterton, and George Bernard Shaw) are characteristic of much of the pre-World War I material found in *The New Age*. Their power lay in their merciless smashing of Victorian and Edwardian idols, and in the incisive, and thorough, puncturing of its great, baggy ideologies. Both England and America are targeted in their lenses, but with Americans there is a deeper alienation, an inhumane association with modernity that renders them both subject and portent for the English reader.

In founding *The English Review* in this period, Ford Madox Ford attempted to "enjoin upon the Englishman a Critical Attitude" (Ford 531). By contrast, Orage's mission, according to Martin, is best expressed in Allen Tate's appraisal of good editing: "An editor owes his first duty to 'his sense of the moral and intellectual order upon which society ought to rest, whether or not society at the moment has an interest in such an order or is even aware of a need for it'; and it was Orage's devotion to this duty which led Tate to name him as one of the great editors of our time" (Martin 15).

The difficulties endemic to a "critical attitude" in pursuing Tate's charge manifest widely in *The New Age*. Francis Grierson, for example, claimed that excessive "scepticism, when it endures beyond two generations, ends in materialism" ("Materialism and Crime" 341–43). In the case of the ancient empires of Greece and Rome, such intellectual decadence created a "national and spiritual disruption" because of its secular materialism, leaving "no faith left on which to build anything" ("Materialism and Crime" 343). He elaborates upon this critique in comments upon George Bernard Shaw, whom he calls "our master cynic[:] . . . Mr. Shaw's weakness lies in the intellectuality of his wit. He can tear down but he cannot construct; he can scatter but he cannot concentrate" ("G. Bernard Shaw" 248–49). The ascendancy of artists like Shaw indicates a lack of the "spiritual" and the ascendancy of commercial values. Grierson sees an "abject fear" behind Shavian skepticism and irony, and identifies a need for a "mystical spirit" or "vitalizing influence" of some kind to stimulate the revival of art, poetry, and literature ("G. Bernard Shaw" 249).

Such a want was widely felt. According to Martin, Orage believed that the purpose of criticism was to formulate a coherent set of values, based on tradition, which would be sufficiently flexible to absorb new forms without being a weather vane of literary novelty (Martin 195).

Grierson's essays in *The New Age* historicize the national characters of the two nations in terms of how they have been shaped by commercialism. For Grierson, the stripping away of sentimentalism has created an American character that, while resembling the English's deep faults, is nevertheless far more monstrous. While the English and American people are supposed to be "the most practical and matter-of-fact races the world has ever known . . . an era of 'aggressive prosperity' in America" has reconfigured their relations: "Where the English looked down on Americans with an air of patronage a few years ago, it is now the American tourist who thinks this air of patronage perfectly justified in his own case when he visits England" ("Anglo-American Animosity" 50–51).

Though turnabout may seem fair play in this relation, for Grierson "the American mind seems to be fixed in a way all its own . . . and screwed on by a new and unheard-of process; it is made to turn, but not to bow; it can think quicker than it can feel" (51). This figure occupies the position of abstract cynicism described earlier: "The opinions of Continental visitors never weighted with the people of London, but the American tourist, stripped of all superfluities, armed with a handbag, two keen, restless eyes, and a sharp tongue, ready to see most things as they are and some things as they ought to be, the time having passed when sentimental considerations play even an insignificant role in the ruling of a judgment; and lo! The Londoners [*sic*] breath is taken away with the cool frankness of a point-of-view never dreamed of" (51). Grierson's mechanistic American tourist mirrors John Bull's stereotypical *sangfroid* but as an uncanny double, soulless through its rejection of all reverence.[2] It is cool, analytical, and inhuman—a character defined by its puncturing of any sense of the value of tradition as mere sentiment; in our terms, as mere ideology. Thus the American tourist represents a "type" in the sense of a representative effect of the material conditions ascendant in the United States; yet that type embodies the dissolution of romantic notions of national character or culture. Such an analysis thus maps America with modernity, and "Americanization" with the alienation created through the denationalization of global capital.

While other *New Age* contributors associated Americans with soulless materialism and effectively developed Grierson's analysis, prewar writing about America occupied a more optimistic register as well. For that position we turn to Ezra Pound who, behind Orage and Beatrice Hastings, may be the most prolific contributor to *The New Age*. He famously remarked that the journal "did more to put food on my plate than anyone else in England," and the range of his contributions—including creative pieces, satirical essays, literary criticism, music and art criticism (often under pseudonyms), and cultural commentary is extraordinary. He participates in the tendency within *The New Age* and elsewhere to map American taste with the material, in the twin senses of commerce and the bodily. As Pound puts it, sounding much like Grierson, "American taste and discrimination will be held ridiculous in the world's eyes until America learns to pay reverence to something better" ("America" 13.2 34). He even mocks pretences to associating America's liberal individualism with taste and "realized cultural value" by travestying the egotism of Walt Whitman: Pound's version reads "I hear America a-singing . . . Fat, sleek, contented with emotions well / Below the far extended diaphragm." (34).

Yet Pound's aesthetic program is not open to the charge of pure cynicism leveled at Shaw. In writings about England and America, he avows a distinctively Arnoldian burden for the intelligentsia and articulates his vision of the necessary preconditions for a cultural renaissance. His "Credo[es]" are that "arts come into prominence . . . when men of a certain catholicity of intelligence come into power . . . [and second,] the awakening comes when men decide that certain lines need no longer be stuck to" ("America" 13.1 10).

Pound stresses the need for "indiscriminate enthusiasm" for the arts among the public and a powerful proculture "propaganda" as the requisite preconditions for the first of these credos—bringing the right people to power. He shares with others the view that England's fixed sensibilities make it unlikely to absorb such propaganda. Despite its Mammonism, the United States is characterized by openness, along with enthusiasm, that set the stage for a renaissance of art and culture. This is a position shared by several other contributors to *The New Age* before the war. Pound anticipates the emergence of several precursory conditions (and he graciously includes England here): "When we get some sense of values, when we come to take a common-sense view of the arts, as something normal, refreshing, sustaining, we may again find artists . . . when the arts shall cease to be regarded as a dope, a drug, a narcotic, as something akin to disease, and when they shall be regarded as sustenance—as clear channels for the transmission of intelligence, then may America and then *even England* may be a place wherein it is fitting that man made in the image of the invisible should draw its breath into his nostrils" (June 5, 1913, 143).

Pound's optimism about America was damaged by Woodrow Wilson's reluctance to join the fight in World War I. By 1915, Pound was expressing "deep chagrin . . . that my country is not at this moment England's ally in war" ("American Chaos" 449). Pound is frustrated with America's prioritization of material self-interest over cultural and spiritual affiliation, yet he claims this tendency has been "imported from England" ("American Chaos" 449). In this instance he attributes "an insoluble ignorance" to a lack "in England or America [of] any sufficient sense of the value of realism in literature, of the value of writing words that conform precisely with fact, of free speech without evasions and circumlocutions" ("American Chaos" 449). If prewar Pound hopes to heap a renaissance atop the propaganda that depicts materialism as a manifestation of the national mission, during the war he's lost all patience for Anglo-American falsifications. The result, interestingly, looks an awful lot like national stereotypes: "The German, I am told, 'lies on system, because he thinks the truth might be dangerous' . . . the Englishman lies unconsciously, because he wants to be considered as holding 'sound opinions' . . . the American falsifies, either because, as men of other and older races, he wishes to sell you a horse . . . or because he wishes to seem genteel, or because of a curious sense of humour" ("American Chaos" 449). The qualification we must make is that Pound is describing his German, Englishman, and American as purveyors of false consciousness, and further, that the roots of said false consciousness involve a particular configuration of individual value within national ideology. Grounded in desire, the relations of the individual to the public sphere have no less impact for being imaginary. In fact, in light of work on nationalism pioneered by Benedict Anderson and

extended through postcolonial theory, Pound's perspective chimes
with certain contemporary positions.

The story, for Pound and *The New Age*, does not end there.
In later volumes, America is associated with notions of "popular
culture" in a novel manner: Charlie Chaplin, the cinema, pulp fiction, popular music, and other elements of mass culture receive
significant attention. Such attentions further expose the modernist
mythos of the great divide, revealing instead both overlaps and the
way engagement with mass culture provided a means of articulating forms of cultural authority that required negation. *The New
Age*'s brand of cultural criticism, indeed, strategically anticipates
recent work in modernist studies for its own purposes. As Ann
Ardis argues, the Guild Socialists writing and editing *The New Age*
critiqued "a commodity culture with which [they] perceive the
modernist avant-garde establishing an all-too-comfortable relationship" (Ardis, *Modernism and Cultural Conflict* 166). The
journal's "commitment to the kind of 'revival of the arts' Guild
Socialists viewed as a 'necessary factor in social salvation' (read, a
socialist revolution) was never satisfied by modernist experimental-
ism" (Ardis, *Modernism and Cultural Conflict* 147).

Nevertheless, modernist figures engaged with the interlays of
mass culture and the Anglo-American relationship in their own
cultural criticism. Ford Madox Ford's founding of *The Transatlantic Review* in 1923 was both a continuation of his earlier attempt,
via *The English Review*, to improve the English reader's critical
faculties[3] and born of a desire to associate the journal with the production of transatlantic connections between America and 1920s
Paris. In the Vorticist manifesto *BLAST*, English stolidity is repeatedly attacked and special vitriol is directed toward the Victorian
period: one target is the "years 1837 to 1900 / Curse abysmal
inexcusable middle-class also Aristocracy and Proletariat" (18).
The character of this vitriol is disdain rather than anxiety, but its
matrix is a distilled version of Arnold's project. So too, is the "Bri-
tannic Aesthete," "CURSE[d] WITH EXPLETIVE OF WHIRL-
WIND" (15). Along with these figures, "FRANCE" is blasted in
part for being a "MECCA OF THE AMERICAN" (14). These
multiple rejections point to the Vorticist's desire to tear down ideological blinders and realize the "timeless, fundamental Artist that
exists in everybody" (39). Yet as *BLAST* moves from its "blast[s]"
and "curse[s]" to its "bless[ings]" and the points of the manifesto,

England continually resurfaces as a subject, especially as a land-scape for the emergence of a new avant-garde. The "Manifesto" claims that "the Modern World is due almost entirely to Anglo-Saxon genius" (39). Marinetti's Futurists are repeatedly rejected (and anticipated by English figures like Wilde and Gissing), and England is envisioned as the space for the development of an avant-garde. The readership, by implication, is English: "Once this consciousness towards the new possibilities of expression in present life has come, however, it will be more the legitimate property of Englishmen than of any other people in Europe" (41). What should we make of this codependency of avant-garde and nation? Is it that, despite the antiprogrammatic claims of *BLAST*, and despite its superficial work of "blast"-ing the nation, its parameters seat it within the discursive history of "action and reaction" it claims to transcend? The nation-obsession is, finally, enmeshed in the positionality of cultivated citizenship and offers pedagogical messages about the state of the nation. Its blasts clearly gesture in the direction of culture, even if they reject visions of utopian realization.

These themes were connected to the emergence of the modern-ists and their forerunners as celebrities in transatlantic print cul-ture—Wilde, the symbolists, and other *fin-de-siècle* figures spring to mind—and of the hardening of avant-garde expressions of dis-taste for "mass culture." The traces of this coupling appeared in D. H. Lawrence's polemical essay "Surgery for the Novel—or a Bomb?" In this piece, Lawrence lambastes both the experimental and the popular novel for the narcissism they foster, the former for its "senile-precocious[ness]" and the latter for its combination of moralism and titillating but light sadomasochism (Lawrence 115). Yet note the selected examples he deploys: the serious novels include "the pulses of *Ulysses* and of Miss Dorothy Richardson and M. Marcel Proust, on the earnest side of Briareus" (114). On the popular side, we find "the throb of *The Sheik* and Mr. Zane Grey, and, if you will, Mr Robert Chalmers and the rest" (114–15). With the exception of Edith Maude Hull's *The Sheik*, the "great divide" falls squarely in the middle of the Atlantic. If we consider Valentino's 1921 film version of *The Sheik* as an American cul-tural product, the mapping is complete. This apparently incidental linking of the United States to mass culture testifies to the subtle manner in which British writers displaced anxieties about changes in their own culture and position in the world. While negative depictions of America and Americans tend toward this "dislocating" and "spatializing" of forces antithetical to British culture, more positive representations also emerged; in *The Plumed Serpent*, Lawrence locates vital New World energies in contrast to Old World exhaustion and in *Studies in Classic American Literature*, Lawrence offers canon-legitimating criticism for American texts.

While the contributors to *The New Age* and British modernist writers thus pursued analyses of America for their own purposes, similar thematics circulated in other cultural realms as well. In particular, the maturation of modern advertising contributed to fears of Americanization. American advertising firms pioneered sloganeering and other innovations, which British advertisers belatedly imitated. In addition, British advertisers deployed American figures as foils in the commodification of British value. Stephen Schwarzkopf describes a further development in figurations of Anglo-American difference around the World War II: "Before the Second World War . . . the terms 'American' and 'America' were . . . used . . . as markers of difference and anchors of self-assertion . . . [but] post-war British advertising discourse began to use 'America' and 'American' as a synonym for 'the other' which needed explanation and cultural translation" (144–45). Critics have begun to explore the complexities of literary British representations of America and Americans in the run-up to and after the World War II. Roger Fagge notes a plurality of perspectives on America from British radical writers in the 1930s, and Tammy Grimshaw sees the emergence of a comic tradition in fiction writing about America. Allen McLaurin makes a particularly compelling argument about a "negative consensus" around the question of Americanization in Dick Hebdige, George Orwell, and Richard Hoggart's work, a thematic that impacts the agenda of British cultural studies in subsequent decades (McLaurin 182). Additionally, the rhetoric of the "Special Relationship," the emergence of well-known analyses of American culture from non-British intellectuals (such as the members of the Frankfurt School), the discourse of globalization, and increasing consciousness of the analysis of America as a well-worn gesture of self-affirmation attenuated the sense of urgency in the subject for most writers.

At the same time, popular U.S.-based British commentator Christopher Hitchens continues to emphasize the two nations' cultural ties and their common foreign policy aspirations as the dominant notes in the Anglo-American relations. In countless films, television programs, songs, and so-called popular culture "events," the legacy of Anglo-American representations are reinscribed and reworked to accommodate the agenda of the particular product. They provide a rich source of sometimes allegorical, sometimes nuanced tropes. This malleable reserve is deployed not so much to make sense of contemporary life, but to code it in readily consumable ways as our participation in the "public sphere" retreats further from the scene of the political, the cultural, and even the interpersonal.

In ending this book, it should be noted that while I do believe the self-consciousness attending national characterization persists in most discourse that could be classed as literary, the features of John Bull that would seem to resist such self-consciousness—stoicism, reverence for authority, and so on—also persist in cultural representation in the twentieth century. The complexity of their iterations is the subject of excellent scholarship in the British cultural studies tradition, but I believe there remain great opportunities for scholarship that considers the evolving image of the cultural critic and his or her identifications through the twentieth and early twenty-first century.

The more texts I read from this period, the more firmly I am convinced that we need to revaluate the relationship between ideology and history. For even if ideological commitments structure our fields of vision and knowledge, this precedence of ideology to history is rarely what determines the shaping of representation. Rather, we move from the "real" encounter with historical objects to the "symbolized" version retrospectively, shutting down the "content" of our musings by applying ideological ways of understanding that fit it within a field of meaning. That is to say, our experience of ideology is one of activation after the event, rather than prior to it.

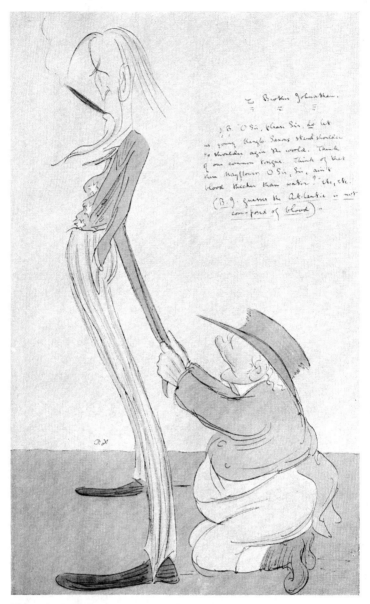

Figure 3 Published in the modernist journal *The New Age*, this image of Anglo-American relations placed England in a supplicatory posture while satirizing the myths of Anglo-American affiliation that had dominated the turn of the century.

NOTES

INTRODUCTION

1. As Ann Ardis notes, Anglo-American is a problematic term for the plural voices that contributed to what others have called the "Atlantic world" ("Staging the Public Sphere" 30). Yet it signifies a frequently invoked attempt to define the public sphere by dominant media and political voices. Sometimes even fashioning themselves as Anglo-Americans, these figures invoke the Anglo-American world in their texts. See Chapter 2 for consideration of the public sphere as a strategic trope.

2. Work from scholars such as Maria DiCenzo, Lucy Delap, Kate Flint, and Margaret McFadden demonstrates the range of scholarship currently being produced about women and other marginalized subjects within a transatlantic framework during this period.

3. Butler sees "educative citizenship" as the province of transatlantic liberals, whose intellectual roots in Unitarianism and the work of John Stuart Mill cause them to valorize self-improvement as a human possibility not limited by class or nation. My use of "educative citizenship" and "cultivation" strays from Butler's focus upon liberalism, for I see "educative" self-presentation and an idealization of the effects of contact with culture in figures from a wide range of backgrounds. I take this positionality to be a dominant trope in British representations of Anglo-American encounters, where Butler sees it as an effect of more specific liberal values. See the section of the introduction on "pedagogic" and "performative" messages in Anglo-American encounters for a justification of this expanded notion of educative citizenship.

4. See Eric Hobsbawm and Terence Ranger's anthology *The Invention of Tradition*, especially the introductory essay and David Cannadine's essay "The Context, Performance and Meaning of Ritual: The British Monarchy and the 'Invention of Tradition', c. 1820–1977."

5. Winston Churchill's American-born mother, Lady Randolph Churchill, born Jennie Jerome, testifies to this dynamic.

6. The failure of the so-called "Sherman amendment," which would have permitted foreign publishers to obtain copyright without commissioning a printing on American soil, illustrates the way the Chace Act represented only a partial success for the seekers of international copyright.

7. This is demonstrated, as Michael Warner argues, by the rhetoric of the Declaration of Independence: "we the people" are a legitimate polity because "we" have a body of documents asserting our legitimacy. This analysis is Michael Warner's in *The Letters of the Republic: Publication and the Public Sphere in Eighteenth-Century America.*

8. One of the interesting subplots in this shift is the way it implicitly made room for non-English writers like Joseph Conrad, Henry James, and many of the modernists.

9. Arnold's advocacy for culture, while directed toward the health of British culture and society, included a cosmopolitan purview. In "The Function of Criticism at the Present Time" (1864), for example, Arnold argues that the English critic must "dwell much on foreign thought" in order to create an "epoch of concentration" in which English literature can flourish (464, 457).

10. Leslie Butler suggests that Arnold should not be held as the progenitor of Victorian visions of culture: "Arnold's work mattered not because it formed a particular orthodoxy but because of his . . . authoritative voice [that] invited men of letters across the Anglo-American world to respond to his critique and to decide whether he might be embraced as a kindred spirit or targeted as a sparring partner" (132).

11. While subsequent chapters will reference the legacy of the Arnoldian cultural project for Anglo-American discourse, a 1900 piece in the *New York Times* testifies to his centrality to British discourse about America and to the important corollary that both British and American readers consumed this discourse. In "Matthew Arnold: His Relation to America—His Visit and Things He Said About Us," A. Blackwood interestingly associates Arnold's style with American tendencies, and focuses upon Arnold's deep sympathies with the United States and his critiques of England.

12. Colley's focus is upon how Catholic Europe, and France in particular, provided this figure for the other.

CHAPTER 1

1. Donne's anxious knowing seems to fit with a larger European tendency in views of America. Susan Scott Parrish argues, in fact, that "because America was a great material curiosity for the Old World and its immigrants to the New, America's unique matrix of contested knowledge making—its polycentric curiosity—was crucially formative of modern European ways of knowing" (7).

2. The emergence of a competing iconic figure, Ally Sloper, in the 1880s manifested Arnold's fears of anarchy. Sloperism—appealing to the lower classes with conservative purposes such as lampooning trade unions—and the emergence of "bread and circus" mass culture, especially English football, was an occasion for unease and a form

of class-containing "pedagogy" in its own right. See Peter Bailey or David Kunzle, "The First Ally Sloper: The Earliest Popular Cartoon Character as a Satire on the Victorian Work Ethic" (esp. 46–48).

3. DeSpain supplements the analysis of Dickens's positionality as an "elevated observer" with a careful reading of the way the first British edition of *American Notes* "represents British ethos and authority" and that "American reprinters would create carnivalesque, ephemeral adaptations of Dickens's tasteful publication that flouted his attempts at control" (41).

CHAPTER 2

1. The American origins of the machines used for newspaper production—first Thorne machines and subsequently the "Linotype"—may have contributed to the sense of a "transatlantic print culture" for newspaper workers. See Alan Lee's chapter on "The Making of a Cheap Press" (42–72).

2. In "Representing the Public Sphere: The New Journalism and Its Historians," Mark Hampton considers the problems endemic to conceptualizing the public sphere in this period, particularly with the birth of the "New Journalism" in the 1880s. For Hampton, "whatever we may say about the nineteenth-century public sphere, by the fin-de-siècle any hope for a unified public sphere by means of the press was seriously undermined by the multiplicity of audiences" (17). In an essay from the same volume, Ann Ardis describes how magazines "Stag[ed] the Public Sphere;" her focus upon the "*external dialogics* of magazines" resonates with the approach in this chapter, particularly "their discursive exchanges with other print media" ("Staging the Public Sphere" 38).

3. This advertisement appeared on July 29, 1875, on page 1 of *The Continental Herald and Swiss Times.*

4. Stead was an active and complex figure whose transatlantic connections spread beyond the reach of this brief section. As an aside, it is interesting to note that Stead died in the sinking of the *Titanic*, literally making a transatlantic passage.

5. The lines are taken from Charles Roberts's poem "The Shannon and the Chesapeake."

6. In 1890, for example, Smith published "The Hatred of America" in the *North American Review*. Andrew Carnegie wrote a reply claiming that some of Smith's assertions were anti-American.

CHAPTER 3

Angus Wilson uses the opening quotation by Lewis Carroll as the epigraph for his satirical 1956 novel, *Anglo-Saxon Attitudes*.

1. John Moser uses this term as his title in his excellent analysis of American Anglophobia in the first half of the twentieth century.
2. Douglas Lorimer makes this point, calling attention to the centrality of James Bryce's lectures on *The Relations of the Advanced and the Backward Races of Mankind* (1902). See Lorimer's "Race, Science, and Culture" (30–31).
3. Harrison credits British historian Edward A. Freeman for this description of a model Englishman, who was also a central figure in Teutonic Origins theory, referenced in the next chapter.
4. Nancy Stepan argues in *The Idea of Race in Science* that "racial scientists called themselves 'evolutionists,' while keeping alive a typological racial science . . . [A] curious synthesis [was] achieved by some anthropologists between radical traditionalism and evolutionism" (84). I'm suggesting that the muddle within the scientific community may have contributed to the muddled transference of "race science" to the cultural sphere.
5. Another prominent Anglo-Saxonist, Lord Rosebery, reversed the terms of masculinity and empire—arguing that "an empire such as ours requires as its first condition an imperial race—a race vigorous and intrepid," he worries that urban life prevents the fulfillment of the empire's racial needs (23).
6. For a more thorough analysis of the reception of Kipling's feted poem, please see Patrick Brantlinger's "Kipling's 'The White Man's Burden' and Its Afterlives" (172–91).

CHAPTER 4

1. In *Dracula's Crypt*, Jack Valente provides an overview of this critical history and examines anti-Semitic representations in the novel alongside anti-Irishness. He argues that "the Irish and the Jews split the distinction of being white-skinned specimens of the other in fin-de-siècle Britain" (68).
2. Buffalo Bill's spectacle played into the articulation of Britishness via Anglo-American representations in a number of registers. In an incisive analysis, Kate Flint argues that "Buffalo Bill's Indians were invoked and deployed . . . as a means of establishing a British sense of national identity and, above all, a distinguishable national culture" (255).
3. Stoker seems to lament the transition from what German political theorists call "*gemeinschaft*" to "*gesellschaft*," or from a society based upon personal relations and organically evolved institutions to one

organized by economic relations and the classification of persons according to their profession.

4. Later in this chapter the connection between Stoker and Matthew Arnold is further developed.

5. Arthur Holmwood, who inherits the title Lord Godalming during the course of the novel, plays an interesting role: his ascension seems to parallel the development of the chivalric band, and his suffering (first for his father's death, then for death of his fiancée, Lucy) authorizes its work. Finally, at crucial junctures he acts as a patron for the group, enabling them both to have money and to get around scrutiny from the police.

6. This description is borrowed from Patrick Brantlinger. For his comments on the "whirlpool" of the count's ideas on blood and aristocracy, see his *Rule of Darkness* (233–34).

CHAPTER 5

1. As Daniel Rodgers observes, "In the Anglo-German-American race for overall manufacturing output, the primacy of the Americans was a settled fact by the century's end. Alarm at the American penetration of customary European markets fed a steady press diet. The 'Americanization of the world,' European journalists called it. It would be fairer to think of it as the Europeanization of America. Better still, to think of it as the manifestation of market processes that sprawled everywhere across the boundary lines neatly marked by statesmen and diplomats" (49). This quote was featured in the Introduction as well.

CHAPTER 6

The opening epigraph from George Sala appeared in a June 24, 1899, article titled "Hotel Culture," *The Anglo-American*, page 1, column 2. The quote seems, in fact, to paraphrase Sala's comments in *America Revisited* (1883): "Close and frequent acquaintance with small juveniles in an American hotel is apt to induce the conviction that, all things considered, you would like the American child best in a pie" (86).

1. A similar British text, Ernest Williams's *Made in Germany*, had appeared five years earlier, underscoring the fact that competition was not limited to the United States. The sense of cultural invasion chronicled subsequently in this chapter does, however, seem particularly pointed with regards to the United States.

2. It is notable that Watson, and many other critics, pose Europe against America, rather than England or Britain. This corresponds to much of Henry James's work, explored later in the chapter.

3. Pells notes that Americanization, with its attendant hopes and anxieties, began half a century earlier: "the term *Americanization* originated in Britain in the 1830s, and it had spread across the rest of Europe by the 1850s. Initially, the word referred to America's mechanical inventions and technological ingenuity, phenomena that both intrigued and repelled Europe's statesmen and intellectuals. But once the United States had matured into a major industrial and military power at the beginning of the twentieth century, Europeans started to pay attention to America's influence and fear its economic and cultural intrusiveness" (7).

4. Henry James, *The Golden Bowl* (1904; New York: Penguin Books, 1987). All parenthetical citations of *The Golden Bowl* employ this edition. This edition features notes by Patricia Crick, which are referred to later in the essay.

5. In recent work, Christopher Hitchens has characterized the Anglo-American relation in related terms—Britain plays "Greece" to America's "Rome."

6. See note 2 of this chapter.

7. I am particularly indebted to two additional sources for ideas that shaped this essay: Sara Blair, *Henry James and the Writing of Race and Nation* (Cambridge: Cambridge UP, 1996); and Winifried Flück, "Power Relations in the Novels of James: The 'Liberal' and the 'Radical' Version," *Enacting History in Henry James*, ed. Gert Buelens (Cambridge: Cambridge UP, 1997).

CONCLUSION

1. Note the discussion of "representative" journalism and my argument about its "presentative" aspects in the Introduction and Chapter 2. Orage's analysis describes the rhetoric of the New Journalism, but his ambitions are consonant with the projects of most of the texts examined in this book.

2. It also resonates with Henry James's image of himself as a restless analyst in *The American Scene* (see Chapter 6).

3. Paul Peppis argues, in fact, that Ford "'modernizes' [Arnold's] universalist conception of 'culture' as a category transcending nationality and the practical sphere" (21).

WORKS CITED

Allen, Walter. *Transatlantic Crossing*. New York: William Morrow, 1971.

"America and England." *The Anglo-American Times*. 2 Dec. 1865: 2.

"American Competition in the Boot Trade." *Times* (London). 5 Nov. 1901: 7.

"The American Dude." *America*. 4 Jul. 1883: 4.

"The American Girl." *The Anglo-American*. 24 Sep. 1898: 6.

"American Invasion: Sir Thomas Lipton's Views." *The Anglo-American Press*. 4 Jan. 1902: 8.

"American Literature in England." *Anglo-American Times*. 24 Nov. 1865: 2.

"America's Sympathy with England." *The Anglo-American*. 3 Mar. 1900: 6.

Anderson, Benedict. *Imagined Communities: Reflections on the Origins and Spread of Nationalism*. New York: Verso P, 1991.

Anderson, Stuart. *Race and Rapprochement: Anglo-Saxonism and Anglo-American Relations, 1895–1904*. Rutherford: Farleigh Dickinson UP, 1982.

Anesko, Michael. *Henry James and the Profession of Authorship*. Oxford: Oxford UP, 1986.

The Anglo-Saxon Review. Ed. Lady Randolph Churchill. Vols. 1–10. New York: G. Putnam and Sons. 1899–1901.

Appadurai, Ajun. *Modernity at Large: Cultural Dimensions of Globalization*. Minneapolis: U of Minnesota P, 1996.

Arata, Stephen. "The Occidental Tourist: Dracula and the Anxiety of Reverse Colonization." *Victorian Studies: A Journal of the Humanities, Arts and Sciences* 33.4 (1990): 621–45.

Arbuthnot, John. *The History of John Bull*. Eds. Alan W. Bower and Robert A. Erickson. Oxford: The Clarendon P, 1976.

Ardis, Ann. *Modernism and Cultural Conflict, 1880–1922* Cambridge: Cambridge UP, 2002.

———. "Staging the Public Sphere: Magazine Dialogism and the Prosthetics of Authorship at the Turn of the Twentieth Century." *Transatlantic Print Culture, 1880–1940*. Eds. Ann Ardis and Patrick Collier. New York: Palgrave Macmillan, 2008. 30–47.

Ardis, Ann, and Patrick Collier. "Introduction." *Transatlantic Print Culture, 1880–1940*. Eds. Ann Ardis and Patrick Collier. New York: Palgrave Macmillan, 2008. 1–15.

Armitage, David, and Michael J. Braddick, eds. *The British Atlantic World*. Basingstoke: Palgrave Macmillan, 2002.

Armstrong, Catherine, Roger Fagge, and Tim Lockley, eds. *America in the British Imagination*. Newcastle-on-Tyne: Cambridge Scholars Publishing, 2007.

Arnold, Matthew. *Culture and Anarchy*. 1867. Ed. Samuel Lipman. New Haven: Yale UP, 1994.

———. *Civilization in the United States: First and Last Impressions of America*. Boston: Applewood, 1888.

———. *Discourses in America*. St. Clair Shores: Scholarly P, 1970.

———. "The Function of Criticism at the Present Time." *Criticism: The Major Texts*. Ed. W. J. Bate. New York: Harcourt Brace Jovanovich, 1970. 452–66.

———. "A Word about America." *The Complete Works of Matthew Arnold. Volume X: Philistinism in England and America*. Ann Arbor: U of Michigan, 1974.

Austin, Alfred. *Alfred the Great: England's Darling*. London: Macmillan, 1901.

Bailey, Peter. *Popular Culture and Performance in the Victorian City*. Cambridge: Cambridge UP, 1998.

Baldick, Chris, and Robert Mighall. "Gothic Criticism." *A Companion to the Gothic*. Ed. David Punter. Oxford: Oxford UP, 1990. 225.

Barrington, John. "Symbiotic Strength: An Eighteenth-Century View of the British-American Relationship." *America in the British Imagination*. Eds. Catherine Armstrong, Roger Fagge, and Tim Lockley. Newcastle: Cambridge Scholars Publishing, 2007. 65–85.

Baucom, Ian. *Out of Place*. Princeton: Princeton UP, 1999.

Beer, Janet, and Bridget Bennett, eds. *Special Relationships: Anglo-American Affinities and Antagonisms 1854–1939*. Manchester: Manchester UP, 2002.

Beerbohm, Max. Supplement: Cartoons by Beerbohm. *The New Age* 9.21 (1911): Supplement. Online access. http://dl.lib.brown.edu/jpegs/1166389725546875.jpg. 11 Aug. 2010.

Belford, Barbara. *Bram Stoker: A Biography of the Author of "Dracula."* New York: Random House, 1996.

———. *Oscar Wilde: A Certain Genius*. New York: Random House, 2000.

Bell, Duncan. *The Idea of Greater Britain*. Princeton: Princeton UP, 2007.

Berberich, Christine. *The Image of the English Gentleman in Twentieth-Century Literature*. Burlington: Ashgate, 2007.

Bergonzi, Bernard. *The Myth of Modernism and Twentieth Century Literature*. New York: St. Martin's, 1983.

Besant, Walter. *The Story of King Alfred*. New York: D. Appleton, 1901.

Bhabha, Homi. *The Location of Culture*. New York: Routledge, 1994.

———, ed. *Nation and Narration*. New York: Routledge, 1990.

Billig, Michael. *Banal Nationalism*. London: Sage, 1995.

Bird, Arthur. *Looking Forward*. New York: L. C. Childs & Son, 1899.

Bivona, Daniel. *British Imperial Literature, 1870–1940: Writing and the Administration of Empire*. New York: Cambridge UP, 1998.

Blackett, R. J. M. *Divided Hearts: Britain and the American Civil War*. Baton Rouge: Louisiana State UP, 2001.

Blackwood, A. "Matthew Arnold: His Relation to America—His Visit and Things He Said About Us." *New York Times*. 18 Aug. 1900: BR 1–2.

Blair, Sara. *Henry James and the Writing of Race and Nation*. Cambridge: Cambridge UP, 1996.

BLAST 1. Ed. Wyndham Lewis. Santa Rosa: Black Sparrow P, 2002.

Boehmer, Elleke. *Empire, the National, and the Postcolonial*. New York: Oxford UP, 2002.

Bourke, Joanna. *Working-Class Cultures in Britain 1890–1960*. New York: Routledge, 1993.

Bowker, Alfred. *Alfred the Great*. London: Adam and Charles Black, 1899.

Bradbury, Malcolm. *Dangerous Pilgrimages*. New York: Penguin, 1998.

Brake, Laurel. "Journalism and Modernism, Continued: The Case of W. T. Stead." *Transatlantic Print Culture, 1880–1940*. Eds. Ann Ardis and Patrick Collier. New York: Palgrave Macmillan, 2008. 149–66.

Brantlinger, Patrick. *Fictions of State: Culture and Credit in Britain, 1694–1994*. Ithaca: Cornell UP, 1996.

———. "Kipling's 'The White Man's Burden' and Its Afterlives." *English Literature in Transition, 1880–1920* 50.2 (2007): 172–91.

———. *The Reading Lesson: The Threat of Mass Literacy in Nineteenth-Century British Fiction*. Bloomington: Indiana UP, 1998.

———. *Rule of Darkness: British Literature and Imperialism, 1930–1914*. New York: Cornell UP, 1990.

Brickhouse, Anna. *Transamerican Literary Relations and the Nineteenth-Century Public Sphere*. Cambridge: Cambridge UP, 2004.

Brothers, Thomas. *The United States of North America as They Are; Not as They are Generally Described: Being a Cure for Radicalism*. London: Longman, Orme, Brown, Green, & Longmans, 1840.

Bryce, James. *The American Commonwealth*. New York: Book Jungle, 2006.

———. *The Relations of the Advanced and the Backward Races of Mankind*. Oxford: Clarendon P, 1902.

Bryden, Inga. "Reinventing Origins: The Victorian Arthur and Racial Myth." *The Victorians and Race*. Ed. Shearer West. Brookfield: Ashgate, 1996. 141–55.

Buchan, John. *The Thirty-Nine Steps*. 1912. Ed. Josef Kraus. Palm Springs: Wexford College P, 2001.

Burne-Jones, Philip. *Dollars and Democracy*. New York: D. Appleton, 1904.

Butler, Leslie. *Critical Americans: Victorian Intellectuals and Transatlantic Liberal Reform*. Chapel Hill: U of North Carolina P, 2007.

Cannadine, David. "The Context, Performance and Meaning of Ritual: The British Monarchy and the 'Invention of Tradition', c. 1820–1977." *The*

Invention of Tradition. Eds. Eric Hobsbawm and Terence Ranger. Cambridge: Cambridge UP, 1992. 101–64.

———. *The Decline and Fall of the British Aristocracy.* New York: Vintage, 1999.

Chamberlain, Douglas. "Anglo-American Elites 1902–1941: An Educational Alliance." Diss. Christ Church Oxford, 2003.

Clarke, I. F. *Voices Prophesying War: Future Wars, 1763–3749.* New York: Oxford UP, 1992.

Cleveland, Grover. Speech of 17 December 1895. "Mr. Cleveland is Dead at 71." *New York Times* 25 June 1908, sec. A1+.

Colby, Robert. "Authors Unite!: An Anglo-American Alliance." *Victorian Periodicals Review* 26.3 (1993): 125–32.

Colley, Linda. *Britons: Forging the Nation 1707–1837.* New Haven: Yale UP, 2009.

Collier, Patrick. "*John O'London's Weekly* and the Modern Author." *Transatlantic Print Culture, 1880–1940.* Eds. Ann Ardis and Patrick Collier. New York: Palgrave Macmillan, 2008. 98–113.

———. *Modernism on Fleet Street.* New York: Ashgate, 2006.

Collini, Stefan. *Public Moralists: Political Thought and Intellectual Life in Britain 1850–1930.* New York: Oxford UP, 1991.

Collins, Marcus. "The Fall of the English Gentleman: The National Character in Decline, c. 1918–1970." *Historical Research* 75 (2002): 90–111.

Collister, Peter. *Writing the Self: Henry James and America.* London: Pickering and Chatto, 2007.

Colls, Robert, and Philip Dodd. *Englishness, Politics and Culture 1880–1920.* London: Croon Helm, 1986.

Comentale, Edward. *Modernism, Cultural Production, and the British Avant-Garde.* Cambridge: Cambridge UP, 2004.

Conrad, Joseph. *Lord Jim.* Ed. Thomas Moser. New York: W. W. Norton, 1996.

———. *Nostromo.* New York: Penguin, 1990.

———. *Notes on Life and Letters.* Eds. John Henry Stape and Andrej Busza. Cambridge: Cambridge UP, 2004.

Conrad, Peter. *Imagining America.* New York: Avon, 1982.

Cooper, Thomas. *Some Information Respecting America.* London, 1794

Cosmopolis: An International Monthly Review. Ed. F. Ortmans. London: T. Fisher Unwin, 1896.

Crick, Patricia. "Notes to *The Golden Bowl*." *The Golden Bowl.* New York: Penguin Classics, 1987.

Cutler, Edward S. *Recovering the New: Transatlantic Roots of Modernism.* Hanover: UP of New England, 2003.

Davenport, Benjamin Rush. *Anglo-Saxons, Onward!* Cleveland: Hubbell, 1898.

DeKoven, Marianne. *Rich and Strange: Gender, History, Modernism.* Princeton: Princeton UP, 1991.

Delap, Lucy, and Maria DiCenzo. "Transatlantic Print Culture: The Anglo-American Feminist Press and Emerging 'Modernities.'" *Transatlantic Print Culture, 1880–1940.* Eds. Ann Ardis and Patrick Collier. New York: Palgrave Macmillan, 2008. 48–65.

Demolins, Edmond. *Anglo-Saxon Superiority: To What It Is Due.* Toronto: Musson, 1899.

DeSpain, Jessica Rae. "Steaming across the Pond: Travel, Transatlantic Literary Culture, and the Nineteenth-Century Book." PhD diss. U of Iowa, 2008.

Dickens, Charles. *American Notes for General Circulation.* 1842. New York: Penguin, 2001.

Dilke, Charles. *Greater Britain.* London: Macmillan, 1869.

Donne, John. "Elegy XIX: To His Mistress Going to Bed." *The Harmony of Muses.* Ed. Robert Chamberlain. London: T. W. for William Gilbertson, 1654. 6–7.

Dunkerley, James. *Americana: The Americas in the World, Around 1850.* London: Verso, 2000.

During, Simon. "Literature—Nationalism's Other? The Case for Revision." *Nations and Narration.* Ed. Homi Bhabha. New York: Routledge, 1990. 138–53.

Dyer, Thomas. *Theodore Roosevelt and the Idea of Race.* Baton Rouge: Louisiana State University P, 1992.

Dzwonkoski, Peter. "Analysis of the provisions of the copyright law of 1891." *American Literary Publishing Houses, 1638–1899.* Vol. 2. Detroit: Gale Research Company, 1986. 570–72.

Easthope, Antony. *Englishness and National Culture.* New York: Routledge, 1999.

Edel, Leon. *Henry James.* Vols. 1–5. New York: Avon Books, 1972.

Ellmann, Richard. *Oscar Wilde.* New York: Knopf, 1988.

"England Going to the Bad." *Anglo-American Times.* 2 Nov. 1865: 1.

Epstein, James. "'America' in Victorian Cultural Imagination." *Anglo-American Perspectives.* Ed. Fred Leventhal and Roland Quinault. Burlington: Ashgate, 2000. 107–23.

Esty, Jed. *A Shrinking Island.* Princeton: Princeton UP, 2003.

Fagge, Roger. "'The Finest or the Damndest Country in the World?': The British Left and America in the 1930s." *America in the British Imagination.* Eds. Catherine Armstrong, Roger Fagge, and Tim Lockley. Newcastle: Cambridge Scholars Publishing, 2007.

Flint, Kate. *The Transatlantic Indian, 1776–1930.* Princeton: Princeton UP, 2008.

Flück, Winifried. "Power Relations in the Novels of Henry James: The 'Liberal' and the 'Radical' Version." *Enacting History in Henry James.* Ed. Gert Buelens. Cambridge: Cambridge UP, 1997.

Ford, Ford Madox. "The Critical Attitude—On the Objection to the Critical Attitude." *The English Review.* Feb. 1910: 531–42.

Frantzen, Allen J., and John D. Niles, eds. *Anglo-Saxonism and the Construction of Social Identity*. Gainesville: UP of Florida, 1997.

Frederickson, George. *The Comparative Imagination*. Berkeley: University of California P, 2000.

Freedman, Jonathan. *Professions of Taste: Henry James, British Aestheticism, and Commodity Culture*. Palo Alto: Stanford UP, 1990.

———. *The Temple of Culture: Assimilation and Anti-Semitism in Literary Anglo-America*. New York: Oxford UP, 2000.

Gerlach, Murney. *British Liberalism and the United States*. New York: Palgrave Macmillan, 2001.

Gibson, Matthew. *Dracula and the Eastern Question*. New York: Palgrave Macmillan, 2006.

Gikandi, Simon. *Maps of Englishness: Writing Identity in the Culture of Colonialism*. New York: Columbia UP, 1996.

Giles, Paul. *Transatlantic Insurrections: British Culture and the Formation of American Literature, 1730–1860*. Philadelphia: U of Pennsylvania P, 2001.

———. *Virtual Americas*. Durham: Duke UP, 2002.

Glover, David. *Vampires, Mummies, and Liberals: Bram Stoker and the Politics of Popular Fiction*. Durham: Duke UP, 1996.

Gorki, Maxime. "An Interview with an American Millionaire." *The New Age* 7.16 (1910): 368–72.

Gosse, Edmund. "Culture and the Small Nations." *Anglo-Saxon Review* 5 (1900): 93–106.

Gossett, Thomas. "Imperialism and the Anglo-Saxon." Ed. Michael Krenn. *Race and U.S. Foreign Policy in the Ages of Territorial and Market Expansion, 1840 to 1900*. New York: Garland, 1998. 208–40.

Greenway, John. "Seward's Folly: *Dracula*'s Critique of 'Normal' Science." *Stanford Literature Review* 3.2 (1986): 213–30.

Grierson, Francis. "Anglo-American Animosity," *The New Age* 5.3 (1909): 50–51.

———. "G. Bernard Shaw," *The New Age* 5.13 (1909): 248–49.

———. "Materialism and Crime," *The New Age* 7.15 (1910): 341–43.

Grimshaw, Tammy. "The Imagining of America in Kingsley Amis's Fiction." *America in the British Imagination*. Eds. Catherine Armstrong, Roger Fagge, and Tim Lockley. Newcastle: Cambridge Scholars Publishing, 2007.

Hall, Catherine. "The Rule of Difference: Gender, Class and Empire in the Making of the 1832 Reform Act." *Gendered Nations: Nationalisms and Gender Order in the Long Nineteenth Century*. Eds. Ida Blom and Karen Hagemann. Oxford: Berg, 2000. 107–36.

Haller, John. *Outcasts from Evolution*. Carbondale: Southern Illinois P, 1995.

Hampton, Mark. "Representing the Public Sphere: The New Journalism and Its Historians." *Transatlantic Print Culture, 1880–1940*. Eds. Ann Ardis and Patrick Collier. New York: Palgrave Macmillan, 2008. 15–29.

———. *Visions of the Press in Britain, 1850–1950*. Urbana: U of Illinois P, 2004.

Harris, Jose. *Private Lives, Public Spirit: Britain 1870–1914*. London: Penguin, 1994.

Harrison, Frederic. *Alfred the Great*. New York: Books for Libraries P, 1971.

Harrison, J. F. C. *Late Victorian Britain 1875–1901*. New York: Routledge, 1990.

Harvie, Christopher. "The Moment of British Nationalism, 1939–1970." *Political Quarterly* 71 (2000): 328–40.

Haseler, Stephen. *The English Tribe: Identity, Nation, and Europe*. Basingstoke: Macmillan, 1996.

Hastings, Adrian. *The Construction of Nationhood: Ethnicity, Religion and Nationalism*. Cambridge: Cambridge UP, 1999.

Heathorn, Stephen. "The Highest Type of Englishman: Gender, War, and the Alfred the Great Millenary Commemoration of 1901." *Canadian Journal of History* 37.3 (2002): 459–84.

Hitchens, Christopher. *Blood, Class, and Empire: The Enduring Anglo-American Relationship*. New York: Nation Books, 2004.

Hobsbawm, Eric. *The Age of Capital 1848–1875*. New York: Charles Scribner's Sons, 1975.

———. *The Age of Empire: 1875–1914*. New York: Vintage Books, 1989.

———. *The Age of Extremes: A History of the World, 1914–1991*. New York: Pantheon Books, 1994.

———. *Industry and Empire: The Making of Modern English Society, 1750 to the Present Day*. New York: Pantheon Books, 1968.

———. *Nations and Nationalism Since 1780: Programme, Myth, Reality*. Cambridge: Cambridge UP, 1990.

Hobsbawm, Eric, and Terence Ranger, eds. *The Invention of Tradition*. Cambridge: Cambridge UP, 1992.

Holroyd, Michael. *Bernard Shaw*. 4 vols. New York: Vintage Books, 1993.

Horsman, Reginald. *Race and Manifest Destiny: The Origins of American Racial Anglo-Saxonism*. Cambridge: Harvard UP, 1981.

Horwill, H. W. "Americanization of England after the Boer War." *Forum* 33 (1902): 235.

"Hotel Culture." *The Anglo-American*. 24 June 1899: 1.

Hughes, William. *Beyond Dracula: Bram Stoker's Fiction and its Cultural Context*. New York: St. Martin's P, 2000.

Hulme, Peter, and Tim Youngs. *The Cambridge Companion to Travel Writing*. Cambridge: Cambridge UP, 2002.

Huyssen, Andreas. *After the Great Divide*. Bloomington: Indiana UP, 1986.

Jaffe, Aaron. *Modernism and the Culture of Celebrity*. Cambridge: Cambridge UP, 2005.

James, Henry. *The American Scene*. 1907. New York: Penguin Classics, 1994.

———. *The Golden Bowl*. 1904. New York: Penguin Classics, 1987.

Jameson, Fredric. "Modernism and Imperialism." *Nationalism, Colonialism, and Literature*. Minneapolis: U of Minnesota P, 1990. 43–66.

———. *The Political Unconscious: Narrative as a Socially Symbolic Act*. Ithaca: Cornell UP, 1981.

———. *Postmodernism, Or, the Cultural Logic of Late Capitalism*. Durham: Duke UP, 1992.

Jennings, Charles. *Them and Us: The American Invasion of British High Society*. Stroud: Sutton, 2007.

"John Bull History." Wells and Young's Ltd. 2010. 25 Jan. 2010. http://www.johnbullpub.co.uk/johnbull/history/

Jones, Greta. "Darwinism and Social Thought." Thesis PhD. London School of Economics, 1979.

Jones, H. S. *Victorian Political Thought*. New York: St. Martin's P, 1999.

Kaplan, Amy. *The Anarchy of Empire in the Making of U.S. Culture*. Cambridge: Harvard UP, 2002.

Kasson, Joy. *Buffalo Bill's Wild West: Celebrity, Memory, and Popular History*. New York: Hill and Wang, 2000.

Kaufmann, Eric. *The Rise and Fall of Anglo-America*. Cambridge: Harvard UP, 2004.

Kidd, Benjamin. *Social Evolution*. New York: Macmillan, 1894.

"The King Alfred Millenary." *Times* (London). 11 Sep. 1901: 5.

Kipling, Rudyard. *American Notes*. Boston: Brown, 1899.

———. *Captains Courageous*. New York: Aerie, 1992.

———. "From Sea to Sea." *The Works of Rudyard Kipling: Stalky and Co.* Vol. 8. Norwood: Norwood P, 1899.

———. "Recessional." *Complete Verse*. New York: Anchor Books, 1988. 327.

———. "The White Man's Burden." *Complete Verse*. New York: Anchor Books, 1988. 321.

Kobre, Sidney. *The Yellow Press and Gilded Age Journalism*. Tallahassee: UP of Florida, 1964.

Kohn, Edward. *This Kindred People: Canadian-American Relations and the Anglo-Saxon Idea, 1895–1903*. Toronto: McGill-Queen's UP, 2004.

Krenn, Michael. *Race and U.S. Foreign Policy in the Ages of Territorial and Market Expansion, 1840 to 1900*. New York: Garland, 1998.

Kroes, Rob. *If You've Seen One, You've Seen the Mall: Europeans and American Mass Culture*. Urbana: U of Illinois P, 1996.

Kroes, Rob, and Maarten van Rossem. *Anti-Americanism in Europe*. Amsterdam: Free UP, 1986.

Kroes, Rob, Robert Rydell, and Doeko Bo. *Cultural Transmissions and Receptions: American Mass Culture in Europe*. Amsterdam: VU UP, 1993.

Kumar, Krishnan. *The Making of English National Identity*. Cambridge: Cambridge UP, 2003.

Kunzle, David. "The First Ally Sloper: The Earliest Popular Cartoon Character as a Satire on the Victorian Work Ethic." *Oxford Art Journal* 8.1, Caricature (1985): 40–48.

Langford, Paul. *Englishness Identified: Manners and Character, 1650–1850.* Oxford: Oxford UP, 2000.

Lawrence, David Herbert (D. H.). *Selected Literary Criticism.* Ed. Anthony Beal. New York: Viking P, 1966.

Leavis, F. R. *Mass Civilisation and Minority Culture.* Cambridge: Minority Pamphlets No. 1, 1930.

Leavis, Q. D. *Collected Essays. Volume 1: The Englishness of the English Novel.* New York: Cambridge UP, 1983.

Lee, Alan. *The Origins of the Popular Press in England, 1855–1914.* London: Croom Helm, 1976.

Lewis, Jane. *Women in England 1870–1950: Sexual Divisions and Social Change.* Bloomington: Indiana UP, 1984.

Livingstone, David. "Science and Society: Nathaniel S. Shaler and Racial Ideology." *Transactions of the Institute of British Geographers, New Series.* 9.2 (1984): 81–210.

Lloyd, J. William. "Theodore Roosevelt: Another Socialist View." *The New Age* 7.11 (1910): 243–44.

Lorimer, Douglas. "Race, Science and Culture: Historical Continuities and Discontinuities, 1850–1914." *The Victorians and Race.* Ed. Shearer West. Brookfield: Ashgate, 1996. 12–33.

———. *Women in Britain since 1945: Family, Work and the State in the Post-War Years.* Cambridge: Blackwell, 1992.

MacDougall, Hugh. *Racial Myth in English History: Trojans, Teutons, and Anglo-Saxons.* Hanover: UP of New England, 1982.

Macpherson, Heidi, and Will Kaufman, eds. *New Perspectives in Transatlantic Studies.* New York: UP of America, 2002.

Mahan, Alfred Thayer. *The Problem of Asia.* 1900. Ed. Francis Sempa. Edison: Transaction Books, 2003.

Manning, Susan, and Andrew Taylor. "Introduction." *Transatlantic Literary Studies: A Reader.* Eds. Susan Manning and Andrew Taylor. Baltimore: The Johns Hopkins UP, 2007. 1–16.

Martin, Wallace. *The New Age Under Orage: Chapters in English Cultural History.* New York: Manchester UP, 1967.

Matthews, Roy. "Britannia and John Bull: From Birth to Maturity." *The Historian* 62 (2000): 799–820.

Mayo, Earl. "Americanization of England." *Forum* 32 (1902): 566.

McFadden, Margaret. *Golden Cables of Sympathy: The Transatlantic Sources of Nineteenth-Century Feminism.* Lexington: UP of Kentucky, 1999.

McKee, Patricia. "Racialization, Capitalism, and Aesthetics in Stoker's *Dracula*." *Novel: A Forum on Fiction* 36.1 (2002): 42–60.

McKenzie, Frederic. *The American Invaders.* London: Grant Richards, 1901.

McKibbin, Ross. *The Ideologies of Class: Social Relations in Britain 1880–1950.* New York: Oxford UP, 1990.

McLaurin, Allen. "'A Tunnel between Two Worlds': Imagining America in British Writing of the 1940s." *America in the British Imagination.* Eds.

Catherine Armstrong, Roger Fagge, and Tim Lockley. Newcastle: Cambridge Scholars Publishing, 2007.

McWhirter, David. *Henry James's New York Edition: The Contruction of Authorship*. Ed. Stanford: Stanford UP, 1995. 1–19.

Mendelssohn, Michele. *Henry James, Oscar Wilde, and Aesthetic Culture*. Edinburgh: Edinburgh UP, 2007.

Middleton, Tim. *Modernism: Critical Concepts in Literary Studies*. 5 vols. New York: Routledge, 2003.

"Militant Ruins a Sargent Picture." Special Cable to *The New York Times*. 5 May 1914: 6. www.nytimes.com. Web.

Morris, Jan. *The Spectacle of Empire: Style, Effect, and the Pax Britannica*. New York: Doubleday, 1982.

Moser, John. *Twisting the Lion's Tail: American Anglophobia between the World Wars*. New York: NYU P, 1998.

"Mr. Bryce on Changes in National Ideals." *Times* (London). 17 Dec. 1900: 13.

"Mr. Cleveland is Dead at 71." *New York Times*. 25 June 1908: A1.

Muirhead, James. *America the Land of Contrasts*. London: Lamson, Wolffe and Company, 1898.

Mulvey, Christopher. *Transatlantic Manners: Social Patterns in Nineteenth-Century Anglo-American Travel Literature*. New York: Cambridge UP, 1990.

Musser, Charles. *Thomas A. Edison and His Kinetographic Motion Pictures*. New Brunswick: Rutgers UP, 1995.

Nairn, Tom. *The Enchanted Glass: Britain and Its Monarchy*. London: Hutchison Radius, 1988.

Nevins, Allan, ed. *America through British Eyes*. London: Oxford UP, 1948.

Nicholas, H. G. *Britain and the USA*. Baltimore: The Johns Hopkins UP, 1963.

Ninkovich, Frank. *The United States and Imperialism*. Oxford: Blackwell, 2001.

Noakes, L. *War and the British: Gender, Memory, and National Identity*. London: I. B. Tauris, 1998.

Orage, A. R. "Unedited Opinions: Concerning 'The New Age.'" *New Age* 28 (January 1909): 280.

"Our 'Raison d'Etre.'" *The London American: A Chronicle of the American Colony in Europe*. 3 April 1895: 9.

Ovendale, Ritchie. *Anglo-American Relations in the Twentieth Century*. New York: St. Martin's P, 1998.

Parrish, Susan Scott. *American Curiosity: Cultures of Natural History in the Colonial British Atlantic World*. Chapel Hill: U of North Carolina P, 2006.

Pease, Donald. "National Narratives, Postnational Narration." *Modern Fiction Studies* 43.1 (Spring 1997): 1–23.

Pells, Richard. *Not Like Us: How Europeans Have Loved, Hated, and Transformed American Culture since World War II*. New York: HarperCollins, 1997.

Peppis, Paul. *Literature, Politics, and the English Avant-Garde*. Cambridge: Cambridge UP, 2000.

Poli, Bernard. *Ford Madox Ford and the Transatlantic Review*. New York: Syracuse UP, 1967.

Porter, Bernard. *The Lion's Share: A Short History of British Imperialism 1850–1995*. 3rd ed. New York: Longman, 1996.

Pound, Ezra. "America: Chances and Remedies." *The New Age* 13.1 (1913): 9–10.

———. "America: Chances and Remedies." *The New Age* 13. 2 (1913): 34.

———. "America: Chances and Remedies." *The New Age* 13.6 (1913): 143.

———. "American Chaos." *The New Age* 17.19 (1915): 449.

Pratt, Mary Louise. *Imperial Eyes: Travel Writing and Transculturation*. New York: Routledge, 1992.

"President McKinley's Message." *Times* (London). 6 Dec. 1900: 6.

"The President's Message." *Times* (London). 4 Dec. 1900: 5.

"Progress of the Season. Americans in England." *America*. 15 Oct. 1883: 8.

Purbrick, Louise, ed. *The Great Exhibition of 1851: New Interdisciplinary Essays*. New York: Manchester UP, 2001.

Rapson, Richard. *Britons View America: Travel Commentary, 1860–1935*. Seattle: U of Washington P, 1971.

Renwick, Robin. *Fighting with Allies: America and Britain in Peace and at War*. New York: Random House, 1998.

Richmond, Velma Bourgeois. "Representations of Anglo-Saxon England in Children's Literature." *Anglo-Saxonism and the Construction of Social Identity*. Gainsville: UP of Florida, 1997. 173–200.

Robbins, Keith. *Great Britain: Identities, Institutions, and the Idea of Britishness*. Harlow: Longman, 1998.

Roberts, Charles G. D. "The Shannon and the Chesapeake." *Orion and Other Poems*. Philadelphia: J. B. Lippincott & Co., 1880. 102.

Rodgers, Daniel T. *Atlantic Crossings: Social Politics in a Progressive Age*. Cambridge: Belknap P of Harvard UP, 1998.

Ross, Edward. *The Old World in the New*. London: Fisher Unwin, 1914.

Ruskin, John. *Unto This Last and Other Writings*. New York: Penguin, 1986.

Said, Edward. *Culture and Imperialism*. New York: Knopf, 1993.

———. *Orientalism*. New York: Pantheon Books, 1978.

Sala, George Augustus. *America Revisited*. London: Vizetelly, 1883.

———. "Hotel Culture." *The Anglo-American*. 24 June 1899: 1.

Sawaya, Francesca. "Philanthropy and Transatlantic Print Culture." *Transatlantic Print Culture, 1880–1940*. Eds. Ann Ardis and Patrick Collier. New York: Palgrave Macmillan, 2008. 83–97.

Samuel, Raphael, ed. *Patriotism: The Making and Unmaking of British National Identity*. 3 vols. London: Routledge, 1989.

Schmitt, Cannon. *Alien Nation: Nineteenth-Century Gothic Fictions and English Nationality*. Philadelphia: U of Pennsylvania P, 1997.

Schneer, Jonathan. *London 1900: The Imperial Metropolis*. New Haven: Yale UP, 1999.

Schwarzkopf, Stefan. "From Barnum to 'Organization Man': Images of 'America' in the British Advertising Discourse, 1850s–1950s." *America in the British Imagination*. Eds. Catherine Armstrong, Roger Fagge, and Tim Lockley. Newcastle: Cambridge Scholars Publishing, 2007.

Scragg, Donald. *Literary Appropriations of the Anglo-Saxons*. New York: Cambridge UP, 2000.

Seeley, J. R. *The Expansion of England*. 1883. Chicago: U of Chicago P, 1971.

Senf, Carol. *Dracula: Between Tradition and Modernism*. New York: Twayne, 1999.

Seville, Catherine. *The Internationalisation of Copyright Law*. New York: Cambridge UP, 2006.

Sharpe, William. "A Pig upon the Town: Charles Dickens in New York." *Nineteenth Century Prose* 23.2 (1996): 12–24.

Shaw, Bernard. "The Apple Cart." *Plays Political*. New York: Penguin Books, 1986. 7–138.

———. "John Bull's Other Island." *Modern Irish Drama*. Ed. John P. Harrington. New York: W. W. Norton, 1991. 119–203.

———. *Major Barbara*. New York: Penguin Books, 1960.

———. "Preface for Politicians." *Plays Political*. New York: Penguin Books, 1986.

"Short Notices." *Times* (London). 13 Sep. 1899: 7.

Simmons, Clare. *Reversing the Conquest: History and Myth in Nineteenth-Century British Literature*. New Brunswick: Rutgers UP, 1990.

Smith, Goldwin. *Commonwealth or Empire? A Bystander's View of the Question*. New York: Macmillan, 1902.

———. "The Hatred of England." *North American Review* 150 (1890). Cedar Falls: University of Northern Iowa: 402.

———. *Lectures on Modern History*. London: J. & J. Parker, 1861.

———. "The Schism in the Anglo-Saxon Race." *Canadian Leaves: History, Art, Science, Literature, Commerce*. New York: Canadian Club of New York, 1888. 19–57.

Spencer, David. *The Yellow Journalism: The Press and America's Emergence as a World Power*. Evanston: Northwestern UP, 2007.

Spender, Stephen. *Love-Hate Relations*. New York: Random House, 1974.

Stead, W. T. *The Americanization of the World*. London: H. Markley, 1902.

Steevens, G. W. *The Land of the Dollar*. London, Blackwood and Sons, 1897.

Stepan, Nancy. *The Idea of Race in Science*. North Haven, CT: Archon, 1982.

Stevenson, Robert Louis. *Across the Plains*. New York: Cosimo, 2005.

Stites, Max. "Dicken's Amputated America." *America in the British Imagination*. Eds. Catherine Armstrong, Roger Fagge, and Tim Lockley. Newcastle-on-Tyne: Cambridge Scholars Publishing, 2007. 102–17.

Stoker, Bram. *A Glimpse of America: A Lecture given at the London Institution*. London: Sampson Low, Marston and Company, 1886.

———. *Dracula.* 1897. New York: W. W. Norton, 1997.

———. Letter to Walt Whitman. 18 February, 1872. Papers of Walt Whitman in the Charles E. Feinberg Collection. Library of Congress, Washington D.C.

———. Letter to Walt Whitman. 14 February, 1876. Papers of Walt Whitman in the Charles E. Feinberg Collection. Library of Congress, Washington D.C.

———. *The Shoulder of Shasta.* 1895. New York: Classic Books, 2000.

Stokes, Claudia. "Copyrighting American History: International Copyright and the Periodization of the Nineteenth Century." *American Literature: A Journal of Literary History, Criticism, and Bibliography* 77.2 (2005): 291–317.

Strinati, Dominic, and Stephen Wagg, eds. *Come on Down: Popular Media Culture in Post-War Britain.* London: Routledge, 1992.

Thomas, Katie-Louise. "Racial Alliance and Postal Networks in Conan Doyle's 'A Study in Scarlet.'" *Journal of Colonialism and Colonial History* 2.1 (Spring 2001). 9–23.

Tocqueville, Alexis de. *Democracy in America.* New York: Penguin Classics, 2003.

Tracy, Louis. *The Final War.* London: Putnam, 1896.

Trotsky, Leon. *Leon Trotsky: Collected Writings and Speeches on Britain.* Vol. 1. London: New Park, 1974. 145–52.

Turner, Frederick Jackson. *The Significance of the Frontier in American History.* New York: Henry Holt and Company, 1921.

Ulmen, Gary. "Universalism Contra Pluralism." *Society* 31.5 (1994): 32–37.

Valente, Jack. *Dracula's Crypt: Bram Stoker, Irishness, and the Question of Blood.* Urbana: U of Illinois P, 2002.

van Elteren, Mel. *Americanism and Americanization: A Critical History of Domestic and Global Influence.* New York: McFarland, 2006.

Vaughan, Leslie. "Cosmopolitanism, Ethnicity and American Identity: Randolph Bourne's 'Trans-National America.'" *Journal of American Studies* 25.3 (Fall 1995): 443–59.

Vernon, James. "Englishness: The Narration of Nation." *Journal of British Studies* 36 (1997): 243–49.

Vogeler, Martha. "Matthew Arnold and Fredric Harrison: The Prophet of Culture and the Prophet of Positivism." *Nineteenth Century* 2.4 (Autumn 1962): 441–62.

Wallace, Elisabeth. "Goldwin Smith on England and America" *The American Historical Review* 59.4 (1954): 884–94.

Ward, Paul. *Britishness Since 1870.* New York: Routledge, 2004.

Warner, Michael. *The Letters of the Republic.* Boston: Harvard UP, 1992.

———. *Publics and Counterpublics.* New York: Zone Books, 2002.

Watson, Barbara Bellow. "The Theater of Love and the Theater of Politics in The Apple Cart." *Shaw: The Annual of Bernard Shaw Studies* 7 (1987): 207–20.

Watson, H. B. M. "The Deleterious Effect of Americanisation upon Woman." *Nineteenth Century and After, a Monthly Review* 54 (1903): 782–92.

Watt, D. Cameron. *Succeeding John Bull: America in Britain's Place 1900–1975.* New York: Cambridge UP, 1984.

Webb, Beatrice. *American Diary. Ed. David Shannon.* Madison: U of Wisconsin P, 1963.

Weight, Richard. *Patriots: National Identity in Britain 1940–2000.* London: Macmillan, 2002.

Weintraub, Stanley. *The London Americans.* New York: Harcourt Brace Jovanovich, 1979.

Wells, H. G. *The Future in America: A Search After Realities.* Leipzig: Bernhard Tauchnitz, 1907.

———. "Roosevelt in Europe." *The New Age* 7.15 (1910): 339–41.

West, James. "The Chace Act and Anglo-American Literary Relations." *Studies in Bibliography* 45 (1992): 303–11.

Wilde, Oscar. Aphorisms. MS W6721M3 P576. Oscar Wilde and his Literary Circle Collection. Box 81. U of California, Los Angeles. MS.

———. *Complete Works of Oscar Wilde.* New York: Harper & Row, 1989.

———. *The Portable Oscar Wilde.* Ed. Richard Aldington. New York: Penguin Books, 1978.

Williams, Raymond. *Marxism and Literature.* New York: Oxford UP, 1978.

Wilson, Angus. *Anglo-Saxon Attitudes.* London: Secker and Warburg, 1956.

Wilson, Edmund. *A Piece of Mind: Reflections at Sixty.* London: W. H. Allen, 1957.

Woodley, William. *The Impressions of an Englishman in America.* New York: William J. Woodley, 1910.

Žižek, Slavoj. *For They Know Not What They Do: Enjoyment as a Political Factor.* London: Verso, 2008.

———. *The Sublime Object of Ideology.* New York: Verso, 1989.

———. *Tarrying with the Negative.* Durham: Duke UP, 1993.

Zwerdling, Alex. *Improvised Europeans.* New York: Basic Books, 1999.

INDEX

Note: Pages followed by *f* indicate figures. The abbreviation chap. indicates the section heading under which a note can be found.

British culture: Anglo-Saxon support for, 108; apex, 133–34; defense for, 145; destruction of, 176; enriching nature of, 203; heritage, 184; national value of, 151; redemptive authority of, 10; repository of, 5; superiority of, 14–15, 27, 54, 75, 86, 92; valorization of, 41, 204. *See also* American culture; culture

British imperialism, 36–38, 153–55; civilizing mission, 157–58; critique of, 163–64; relationship to tradition, 170; self-legitimation, 190; threats to, 164, 165. *See also* imperialism

Britishness, 26, 58, 85; contrast to Americanness, 146; essence of, 136; idealized, 150; ideals of, 155; imitations of, 136; indeterminate nature of, 146; indifference of, 52, 114; literacy, 149; paradoxical nature of, 139; representations of, 72, 149. *See also* British character

British serial publications: *BLAST*, 214–15; *Boy's Own Paper*, 102; *English Review*, 210; *Forum*, 175; *McClure's Magazine*, 121; *New Age*, 205–16, 218*f*; *Nineteenth Century and After, a Monthly Review*, 176; *Pall Mall Gazette*, 80–81; *Punch*, 28–29; *Spectator*, 70; *Times* (of London), 79, 129. *See also* American serial publications; Anglo-American serial publications; journalism

Bryce, James, 14, 39–41, 222n2 (chap. 3); *The American Commonwealth*, 39; *The Relations of the Advanced and the Backward Races of Mankind*, 106–7

Buchan, John: *The Thirty-Nine Steps*, 136

Burke, Edmund, 86, 148, 200

Burne-Jones, Philip, 54; *Dollars and Democracy*, 47–50

Burns, John, 39

Butler, Leslie, 3, 219n3, 220n10

Cannadine, David, 37, 219n4

capitalism: American dominance, 81, 189; business mentality, 193; commodity, 174, 177, 178–79; as duty, 137–38; embracing of, 27; expansion of, 167; finance, 36, 157; and imperialism, 119, 154–55, 157–60, 165–71, 199; legitimization of, 159; leveling of tradition by, 185; as religion, 158–60; threats of, 40, 178–79; vanguard of, 22, 167. *See also* liberalism

Carlyle, Thomas, 103

Carnegie, Andrew, 71

Carroll, Lewis, 93, 222

Celts, 89–90, 102, 125. *See also* Ireland

Chace Act, 8–9, 219n6. *See also* copyright, Sherman amendment

Chamberlain, Joseph, 86–87

chivalry, 33, 132, 139, 143, 142; as code, 140, 137; as ideal, 131, 137–38, 143

Churchill, Lady Randolph (née Jennie Jerome), 123, 129

Churchill, Winston, 8

civilization: advancement of, 57; Arnoldian, 11–15, 84; British superiority of, 105, 134–35; and commerce, 56–57, 152*f*; degenerative effects of, 119; and imperialism, 121; and intellectualism, 164; preservation of, 107; threats to, 35, 49, 55; vanguard of, 74, 86; world, 77, 86

Civil War (American), 7, 68, 70, 91, 115, 155–56

class, 30–31; attitudes about, 53; composition of, 12; distinctions among, 35, 52, 140; hierarchies, 100, 108, 110; loss of distinction, 140; lower, 109, 116, 150; middle, 29–30, 38, 99, 109; mobility, 140; prejudices toward, 35; social, 12, 25, 30–31. *See also* aristocracy

Cleveland, Grover, 166, 180

Cobden, Richard, 81

Cody, William (Buffalo Bill), 60, 133, 222n2 (chap. 4)

Cogliani, Francis, 205